OF STARS & DRAGONS

THE ASTRALA SAGA
BOOK ONE

D.A. WHITE

Cover design and Interior Art by: Reece-Alexander Norris-Paterson

Map by: Travis Hummelmeier Worldwyrm on Etsy

Editing and Interior design by: Vanessa Mena, Inkspark Digital

First Edition

To my princess, may you always strive for the light, rebuke the darkness, and remember the love I have for you. To my Wife, thank you for always believing in me, pushing me to break through self doubt, and making me a father.

Emerald Forest
Stonefire Mountains
Rockbar
Amakiir Forest
N
W
E

BRIGHTSPIRE
Jade Forest
Rockhaven
hadyvale
RIVERLANDS
The High Road
The GREAT PLAINS
THE WORLD OF ETONYA

TRIGGER WARNINGS

- Animal Injury
- Explicit battle scenes
- Explicit sexual situations
- Dismemberment & Gore
- Loss of Life
- Possession by entity
- Violence
- Death & Grief
- Mental Trauma
- Alcohol consumption

ACT I

PROLOGUE
ANOTHER WAR

The night sky crackled with flashes of spellbound energy as Aryeh ushered the last terrified refugee into the damp cave. His golden fur was matted with blood and dirt, his lion-like face grim. Outside, the roars of Dragons and the thunderous blasts of mage fire echoed.

"Quickly now, into the depths!" Aryeh growled, his voice a deep rumble. "Stay to the back and keep the children quiet."

Wide-eyed and trembling, the refugees huddled together in the darkness, flinching at every explosion that shook the cave. Aryeh turned to Kael, the Astralan battlemage standing at the entrance. Kael's eyes glowed with magic, his armor still smoldering from a deflected blast.

"The Stormbringers are holding the line, but they won't last much longer," Kael said grimly. "I must return and help them push back until reinforcements arrive."

Aryeh nodded. "I will keep them safe and calm. Go, join the defense. May Astrala's light guide you."

As Kael rushed out into the chaos of battle, Aryeh turned to the refugees, his broad frame blocking the cave entrance. The cave's crystalline walls flickered with mage-light, casting a glow on his golden eyes when he turned to smile warmly at them.

"Be at ease," he said, his deep voice resonating off the cave walls. "You are safe here for now. The Stormbringers will let no harm come to you."

A small girl with pointed ears peeked out from behind her mother's leg. "W-what's happening out there?" she asked, her lip quivering.

Aryeh smiled sadly at her. "A terrible war, little one. Those scaled beasts are called Dragons, and those mages are my friends. Together, we fight to protect all those who would otherwise be conquered. If left unchecked, the Dragons would tear your world asunder."

Murmurs of dismay rippled through the refugees. Aryeh held up a gauntleted hand for silence.

"Even in this dark time, there is still hope. Hope in heroes like The Spellsword. Would you like to hear his story?"

Nods and hushed sounds of assent echoed in the cave. Aryeh shifted into a more comfortable position and began. "Astrala was a world which spun into existence from the arcane, pure and powerful. Its people, the Astralan, were born into a world already blessed by magic. As they grew, their language developed as a tool to harness the abundance of magic that surrounded them. In time, their power grew so vast that it carried them to the stars in search of what lay beyond. Weaving powerful spells by simply speaking, they traveled the cosmos as peaceful explorers."

As Aryeh wove the tale of Rider's ascent from commoner to commander, the battle raged on, but the refugees listened with rapt attention, their fears momentarily forgotten. For a time, there was no war, no death - only the story of a hero and the promise that dawn would break.

CHAPTER I
THE QUEEN'S SUMMONS

As Rider traveled, his ears picked up the clash of steel. Rider urged his steadfast mare, Eve, into a gallop down the road and around the lower bend. Ten rough-looking men in mismatched armor locked in battle with a group of heavily armed guards protecting a carriage.

Rider leaped from Eve's saddle, his longsword singing as it slid free from its sheath. He crashed into the fray like a wave, the clang of steel-on-steel ringing through the air. Rider parried a vicious slash and countered with a thrust, his blade finding the gap between a bandit's chest plate and shoulder pauldron. Hot blood spurted as he wrenched it free, the man collapsing with a gurgle.

To his right, a guard bashed a bandit with his shield before delivering a devastating overhand chop, cleaving into the man from above his shoulder. Blood sprayed as the guard yanked his blade free, the bandit crumpled to the ground. Two guards fought back-to-back, fending off two more bandits who sought to flank them. One guard took a cut across the thigh but kept fighting, his sword finding a bandit's throat, releasing a crimson spray.

Rider whirled to engage another foe, steel clanging as they exchanged a flurry of blows. Rider feinted left, then spun right, his blade severing the bandit's sword hand off at the wrist. The man stared at the spouting stump in shock before Rider's backswing separated head from shoulders.

The remaining bandits, seeing over half their number cut down in a matter of moments, fled into the trees. Rider turned to give chase, but the guard captain called him back.

"Let them go," the big man growled, wiping his blade clean. "They'll think twice before trying that again." He turned to Rider, respect grudgingly showing in his eyes. "My thanks, swordsman. That could have gone badly without you."

Rider nodded, breathing heavily as he wiped his sword on a fallen bandit's cloak before sliding it back into its sheath. The coppery scent of blood hung thick in the air, the dirt churned and muddy with it. He surveyed the carnage, suppressing a grimace at the tangled pile of corpses.

"Seems the Queen's road isn't quite as safe as I've been led to believe," Rider said.

"Indeed. These are dangerous times." The guard captain's breathing was still heavy from battle. "There's been an alarming rise in bandit attacks along the Queen's Road. Every noble and their grandmother wants extra protection these days, rightfully so." He extended a calloused hand. "Name's Brakken. Captain of the Silverlight family guard. By the looks of ya, you might just be the kind of man the city needs right now."

Rider clasped Brakken's forearm in a warrior's greeting. "Rider, formerly of the Blades mercenary company. A pleasure."

Brakken grunted in approval. "The Blades, eh? Heard good things about you lot. Listen, once you're settled in the city, come find me at The Silverlight Manor. I'd be happy to put in a good word for you, might even have some work for a capable sword like yourself."

"Aye, I may do just that," Rider said with a grin. "My thanks, Brakken."

The guard captain nodded curtly before returning to his men, barking orders to tighten up the formation around the carriage and to secure the bodies.

Rider returned to Eve and swung atop her saddle before clicking his tongue, urging her forward.

As Rider reached the last stretch of the winding forest path, the outskirts of Brightspire's port emerged before him like a vision conjured from the pages of an ancient tome. The city shimmered with iridescent hues above, its walls embedded with pulsating crystals, their colors synchronized with the heartbeat of magic that permeated everything.

"By the Ancients," he murmured, eyes wide with wonder. The ground hummed with the city's energy, beckoning all who dared to dream of magic.

At the elaborate gates, constructed of intertwining branches and silver vines, Rider dismounted before walking Eve to the stables nestled just inside the city.

The stable itself was a wonder—crafted from living wood that continued to grow, sprouting small leaves and flowers which perfumed the air with a sweet, earthy fragrance. Each stall formed an individual grove, offering its equine occupant a serene space filled with soft, green light.

With a gentle pat to Eve's flank and a whispered promise of return, Rider left her in the care of an Elven woman whose silver hair shimmered like moonlight and whose eyes gleamed like polished emeralds. She bowed slightly, her movements slow and graceful as wind through willows.

Rider made his way to the heart of Brightspire, crossing the wondrous air bridge to the city proper. Below him, magical platforms floated effortlessly, moving up, down, and across in a ballet of aerial ferries transporting people and goods through the vertical cityscape. The planks beneath his boots hummed a tune—a melody composed by harmonically enchanted wood infused with ethereal power.

Reaching the floating island's solid ground, he marveled at how magic appeared to be integrated into every aspect of Brightspire's architecture and daily life. Buildings twisted skyward in spirals of alabaster and gold, their surfaces etched with glowing runes. Aqueducts filled with glowing water arched gracefully overhead, distributing not just water, but liquid mana, nourishing both the city's inhabitants and its flora.

The citizens of Brightspire passed by in flowing robes of impossibly vivid colors; their hands tracing sigils in the air that sparked brief but beautiful effects—from blooming flowers to shimmering shields against sudden drizzles. Children laughed as they levitated toys between each other, their joyous shrieks mingling with chimes of floating crystals attuned to harmonize with natural energy flows.

Rider's path eventually led to a central plaza where towering statues of Elven mages stood around an enormous fountain. The sculpture at the center depicted an ancient Elven sorceress, her arms spread wide as if she summoned the streams of sparkling water that danced skyward. Among these marvels, Rider began to grasp just how deeply magic coursed through Brightspire's veins.

Everywhere, the mundane and magical blended seamlessly. Lamps glowed, not by fire, but by captive sunbeams. Street vendors sold fruits that sang of their ripeness. Scholars debated as animated scrolls fluttered around them like wise birds eager to impart knowledge.

The air crackled with enchantment and the clamor of the city enveloped him: the clink of coins, the murmur of clandestine negotiations, and the sizzle of spellwork. Merchants hawked glowing wares, while street performers conjured illusions that danced like fireflies in the daylight.

"Step right up! Behold the elixirs of eternal youth," a vendor called, brandishing vials shimmering with liquid starlight.

"Treasures from the Dragon's hoard, just this way," another beckoned, pointing toward a collection of artifacts pulsing with an otherworldly aura.

Rider's senses were alight. The scent of roasting meats mingled with aromas of exotic spices, competing with the rich fragrance of aged parchment wafting from a nearby scroll shop.

His fingers brushed against a tapestry that rippled with illusory scenes of historic battles. The hum of arcane energy passed through him, an invisible current connecting every stone, every being within the city limits.

"Remarkable," he whispered as he pocketed a coin he found on the cobblestone. It vibrated with latent magic "A lucky charm for the road ahead," he mused.

Here, knowledge equaled power, and power was the currency of the realms.

Rider continued his stroll through the city's markets for a few hours, taking in the sights, sounds, and magic of this wondrous place. As he walked, the transition from bustling markets to stately manors was gradual, the cobblestone path widening and the buildings growing more opulent. Towering estates crafted from shimmering stone and living wood lined the street, their gardens overflowing with luminous flowers chiming softly in the breeze.

Rider's eyes finally caught sight of a large family crest resembling the image on the carriages. It was hanging above a gate made of an intricate web of silver branches. As he neared the grand entrance, one of the family's guards stepped forward. The Elf's armor gleamed with inlaid moonstone, his hand resting on the hilt of a slender blade at his hip.

"Hail, traveler," the guard said, his voice melodic. "What business have you with House Silverlight?"

Rider inclined his head respectfully. "I am Rider, formerly of the Blades. Captain Brakken requested my presence."

Recognition flickered in the guard's eyes. "Ah, yes. The swordsman from the Queen's Road. We've been expecting you." He gestured toward the manor. "Please, follow me. I shall escort you to the captain."

The branches shifted, parting as if sensing his invitation. The path to the main house was lined with glowing orbs that hovered above well-manicured hedges, casting a soft light.

Inside, the guard led Rider through an airy foyer, their footsteps echoing on the polished marble inlaid with silver veins that pulsed softly. Along the walls, tapestries depicting the Silverlight family history subtly shifted, their figures moving as though in perpetual reenactment.

They arrived at a set of double doors carved with intricate runes. The guard knocked twice, the sound resonating with a melodic tone. The doors swung open, revealing a study bathed in the warm glow of a chandelier. Tome filled bookshelves lined the walls, boasting the generations of knowledge contained within them.

Brakken stood near the far window, his silhouette

outlined by the diffused light filtering through the stained glass. As Rider entered, he turned, a smile crinkling the corners of his eyes.

"Rider, good to see you again." He strode forward to clasp Rider's arm in a warrior's greeting. "I'm glad you took me up on my offer."

"How could I refuse?" Rider grinned. "A chance to explore this city and put my blade to good use?"

Brakken chuckled, the sound a deep rumble. "Aye, there's no shortage of work for a skilled swordsman in Brightspire these days. And your timing is impeccable." He motioned for Rider to sit in one of the plush armchairs near the hearth. "I just finished reading the latest notices from the manor. It seems our Queen has issued a summons for warriors hailing from families loyal to the crown."

Rider leaned forward, his elbows resting on his knees. "A royal summons? Sounds serious."

"Indeed." Brakken's expression grew somber. "There have been whispers of a growing threat." He shook his head. "But the details are scarce. Her Majesty is playing this one close to the chest."

"And you think I could be of service?"

"I do and I can't think of a better way to repay you." Brakken met Rider's gaze, his expression grave. "After today's losses, I cannot spare any of my own men. But you... I saw how you fought on the Queen's Road. You have skill. More importantly, you have honor. Those are qualities sorely needed right now."

Rider considered the offer. His coin pouch hadn't been this light in years, and he no longer had the steady flow of pay promised by the Blades. Completing a job directly for the Queen of Brightspire could do more than fill a few coffers, it could bolster his reputation and promise a brighter future than he'd ever imagined.

A slow grin began to form on Rider's face as he nodded. "Alright. I'm in. What do I need to do?"

Brakken smiled, clapping Rider on the shoulder. "I knew you'd rise to the occasion. I'll send word to the palace that House Silverlight will be represented by a swordsman of great caliber." He crossed to the desk, retrieving a sealed scroll. "Take this to the palace gates at dawn. It bears this house's seal and my signature. It will grant you entry."

Rider accepted the scroll, feeling the weight of the new path set before him. "You have my thanks, Brakken. I won't let you down."

"I know you won't." Brakken's eyes shone with confidence. "Now, go get some rest in the bunkhouse. You'll need to be sharp for what lies ahead."

Rider clasped Brakken's hand firmly. "Until dawn, then."

As he left the main manor, Rider couldn't help but feel a thrill of anticipation. The Queen's summons, a growing threat, a city steeped in magic — it was something out of the tales he loved as a child. And now, he was to be a part of it.

He looked up at the twilit sky, the first stars glimmering above the city's spires. "Well, Eve," he murmured, thinking of his faithful companion. "Looks like our next journey is just beginning."

CHAPTER II
THE ROYAL COURT

As dawn arrived, Rider made his way to the courtyard, where a figure was already waiting for him.

"An impressive presence," Rider murmured to himself.

"Indeed," came a melodic response.

Shocked that the individual had heard him, Rider picked up his pace and found himself face-to-face with a beautiful High Elf woman. Her waist-length auburn hair framed her like an autumnal flame, and stunning violet eyes held a depth that spoke of wisdom and undiscovered stories.

"Forgive my forwardness," she said, a playful smile on her lips. "I'm curious to see if you're as good as Brakken has made you out to be."

"Curiosity is often its own reward," Rider replied cautiously. "Yet I find myself at a loss. Would you enlighten a stranger to your city?"

"Ah, of course. Where are my manners? I am Lady Ariella Moonwhisper. Brakken has asked that I take you to meet Queen Vyshaan, the Iron Sorceress herself." Ariella's voice dipped ever so slightly when she mentioned the queen, betraying a hint of something concealed beneath her diplomatic veneer.

"Queen Vyshaan?" Rider echoed.

"None other," confirmed Ariella, her gaze still assessing him. "She is the beacon that guides Brightspire, the force behind our prosperity."

"Is that pride or concern I detect in your tone?" inquired Rider, his eyes locking onto Ariella's.

"Observant, aren't we?" A light laugh escaped Ariella. "Let's say I hold a profound respect for our queen, tempered by a healthy awareness of the realities of rule."

"Realities such as?" prodded Rider, sensing an undercurrent to her words.

"History has many faces," she stated cryptically. "Come, you have a lot to learn, and we have a long way to travel. I don't intend to be late."

As they strolled through the avenues, Ariella spun stories of ancient pacts, grand triumphs, and the intricate dance of politics. With each tale, Rider's understanding of Brightspire deepened, the vibrant tapestry of the city coming alive through her descriptions.

"Your words paint a vivid picture, Lady Moonwhisper," said Rider, his mind leveraging the new knowledge into his plans. "Brightspire is indeed a realm of wonders."

"Yet wonders often come at a cost," Ariella added softly, her eyes reflecting a history both brilliant and dark. "For those who seek to delve deeper, the true nature of Brightspire may reveal itself. But tell me, what brings you to our floating city?"

"Adventure. Opportunity. Perhaps the chance to align with powers that shape the world," Rider replied.

"Then you may find yourself well-met in Brightspire," Ariella said, a knowing glint in her eye. "For this city, and

those who rule it, are in need of individuals with... particular talents."

Their conversation flowed as easily as wine at a royal
banquet. Soon enough, they approached the grandeur of
the main trade district.

"Behold," Ariella said, sweeping her hand toward a
myriad of stalls displaying glowing artifacts and shimmering potions. "Brightspire's heartbeat is its trade. It
pulses with every exchange, every spell cast for coin. Our
prosperity is unmatched, as is our command over magical
commerce."

Rider glanced at the merchants, their hands weaving
spells into objects with practiced ease. He could feel the
raw power thrumming through the marketplace beneath
the din of haggling.

"Control over such power must require...vigilance,"
Rider mused, watching a merchant imbue a crystal with a
soft luminescence.

"More than you can imagine," Ariella murmured. Her
eyes flicked across the marketplace as if seeking unseen
watchers. "Queen Vyshaan's gaze extends beyond our
borders. Every realm feels the weight of her scrutiny,
ensuring no threat arises unnoticed."

"Seems oppressive," Rider observed, the words like the
bitter pith of sour fruit in his mouth.

"Security demands sacrifice," she conceded. "But there
are those who chafe under such watchfulness."

"Such as?" Rider asked, intrigued by the tension
beneath her words.

"Hmph." Ariella replied briefly while looking over
Rider once more. "If the Queen deems you worthy, all will
be revealed."

They traversed through the city streets, crossing

adorned bridges and riding multiple floating platforms until arriving at Queen Vyshaan's magnificent castle.

As they approached the gates of the palace, Rider's eyes widened at the grandeur before him. The palace seemed to grow out of the very earth, twisting spires of alabaster stone intertwined with living wood. The air shimmered around the structure with raw magic, scattering goosebumps across his skin.

As they neared the gate, Rider noticed the abnormally large presence of royal knights patrolling the grounds and guarding the entrance. Their armor gleamed with enchantments, and they carried swords and spears that hummed as they vibrated with contained power. The atmosphere was tense, a stark contrast to the city's lively streets and far from what he expected.

Two guards stepped forward as the pair approached, their eyes assessing them with cool professionalism. "Halt," one said, his voice ringing with authority. "State your business."

Rider bowed his head respectfully, producing the scroll given to him by Brakken. "I am Rider, formerly of the Blades mercenary company, here on behalf of House Silverlight. I bear an invitation from Queen Vyshaan herself."

Ariella bowed slightly in agreement before producing a scroll of her own and handing it over to the guards.

The guards examined the scrolls, the seals glowing briefly as they confirmed their authenticity. They exchanged a glance, then nodded. "Very well," one said as they stepped aside "You may enter."

Without a sound, the gates swung open. Ariella led as she and Rider strode through, his boots clicking against the polished stone path. The gardens surrounding the palace were a riot of color and scent, exotic flowers blooming alongside pulsing crystals that chimed softly in the breeze. Water flowed through levitating channels, defying gravity as it wound its way towards shimmering pools.

As they ascended the steps to the main entrance, the massive doors swung open. A servant in shimmering livery bowed deeply, took the scrolls, and read their contents before continuing, "Welcome, Sir Rider and Lady Ariella. Her Majesty awaits you in the throne room. Please, follow me."

The palace's interior was no less magnificent than its exterior. Rider's eyes drank in the soaring ceilings, intricate tapestries, and floating lights that illuminated every corner. Magic was woven into every surface, from the living wood of the walls to the shimmering mosaics on the floor which depicted scenes from Elven history.

The servant led them through a labyrinth of opulent corridors, each grander than the last. Finally, they arrived at a set of towering doors emblazoned with the royal crest - a silver tree with roots twisted into arcane runes. The doors swung open, and they stepped into the throne room. At the far end, Queen Vyshaan sat upon a dais floating above a pool of liquid starlight. Her piercing blue eyes locked onto Rider, their assessing gaze as sharp as winter's first frost. Advisors in robes woven with magic and guards clad in enchanted armor flanked her.

"Approach," Queen Vyshaan commanded, her voice a melodic force that compelled obedience.

Rider marveled at her presence. Her elegant robes, embroidered with softly pulsing runes, cast an ethereal glow upon her alabaster skin. The Iron Sorceress lived up to her moniker, radiating an aura of strength that belied her delicate appearance.

"Your Majesty," Ariella began with a courteous bow, "we have come to accept the mission posed by the crown."

"Indeed." The queen's gaze never left Rider. "You stand before me because Brightspire faces an encroaching darkness at the edges of our light. An insidious and vile cult seeks to unravel the very fabric of our kingdom." Her words fell like hammer blows, their echoes heavy with urgency.

"Please, speak plainly, Your Grace," Rider said, meeting her gaze with a resolve hardened by years of questing. "What perils await those who would stand against this threat?"

"Perils aplenty," Queen Vyshaan intoned. "This cult has turned many in my kingdom against me. My knights and informants confirm the use of necromancy. Those they cannot sway, they kill and raise them in undeath as hidden allies and soldiers. If not stopped, they will plunge us into chaos."

"What we have learned is troubling enough. They worship the Dragon Lord's memory and his promises of power through draconic transformation. However, I fear their true intentions remain shrouded."

Queen Vyshaan rose from her gilded throne, which floated gracefully to the floor. Her piercing blue eyes swept over Lady Moonwhisper, imparting the gravity of what she was about to share.

"Ariella," she began, her tone softening slightly, "your lineage has long been loyal to the crown of Brightspire. Your ancestors served with honor and distinction in these very halls." Her gaze flicked briefly toward a grand tapestry depicting legendary battles, the embroidered warriors seemingly ready to leap from the fabric in their fervor to protect the kingdom. "And you, Human," the Queen continued. "I have been told you defended the Silverlight family from an ambush. Is that correct?"

"That is correct, Your Majesty," Rider affirmed, bowing slightly.

"Very well, then," the Queen continued, shifting her attention back to Ariella. "It is on this foundation of faithfulness that I place my trust in you, Ariella—and in your companion."

Queen Vyshaan's expression darkened. "Our situation is dire. I sent spies to investigate a known haven, but they were disposed of with calculated malice and the cult has since moved on." She paused, letting the silence fill the chamber. "They worship revenants and ghoulish ideals propped up by the Dragon Lord, yes, but before my spies were discovered, they reported the cult conspired to infiltrate this very court." Her voice dropped to a chilling whisper before she continued, "We must act swiftly and silently."

Rider shifted his weight before speaking. "How may we serve, Your Grace?"

The queen walked down from her now-landed throne. "You will venture forth in secret. I've ensured a room at The Silver Harp. You will keep up appearances and operate as standard adventurers. You are to find the cult's new sanctuary and uncover their plans," Vyshaan instructed. "Any information you discover is to be relayed directly to me. No other."

She leaned closer, lowering her voice to ensure that only Ariella and Rider could hear. "Tread carefully. This cult has eyes and ears everywhere and their undead are hidden from conventional detection."

"And the rewards your summons spoke of for such service?" Rider probed.

"For those who require it, riches beyond measure, titles honored across the realms, and perhaps, most precious of all, my favor," Queen Vyshaan said, her words painting a vivid tapestry of potential glory. "But let me be clear," her tone sharpened, "failure is not an option. Should you falter, know that my wrath is as fearsome as my generosity is great."

The threat hung in the air, a palpable presence sending a shiver down Rider's spine. Yet, the challenge set his heart ablaze. The prospect of venturing into the unknown, where the fate of a kingdom and the secrets of an age lay waiting to be uncovered.

"Your Majesty," Rider spoke with the poise of someone who had faced numerous perils before. "Consider us your instruments. We shall seek out the cult and ensure your court remains untarnished."

"Indeed," Ariella added, her voice carrying the melodic lilt of conviction. "My allegiance to you is unwavering, and I will protect our realm from the shadows that seek to subvert it."

Queen Vyshaan regarded them, the weight of her scrutiny almost tangible. "Let your actions reflect the oaths you've sworn," she said, her voice reverberating through the vastness of the throne room.

As they left, Queen Vyshaan turned toward a window overlooking her kingdom. The floating islands shimmered like jewels suspended in a fading sky, yet her expression was as turbulent as the storm clouds gathering on the horizon.

In the hall, Rider felt Ariella's gaze on him. They traversed a road paved with peril, where trust would be both shield and sword against the threats of treachery and dark sorcery.

"Are you ready for what lies ahead?" Rider asked as they exited the castle, leaving behind the aura of majesty for the uncertain whispers of the outside world.

"More than ready," Ariella responded. "My heart beats for the preservation of my homeland."

Their footsteps echoed softly on stone as they moved through the labyrinthine roads of Brightspire, winding like the roots of an ancient tree. A cool breeze caressed their faces, carrying the mingled aromas of the city and the sea beyond its walls.

"Joining this fight... what drives you to such lengths?" Rider inquired, intent on understanding her resolve.

"Compassion, perhaps. Or folly," Ariella said with a wry tilt of her lips. "But I cannot stand idle while darkness festers. If I can lend my bow and my knowledge to protect Brightspire, then that is the path I must walk, no matter where it leads. The Queen offers me a chance to restore my family's favor at court. I see no reason why I cannot accomplish both tasks at once."

A pause lingered between them, filled with the vibrant sounds of the city. The rhythmic clatter of hooves on stone, the melodious incantations of street sorcerers, and the sizzle of enchanted trinkets being peddled to wide-eyed patrons created a display of life and power, both inviting and ominous.

Rider felt a swell of respect for Ariella's conviction, her willingness to stand against the shadows that threatened her beloved city. "The Queen is wise to call upon her allies, if she can count on all of them to be as loyal as you," he said, meeting her gaze with a steady intensity. "I'm glad I was able to lend my blade to you and your Queen. But after all, every sellsword needs a worthy job, right?" he added with a grin.

"Bold words," she said, a smile breaking through her solemnity. "Let us hope our deeds prove to be as bold when the time comes."

As they made their way through the lengthening evening shadows, Ariella led them with practiced ease through the city streets. Rider hoisted his pack onto a broad shoulder, the leather straps worn from countless journeys.

"Rider, we must mask our quest in secrecy," she reminded him as she tucked an amulet bearing her family's seal next to her heart, concealing it beneath her cloak.

"I understand," Rider replied, his fingers deftly checking the clasps on his cloak. "A secretive cult of Dragon Lord worshipers," he quipped with the hint of a smirk. "Just another day in the life."

"It's not just about the thrill of adventure or the promise of gold for me, Rider, " Ariella said, her expression turning somber. "There's a complex web of politics and power here. Maintaining that balance is delicate. One wrong move could send everything crashing down around us."

"Then we won't make a wrong move," Rider declared.

Ariella stepped closer, her tone unwavering. "We're going to need to trust each other. I need to know you're in this until the end."

Rider allowed himself a moment to appreciate the bond forming between them. "You have my word, Lady Moonwhisper."

"Good." Ariella replied as she glanced upward, where the first stars began to prickle the darkening sky. She shifted her attention to the path that stretched before them.

"Toward destiny, then," Ariella said as she fell into step alongside Rider.

"Toward destiny," Rider affirmed.

CHAPTER III
THE SILVER HARP

The Silver Harp loomed before Rider and Ariella, a grand three-story structure with white stone and polished silver-wood beams. Raucous laughter and jovial voices drifted out the open windows into the bustling city street. The inn's ornate wooden door, carved with intricate vines and musical instruments, stood invitingly open.

"Quite the lively place," Rider remarked, taking in the steady stream of patrons flowing in and out the ornate silver doors. Humans, Elves, Dwarves, and more packed the establishment to the brim.

Ariella paused and turned to Rider. "This place is the go-to watering hole for adventurers, mercenaries, and anyone looking to make a name for themselves or earn some extra coin while passing through Brightspire. Quests, companions, or trouble, you can find them all here, depending on your luck." Her violet eyes sparkled in the warm glow from within.

Rider took in the imposing three-story structure. Lanterns hung from the eaves, casting soft light on the pale stone walls. "Aye, I've heard stories about The Harp.

Though I admit, it's still bigger than I imagined." He adjusted his sword's shoulder strap. Flashing a roguish grin, he gestured toward the entrance. "Shall we see what fortune awaits us inside, my lady?"

Ariella smirked and strode forward, her auburn tresses shimmering in the fading sunset. "We shall, but don't call me 'my lady' again or your luck will turn for the worse."

They ascended the marble steps into the lively din of the fabled Silver Harp, anticipating what the night might bring, and were immediately enveloped by a whirlwind of sound and motion.

Boisterous laughter boomed over the clinking of steins. Patrons filled the space, deep in drunken contests and raucous conversation. Servers deftly wove through the crowds, balancing trays laden with overflowing tankards and aromatic dishes. A bard perched upon a small, elevated stage plucked a lyre with nimble fingers, notes twining like ivy around the rafter beams. His melody, lively and intricate, spun through the tavern, weaving an auditory tapestry that bound the chaos into something almost harmonious.

Ariella scanned the room, her keen eyes taking in every detail. She spied a bulletin board covered in flyers and notices on the back wall. "There. That board is where locals post jobs like deliveries, bounties, bodyguarding. The kind of things that require a particular set of skills."

As they approached, Rider caught snippets of conversation:

"...heard the Jade is infested with giant spiders now. Some even say a broodmother..."

"...damned bandits are growing bolder, attacking caravans on the high road..."

"...have you seen those flyers around the city? Something about a new religion..."

Rider's scanned the myriad of parchments and notices pinned haphazardly to the board. One flyer in particular caught his attention. Penned in an elegant script on thick, cream-colored paper.

He reached out and plucked it from the board, reading aloud: "Daring adventurers sought to infiltrate and eliminate a group of bandits terrorizing the foothills outside Brightspire. Handsome reward of one hundred gold coins offered."

"Seems straightforward enough," he mused.

Ariella peered over his shoulder, her warm breath tickling his neck. "Keep reading," she urged, a hint of caution lacing her melodic voice.

Rider's eyes traveled further down the page. "Warning: the last brave soul who attempted this task barely escaped with their life. Proceed with utmost caution." He let out a low whistle. "A failed attempt? These aren't your average bandits, it seems."

Ariella's delicate hand came to rest on Rider's forearm, her touch electric even through his leather bracer. "Such a substantial reward could greatly aid our cause," she murmured, her violet eyes locking with his. "But as they say, some rewards are too good to be true."

Rider nodded, his thumb absentmindedly tracing the parchment's edge. Around them, the tavern's clamor faded as he weighed the potential risks. The gold's allure was undeniable, but was it worth the cost?

His gaze drifted to a second flyer, this one weathered and torn at the edges. The parchment was stained with what looked suspiciously like old blood. Rider plucked the flyer, a frown creasing his brow as he scanned the faded ink. He held it up, squinting to make the writing out. "Footpads wanted for crimes against the Crown. Last seen fleeing south along the Queen's Road. Reward of seventy-five gold coins for their live capture and return to the City Guard," he paused, considering this new request. "Hmm, seems the authorities are having trouble with some light-fingered miscreants."

Ariella leaned in, her hair brushing Rider's shoulder, studying the notice. "This one is posted by the City Guard directly. That offers some assurance of payment, even if our bandit-hunting benefactor proves reluctant to part with his gold." Her brow furrowed. "Although, I wonder what sort of thieves would be so brazen as to operate on the Queen's Road. That route is heavily patrolled."

Rider folded the flyer and tucked it into his belt pouch alongside the first. "Well, well. Two tantalizing prospects. Daring bandit raid or wily footpad hunt." He flashed Ariella a roguish grin. "What say you, my Elven enchantress? Shall we pursue glory, justice, or both? Adventure awaits, regardless of the path we tread."

Ariella rolled her eyes at Rider's dramatic flair, but a smile tugged at the corner of her lips. "While I appreciate your enthusiasm, perhaps we should gather more information before charging headlong into danger." She nodded towards the bar. "Buy me an Elven wine and I'll see what rumors I can coax from the locals. Drunken lips often let secrets slip."

Rider bowed with a flourish. "As my lady commands." He winked as Ariella shot him a glare. "I shall procure the finest vintage this establishment has to offer and endeavor to loosen a few tongues myself."

He sauntered off towards the bar, his easy smile and confident swagger drawing appreciative glances from several female patrons. Ariella shook her head and melted into the crowd.

Leaning against the polished mahogany bar, he

couldn't help but feel a thrill of excitement at the prospect of the challenges ahead.

A barmaid sauntered over, her ample cleavage nearly spilling from her bodice. "Well, hello handsome. Haven't seen you around here." she asked, voice husky, eyes roving appreciatively over Rider's form. "Name's Isabella. What'll it be, love?"

Rider offered the barmaid a charming grin. "That's 'cause I'm new around here, love. Maybe you could show me where all the fun is at?"

The barmaid smiled devilishly as she leaned over the bar toward Rider. "Oh, you're gonna be trouble," she let out with a light laugh.

Rider chuckled and proceeded with his order. "Just a glass of your finest Elven red and one ale, if you please."

The barmaid winked saucily. "Coming right up, handsome." She sashayed away, and promptly returned with the drinks.

Rider wove through the crowded tavern and met Ariella at a small table in the dim back corner.

She snorted delicately as he sat. "You certainly have a way with the fairer sex."

Rider shrugged, leaning back in his chair, one arm draped casually over the back. "It's a gift and a curse, my dear." His eyes gleamed in the candlelight.

Ariella rolled her eyes but smiled. She leaned forward, elbows on the scarred tabletop. "So, the Guard's bounty first? We could ask around, see if anyone here has heard whispers of these footpads."

Rider nodded, taking a swig of ale. "Aye, let's start there. Folks here seem like the type to keep their ears to the ground." He scanned the room, his gaze settling on a table of rough-looking men engaged in a dice game. "Those lads might know something. Shall I go have a friendly chat?"

Ariella followed his gaze, her brow furrowing slightly. "Just be careful. They look like they're not afraid to start trouble." She sipped her wine, the rich ruby liquid staining her lips. "I'll mingle with the crowd, see what gossip I can glean."

Rider stood, his chair scraping against the worn floorboards. "Meet back here when the minstrel starts his next set?" At Ariella's nod, he made his way toward the gamblers' table.

Laughter erupted as he approached. A hulking man with a shaved head and a jagged scar running down his cheek slammed his fist on the table. "You cheating bastard!" he roared at his wiry, shifty-eyed companion.

Rider stepped up to the table, his easy smile belying the coiled tension in his belly. "Gentlemen," he greeted, his deep voice cutting through the din. "Mind if I join you for a round?"

Meanwhile, Ariella slipped into the crowd, her keen violet eyes scanning for potential sources of information.

———

An hour later, Rider and Ariella reconvened at the main bar. The tavern was still in full swing, the air thick with pipe smoke, laughter, and the clatter of tankards.

Rider leaned his muscular frame against the polished mahogany bar and caught Isabella's eye. The buxom barmaid sauntered over, a playful smirk on her painted lips. "Back for more, handsome?" she purred, leaning forward just enough to give Rider another ample view of her straining cleavage.

"Actually, I was hoping you could provide me with something else," Rider replied smoothly, blue eyes twinkling mischievously. "The key to my room. It should be reserved under the name Rider."

Isabella's smirk faltered slightly as she glanced past Rider to Ariella. The Elf's serious gaze fixed on Rider.

"Ah, I see you've already found someone to '*show you where all the fun is at*'," Isabella pouted Rider's earlier flirtatious banter, painted lips pursing. She reached under the bar and produced an iron key, sliding it across the countertop. "Up the stairs, third door on the right. Enjoy your stay." With a last lingering look, she turned to serve another patron.

Rider scooped up the key with a wink and turned to face Ariella. "Shall we retire to somewhere more private, my lady?"

"There better be two beds," she replied as she took the key from him.

The creaky wooden stairs groaned beneath their steps, the noise of the tavern fading as they reached the upper landing. Ariella unlocked the door to their room and pushed it open. The space was small but clean, with a simple bed, and a worn table and chairs.

Rider closed the door behind them and turned the lock with a soft click. He shrugged off his coat and draped it over the back of a chair before sinking down onto the room's lone bed with a contented sigh. "So, what did you manage to uncover from those loose-lipped mercenaries?"

Ariella leaned against the mantle, firelight dancing across her fine-boned features. "Quite a bit, actually. Apparently, this group of bandits call themselves the Crimson Cloth and they've been growing bolder in their attacks. The mercenaries seem to think both jobs are linked to the same group. Someone with an interest in disrupting trade on the Queen's Road may be aiding them."

Rider rubbed his stubbled chin thoughtfully. "Interesting, looks like we're going to the foothills." He stretched out on the bed, clasping his hands behind his head as he glanced over at Ariella, a playful smirk tugging at his lips. "So, looks like it's just the one bed ..."

Ariella scoffed and sauntered over to the bed, her hips swaying. She reached down and swiftly yanked the pillow out from under Rider's head. "I'm sure a rugged adventurer like yourself has spent plenty a night on floors much worse than the Harp's," she quipped, tossing the pillow towards the hearth.

Rider chuckled and sat up, running a hand through his tousled hair. "Aye, that I have. Though I must say, the company is usually far less alluring." His sapphire gaze raked over Ariella's form appreciatively.

She rolled her eyes but couldn't suppress the hint of a smile tugging at her lips. "Flattery will get you nowhere, Rider." She began unbuckling her leather armor, nimble fingers making quick work of the straps.

The next morning, Ariella and Rider rode a full day's journey to the southeast foothills. The dense green forest gradually thinned to shrub-covered hills as they followed a recently made winding dirt track. By late afternoon, Brightspire glittered like a jewel on the horizon behind them, dwindled to a mere speck in the distance.

As dusk painted the sky in hues of orange and purple, they came upon signs of recent violence - broken carts abandoned by the roadside, their contents strewn about as if rifled through in haste. Dark, rusty stains splattered the dirt, and a few arrows jutted from splintered wood. The air hung heavy with unsettling stillness.

Ariella reined in her chestnut mare beside one of the decimated carts and dismounted gracefully. Her eyes scanned the wreckage as she knelt to examine the stains.

"Blood," she declared grimly. "Not more than a day old. This attack was recent."

Rider remained astride his black stallion, his expression hardening as he took in the scene.

Ariella's hand drifted to the elegant curve of her longbow. "We'd best be on our guard."

They continued, senses heightened and weapons at the ready. As they navigated the twisting path, a flicker of sound from atop the ridge caught Ariella's Elven senses.

She lifted a hand, signaling for Rider to halt. In one fluid motion, he dismounted and drew his blade as Ariella notched an arrow to her bowstring, keen eyes scanning the ledges above.

Her eyes swept the rocky outcroppings, her bow held ready. The fading light cast long shadows across the uneven terrain, providing ample hiding spots for potential ambushers.

Beside her, Rider adjusted his grip on his longsword in a battle-ready stance, his body coiled with tension. "See anything?" he murmured, his deep voice barely audible over the soft snorts of their mounts.

Ariella shook her head almost imperceptibly, auburn tresses swaying. "Nothing yet, but I heard movement." Her gaze darted from ledge to ledge, scanning for any hint of danger lurking in the growing dusk.

Suddenly, a flicker of motion caught her eye. The barest shift of a shadow behind a large boulder. As if on cue, a volley of arrows hissed through the air toward them, the deadly points glinting in the fading light.

"Get down!" Ariella shouted, already diving into a controlled roll. She came up on one knee and loosed an arrow in one fluid motion. The shaft flew true, burying itself in the throat of a bandit as he rose from behind his rocky cover.

Rider moved with the efficiency of a seasoned warrior, his blade a blur of steel. He deflected two arrows with lightning-fast swipes before charging forward, a roar ripping from his throat.

More bandits burst from the shadows, their blades flashing. They were an organized bunch, wielding an array of polished weapons and uniformed leathers. A hulking brute with a wild black beard swung a massive war hammer at Rider's head.

Rider ducked beneath the hammer's arc. He lashed out with his sword, opening a deep gash across the brute's chest. The man stumbled back, bellowing in pain before collapsing, blood soaking his jerkin.

Ariella picked off bandits one by one, each arrow finding its mark with lethal grace. One shaft sprouted from a lean man's eye, another punched through a second's throat in a spray of crimson. Rider was a whirlwind of flashing steel. His blade seemed to be in multiple places at once. He hamstrung one attacker, nearly severing the man's leg at the knee then pivoted to block a vicious axe swipe. The clang of metal echoed in the early evening air. With a twist of his wrist, he sent his opponent's weapon flying before plunging his sword into his chest and savagely kicking the corpse from his sword.

The last bandit fell with a gurgle as Ariella's arrow lodged in his throat. The man crumpled, hands scrabbling feebly at the shaft before going still, glassy eyes staring unseeing at the twilight sky.

Silence settled, broken only by his and Ariella's labored breathing, occasionally punctuated by a wet cough coming from the brute Rider felled earlier. They stood amidst the carnage, blood-spattered and tense, eyes darting warily for any further signs of attack.

After a long moment, Rider lowered his blade, the steel dripping crimson. "I think that's the last of them," he panted, sapphire eyes still hard and battle-bright.

Ariella nodded, lowering her bow but keeping an arrow nocked. She moved to stand beside Rider, her lithe muscles still coiled with tension. "These are no ordinary bandits," she murmured, her violet gaze sweeping over the fallen bodies, taking note of the quality of their arms and armor, far finer than the motley gear of a common brigand.

Rider's brow tensed as he wiped his blade on a dead man's tunic. "You think they were hired?"

Ariella shook her head, auburn tresses swaying. "I intend to find out."

Ariella strode purposefully over to the hulking brute whose breath came in wet gasps in a spreading pool of his own blood. "Who hired you?" she demanded, her melodic voice edged with steel.

The brute glared up at her, his beady eyes glinting with equal parts pain and malice. He let out a rattling, wheezing laugh that quickly devolved into a coughing fit, flecks of blood spraying from his lips. "Go to hell, knife-ear," he rasped, chest heaving with labored breaths.

In one vicious movement, Rider grabbed an arrow from Ariella's quill and drove it into the brute's shoulder before twisting it. "Let's try this again," he growled, leaning close. "Who. Hired. You?"

The bandit writhed, meaty wet hands scrabbling at Rider's iron grip. "Ach! 'Right," he screamed, face contorted in pain. "The Speaker. He hired us to waylay travelers on the road. Wants to sow fear and confusion."

Rider leaned in, looming over the fallen man. "The Speaker? Who in the nine hells is that?" he growled, leaning into the arrow.

"I don't know!" the brute whimpered, eyes rolling wildly. "I swear. Never seen 'im. Always wears a mask. A kinda metal plate." He coughed again, blood trickling from his mouth. "Please. Mercy. Take the carriages. The goods —it's all yours. The others will be back soon. We'll leave and not return."

Ariella's lips curled in disgust. "A masked man, using bandits to terrorize the roads?" She shook her head, brow furrowed in thought. "This bodes ill. There is more at play here, it has to be connected."

Rider released the arrow and nodded grimly before sheathing his sword. "Aye. And I aim to find out how." He glanced down at the wheezing brute dispassionately. "What should we do with this one?"

Ariella met the man's pleading gaze, her expression unreadable. "Leave him. He'll be dead soon enough." She turned and strode towards their waiting mounts.

Rider cast one last look at the dying brigand before following Ariella, his boots crunching on the bloody dirt.

The duo strapped their horses to one of the stolen carriages, loaded it with some of the stolen goods, and headed south towards the Queen's Road. They posed as merchants, their cart laden with barrels and sacks rattled with each bump in the road.

It wasn't long before a group of thieves darted from their woodland cover like foxes after prey. The confrontation was brief but intense. Rider's blade rang as he parried a knife aimed at his heart. His movements were vicious but efficient as he worked with Ariella to render the group unconscious. They loaded the group into their commandeered vehicle and returned to Brightspire, delivering the thieves and collecting their reward from the local bounty office.

With their coin purses now heavier, they returned to the Silver Harp for refreshment and rest.

CHAPTER IV

HIDDEN IN THE NIGHT

Rider and Ariella slipped through the edges of the bustling tavern, sidestepping a raucous group of Humans and Elves clinking mugs in salute.

A cloud of pipe smoke wafted lazily toward the rafters, carrying hints of tobacco from distant lands.

In a shadowed corner, Rider pulled out a chair for Ariella. The worn wood of the table was cool to the touch, a testimony to its rare use this far from the bar.

"Thank you," she said, adjusting her emerald cloak as she sat. Her auburn hair cascaded over her shoulders, a striking contrast against the rich fabric.

"Of course, Ari," Rider replied, trying a new nickname. "Now, regarding our next move—" Rider began.

Ariella leaned forward, her voice low and tinged with urgency. "We need to tread carefully. I'm not sure we're as safe here as we originally thought." She glanced discreetly at the patrons, seeking signs of prying ears amidst the revelers. "Those bandits were hired by someone in Brightspire, so it stands to reason they've employed local adventurers as well."

"Well then," Rider murmured, thumbing the edge of the lucky coin in his pocket. "We could ask around, see if anyone's *hiring* and strike swiftly."

"I'm not joking, Rider. I'm more concerned for Brightspire now than I was when we started out. I'd hoped we'd have a clearer lead by now," Ariella grieved, her lips pressed into a determined line. "We must balance our approach. Gather information before we act."

"Balance," Rider echoed, smirking. "That's why we make such an excellent pair, Ari. Your caution tempers my... enthusiasm."

"Enthusiasm," she chuckled softly. "Is that what you call your penchant for flirtatious banter with every soft-featured lady we meet, or perhaps it's your risky decisions and overconfident use of that sword on your back?"

"Perhaps," he winked. "But it's gotten us this far, hasn't it?"

Ariella groaned. "Let's not forget what's at stake."

"Will it be the usual, a Red for the lady and an ale for you, handsome? Or does tonight call for something stronger?" Isabella's voice sliced through the din of the tavern as she approached Rider and Ariella's secluded table. She flashed a smile at Rider, her eyes glinting with a hint of mischief beneath tendrils of chestnut hair that escaped from her loose braid.

Ariella rolled her eyes slightly before she tilted her head, considering. "The mulled wine, if you please. Oh, and a bowl of whatever stew the kitchen has."

"Make it two, and another room please," Rider added, his flirtatious gaze lingering on Isabella. Her fingers grazed the tabletop, so lightly it seemed accidental. When she withdrew, a tiny, folded piece of parchment lay in her wake.

"Two mulled wines and the hunter's stew coming right up," she chirped before disappearing into the crowd, her skirts swishing around her ankles.

Once the barmaid was out of earshot, Rider snatched the note, his fingertips brushing over the emblem pressed into the wax seal—a sigil known only to those who served Queen Vyshaan directly. With a flick of his fingers, he broke the seal.

Room seven holds the key; let the shadows guide thee.

"Instructions from our patron?" Ariella arched an eyebrow. "Intriguing."

"Or troubling," Rider replied, tucking the note into his vest. "Depends on what we find in room seven."

"Only one way to find out." Ariella's eyes sparkled.

Hours slipped away like sand through fingers. The tavern's raucous energy gradually faded into a sleepy murmur. Patrons staggered out, their laughter trailing off into the night. When Isabella snuffed the last candle, the tavern stood silent but for the soft crackle of the dying hearth.

"Time to uncover the Iron Sorceress's secrets," Rider whispered, as the duo retired to room seven.

A large, unlit chandelier hung above them, its crystals diffracting the moonlight that spilled through the window. As the door closed behind Ariella, Rider's assessing gaze caught a figure waiting in the darkness.

Instinct took over. Rider moved Ariella behind him as

he placed his free hand on the hilt of his sword, ready for whatever came next. The silence pressed upon them as a shadow unfurled from the darkest corner with unnatural grace. A slender, pale-skinned High Elf woman stepped into the scattered moonlight, as if emerging from another realm.

The woman's attire was a whisper of midnight fabric, melding seamlessly with the shadows that clung to her like loyal subjects. She carried blades at her waist, their deadly edges evidence of a life spent in the service of secrecy and swift justice. Her jet-black hair, cropped short against the nape of her neck, framed her sharp features which added to the intensity of her gaze.

Rider tensed, his hand tightening around the hilt of his blade.

Ariella stepped out from behind him and raised a hand in a gesture of peace. "Zara Nightshadow," she said, her voice steady but filled with a respectful caution. "I've heard of your exploits from Queen Vyshaan's court."

Zara's lips twitched, not quite a smile, but an acknowledgment of Ariella's familiarity. "Lady Ariella," she replied, her voice low and melodic, yet as sharp as a knife. "It has been many years since courtly intrigues were my concern. The shadows whisper different stories now."

Zara Nightshadow, the Queen's trusted spy and assassin, regarded them with pitch-dark eyes that missed nothing as she moved towards them, controlled and deliberate. Zara reached into the folds of her cloak and produced several items: a tattered banner emblazoned with a Dragon coiled around a black sun, and small eerie trinkets that pulsed with a dark energy.

"These are fragments of the growing threat," she explained, laying them out on the stone table among the remnants of a forgotten meal. "The guards find more each week. The dungeons grow crowded with those who preach Dragon worship, the cult is gaining strength in numbers and boldness."

Ariella frowned, examining a small, rune-etched stone that shifted under her gaze.

"How deeply have they infiltrated our lands?" she asked.

"Deeper than we feared," Zara responded. "And they are not merely peasants and madmen. The number of nobles and scholars drawn to the promises of power is growing."

"What does Queen Vyshaan ask of us now?" Rider asked.

Zara's eyes met his. "Same as before, but I come bearing new information and leads Queen Vyshaan demands you follow."

"Tell us what you know," Rider urged.

"This cult has an established hierarchy, each member a piece in a larger puzzle," Zara began. "They believe they are the lifeblood of the Dragon Lord's spirit, and they seek vessels for his return."

"His return?" Ariella's voice was skeptical. "Is that even possible?"

"We fear it is," Zara said. "Their numbers keep growing, and they've proven their ability to dominate minds and resurrect those they kill after failing to turn them. They operate in shadows—much like I—but for far darker purposes."

"Then we shall be the light that reveals them," Rider declared.

"Don't rush recklessly into this. They are more skilled in deceit than you know," Zara warned, quiet but firm. "Remember, your primary mission is to gather information. We've received rumors that the cult has infiltrated the guard. Your task is to discover any truth behind these rumors and if so, who in our ranks have been turned."

"This, however, will require subtlety" Zara turned around toward a large wooden trunk, "If you must dispatch any who serve the cult, these should help you do so in silence and without drawing suspicion."

Inside the trunk was an array of weapons and tools. "Each item here was chosen with care," Zara said, her tone reverent. She lifted a cloak from the pile, its fabric shifting colors like oil on water. "This will blend your Human form into any shadow, any background. It's protection as much as any armor."

Rider reached out, the cloth cool and weightless between his fingers. As he draped it over his shoulders, the room seemed to swallow his form, leaving only a faint outline where he stood.

"Remarkable," breathed Ariella, her keen eyes wide with a mix of awe and longing.

Zara moved on, presenting a slender blade with a handle wrought like twisted vines. "This blade seeks weakness. It will find the weakest point in armor and flesh alike."

"Incredible..." Rider murmured, turning the dagger in his hand, feeling its balance. He performed a few slices against imagined foes, feeling its promise of lethality in its whispering slices through the air.

Zara handed Ariella scrolls sealed with wax. "Healing magic. Crafted by the Queen herself. In your journey, wounds will come, both seen and unseen. The magical training you received as part of your courtly upbringing will allow you to use these to mend flesh and fortify spirit."

"Thank you, Zara," Ariella said, her hands steady as she took possession of the scrolls, treating them as sacred relics.

"Your skill with a bow is beyond doubt, but there will come times when a more... personal approach is necessary," Zara remarked, locking eyes with Ariella. "In those instances, these blades will prove invaluable," Zara handed the huntress two Elven short-swords forged from mithril. "Light as feathers yet stronger than steel. Keep them close," she instructed.

Ariella nodded.

The pieces were not just tools, but symbols of earned trust and a shared mission.

"Rest now," Zara said, stepping away from the duo. "Your mission continues at dawn." With a wave of her hand, the air seemed to shimmer like water disturbed by a stone. A portal appeared, its edges flickering with an ethereal gray light. Rider felt a chill emanating from the void, the hairs on his arms standing at attention.

"Do not fail the Queen." Zara commanded. "I don't want our next meeting to be on less friendly terms." Then she was gone. The portal collapsed in on itself, , its shimmering edges fading back into the shadows as it disappeared.

The next morning, amber light from the morning sun penetrated the windows and washed over the rustic interior of the Silver Harp. Rider and Ariella were met by the sounds of breakfast-seekers discussing their plans and the scents of freshly fried eggs, sizzling pork, and morning brew mingling with the smoky tinge of burning wood from the freshly lit hearth.

"A round of morning brew," Rider motioned to the morning barkeep, his voice barely rising above the din.

"Make it strong," Ariella added, her eyes scanning the

room as if trying to memorize the face of every early patron.

The drinks arrived, a potent brew that warmed their insides with each sip, carrying hints of cinnamon and nutmeg. The food was a rustic platter of the aforementioned pork, firm but not overcooked, served alongside scrambled eggs seasoned with herbs from the surrounding Brightspire forests.

Rider and Ariella spent the day melding into crowds like phantoms. They lingered near groups of guards, seemingly engrossed in market stalls or idle chatter, while they listened for secrets.

They overheard one guard gossip quietly with his partner. "Did you hear what the others are saying about the chief? Apparently he's releasing some of the prisoners without reporting it."

"If the rumors are true, they all had the same tattoo and were brought in as part of last month's raid."

"Best not to ask questions, Rookie," his partner replied. "Not unless you fancy being one of the next bodies we find with a dagger in its back."

"The chief is too busy spending most of his nights at The Grand Opulent Theater to put a dagger in anyone's back."

Each scrap of conversation overheard added another thread to the web of conspiracy tightening around Brightspire. Rider exchanged a look with Ariella. It was time to delve deeper into the shadows.

"Go get your best dress, I'm taking you to the theater tonight." Rider stated in a low, authoritative tone.

"Yes, sir." Ari replied with a sultry look and smile escaping the side of her lips.

As the sun began to dip below the horizon, painting the sky in hues of orange and pink, Rider waited in the Silver

Harp's dining area. His fingers drummed impatiently on the worn wooden table, his mind focused on the mission ahead—and the captivating partner who would accompany him.

The creak of the stairs drew his attention, and as he looked up, the room seemed to melt away. Ariella appeared at the top of the staircase, a vision in a form-fitting black High-Elf dress that clung to her curves like a second skin. The plunging neckline dipped dangerously low, revealing the tantalizing swell of her breasts and the valley of her cleavage. The smooth, pale skin of her decolletage was a striking contrast against the dark fabric that shimmered in the candlelight, accentuating her every movement as she descended the stairs.

Rider stood abruptly, his chair scraping against the floorboards. His breath caught in his throat as his eyes traced the way the dress hugged her slim waist and how her auburn hair cascaded down her back in soft waves, exposing the slender column of her neck and the delicate points of her ears.

As she reached the bottom of the stairs, Ariella's eyes locked with Rider's. Rider was spellbound, unable to look away from the captivating depths of her gaze. A hint of a smile played at the corner of Ariella's full lips, a smile that promised both danger and delight.

Rider's world narrowed as he stepped forward, mesmerized by the violet of her eyes, the fullness of her lips, and the intoxicating scent of jasmine and sandalwood. "You look stunning, Ari," he murmured as he offered his arm, his voice rough with barely contained desire.

Ariella smiled, a slow, sensual curve of her lips. "You clean up well yourself," she purred, her eyes roaming appreciatively over his tailored black suit and the way it accentuated his broad shoulders and lean build.

As they stepped out into the bustling streets of Bright-spire, Rider's hand placed firmly on the small of her back, heads turned to follow their progress. Whispers rippled through the crowd, admiring the striking couple. But Rider and Ariella paid them no heed, their focus solely on each other and the mission that lay ahead.

CHAPTER V
ELVES DON'T FORGET

Rider marveled at the Grand Theater of Brightspire, its marble pillars gleaming in the twilight glow, each topped with a golden likeness of legendary heroes. The building loomed with an air of timeless grandeur, its velvet-lined balconies arched gracefully overheard. Enchanted murals adorned the walls, their vivid colors flickering under the torchlights.

As they stepped into the opulent lobby, Rider examined the images. One in particular caught his attention. A battle frozen in time between a knight astride a Griffin and a colossal Dragon, its scales shimmering like rubies.

"These paintings… they're remarkable." Rider murmured.

"They represent the Battle of Stonefire," Ariella pointed out. "Not many of the other races remember the details as vividly as we Elves do. Queen Vyshaan herself witnessed The Great War first-hand seven centuries ago."

"Incredible. I always considered most of what I learned about the war to be more myth or tall-tale than fact,"

Rider replied as his eyes traveled across the intricate painting.

"I assure you, Rider. The Dragon Lord was real. If the High Elves hadn't joined the cause when we did, the other great kingdoms would surely have fallen. You may actually learn something tonight," Ariella smirked, taking the opportunity to playfully act his superior.

They moved through the throngs of patrons, avoiding contact and notice through subtle techniques. Their presence was inconspicuous to the oblivious guests, who were more concerned with social niceties and the forthcoming performance.

From a corner where the laughter and music seemed most distant, they watched, their attention fixed on a man of considerable stature, his uniform adorned with medals that caught the light with every confident stride.

"Rider, look," Ari alerted, "The Chief of the City Guard."

Rider's eyes scanned toward Ariella's side of the room before he caught sight of the Elf. "I got him," he responded.

"See how he avoids certain individuals?" Ariella noted, her eyes still following the official's calculated movements. "How he steers clear of certain conversations? Yet he's never far from those other highborn," Ariella added quietly. "He's cautious, but informed. Clever."

Rider and Ariella blended with the crowd as it entered the theater to take their seats. They listened intently, ears tuned to whispers that might betray cultists hiding in plain sight. A phrase here, a word there, it was a verbal dance as intricate as any performance on stage.

"Have you prepared the offering?"

"Of course. The ceremony won't be delayed this time."

"Good. We'll head to the gathering after the performance then."

A chill ran down Rider's spine. These were no ordinary theatergoers. Their ominous conversation pointed at something sinister.

"I think we might have tumbled into the viper's nest," Rider whispered.

"Indeed," Ariella replied. "Now, we watch and wait."

Rider shifted forward, straining to hear the hushed tones of a caped figure three rows in front of him. Just behind a gilded pillar, a seated pair came into view. Something about them caught his attention.

"Are you certain you know the way?" one murmured, his voice quivering with anxiety.

"Of course," the other responded tersely.

"A meeting of the serpents," the nervous one whispered. "I can't believe we're actually going to be official."

"Tonight, after the opera," confirmed the other, a sly smile curling his lips.

Rider touched Ariella's wrist and exchanged a glance with her. Silently, he arched an eyebrow in the direction of the pillar. These were their quarry. Two soon-to-be members of the elusive cult. With a subtle nod, they prepared themselves for the pursuit.

Rider and Ariella took their seats behind the suspicious duo and settled in to enjoy the performance, as the master of ceremonies took the stage.

The emcee bowed deeply, his velvet jacket catching the light. "Lords and ladies, distinguished guests," he began, his voice carrying across the hushed theater. "Tonight, we present a tale of bravery, sacrifice, and the triumph of good over evil. I give you, The Dragon Lord and the Battle of Stonefire!"

The curtains parted, revealing an exaggeratedly large

figure shielded in heavy black armor. "Before the dawn of the new age, a figure loomed over the land. Drakzeneth, a dark sorcerer who along with his evil army of monstrous creatures, wrote the darkest saga in Etonya's history." As the emcee's voice rang through the hall, the stage transformed into a battlefield.

The emcee stepped forward, gesturing dramatically as each Dragon made its entrance.

"The Ebony Dragons, their scales as dark as the abyss, unleash a caustic acid that melts flesh from bone." On cue, an obsidian-scaled Dragon soared overhead spewing a torrent of sizzling green acid which left seared scars on stage.

"The Emerald Dragons, cloaked in verdant scales, exhale a miasma of toxic gases, choking the life from their victims." An emerald beast glided past, noxious clouds billowing in its wake. Extras playing soldiers crumpled to the ground, clutching their throats.

"The Sapphire Dragons crackle with the power of the storm itself, their breath a maelstrom of lightning." A Dragon with glittering blue scales reared up. Electricity arcing from its jaws, sending extras scattering in a frenzied dance for cover.

"And the Ruby Dragons, their scales gleaming like the blood they spill, vomit torrents of liquid fire, setting the very air ablaze." A crimson terror swooped low, jets of illusionary flame engulfing swaths of the stage.

As the play unfolded, Rider found himself drawn into the story despite his focus needing to be solely on their mission.

The actors portrayed the desperation of the dwarves as they fought against the relentless onslaught of the Dragon Lord's armies. Black-armored Orcs adorned with draconic symbols swarmed the stage, their snarls and battle cries echoing through the theater.

Just as all seemed lost, a horn blast cut through the chaos. The Dwarven king, his beard streaked with gray and his crown sitting heavy upon his brow, looked up with hope in his eyes.

"The Elves of Brightspire have come!" he declared, his voice booming. "We are saved!"

A silver banner unfurled from the rafters, catching the glow of the stage lights. From the wings, a contingent of Elven warriors emerged, their silver and gold armor gleaming like starlight.

Leading them was Queen Vyshaan herself, resplendent in a gown of shimmering silk, a delicate crown of stars upon her brow. Despite the delicate finery, there was no mistaking her presence in the melee for anything but regal authority.

"Brightspire!... Advance!" She cried out with authority. In unison, High Elf warriors and mages began shouting and casting spells that imitated the intense battle of old.

As the Elven forces joined the fray, the tide of battle turned. Dragons swooped from the rafters, their wings spread wide as they breathed plumes of arcane fire across the stage. But the combined might of Elf, Man, and Dwarf proved too much.

Rider leaned forward in his seat, transfixed by the spectacle. The Dragons were marvels of stagecraft and illusion, and yet, a part of him knew the real beasts had been even more terrifying. Beside him, Ariella's fingers tightened on the armrests. Her eyes bright with memories of tales told by her people. The High Elves did not forget.

The battle reached its crescendo. Queen Vyshaan pointed her staff at the volcanic prop of Mount Stonefire. A gout of crimson fabric burst from the mountain with a deafening roar from the orchestra. The actor portraying Drakzeneth fell beneath the stage as the Dragons scattered, fleeing into the shadows. The Elven hero stood triumphant amidst the scorched and tattered battlefield.

The audience erupted into applause, rising to their feet in a standing ovation. Ariella and Rider joined in.

As the curtains fell, the entrancing spell of the reenactment was broken. The illusions dispelled, the past fading once again into legend. Rider's focus snapped back to reality. He glanced at Ariella, flicking his gaze toward the retreating figures ahead.

As the crowd dispersed, they melted into the crowd behind the novice cultists. They followed the suspects through city streets, across bridges, and eventually down to the port below.

The pair of neophyte cultists made their way toward the forest. Ariella and Rider bided their time, letting the pair disappear beneath the looming canopy before pursuing their marks.

The forest swallowed the last vestiges of twilight like an abyss. The earthy aroma of moss and pine needles filled their nostrils as they ventured into the wooded darkness.

"Stay sharp," Ariella breathed.

Ariella led Rider through twisted underbrush and over gnarled roots as she tracked the unsuspecting duo's trail. Moonlight filtered through the trees, casting ghostly silver beams that sliced the shadows.

Rider's heartbeat matched the steady nocturnal rhythm of the forest around him.

Ahead, murmured voices and flickering flames. The cultists stood at the grove's edge next to a campfire that sent sparks spiraling toward the star-studded sky. The smell of burning wood hung sharp and pungent.

"Something's not right," Ariella said, her body taut as a drawn bowstring. "Why meet here, in the open?"

"I don't think it's as open as it seems, Ari."

From the darkness, shadows stirred. Cloaked figures appeared from the opposite side of the woods. They fanned out, moving with purpose to close the circle.

Rider crouched beside Ariella behind a thick veil of brush.

The cultists raised their hands toward the waterfall. A chant rose, low and thrumming, the cadence resonating with the very earth beneath them.

"Look at their hands," Ariella whispered, pointing.

Tattoos spiraled up the cultists' arms, glowing faintly with an otherworldly light.

Rider frowned. "Didn't that guard mention something about tattoos? When he mentioned the chief releasing prisoners?"

Before Ariella could answer, the waterfall slowed. The wall of water parted. A dark cavern appeared behind the liquid curtains.

"An entrance guarded by water and spellwork." Rider's gaze lingered on the cave. "We've got our mark. Let's move." Rider reached for the handle of his concealed dagger as he turned to Ariella, her gaze steady.

"No, Rider. We're here to watch, learn, and strike only when victory is certain."

"Ari, there's only five of them. Between you and me? They'd never know what hit them. This is why I'm here. That's our mission."

"And we were warned about the consequences of failure," Ariella countered.

"Then we wait and watch," he sighed, easing into a more comfortable position.

The pair watched the cultists complete their ritual and

enter the cave before turning their backs on the site and retracing their steps. Their boots sank into the damp earth as Rider and Ariella hastened through the forest, the air thick with the musk of rain-soaked foliage. Around them, the nocturnal chorus of crickets and the rustling leaves whispered secrets into the dark as the silver moon cast a spectral glow over their path, illuminating the way back to Brightspire.

In the week that followed, the city's stone spires and gilded domes loomed above as Rider and Ariella scoured the streets for leads. Eventually, they found a promising target. A local high-born displaying unusual changes in behavior and cloaked late-night visitors to his large home.

The moon, now a slender crescent, barely illuminated the cobbled streets of Brightspire as Rider and Ariella scaled the second story balcony on his house. They slipped inside through unlocked doors, moving with practiced silence, their soft leather boots whispering against the floor.

The musty scent of ancient parchment and ink enveloped them as they entered a large study. Faint moonlight trickled through the high windows, casting long, slithering shadows along the rows of towering bookshelves. Their senses heightened in the hush that hung like a cloak over the vast chamber.

"Keep an eye out for any wards or enchantments," Ariella whispered.

They split up, eyes skimming over the spines of tomes and scrolls. Rider paused occasionally, running his fingers over titles etched in gold leaf, searching for anything out of place.

"Here," Ariella's voice, a mere scratch in the stillness, beckoned from across the room.

Rider approached and found her standing before a bookshelf that seemed no different from the rest. Ariella's keen gaze caught a subtle discrepancy—a single volume, slightly askew, its binding not quite matching the surrounding works.

"Good catch," Rider murmured, reaching out to adjust the errant book. The soft, mechanical sound barely registered before a section of the shelf swung outward, revealing a hidden compartment.

An old journal lay inside, its cover a somber leather with no title to betray its contents. Rider carefully removed it. He exchanged a glance with Ariella before adjusting his hands to open the book. The cover, however, refused to separate from its pages.

"Give it here," Ariella said, "Let me try something."

Ariella took the journal from Rider, held it between her palms, and chanted in High Elvish. A small light flared between her palms and the journal.

"There. That may have done the trick," she whispered as she opened the journal.

"What did you do?" Rider asked.

"A simple dispelling charm," Ariella muttered nonchalantly as she flicked through the pages. "A trick I picked up during my studies before my family lost favor at court."

She flipped through a few pages. "This holds entries about the cult. Their movements and some sort of dark ritual."

Rider leaned closer, his breath mingling with hers as they poured over the cryptic lines written in an elegant scrawl. References to secret meetings, locations known only to the initiated, and chilling details about the cult's plans filled the pages.

"Look at this symbol," Ariella pointed to a recurring sigil, a winged serpent entwined around a triangular shape. "It's the same one we saw on the cultists' arms."

Rider traced the symbol with his finger. "This journal, he has to be a member of the cult. We need to act, Ari. Let's get back to that cave and end this."

"While I agree that we are closer to the heart of the serpent's nest than we thought," Ariella admitted, a fierce determination hardening her features. "We must tread even more carefully now."

"Ari, we can't just sit around." Rider said, his mind racing with the gravity of their discovery. "Every word in this accursed book brings us a step closer to ending this cult."

"Then we take it with us. We study it. Then we decide on our next course of action," she countered as she carefully placed the journal into her waist pouch before closing the secret compartment.

Ariella slid the panel back into place, ensuring the bookshelf appeared untouched by their intrusion. She ran a slender finger along the spine of the neighboring tome, checking for dust disturbed in their search.

They made their way back toward their exit, each measured step deliberate upon the plush carpet. As they reached the door, Rider paused, placing a hand on the cool metal of the handle. "This information... it could change everything."

"Let us hope it changes things for the better," Ariella replied.

Rider pushed the door open just wide enough for them to slip through. They emerged into the night, the brisk air filling their lungs as they left the cloistered manor behind.

Their pace was swift but cautious as they wove through the city's slumbering streets. The sense of accomplishment melded with anticipation, creating a heady mixture that quickened Rider's pulse.

Rider murmured, "With this knowledge, we hold the power to strike at the heart of the cult."

"Indeed, and may our aim be true when that moment comes," Ariella replied.

The Silver Harp's warm glow beckoned Rider and Ariella. The now familiar medley of scents—roasted meats, spiced ale, and the underlying musk of wood smoke—wrapped around them like a welcoming embrace. Laughter and conversation mingled with the lilting melody of a lute played by a bard, carefree and warm.

Rider and Ariella settled into a corner table, the worn wood carrying the warmth of the hearth.

A waitress, her hair tied back with a green ribbon, approached with a friendly smile. "What'll it be, handsome?"

Rider met her gaze with a flirtatious but appreciative nod. "A hearty stew. You know, something to keep me warm tonight," Rider quipped, flashing a grin as he raised an eyebrow.

"And mulled wine," Ariella cut in. "Heavy on the cinnamon and cloves."

The girl winked at Rider. "Coming right up," she said before mingling into the boisterous crowd.

As they waited, they withdrew the journal from Ariella's satchel. The pages seemed to whisper their dark secrets, the words shimmering faintly in the candlelight.

"So much information," Ariella mused, her slender fingers tracing over the serpentine sigils. "Locations, rituals, secret symbols… it's as if we're holding the very foundation of the cult in our hands."

Their conversation halted as the woman returned, setting down bowls of steaming stew and two large tankards of mulled wine. The aroma of tender meat and rich broth mingled with the heady scent of spices, making their mouths water.

"Anything else I can do for you?" the girl asked, her eyes warm and inviting as she not so subtly tilted her body toward Rider, her breasts pushed toward his eyeline.

Rider began to turn toward her, grinning.

"Thanks, that'll be all tonight," Ariella interrupted once again, her tone flat and stern.

Rider's grin slowly disappeared as he shook his head, offering a grateful smile. "This is perfect, thank you."

As the girl departed, Ariella lifted her tankard, drawing Rider's attention back to her. "To small comforts in trying times," she toasted, clinking her cup against Rider's.

"I'm pretty sure that's what she was offering," Rider replied with a smirk.

Ariella rolled her eyes and took a long sip of the mulled wine, savoring the warmth that spread through her body. Setting her cup down, she fixed Rider with an exasperated look. "Focus, Rider. We have more important matters at hand than your dalliances with tavern wenches."

Rider chuckled and held up his hands in mock surrender. "Alright, alright. You're right, as usual." He took a hearty spoonful of stew, relishing the rich flavors. After swallowing, he leaned forward, his expression turning serious. "So, what's our next move? We can't just sit on this information."

Ariella absently stirred her stew as she considered their options. "We take this discussion away from prying eyes and ears."

CHAPTER VI
THE SERPENT'S DEN

The flickering light of a single candle cast elongated shadows against the walls as Rider and Ariella hunched over the journal spread open between them. The parchment seemed to shimmer as they dove deeper into its secrets.

Rider's eyes scanned the ancient text, a mix of awe and fear tightening in his chest. "This says that ley lines are the veins of Etonya's magic. Raw energy, the heartbeat of our world. Every spell we cast drains from these sources, but they renew themselves over time," he voiced his concern in hushed words.

"I remember hearing whispers of this in our studies at Brightspire, but it was all dismissed as Dragon Lord propaganda," she replied, her voice tinged with doubt.

"Not according to this, Ari," Rider insisted, pointing to a passage that made his heart race. "It says that if someone controls the ley lines, they could have the power to tear open the very fabric of our reality and bring forth beings from other realms. Or transform others into whatever they please." The weight of the words hung in the air, a terrifying prospect.

"That would explain how they've been able to reanimate corpses, forcing them to serve," Ariella admitted. Her normally vibrant violet eyes now reflected the seriousness of their discovery. "If we don't intervene, the cult could tear Etonya apart."

Silence hung between them as they pondered the possibility.

Rider spoke up. "Look here," he tapped the text. "They call that cave behind that waterfall The Serpent's Den. It looks like they're gathering tomorrow night for another ritual of initiation. We have to find a way in there."

"We must inform the queen," Ariella said.

"If our information is incorrect, and she makes a move too soon," Rider countered, "it could be months before she finds another lead." He swallowed as he gathered up the parchment. "You're the one who reminded me about the consequences of failure. We need more evidence."

"Tomorrow evening then." Ariella sighed.

The forest teemed with its own nocturnal symphony when Rider, shielded in the magical cloak Zara had given him, approached the waterfall cautiously. His senses were heightened, attuned to the slightest rustle of leaves or snap of a twig underfoot. He moved with stealthy intention, the cloak blending seamlessly with the shadows that danced beneath the moon's silver gaze.

"Easy," Rider whispered to himself, his ears picking up the distant call of an owl. "Just another shadow."

A cool breeze carried the scent of damp moss mixed

with the earthy musk of the forest floor. With each measured step toward the waterfall's roar, Rider's hand brushed against the hilt of his dagger – a silent promise of protection. He knew what awaited within The Serpent's Den would be challenging, but it was a risk he was willing to take.

A sudden crackle echoed to the left. Rider froze, breath caught in his throat, heart pounding.

A small creature skittered across the underbrush. Exhaling slowly, he continued forward.

Mist from the waterfall teased his skin as he drew near; the crashing cascade masked the sound of his movements. Hidden by Zara's enchanted cloak, Rider observed the entrance. Mist obscured his view, but he made out the cultists' dark outlines. Their torches flickered, illuminating the serpent sigil embroidered on their identical robes, just as described in the journal's pages.

The cult's sentries parted ways, their footfalls drowned beneath the relentless roar of the falls as they made separate patrols around the grove.

This was the moment Rider had anticipated.

Rider's dagger felt like an extension of himself as he drew it from its sheath. The blade, imbued with magic, thrummed softly.

His heartbeat steady, he thrilled in the hunt but feared the sobering reality of what failure could mean. He drew a shallow breath, the night air filling his lungs.

In one fluid motion, Rider clamped a hand over the cultist's mouth. The dagger found its mark, slipping between ribs with clinical precision. There was no struggle, only the soft thud of a body meeting the earth.

"Rest now, in the void," Rider murmured.

Silently, he withdrew the blade, cleaning it on the fallen cultist's robe before vanishing into the shadows once more.

Each movement was deliberate, a ghostly dance through darkness as he prepared to strike again. His senses remained razor-sharp, attuned to the merest hint of danger.

Thank you, Zara, Rider adjusted his grip on the dagger. *Now, to deal with the other.*

The moon hung high, casting an eerie glow upon the forest clearing as he crept toward the second guard. A wolf's mournful howl pierced the silence, and the guard snapped his head toward Rider's path.

Eyes met.

Time stood still.

Then, chaos erupted.

"Who goes there?" the guard bellowed as he rushed at Rider, summoning a greatsword that shimmered with malevolence. Dark magic pulsed from the blade, its sinister aura empowering the cultist with unnatural strength as his muscles grew and his size increased.

No time for subtlety. Rider drew his own sword and engaged. Each clash felt like striking a stone wall. Sparks flew as his sword met darkened steel, the force reverberating up his arms.

The guard pressed forward, his attacks relentless. Overhead strikes rained down, each one threatening to cleave Rider in two.

Panic and desperation began to set in as Rider felt his arms begin to fail under the repeated blows. Instinct kicked in and something within him changed. Rider's left hand shot out toward the sentry, palm outstretched. A burst of raw energy surged forth, crashing into the dark steel greatsword. The guard's boot heels left ruts in the ground as he was pushed backwards.

"Is that all you've got?" the guard sneered, a twisted smile set across his face as he regained his footing.

Before Rider could muster a word, an arrow zipped from the shadows. The sentry crumpled without another word, an arrow buried in his temple, the threat extinguished by precise intervention.

"No," Ariella retorted. "He's got me." She stepped from the shadows of a nearby tree.

"Did...did you see that?" Rider's chest heaved, his gaze locked on his trembling hand.

Ariella approached, her violet eyes wide with astonishment. "What the hell was that? I've never seen anything like it, especially not from you."

"Neither have I," Rider admitted, wonder and unease warring in his expression.

"Do you still want to press forward or should we turn back and figure out whatever in the hells *that* was?"

"It's too late, if we turn back now we may never get a chance like this again. Just put his robes on," Rider said. "I'll get the others and we can hide their bodies in the brush."

Ariella's slender fingers fumbled with the hem of one of the bloodstained robes, the coarse fabric chafing against her skin as she draped it over her slender frame.

Beside her, Rider adjusted his hood, as his eyes scanned their surroundings with a mix of caution and curiosity.

"I'm not certain this will fool them," Ariella whispered, her voice barely audible over the sound of the crashing falls.

"Only one way to find out." He pulled his hood lower, shadowing his features. "Stay close."

They slipped around the veil of water, the frigid mist dampening their borrowed attire, and entered the cave's gaping mouth. The air within was dank, carrying an undercurrent of something ancient and decayed. It tasted metallic, like iron, as if the very atmosphere was tainted with old blood.

"By the light..." Ariella breathed, her Elven eyes widening.

The Serpent's Den unfolded before them, far grander than any cave hideout had a right to be. It was a labyrinth of tunnels. Each twist and turn revealed more alcoves filled with scroll-lined shelves, stacks of crates, and racks upon racks of sinister-looking weapons. Distant chanting echoed, the words indecipherable but laden with dark intent.

"Look at all this," Rider murmured, his gaze sweeping across the vast space. "They must've been here for years."

"Long enough to amass quite the hoard," Ariella agreed.

They ventured deeper, until they came across a chamber that served as a shrine to conquest and power.

A life-size statue of a helmed dark knight stood, dominating the room with its massive stone sword and shield held in eternal readiness. A painted battle scene stretched across the wall behind it, depicting a fiery sky torn asunder by Dragons of various colors descending upon a scorched land.

"Is that—" Ariella began, but Rider already stepped closer to the open-faced tome on a pedestal, his fingers tracing the brittle pages reverently.

"Listen to this," he said, his voice low but clear as he read aloud. "*And so it came to pass that the Dragon flights, once proud and unyielding, fell into servitude beneath the Dragon Lord's iron will. With magic and bloodshed, he carved a path of ruin through the southern reaches of Etonya, his dominion unchallenged, his enemies laid to waste.*"

Ariella nodded solemnly, the weight of centuries bearing down upon her. She could almost smell the charred aftermath of those ancient battles, the stench mingling with the earthy dampness of the chamber.

Ariella's gaze lingered on the helmed dark knight, its stone visage frozen in an eternal grimace. "Rider," she whispered, her voice barely audible over the distant drip of water echoing through the cavernous den. "We can't let them succeed."

Before Rider could respond, the sound of footsteps alerted them both to the approach of cult members. Two figures emerged from the shadows, their robes identical to those Ariella and Rider now wore. With a practiced ease, they set down crates, the wood thudding softly against the stone floor.

"Hail the Serpent's embrace," one member intoned, raising his arms in a fluid gesture that hinted at ritual significance.

"Embrace... the Serpent," Ariella ventured hesitantly, mimicking the motion with forced confidence. Beside her, Rider echoed the phrase, his accent slightly coloring the words.

The cultists' eyes narrowed, a silent exchange passing between them. The first member murmured something low enough only his companion could hear. His hand subtly gestured toward the tunnel behind them.

"More crates to move," his comrade said, his stare lingering at the duo. They exited without another glance, their steps quickening as they vanished into the tunnels beyond.

Ariella exhaled, her heart pounding. "We must move. Now."

"We're close, Ari," Rider responded. "We need to put an end to whatever is happening within."

Rider and Ariella pressed forward, the scent of old

incense and cold stone guiding them further into the heart of The Serpent's Den.

The walls of the tunnel were damp and cold to the touch narrowed around them, a stark reminder of the maze they willingly entered.

"Rider, do you think they recognized us as outsiders?" Ariella's voice was barely above a murmur, her breaths shallow in the confined space.

"Even if they didn't, they know something is amiss," he replied, eyes scanning the labyrinthine shadows for signs of pursuit.

Every few paces, Ariella paused, her Elven eyes piercing the darkness for subtle cues that might betray an ambush or a hidden watcher.

"Listen," she said suddenly, tilting her head. A rhythmic chant filtered through the tunnels.

Silently, they pressed forward with the barest of glances exchanged. The chants grew steadily louder with each turn and twist of the winding passages.

Flickering torchlight grew brighter as they approached the chants. The smell of burning resins and spices filled their noses.

"Careful," Rider cautioned as they neared an archway. Peering around the corner, they saw a vast chamber ahead, the source of the chants. Shadows of gathered figures swayed across the damp stone walls, lost in their ritualistic fervor.

"Can you make out what they're saying?" Rider asked.

"Something about awakening and offerings," Ariella replied, her face set in a grim line. "We need to find out—."

"Intruders!" the shout echoed off the stone walls.

Rider spun and found himself facing five cultists, their twisted weapons wielded with menace. He ducked under a wild swing and parried a thrust, countering with a swift jab to the assailant's throat.

Another cultist lunged.

Rider sidestepped, pivoted, and slashed his dagger's edge across the man's hamstring.

One by one, the cultists fell. They lacked the sentries' dark strength and martial training.

Ariella's silhouette moved with lethal grace among the shadows.

Five cultists surged forward from the passage on her right, their faces twisted masks of hatred and malice.

Ariella's form weaved through the dim light like a wraith, her movements a blur to the untrained eye. "Come and die, then," she taunted, her voice ringing clear above the din of battle.

The first cultist lunged, a crude dagger aimed for her heart.

She slipped to the side, brandishing an arrow. In a fluid motion, she pivoted, driving the shaft deep between his ribs.

He crumpled to the cold cave floor without a sound.

The others closed ranks, their eyes wide.

Ariella was already moving. She nocked and loosed an arrow with preternatural speed. Her bowstring sang twice more, one fell with an arrow in his eye, the other clutched his throat as he fell.

"Ari, duck!" Rider shouted.

Without hesitation, she dropped to her knees. The dark sorcery of a cultist's bolt seared the air where her head had been. She rolled, coming up with daggers drawn—a gleam of silver in each hand.

The remaining cultists closed in, emboldened by their numbers.

"Your tricks won't save you now, Elf," taunted one, raising his weapon.

"Tricks?" Ariella's laugh was a silvery peal, a stark contrast in the grim setting. "This is skill." She met them head-on, her twin blades flashing. A parry, a twist, and her blade sank into flesh.

She pivoted, using her assailant's body as a shield against another's wild swing. One swift pull and her blade slid free, sending another cultist to the ground.

Rider moved in beside her. They battled together against the darkness, a deadly duet in the heart of the Serpent's Den.

"Enough!" The last cultist standing cried out, desperation dripping in his voice. His hands wove an intricate pattern in the air, darkness gathered like storm clouds, and coalesced into a barrier shimmering with dark energy. Magical arcs struck all around.

The dead stirred, their darkened souls struggling to crawl from their husks.

"Ari!" Rider called out, pivoting to face their remaining adversary.

But it was too late. The barrier separated the two heroes on opposite sides of the room.

Ariella released a series of arrows against the Sorcerer's dark barrier, to no avail. "I can't get through!" she announced, her eyes reflecting the glow of the dark barrier.

The air crackled with raw power as Rider darted between rising wraiths, his cloak billowing as he weaved through the chaos. His blade became an extension of will and instinct, each movement faster than the one before, a calculated dance of steel.

Beyond the melee, the sorcerer unleashed a barrage of

magic blasts, forcing Ariella to take cover behind a fallen pillar. Magic runes appeared across the floor.

The cavern's air crackled with energy as the last undead swordsmen fell.

Rider panted, exhaustion weighing him down and looked to find Ariella before his attention was drawn to the sorcerer's deep voice.

"Your victory is an illusion," the sorcerer hissed.

Before Rider could react, strands of bright red magic wrapped around him like an ethereal python, searing his amor and flesh as it squeezed. Pain exploded everywhere. A scream tore from his throat, raw and desperate.

"No!" Ariella's cry echoed through the stone chamber. She drew her bow. As if responding to her urgency, a luminescent aura swirled around the arrow, growing brighter with each passing second.

She released.

A streak of blinding light collided with the barrier.

For a moment, the two forces clashed in a chaos of energies. Then, with a resounding crack, the barrier shattered like glass and the arrow continued. It struck true and the cultist staggered, the spell on his lips dying with him.

"Rider!" Ariella yelled, rushing to kneel at his side. Her fingers brushed against his singed clothes, revealing skin marred by dark, arcane burns. She fought back tears as Rider's breaths came shallow and uneven.

"Stay with me," she pleaded, frantically pulling the healing scroll from her quiver. Her hands trembled as she unfurled the delicate parchment, its glyphs shimmering faintly.

"By the Queen's light, heal this flesh, bind this soul," Ariella chanted, the words flowing over Rider like a soothing balm.

The script ignited with a soft, golden glow. Tendrils of

warm healing magic weaved around Rider's wounds. Flesh knitted together and charred marks faded like shadows chased away by dawn's first light.

"Better?" Ariella asked, her voice barely a whisper as Rider's eyes fluttered open, their usual intensity returning.

"Thanks to you," he groaned, though the agony was receding.

Together, they rose, bodies weary but spirits unbroken. They surveyed the cavern, the fallen cultists, and the broken room.

Their mission was far from over, but for now, they had proven they were a team—and that was enough.

They delved deeper into the chamber, their senses alert for any threat. Rider's fingers traced over an ornate chest, its surface cool to the touch. With a deft flick, the latch opened. Inside, an assortment of artifacts: scrolls of parchment, a cracked mask, a dagger with a hilt of bone, and a dark tome bound in worn leather.

Rider's hands sifted through the scrolls, each one inscribed with runic symbols that thrummed faintly against his fingertips. "Look at this." He held up a brittle scroll, its edges singed but the script still legible.

Ariella leaned over, her eyes scanning the ancient text. "By the gods. This is a summoning ritual." She swallowed, an icy shakiness gripping her. "For Drakzeneth Maleficarum's spirit."

"Then we were right. They're closer than we thought to bringing him back." Rider's words hung heavy in the air as he tucked the scroll back into the chest. "We need to get this to Queen Vyshaan."

Ariella reached for the tome and scanned its pages. "This speaks of possible alliances, pacts with Dragons, and names I've never heard of." She shut the book and slid it back into place.

"We've got what we came for. Let's go."

They retraced their steps, the echo of their passage absorbed by the cavern walls.

"Are we ready?" Ari whispered, her hand resting briefly on Rider's arm—a silent vow shared between warriors. Partners. Maybe something more.

"Together, we are." he replied.

The chill of the evening air enveloped them as Rider and Ariella stepped out from the shadow of the waterfall, the mist clinging to them like a shroud. They paused, the sounds of the forest surrounding them a reminder they were not yet safe from the lurking dangers in the night.

The towering spires of Brightspire reached toward the sky as they approached the castle. Queen Vyshaan waited in her throne room, the vast chamber and intricate tapestries never ceasing to amaze.

"Your Majesty," Rider began, bowing deeply as they presented the chest. "We bring news of the cult's intentions and their planned alliances."

Ariella, graceful despite the fatigue etched on her face, added, "And evidence of rituals meant to revive the Dragon Lord's spirit from death."

Queen Vyshaan nodded courteously before replying, "You have done well. Rest now. By tomorrow's light, I will unveil the next chapter of your endeavor."

As they left, Ariella remained close to Rider. A soft touch lingered a moment too long as she brushed away a streak of dried blood from his cheek. "You're still hurt," she murmured.

"Battle scars." Rider shrugged, though the movement brought fresh pain. "Nothing I haven't weathered before."

"Still," Ariella insisted, her fingers gently closing on his upper arm. "You should be careful—"

"Careful?" Rider smiled, the glint of mischief returning to his eyes. "I'm indestructible," he finished with a flirtatious smirk.

Ariella exhaled, half amusement, half exasperation. "Then let it be so," Ariella smiled faintly, her concern not quite masked by the playfulness in her voice.

As they retired to the quarters provided for them within the castle, Rider felt Ariella's gaze on him. She was his team, but she was beginning to feel like something more.

ACT II

CHAPTER VII
THE KINGDOM OF STONE AND FIRE

As Rider and Ariella approached a private chamber within Queen Vyshaan's castle, the air was thick with the scent of ancient stone and blossoming nightshade. The heavy oak doors swung inward, revealing the Council Chamber where two of the Queen's Council of eight Elven Magi stood waiting.

Each bore the beauty of their kind, their bodies slender and graceful. Their attire shimmered with an otherworldly light; robes spun from magical silk and linen, adorned with gemstones that pulsed with magical energy. Their intricately braided hair, one a cascade of midnight blue and the other a mixture of brown and gold, signified their high status.

"Welcome," greeted one of the Magi with a smooth polished voice. "Her Majesty awaits your presence."

As they reached the central chamber, their passage through the lofty corridors was silent save for the whisper of silk and soft footfalls on marble floors. Five Magi stood around a glowing geometric matrix, their hands raised in unison, fingers weaving a tapestry of incantations through the air.

The sixth, a commanding figure, was the Head Magi. Silver hair flowed over his shoulders as his eyes remained fixed on the spell's center, the swirling enchantment revealing dwarves laboring over an intricate machine, its purpose obscured by distance and magic.

"What are they doing?" Rider whispered to Ariella, his gaze transfixed by the arcane display.

"Scrying," Ariella murmured back, her violet eyes alight with a mixture of awe and unease. "Magical surveillance. It's how the Queen keeps her watchful eye on the other kingdoms. Speak nothing of it," she cautioned with a glance that cut sharper than any blade.

At their arrival, the two council members announced Rider and Ariella's entrance, and the enchantment shuddered to a halt. The Magis' hands lowered, and the room's atmosphere shifted from one of intense focus to formal reception.

"Rider, Ariella," the Head Magi addressed them, his voice resonating with quiet power. "Your deeds have earned you a place of trust within these walls."

With a grandeur befitting his station, he led them to the Queen's courtroom.

"Your Majesty," the Head Magi bowed deeply once they arrived in Queen Vyshaan's throne room. The Iron Sorceress sat upon her throne of intertwined thorns and silver, her piercing blue eyes missing nothing as she regarded them.

"Rider, Ariella," she began, her voice cold and direct. "This blight spreads across our lands, the cult's tendrils continue to reach far and wide."

"Here," said a council member, stepping forward to present them with a portion of the recovered artifacts: a cracked mask, a dagger with a hilt of bone, and scrolls bearing eldritch symbols. "Pieces of evidence you recovered from that forsaken lair."

"You must study these well," Queen Vyshaan continued, her gaze locked onto Ariella's. "For you must now seek out those who would stand against this darkness with us."

"Your path is perilous," the Head Magi added solemnly, "but necessary. The future of all Etonya hangs in the balance."

The Queen's words hung heavy in the air. Rider could feel the gravity of their task settling upon his shoulders. He shared a look with Ariella, one of resolve and quiet apprehension. The road ahead would test them in ways they'd yet to imagine.

"My Magi have confirmed your findings. The cult seeks to resurrect Drakzeneth and assist him in regaining his power," the Queen confirmed, her voice laced with concern.

"How could anyone willingly pursue this?" Ariella questioned. "Don't they understand the horrors of what he did? The scars that still haunt our world because of him?"

"Not all races of our world possess our wisdom or remember as far back as we do, my child," the queen answered coldly, her gaze now fixated on Rider's Human form.

"Even now," she continued, "I watch as the Dwarves fulfill the prophecy I decreed many years ago. They heedlessly delve deeper into their mountain, without care for the evils lurking deep in the dark."

"Your majesty—" Rider said, attempting to interject.

"Regardless," Queen Vyshaan interrupted commandingly. "Your new charge is to seek out an audience with the Kings of Stonefire and Amakiir. You must convince them of the threat this cult poses to us all and rekindle the alliance of old."

"As you command, my Queen," Ariella accepted with a respectful bow.

"And you, Rider," Vyshaan turned to him with piercing eyes. "Do you swear to follow through with this quest and guard Ariella in my name?"

Rider met her stare, unwavering. "I will see this threat undone," Rider replied, turning his gaze to Ariella as he continued, "and I will offer my life to protect her, Your Grace. In this, you have my solemn vow."

Ariella felt a surge of emotion at Rider's unwavering pledge. Never had a friend been so loyal, nor a companion as devoted. Was this this pride, or something beyond their shared duty?

With a wave of her hand, the head magi approached once more and bestowed the duo with a pair of royal letters requesting Stonefire and Amakiir's aid.

"Very well," Vyshaan said from her throne. "Do not return until your quest is complete or the cult has been eradicated."

And with that, Rider and Ariella turned to exit the courtroom and continue their quest.

Their boots strided against the pathways and enchanted bridges as they made their way through Bright-spire's bustling cityscape, the light casting shadows between the spires of the grand city. The scent of sweet honeydew wafted through the air, mingling with the distant echo of minstrels playing in the square.

"Queen Vyshaan trusts us with a grave task," Ariella murmured, her eyes reflecting the urgency of their mission. "Stonefire Mountain and Amakiir await."

"Indeed," Rider replied, adjusting his sword's leather

grip. "The weight of the words in these letters! Let's hope they carry enough sway to unite kings."

Their path led them down to the royal stables in the port, where the familiar smell of hay and polished leather greeted them. Rider whistled softly, and from the depths of the stable, his robust chestnut mare emerged. Eve snorted affectionately at Rider's approach, her dark mane braided with metallic bands that jingled melodically. She nuzzled her master's palm as he stroked her broad forehead, a silent exchange of trust and familiarity passing between them.

"Sturdy as ever, aren't you, Eve?" Rider praised, his hand running along her muscular flank. He admired her readiness, knowing the journey ahead would demand every ounce of her war-trained endurance.

"Your papers, if you please?" the stable master called out, extending a hand towards Ariella.

"Of course," she replied, presenting the necessary documents. The man nodded, leading out a magnificent white horse adorned with the Queen's sigil. Its coat gleamed like fresh snow under the dying sun, its muscles rippling with restrained power.

"Fit for a queen, or at least a High Elf," Rider jested lightly, eyeing the regal beast.

"Let us depart," Ariella said, mounting with an effortless grace only an Elf could possess. She guided her mount beside Eve, ready for the vast expanse that lay beyond the city gates.

As the spires of Brightspire faded into the horizon behind them, Rider and Ariella found themselves enveloped by the scent of moss and wildflowers of the Emerald Forest. They rode in companionable silence for a time, the rhythmic clopping of their horses' hooves against the soft earth the only sound. Ariella's eyes drifted over the lush surroundings, drinking in the vibrant hues of the foliage. It was a stark contrast to the gleaming marble and glass of Brightspire, and she found herself relishing the change of scenery.

Rider, too, seemed at ease in the wilderness, his posture relaxed yet alert in the saddle. He scanned the trees with the gaze of a seasoned traveler, ever watchful for signs of danger.

As the sun sank towards the amber and crimson horizon, Ariella broke the silence. "Rider," she began, her voice soft yet curious. "I've been meaning to ask... how did you become such a skilled swordsman? Your skill in battle is remarkable."

Rider glanced over at her, a flicker of surprise in his eyes at the unexpected question. He was quiet for a moment as he gathered his thoughts.

"Well, that's a long story," Rider began, his voice taking on a nostalgic tone. "I grew up an orphan in the seaside village of Rockhaven. Life was hard. We scraped by on what little the fishermen and traders could spare. By fifteen, I knew the only way I'd ever make something of myself was to seize opportunity when it came."

A faint smile playing at the corners of his mouth. "One day, The Blades rode into town. I watched them stroll through the village, their swords flashing in the sunlight. People moving out of their way as they approached. I didn't care if it was from fear or respect, I knew right then that I wanted to be one of them."

Ariella listened intently, her violet eyes studying Rider's profile as he spoke. She had always sensed a depth to him, a deeper history than the flirtatious façade he portrayed, something that had shaped him into the formidable warrior she'd caught glimpses of.

"So I approached their captain, a grizzled old veteran named Giles," Rider laughed before continuing. "I told him I was joining them," Rider continued. "He laughed in my face at first, told me I was too scrawny, too green. But I was persistent. Every morning, I'd wake up early and sneak to their training grounds outside the city, mimicking their moves with a stick."

He chuckled softly at the memory.

"Eventually, Giles must have taken pity on me, or maybe he just got tired of me pestering him. He agreed to teach me the basics, on the condition that I kept the camp and gear clean and didn't get in the way." Rider's eyes took on a distant look.

"Those were some of the hardest years of my life. Giles ran me through drills from dawn till dusk. My muscles would ache constantly, my hands blistered and bled, but I never complained. I knew that was my one shot at a better life."

Ariella nodded, a newfound respect blooming in her chest. She could picture a younger, wiry Rider, pushing himself to his limits day after day.

"So how did you go from apprentice to full-fledged member of The Blades?" she asked, genuinely curious.

Rider's expression darkened slightly. "It was during a job. We were hired to take out a group of bandits that had been terrorizing a nearby village. It should have been a straightforward mission, but we underestimated their numbers."

He sighed heavily, the memories clearly still painful. "We were outnumbered and outflanked. Giles took a crossbow bolt to the chest. I saw him go down and some-thing just...snapped inside me. I fought like a man possessed, cutting down bandits left and right until my sword was slick with blood. By the time it was over, the bandits lay dead...but so did half the Blades."

Rider fell silent for a moment, his jaw clenching at the painful recollection. Ariella reached out instinctively, placing a comforting hand on his arm. He glanced at her, a flicker of gratitude in his eyes before he continued.

"After Giles passed, things changed. The Blades lost their way, became more interested in coin than honor. I stayed for a while. I was nineteen, it's all I knew." Shaking his head, he continued. "But, I couldn't agree with what they'd become. So, I packed my things and resigned. I've spent the past two years accepting odd jobs and trying to keep true to what The Blades once stood for."

Ariella squeezed Rider's arm gently, her touch a silent offer of comfort and understanding. She could sense the pain and conflict in his words, the weight of his past bearing down on him.

"I'm sorry, Rider," she said softly, her eyes shimmering with empathy. "I can't imagine how difficult that must have been."

Rider met her gaze, a flicker of vulnerability passing across his handsome features. It was a side of him she rarely saw, cracks in his normally confident and flirtatious demeanor.

"It was," he admitted, his voice rough with emotion. "Giles was the closest thing I'd ever had to a father. Losing him, and then seeing The Blades turn into something he would have despised..." he stopped, catching his emotions in his throat.

Ariella nodded, understanding all too well the pain of loss and the struggle to find one's place in the world again after drastic change.

"But you didn't lose yourself," she pointed out gently.

"You held true to your values, even when it meant walking away from the only life you knew. That takes a rare and admirable strength."

Rider smiled, a genuine, heartfelt expression. "I appreciate that, truly." He glanced up at the sky, noting the deepening hues of sunset. "We should probably think about making camp for the night."

Ariella nodded in agreement. They guided their horses off the main path, finding a small clearing on the precipice of the great forest that bordered Stonefire's domain. While Rider set about pitching their camp, collecting wood for a fire whose crackle soon pierced the twilight hush, Ariella slipped soundlessly into the trees.

"Be swift," Rider called after her, hammering the last peg into the soft earth.

"Swift as the wind," she promised before disappearing amongst the foliage.

Ariella's steps were silent, her Elven senses attuned to the faintest shift in the forest's pulse. Her pointed ears caught the distant heartbeat of her prey, a stag unaware of the huntress in its midst. She drew her bow, the string singing a faint note as she pulled it taut.

"Forgive me," she whispered, loosing the arrow. The arrow flew, slicing through the dim light. The deer fell gracefully, as if conceding to a dance that had long been written by nature itself.

"Even in death, you are majestic," Ariella proclaimed solemnly, kneeling beside the fallen animal.

Upon her return, Rider had transformed their small clearing into a semblance of home, the fire casting a warm glow on his rugged features. He looked up, a smile of welcome spreading across his face as Ariella approached with their bounty.

"Your skills never cease to impress," he complimented,

rising to help her prepare the meat for cooking and preserving.

"Your ability to make a camp feel like a haven is impressive as well," she returned the sentiment, her gaze soft with gratitude.

As night enveloped their camp, the savory aroma of roasting venison filled the air, mingling with the earthy scent of pine and woodsmoke. Together, they feasted beneath the twinkling stars, the forest a silent witness to their resolve and the vital quest that awaited them beyond dawn's light.

The crackle of the fire mingled with the gentle hiss of excess meat cooking over the flames. Rider lay back against his saddle, using it as a makeshift pillow. His eyes were heavy-lidded, the fatigue of the day's journey coaxing him into slumber. The world around him faded to darkness, and soon he was enveloped by the embrace of an uneasy dream.

Visions swirled in Rider's mind, a maelstrom of fire and smoke. He stood upon Stonefire Mountain, its very name a harbinger of what was to unfold. Dwarves—hundreds of them—were in retreat, their faces streaked with soot and despair. Mighty kingdoms had fallen like sandcastles before the tide, and now they huddled here on the brink of extinction.

A figure emerged from the throng. A Dwarf whose presence commanded attention despite the chaos. It was Ragnoc Blackhammer, his visage etched with steely resolve. His legendary warhammer, worn by countless battles, was gripped tight in his calloused hands. The ground trembled as he approached the volcano's edge. With a roar that rivaled the mountain's fury, he drove his weapon into the earth.

The volcano answered his call. Fire belched forth, a cataclysmic explosion that sent rivers of molten rock cascading down the slopes. Enemy forces, once a threatening swarm at the base of the mountain, were engulfed and obliterated. The plains below became a fiery grave for those who sought to end the Dwarven race.

But amidst the inferno, a shadow loomed over the battlefield. A silhouette darker than the surrounding devastation. It slammed its own sword down, mimicking Ragnoc's defiant act, and from it, a surge of fire rushed outward, consuming all in its path.

Rider's heart pounded, the echo of the roaring fire reverberating through his bones. He jolted awake, gasping for air, the dream's intensity still clawing at the edges of his consciousness.

"A nightmare?" Ariella's calm voice cut through the night, her violet eyes reflecting the flickering firelight as she sat across from him, tending to the meats.

"More than that, I think," Rider replied, running a hand through his hair. "I saw the last Great War... Ragnoc Blackhammer calling the fire of the mountain to save his people."

"Legends say he's lived for eight centuries," Ariella murmured thoughtfully.

"Six longer than any Dwarf should," Rider added.

"Imagine the weight of such a life …the burdens carried, the decisions made."

"Eight hundred years..." Rider echoed, the enormity of such a span weighing on him. "And yet, here we are, hoping he'll aid us after all this time."

"Stonefire's people are hard to sway," Ariella said, skewering a strip of venison and holding it out to him.

"Even Queen Vyshaan's Prophecy of Doom for their Kingdom hasn't stopped them from digging for earthen treasures."

"Prophecies can be double-edged," Rider mused, accepting the food. "They instill fear but also create legends."

"True," Ariella conceded, her gaze distant. "But fear can be a powerful motivator—it can either unite or divide."

Rider chewed slowly, the savory taste of the meat doing little to distract from his thoughts.

The warmth of the fire did not reach the chill that had settled in his bones from the vision. Deep within, he knew that their journey would test them. But for now, under the watchful stars and the sentinel trees, he found solace in the quiet camaraderie between them.

The morning dew had barely lifted when Rider and Ariella packed their camp. They rolled their bedrolls and doused the fire pit, leaving no trace but flattened grass. Eve snorted in anticipation, her hooves pawing at the earth while Ariella readied her white steed. Without a word, the pair mounted and set off toward Stonefire Mountain.

The forest thinned over following days, eventually giving way to blackened earth and stone. The air grew warmer, tinged with the scent of sulfur and ash. The trees retreated entirely, revealing the imposing sight of the mountain before them. It rose into the sky like the spine of a slumbering Dragon, its peak lost to the clouds.

"Giants frozen in time," Ariella murmured, awe coloring her voice.

Before them stood four giant statues guarding the

mountain's approach. They were Dwarven warriors carved from the mountain itself. Each bore the distinctive mark of their craft and valor: one with a warhammer held aloft, another with axes crossed at his chest, a third clutching a two-handed axe, its blade glinting even under the dim sun. But it was the fourth, tallest of all, that captured their attention—a regal figure wielding a mighty warhammer, the very visage of King Ragnoc Blackhammer, forever watching over his domain with eyes of stone.

"State your business!" The sharp command snapped them out of their reverie. Two Stonefire guards stood at the ready, armored in plates etched with the same intricate designs adorning the colossal statues.

"We come bearing a message from Queen Vyshaan of Brightspire," Rider called out, retrieving the sealed letter from his saddlebag. He extended the parchment towards the guards, his posture relaxed yet alert.

One guard took the letter, examining the seal with a scrutinous eye before nodding to his companion. "Follow us. We'll take you to the royal court."

The clanking of armor and the steady clip-clop of hooves against stone filled the silence as they ascended the path towards the heart of Stonefire Mountain. The sheer scale of the gates that loomed before them was enough to make Rider feel like an ant at the threshold of a fortress.

Inside, the royal court bustled with activity. Dwarves moved with purpose, their voices a mix of orders and reports. At the center of it all, sat King Ragnoc on a throne carved from obsidian, his grey eyes sharp as flint beneath bushy white brows.

"Queen Vyshaan sends children to speak for her?" Ragnoc's voice boomed across the hall, skepticism evident in his tone.

"Your Majesty," Ariella began, her tone respectful yet

firm, "We come not as children, but as envoys bearing grave news. A cult seeks to resurrect the Dragon Lord, a threat to all our kingdoms."

"Ha!" Ragnoc scoffed. "And why should I trust the word of Brightspire? You've monopolized magic for generations, hoarding relics while others suffer!" The king's disdain was palpable.

"True, tensions exist," Rider interjected, meeting the king's gaze with confidence. "But we bring proof. Evidence gathered from the cult's lair." He presented the documents and artifacts, laying them out for all to see.

As Rider concluded the presentation of their findings, King Ragnoc's scowl deepened like a chasm in his weathered face. He leaned forward, his warhammer resting beside the throne, as he inspected the items before him. The court fell silent, every Dwarf holding their breath as their king considered the evidence.

He rose from his throne with a deliberate slowness that contradicted the simmering fury beneath his surface. His massive warhammer, a legendary weapon whispered about in tales spread far beyond the borders of Stonefire Mountain, was lifted with ease, not a fearsome instrument of war.

"Espionage!" Ragnoc thundered, slamming the obsidian Dragonhead of his hammer onto the stone floor of the court. The impact sent a tremor through the room, and an almost imperceptible vibration traveled up through the soles of Rider's boots.

The air grew oppressive with heat, a suffocating wave that left beads of sweat glistening on brow and beard alike. It was a reminder that the king's magical connection was bound to the mountain's fiery heart.

"Your Majesty," Ariella implored, her voice steady

despite the sweltering heat, "we seek only to warn you, to unite against a common foe."

Rider watched as the king's chest heaved, his gaze shifting between the evidence they had provided and the two envoys before him. Finally, with a nod more to himself than anyone else, Ragnoc's features softened just enough to show a begrudging acceptance.

"Stonefire cannot turn a blind eye to threats, even those heralded by potential deceivers," Ragnoc admitted gruffly.

He turned sharply. "Baelgor Stoneheart," he beckoned to a robust Dwarf standing at the edge of the court, "you will join these emissaries. Aid them, protect our interests, and report back what you find."

Baelgor stepped forward, his red beard catching the torchlight like embers. His eyes, bright as forged rubies, held respect for his king. He bowed deeply, the iron rings in his beard chiming softly.

"By your word, my liege," Baelgor affirmed, his voice resonant within the hallowed hall.

CHAPTER VIII
THE MOUNTAIN'S BLESSING

Rider and Ariella spent the next week among the marketplaces of Stonefire, gathering supplies and waiting for Baelgor to be ready for the journey. The scent of roasted meats mingled with earthy fragrances, while the clamor of bartering filled the air. They visited Baelgor's workshop, just as they'd done almost every day since receiving the King's blessing. As they entered the workshop, the sounds of hammer and anvil rang out like a rhythmic battle song, sparks dancing in the dim light of the forge.

"Ah, my finest work yet," Baelgor announced, withdrawing a long blade from the sizzling quench. Baelgor's eye caught sight of the pair as he sheathed the blade, his muscular arms bared to the elbow with streaks of soot from his forge. "Come, I wish to share a meal with you at my home. A proper send-off."

That evening, they arrived at Baelgor's manor, a large decorated building nestled near the edge of the smithing district. The aroma of hearty stew welcomed them, and the warmth of his hearth and home enveloped them as they entered. Baelgor's home was a testament to Dwarven craftsmanship, with stone walls adorned with intricately carved reliefs depicting the storied history of Stonefire.

"Sit, eat," Baelgor urged, placing bowls brimming with stew before them. "Tomorrow we depart, but tonight, we feast as kin."

As they ate, the stout Dwarf regaled them with tales of Stonefire's glory, his voice rich and captivating. The food was robust and filling, a stark contrast to the delicate flavors Rider knew Ariella favored. Yet she ate with genuine appreciation, acknowledging the hospitality with a grace that spoke of her Elven heritage.

Rider's fork clinked against the earthenware as he scooped up the last hearty bite of stew, the rich flavors of root vegetables and tender meat still dancing on his tongue. The warmth of the Stoneheart hearth had seeped into his bones, a welcome reprieve.

"Your home is a fortress of comfort, Baelgor," Rider remarked with genuine contentment, his eyes roving over the stout wooden beams and the glow of the fire reflecting off polished metalwork.

"Aye, it's served us well through winters and woes alike," replied Baelgor, pride resonating in his deep voice as his bushy beard twitched with a smile. His wife cleared away the empty bowls, her movements efficient in the cozy domesticity of their stone abode.

They talked late into the evening, sharing stories and forging bonds that would, with hope, withstand the trials of their quest.

"Speaking of journeys," Ariella interjected smoothly, "we seek your guidance, Master Baelgor. The path to Amakiir Woodlands is long and treacherous by the surface. Is there another way?"

"Aye." Baelgor's red eyes glinted with a conspiratorial

gleam. "The old mining tunnels weave through the belly of the mountains like the roots of an ancient tree. They could cut our travel to mere shards of time."

"Underground?" Rider raised an eyebrow, intrigued. "But surely—"

"King Ragnoc's permission is needed," Baelgor finished for him. "Venturing deep into the mountain's heart is no light matter."

After dinner, they retired to the sitting area, where Baelgor fetched a dusty bottle from a high shelf. He poured a dark, amber liquid into thick-bottomed glasses, the ale's robust aroma filling the room, starkly different from the floral scents of Elven wine.

"Stonefire brew," he announced, handing them each a glass. "It warms the insides like molten rock and has a bite that'll remind ye you're alive."

Rider sipped cautiously, the liquid bold and earthy on his palate, a stark contrast to the Elven drinks he'd shared with Ariella under the moonlit canopies of Brightspire. A slow heat radiated down his throat, bringing a grunt of surprise and approval.

"Strong," he coughed, a grin spreading across his face. "Very strong."

Ariella's laugh was musical, echoing softly around the room as she savored her own drink with grace despite its potency.

"Truth be told," Baelgor began, lowering his voice once his children were out of earshot. "The distrust between Ragnoc and Brightspire weighs heavy on us all. We've found cult tracts even here, writings promising a new age and power to those who will serve them."

"Dark times indeed," murmured Ariella, her violet eyes clouding with concern.

Baelgor nodded. "Which is why we've been building

new paths in secret. Passageways, for a steam-powered carriage we will one day use to carry us through the darkness."

"An underground, steam-powered mode of transportation?" Rider leaned in, interest piqued. "That's ambitious, even for Dwarves."

"Unfinished, though," Baelgor warned, his gaze hardening. "The shadows within the mountain hold dangers untold."

"Yet if it shaves weeks off our journey..." Ariella pondered aloud, meeting Rider's gaze.

"Then we must seek the King's leave," concluded Rider, setting his empty glass down with a decisive clack.

"Tomorrow, we ask for the mountain's blessing," Baelgor affirmed, nodding solemnly. "And may the stone sing our safe passage."

The next day, the trio stood before King Ragnoc Blackhammer, whose scrutinizing gaze seemed to pierce the very stone upon which they stood. Baelgor, his voice steady, made the request himself.

"Your Grace," he began, "I ask permission to guide these allies through the old mining tunnels. If we travel through the passages where our craftsmen are currently working toward the power of steam, we can hasten our journey and thwart the cult's dark designs faster."

King Ragnoc's steely eyes flickered to Rider and Ariella, weighing them, measuring their worth. The silence hung profound, like the burden of centuries upon his armored shoulders. After what felt like an eternity, he nodded once.

"Go then, with my blessing," he rumbled, his voice echoing off the high-vaulted chamber. "But return victorious, for you carry Stonefire's honor with you."

"Thank you, Your Grace," Ariella said, her voice a

melodious contrast to the Dwarves' deep timbre. "We shall not fail."

With a final, respectful bow, they turned away from the throne and made their way towards the halls deep within the castle.

The entrance of the ancient tunnels was guarded by two giant stone doors. The moment they crossed the threshold, the world changed. Baelgor's torch cast long shadows on the rough-hewn walls, the flames dancing eerily as if alive. The air was cool and damp against their skin, carrying the scent of rock and ore. They moved in wordless communion, broken only by the occasional skitter of pebbles underfoot or the distant drip of water seeping through rock.

"Keep close," Baelgor instructed, his voice barely above a whisper. "The path is treacherous and unforgiving."

"Like navigating the intrigues of court," Ariella murmured, half to herself. "Yet here, the darkness holds no lies." Her eyes adjusted to the gloom, catching the glint of minerals embedded in the walls.

They progressed in wordless communion, senses heightened in the oppressive silence. Here a broken rail, there an abandoned pickaxe—the debris of miners long gone spoke of the relentless pursuit of precious gems and metals.

"Watch your step," Baelgor cautioned as he sidestepped a collapsed beam.

Rider crouched to examine the beam, his fingers tracing the age-worn wood. "This must have been part of the original supports."

"Indeed," Baelgor confirmed. "We stand on the bones of our forebears' labor."

"Feels like walking through history," Rider said, standing back up and brushing his hands together.

"History that will not forgive a misstep," Ariella chimed in, her keen eyes scanning ahead.

As they delved ever deeper, the air grew thicker, the weight of the mountain pressing down upon them like a tangible force. The path twisted and turned, a labyrinthine descent into the belly of the earth.

"Here." Baelgor halted. A narrow crevice split the rock face before them. "We'll need to pass through."

"Looks barely wide enough," Ariella observed, sizing up the gap.

"Well, you'll just have to try and squeeze those '*weapons*' of yours a little tighter against that armor of yours," Rider said with a wink as he took the lead. He forced himself through the opening, feeling the coarse stone scrape against his arms.

On the other side, they found themselves in a cavernous space, the ceiling lost to darkness, the extent of it beyond the reach of his torch's light. A palpable sense of solitude wrapped around him.

"Remarkable..." Ariella exhaled, her voice a hushed awe.

"Stay alert," Baelgor reminded them, his gaze fixed on the path that lay ahead.

"Always," Rider replied. "After all, who knows what stories these stones might tell if they could speak?"

"Let us hope they remain silent witnesses to our passage." Ariella's lips quirked into a wry smile.

The ground shuddered, a rumble that echoed through the cavernous expanse. Rider steadied himself against the rough wall, his heart pounding in rhythm with the tremors.

Baelgor grunted, squinting at the gaping chasm before them. The bridge that once spanned the abyss lay raised on the far side, unreachable and taunting.

"Is there another way around?" Ariella's voice cut through the silence, her eyes scanning for any sign of hope.

Baelgor shook his head, his bushy beard bristling. "Nay, lass. But I have ways with the earth." He approached the edge and knelt, placing his palms flat against the stone floor. The inked designs on his arms glowed faintly, and he began to chant in a deep, resonant tone that seemed to vibrate through the very rock.

Baelgor's body softened like wax melting into the rock. Then, he was gone. Moments later, on the opposite end of the chasm, the earth rippled and Baelgor emerged. He gave them a reassuring nod and set to work on the levers, each pull accompanied by a heavy clunk of gears.

"By the gods," Ariella whispered, her eyes wide with wonder.

"Earth-melding," Rider murmured. "I've heard tales, but to witness it..."

"More than tales, my friends," Baelgor's gravelly voice called out. The bridge began to descend with a groan of weathered ropes and ancient pulleys. When it finally thudded into place, they crossed quickly, eager to leave the open vulnerability behind.

"Come," Baelgor beckoned, leading them deeper into the mountain's bowels. They traversed halls so vast, their torchlight could not reach the distant walls. Pillars rose like stoic guardians, each one carved with the visages of Dwarf ancestors, their eyes set with glittering gemstones that reflected the flickering flames.

"Was all this built by your people?" Rider asked, his voice a hushed whisper.

"Every stone," Baelgor declared, pride swelling in his

chest. "We sought to carve a kingdom that would stretch even further into the depths. But we were not alone down here."

"Creatures of the dark?" Ariella queried, her hand reflexively reaching for an arrow.

"Goblins," Baelgor spat the word as if it left a sour taste. "Vile things. We fought them for years, pushing them back into the shadows whence they came. But now, they might be stirring again, meddling with our works."

"Have you seen them recently?" Rider's fingers curled around the hilt of his sword, seeking comfort in its familiar weight.

"Not in any sizable force for years, but trouble with the railway has us wary. We suspect they're clawing back from the abyss," Baelgor said, his red eyes narrowing.

"Then we must tread carefully," Ariella concluded, her senses attuned to any sign of movement in the darkness.

"Carefully, and with haste," Baelgor agreed. Their steps quickened, the sense of unseen danger driving them deeper into the mountain's secrets, where history lay etched in stone.

Rider's boots crunched on gravel as the trio emerged into a vast cavern, the air thick with the scent of iron and soot. Above them, massive beams supported the ceiling, and ahead, gleaming tracks disappeared into the dimly lit distance. The rhythmic chuffing of steam engines echoed off the walls, melding with the clang of metal on rock.

"By the Ancients," Ariella breathed, her gaze sweeping over the intricate network of scaffolding and pulleys. "Your people's ingenuity never ceases to astound me."

Baelgor grunted, his eyes scanning every shadow. "Aye, but this marvel is yet half-born. The rails lead far, but many a span remains unfinished. And where there's a gap in stone, trouble brews."

Rider followed Baelgor's gaze to the hulking machinery, pistons pumping and wheels spinning as Dwarven engineers shouted orders amidst clouds of steam. He felt the hum of activity rattling in his chest, the palpable energy of creation and toil.

"Mind your steps," Baelgor cautioned, leading them along the railway's edge. The earth beneath them, a quiet reminder of the power coursing through the depths. "We tread on dreams not yet fully realized, and nightmares that wish to see them crumble."

Ariella's fingers danced along the fletching of her arrows, her eyes sharp as she scanned the darkness beyond the light's reach. "If Goblins are behind this, they will find no easy prey in us."

"Nor in me," Baelgor added, the weight of his hammer a constant presence at his side. "But let's pray our steel stays sheathed. The darkness here can swallow whole armies."

As they progressed, the air grew hotter, tinged with the acrid smell of burning coal. The ground beneath their feet grew uneven, loose stones tumbling into the abyss.

"Is that... singing?" Rider paused, tilting his head. A faint melody drifted towards them, mournful and distant, the words indistinguishable but laden with a haunting beauty.

"An old miners' chanty," Baelgor explained, his voice softening. "It's said to soothe the wrathful spirits of the deep and keep the miners' hearts from dark thoughts."

"Let's hope it works," Ariella whispered, her keen eyes still watching the shadows.

The deeper they went, the more pronounced the signs of destruction became. Broken carts lay abandoned, their contents spilled across the stone. In several places, the railway had been torn up, the ends of the rails twisted grotesquely.

"Look there," Baelgor pointed to a section of rail hanging precariously over an open chasm. "That wasn't done by any stone or pickaxe."

"Then we must be vigilant," Rider stated, his hand resting on the dagger at his hip. The memories of his vision returned unbidden—the heat of the erupting volcano, the shadowy figure, and the encroaching tide of fire.

"Ever vigilant," Ariella agreed, her voice barely above a whisper. She crouched low, her ears twitching as she listened to the secrets carried on the stale air.

Days passed as they delved deeper into the bowels of Etonya, each step taking them further from the realm of the living and deeper into the domain of history.

CHAPTER IX
THE DARK

The mountain's natural stone began to change as the ground beneath them transitioned to rugged cobblestones and mosaics began to appear upon the walls, each revealing their trespass into the ruins of Rockbar. Walls that once gleamed with the luminance of enchanted torches now stood in the solemnity of time's embrace, adorned with sculptures depicting Dwarven heroes of yore.

Baelgor ran his gnarled fingers across a particularly intricate carving, the lines of his rough skin tracing the arcs and swirls of the stonework. "Look at this," he rumbled, his voice echoing softly through the hallowed halls. "This was carved before our fathers' fathers were born. By Moradin's beard, they don't make 'em like this anymore."

Ariella, her eyes wide with admiration, couldn't help but marvel at the craftsmanship. "It's breathtaking, Baelgor."

"Beauty it may be, lass, but keep your senses sharp," Baelgor replied, his gaze scanning the shadows that danced just beyond the reach of their light. "This beauty can hide treachery as easily as a Goblin's grin."

As if summoned by his words, the path ahead opened up to a vast chasm, bridged by a gargantuan slab of natural stone that arched daringly over the abyss. Far below, almost beyond what the eyes could see, a river of molten rock flowed, its primordial glow casting an otherworldly radiance upward from the abyss. The air thickened, the scent of sulfur and heat mingling with the mustiness of untouched corridors.

"By all the forges..." Ariella breathed, her hand instinctively reaching for the comforting grip of her bow.

"Mind where ye step," Baelgor warned, peering over the edge into the fiery depths. "The belly of Etonya is a mystery, even to us. And unless ye've sprouted wings when I wasn't lookin', a fall here would be your last."

"Is there no end to the wonders of your home?" asked Rider, his voice tinged with awe, though he remained tense and wary.

"Nor to its dangers," Baelgor grunted, stepping onto the bridge with a confidence born of countless years treading such paths. "Stay close. We'll cross this relic of the ancients together."

With careful steps, they ventured onto the bridge. The vastness of the chasm swallowed any sound save for the distant roar of the lava and the hollow echo of their own footfalls. Despite the warmth rising up to meet them, a chill of foreboding settled in —a silent reminder of the treacherous journey ahead.

"Once we cross," Baelgor's deep voice resonated through the cavernous expanse, "we tread upon the soil of Rockbar." His eyes, twin embers of remembrance, flickered with a sorrowful light. "A kingdom fallen but not forgotten."

Ariella's violet gaze softened, her voice a whisper amidst the echoes of their steps. "Your kinsmen fought with honor, Baelgor. May their spirits find solace in the stone."

"Tell me of Rockbar," Rider urged, his curiosity casting a net into the shadowed depths of history. "What force could drive such strong folk from their hallowed halls?"

"Rockbar..." Baelgor paused, his hand tightening into a fist. "Rockbar was a bastion of our people, a stronghold unyielding. For years, it withstood the Dragon Lord's vile legions. But when he sent the Black Dragons, the skies themselves turned against them. Black fire rained down upon Rockbar. Its proud walls crumbled under the fury of Dragons."

"By the ancestors," Ariella throat tightened, her heart heavy with the weight of shared loss.

"Legend has it," Baelgor continued, "that Queen Rockbar herself, wielding the ancient magics of our clan, held the line. She conjured flame and forged mountains anew, allowing her kin to flee towards Stonefire's sanctuary."

The trio pressed on, their path lit by the faint glow of the lava below and the lanterns they carried. As they journeyed deeper into the realm of Rockbar, signs of an age-old struggle emerged. Cobwebs clung to skeletal remains. Dwarven armor lay sundered. The dust itself spoke of battles long past.

"Others have been here," Ariella noted, her keen eyes discerning disturbances in their surroundings—a scuff mark here, an uneven layer of dust there. "Not all these footprints belong to the dead."

"Stay sharp," Baelgor grunted, gripping his warhammer.

Ariella stilled, her ears twitching at a sound beyond the range of Human or Dwarven hearing. In one fluid motion, she nocked and loosed two arrows into the gloom. A metallic clang rang, followed by the squeals of guttural gibberish shattered the relative silence.

"Move!" Rider shouted, drawing his sword as they advanced cautiously toward the source of the commotion.

Slumped against the wall, lay a Goblin pierced by one of Ariella's shafts. Its crude armor had failed it, the arrow finding the narrow chink between plates with lethal precision. A dark trail of blood snaked away from the corpse, leading further into the darkness.

"Seems we're not alone," Ariella stated, her bow still trained on the shadows ahead. "Whatever else lurks here, be it beast or remnants of the Dragon Lord's filth, we must face it together."

"Then onward we march," Baelgor declared. "For honor, for Rockbar, and for those who can no longer wield axe or spell in defense of their homeland."

They followed the bloodied path, each step a silent vow to unearth Rockbar's lost secrets and face whatever dangers lay hidden within its forsaken chambers.

The scent of iron and earth clung to the air as the dark smudges of blood led the trio to a precipice overlooking the abyss. Guttural voices echoed from above, betraying the presence of the Goblin scouts.

A trap.

With no warning, crude arrows sliced through the dimness towards them.

"Shield wall!" Baelgor roared, raising his warhammer skyward. The ground beneath his feet trembled, and up rose a barricade of jagged stone, intercepting the volley.

"Swift as the wind," Ariella whispered, her fingers dancing over the strings of her bow. Her eyes—a jeweled blaze in the half-light—tracked the scouting party's movements before arrows flew from her bow, each finding its mark in Goblin flesh. They fell in swift, silent death, their grotesque forms crumpling to the stone floor.

Rider moved like a torrent, his sword and dagger extensions of his will. He wove through the fray, a blur of parries and thrusts a ballet of battle that left Goblins dismembered and dispatched.

A Goblin blade found its way through Rider's defenses, biting into his left arm. A grimace flashed across his features as he withdrew his arm back toward his chest before taking down his attacker.

Baelgor's magic surged, a primal force that commanded stone and ore to heed his call. His warhammer struck the ground, and the very bones of Etonya answered. Stone rose to crush, divide, and shield. Goblins screamed as they were ensnared by the living rock, their bodies broken against the implacable might of the earth.

The clatter of weapons being sheathed marked the end of conflict. Ariella's eyes swept over Rider and Baelgor, taking in the weariness that clung to their frames like the dust from shattered Goblin bones.

"Rider," she called softly, her gaze fixing upon the jagged tear in his flesh where dark blood welled. "Your arm."

"Ah, it's nothing." Rider's dismissive chuckle couldn't mask the wince as he flexed his limb. "Just a scratch."

Baelgor grunted, moving closer with a furrowed brow. "Let me see it. Goblin blades are often laced with filth and rot. We can't afford an infection, not down here."

Ariella watched as Baelgor's calloused fingers probed the injury with surprising gentleness, his bushy beard twitching in concentration. The dwarf produced a cloth from his pouch, dampened it with a vial of clear liquid, and cleansed the wound.

"Ahh, it stings!" Rider hissed between clenched teeth.

"Better than losing the arm," Baelgor retorted, securing a bandage tightly around the injury. "Rest now. You'll need your strength, and all your limbs," he chuckled before adding, "for what lies ahead."

Ariella's Elven eyes scanned the area, noting the Goblin corpses strewn about. She knelt beside one and rifled through its pockets.

"Look at this," Ariella murmured, holding up a crumpled schematic that bore the unmistakable lines of Dwarven engineering. "Your people were right. These vermin have been preying upon your construction sites, sowing chaos in the darkness."

"Despicable creatures," Baelgor spat, his red eyes flaring with anger. "They defile even the dead with their presence."

"Let's set camp," said Ariella, rising gracefully to her feet. "We shall guard our rest in shifts. Who knows how deep this infestation runs."

"Agreed," Rider nodded, suppressing a yawn. "Though I wouldn't mind watching the first watch pass from the inside of my eyelids."

They settled amidst the ancient stone, the air heavy with the scent of earth and light embers. A small fire was kindled, casting dancing shadows upon the walls, shadows that held memories of a time when these tunnels thrummed with Dwarven life.

"Hard to believe," Ariella mused aloud, "that such silence could follow the clamor of battle."

"Silence is a treasure seldom appreciated," Baelgor replied, his voice tinged with reverence. "In it, we hear the whispers of the stone and the stories of old."

"Stories for another time," Rider interjected, easing

himself down with a groan. "For now, let's just try to survive this night."

The trio nestled into their makeshift camp, the weight of their journey pressing down upon them like the mountain itself. In the darkness, far from the sky's embrace, they found respite in the rhythm of each other's breathing, a reminder that they were not alone in the vastness of the underground.

Rider's sleep was tempestuous. In the depths of slumber, he beheld the shadowy figure once more, massive and menacing, its warhammer raised high before slamming down upon the earth. The ground ruptured once again, belching forth a tsunami of flames that engulfed Stonefire Mountain's surroundings, painting the world in a furious blaze.

As the inferno receded, two Dragons emerged, gliding with predatory majesty around the mountain's peak. Their scales shimmered like molten gold beneath an unseen sun, their roars a symphony of power that made the skies tremble.

The dream tapestry shifted, revealing a stout and indomitable figure. A broad-shouldered Dwarven woman with the strength of mountains stood amongst the chaos. With commanding shouts, she conjured torrents of fire and cascades of stone, shaping them into lethal projectiles that struck at the swarming Goblins and orcs.

But then, a shadow loomed overhead. A black Dragon, gargantuan and wrathful, reared its head, unleashing a torrent of dark acid directly at Rider. The world dissolved into chaos—

"Rider!" Ariella's voice sliced through the nightmare.

Rider jolted awake with ragged gasps, the acrid taste of fear lingering on his tongue. He blinked away the remnants of the dream, the real world slowly coming into focus.

"Another one?" Ariella's concerned eyes searched his face. Her hand rested lightly on his shoulder, her touch as comforting as it was grounding.

"More frequent," he admitted hoarsely. "And more vivid."

Baelgor knelt by Rider's side, his red eyes examining the wound on Rider's arm with a practiced gaze. "No sign of festering," he grumbled, his fingers careful as they prodded the bandaged flesh. "You're clean, lad. It's the weight of prophecy, not poison."

"Prophecy..." Rider trailed off as he began to search his mind for anything he could remember about his prior nightmares.

"Come," Baelgor said firmly, standing to his full, though modest, height. "Whatever fate you saw will not wait, nor will the trail grow any warmer with time."

They packed their belongings swiftly, leaving no trace of their stay but ash and silence.

The gloom of the tunnels gave way to an expansive land bridge, stretching across an abyss that yawned hungrily below. At its end stood a giant gate wrought from iron and stone, a testament to the grandeur of the fallen Rockbar fortress.

"Ancestors..." Baelgor's voice was barely above a whisper as he took in the sight of piled remains—bones stripped of dignity, devoid of the armor and weapons once proudly borne by kin long deceased.

"Press on," Ariella urged softly, her bow gripped tightly

in her hand. "We honor them best by completing our quest."

"Indeed," Rider agreed, drawing his blades with quiet resolve. "Let's find what secrets Rockbar still guards."

Together, they crossed the bridge, stepping over the bones of history, their path lit only by the steadfast flame of their mission—and the unyielding spark of hope that still burned within their hearts.

Baelgor's thick fingers curled into fists, his knuckles white as the ancient bones strewn about them. "Cursed scavengers," he growled, voice reverberating off the stone around them. "They defile the resting places of the honored dead with their filth and disrespect. No decency resides in the souls of these creatures!"

Ariella placed a calming hand upon Baelgor's shoulder. "Peace, Baelgor. Wrath will not shield us here. We must tread lightly if we are to—"

Her words caught like a snagged thread as Rider raised a hand in silent warning, his eyes narrowing on the shadowed ramparts above. "It seems stealth is a luxury no longer afforded to us," he announced, blades singing as they slid from their sheaths.

Battle had found them once more.

Goblins, grotesque parodies of life, slithered down the walls with unnatural agility, their inky eyes alight with malice. The noise of their weapons rang out like a chaotic cacophony, mirroring the violence in their hearts.

The air hissed with tension, a prelude to the chaos that would soon erupt. Ariella, poised as a huntress in the dark, drew an arrow. Her movements were a fluid stream of precision and grace. With the ghost of a whisper, the bowstring released its pent-up fury, sending death to claim Goblin after Goblin.

Rider became a tempest, steel flashing like lightning

across a storm-ravaged sky. His longsword cleaved through the air, turning aside the crude weapons of the larger brutes. Pain seared beneath the bandaged wound. He shifted his grip, favoring his uninjured arm. Weaving through the gaps in the Goblin ranks, each thrust and parry was a testament to his relentless training.

Baelgor invoked the ancient rites of rock and ore, his warhammer aglow with eldritch power. With each resounding crack, boulders obeyed his call, plummeting from the cavernous heights to sow despair among the Goblin hordes. A thunderous blow sent adversaries tumbling into oblivion, their screams swallowed by the abyss.

"Steel and stone!" Baelgor roared, as the battle raged around them. "We stand firm!"

The battle was a grim spectacle, yet within it lay a beauty—a tragic symphony played out with bow, blade, and hammer. They were harmonious in their discord, painting a tapestry of survival against the dark canvas of the underground.

In the midst of the fray, the scent of blood mingled with the acrid taste of fear, as the air vibrated with the cries of the fallen. But still, our heroes pressed forward, their every sense alert, their every breath a defiance of the darkness that sought to envelop them.

The air trembled when a dark silhouette emerged against the flickering torchlight atop the gate.

The Goblin King.

His voice cackled across the battlefield. "Go forth, my precious, and feast!"

A beast of nightmares burst through the ancient gate, splintering it like kindling. A young Dragon, a wyrmling, let loose a roar that shook the foundations of where they stood. The beast's eruption through the gate sent Goblins scattering; as some of their spindly bodies flung into the abyss below. This wyrmling was much smaller than the Dragons of legend, but no less fearsome. As its mutilated wings outstretched, they could see that flesh was missing from between its wing bones. This was a grotesque mockery of its Dragon ancestors, not fully or properly formed, but it still hungered for their flesh nonetheless.

"By the stars," Ariella stared, her eyes wide with a mix of pity and horror.

"Steel yourselves!" Baelgor bellowed, his warhammer ready as the wyrmling's presence began to loom before them.

The Wyrmling swung its tail with brute force, launching dead Goblins towards the party. The thud of decaying flesh met Baelgor's hammer, the impact echoing like distant thunder. Rider, with a fluid motion, cleaved one cadaver mid-air, halves spiraling away in a grisly dance. Ariella twirled, the corpses passing by as if she moved with the wind itself.

The Wyrmling raised its chest as it gathered an angered breath.

"RUN!" Baelgor's roared command sent them scrambling just as the Dragon readied its toxic assault.

With an incantation made out of more reflex than thought, Baelgor summoned the earth to their defense. A wall of stone rose, strong but fleeting. Acid devoured the protection Baelgor raised in their defense. The stench of vaporized rock stung their nostrils as the heat burned their lungs.

"I don't know… how many more of those I can pull off, lad," Baelgor exhaled, his strength waning.

Rider's gaze hardened as he raised his left palm to meet his gaze, a dangerous plan forming in his mind.

"Rider, no! You don't know how to control it!" Ariella's

voice trembled, her usually composed demeanor crumbling.

A twisted smirk spread across Rider's face as he turned his eyes to meet Ariella, determined to prove her wrong.

"Baelgor," Rider began, as he switched his gaze toward the Dwarf. "I'm gonna need a few stairs." With a burst of adrenaline, Rider sprang from behind their failing earthen shield.

Empowered by Rider's actions, Baelgor readied himself for one final conjuring.

"Now!" Rider shouted as he leaped skyward, anticipating his allies' actions.

Baelgor summoned two towering pillars of earth in response. One shot up beneath Rider's boots, launching him even higher. The second created a platform for Rider to ascend to and gain his advantage.

As he rose upwards, the raw energy originating from Rider's palm crackled around him like a raging storm. With a primal scream, he unleashed the full force of his magic against the bridge below. Rider's blast launched him backwards towards his allies as it shattered the ground beneath the Dragon's feet. Chunks of stone began to break apart and crumble into the abyss below.

Baelgor reacting quickly, softened the earth below into a slippery slide of cool mud, catching Rider just in time. The Dragon let out a deafening screech that echoed through the chasm as his mutilated wings refused to catch flight, the sound of defeat and death dimming as it plummeted below.

Their moment of triumph was short-lived as arrows whistled like vengeful spirits through the dimly lit tunnels, ricocheting off stone walls with deadly intent. The Goblin King's shrill command carried over the clamor, a death sentence echoed by the twangs of bowstrings.

"KILL THEM, KILL THEM ALL!"

Ariella dove behind a jutting stalagmite, an arrow grazing her ear and snagging a strand of auburn hair. "This way!" she hissed, darting into the darkness, the others at her heels.

Rider stumbled after her, breath ragged. The narrow beam of his vision focused on the sway of her hair as it whipped behind her, a beacon in the gloom. They plunged deeper into the bowels of the earth, the battle fading into a murmur behind them.

"Careless!" Ariella snapped suddenly, her voice low but laced with anger. She spun on her heel to face Rider, her silhouette etched against the dimness like a specter of war. "You could have died! Do you understand that?"

Rider raised his hands placatingly, though his eyes sparkled with the thrill of their recent victory. "I took a chance—"

"A chance?" Ariella cut him off sharply. Her gaze was piercing, and even in the scant light, he could see the concern etched deep within. "What value is your treasure if you're not alive to spend it? We need you. *I* need you— whole and breathing."

"Let's keep moving," Baelgor added gruffly, turning away to lead the search for another path—one that he hoped would bear them safely to the Amakiir forest. His sturdy form seemed to carve through the dark, leaving a trail for them to follow.

Rider looked back at Ariella, her figure bathed in the faint glow of luminescent fungi sprouting from the damp walls. He saw not just the warrior in her but the fragility of genuine fear. Her frustration wasn't born of anger but of something far more intimate—a bond that had grown amidst the chaos of their quest.

"Alright," Rider conceded, his voice softened. "We do this together. No more reckless heroics."

"Promise me," Ariella pressed, her eyes searching his.

"Promise," he affirmed. They followed Baelgor's steady steps, delving further into the ancient tunnels, where echoes of the past whispered secrets in the dark.

The damp chill of the subterranean air wrapped around them as they approached a fork in the tunnel. Baelgor halted, his gaze shifting between the two paths that lay ahead, each one disappearing into an abyss of darkness. The silence was heavy, filled only by the distant drip of water and the collective breath of his companions.

"Wait," Baelgor commanded, holding up a hand to signal a pause. He closed his eyes and bowed his head, lips moving in silent communion with the ancestors of his line.

A low, resonant hum emanated from his throat, a primal chant that vibrated through the very stone beneath their feet. Long, sustained notes drifted on the stale air, mingling with the earthy scents of damp rock and minerals.

As the melody deepened, so too did the transformation. Baelgor's skin adopted the texture of granite, his body becoming as still and solid as the ancient walls that enclosed them.

Time stretched and folded upon itself until the dwarf, now fully transmuted into a statue, burst back to life with eyes aflame, glowing like molten rock within a forge. A hard and unyielding form settled upon his features.

"This way," he said, his voice rich with newfound purpose as he pointed decisively down the left-hand passage. "The ancestors have spoken."

They trudged through the labyrinthine tunnels, guided by Baelgor's unwavering certainty, for what they could only assume were three or more days. They rested whenever they could traverse no longer. Fatigue clawed at their limbs, yet anticipation quickened their pace and shortened their rests.

"Can you smell that?" Ariella whispered, her keen senses picking up the subtle change in the air. "The scent of pine... and open sky."

Rider breathed out, allowing himself a small smile. "We're close."

They stepped out from the shadowed confines of Stonefire Mountain into the fading light of dusk. The horizon was painted with the soft blush of twilight, the sky stretching wide and endless above them. Below, the expanse of Amakiir forest unfurled, a sea of greenery that promised both danger and the hope of allies.

"By my beard," Baelgor muttered, squinting against the dying light, "we've made it."

"Thanks to your guidance," Rider clapped the dwarf on the shoulder, a gesture of gratitude and camaraderie.

"Let's not forget the ancestors." Baelgor gave a reverent nod towards the mountain's entrance, now a mere shadow behind them.

"And to each other," Ariella added, her gaze lingering on Rider with a mix of relief and resolve.

Battle-worn but unbowed, the trio stood at the threshold of a new chapter in their journey, the whispers of the past at their backs and the unknown sprawled before them. Their quest for the Amakiir forest—and whatever trials awaited within—beckoned ahead.

CHAPTER X

AMAKIIR'S EMBRACE

Rider's boots crunched softly on the forest floor, the earthy scent of damp soil mingling with the sharp tang of pine. Behind them, the mountain loomed like a slumbering giant, its shadow stretching over Amakiir Forest as dusk settled in. He glanced back once more, half-expecting the screech of Goblins to rip through the serenity of twilight.

"Keep moving," he muttered under his breath, his hand resting on the hilt of his sword. Fatigue pulled at his limbs, but the thought of being tracked by those vile creatures sharpened his stride.

"Rider, we should make camp soon," Ariella's voice was soft yet carried the weight of command, her violet eyes scanning the thickening shadows between the trees.

"Agreed," Rider said, "but let's find some cover first."

The forest embraced them as they ventured deeper. The canopy above was woven so tightly that only slivers of starlight pierced through, dancing on the mossy canvas below. Rustling leaves and creaking branches played around them, the cool breeze carrying whispers of the woodland spirits.

"Look at this," Ariella breathed, stepping into a small clearing. The grass was lush and inviting, a soft carpet that beckoned them to rest. Berries, plump and ripe, hung from nearby bushes, while fruit-laden trees bowed under their sweet bounty.

"Never seen anything like it," Rider admitted, plucking a berry and rolling it between his fingers before tasting its burst of sweetness.

"Nor I," Ariella agreed, her usual vigilance softened by wonder. "This place... it's a gift."

"Then let's accept it," Rider replied, unrolling his pack. The clearing allowed room for two tents, while ensuring enough space for a modest campfire whose smoke would ascend to the heavens through the canopy above.

As night settled, the fire crackled to life, its warm glow casting a protective circle around them. The simple pleasures of the wild – the taste of berries, the softness of the grass, the sounds of the forest – offered a respite from the dangers they had faced in the mountain.

The air was rich with the scent of roasted hazelnuts and wild strawberries as the trio settled by the crackling campfire. Baelgor skewered a collection of mushrooms, their earthy aroma mingling with the smoky wood. Ariella had woven a basket from supple twigs, now filled with an assortment of forest bounty: glossy blueberries, tart raspberries, and the juicy, golden orbs of peaches.

"By my beard, these fruits could sweeten the sourest of Dwarven moods," Baelgor chuckled, tossing a berry into his mouth.

"Indeed," Rider agreed, taking a generous bite of a peach, its nectar trailing down his chin. "Nothing like this grows back in the villages."

"Or in the Elven groves," Ariella added, her lips stained purple from the berries.

Their laughter softened the shadows around them, and tales of their recent battles echoed through the clearing. Rider animatedly recounted how they had maneuvered within the mountain's treacherous confines, narrowly avoiding the seething breath of the Black Wyrmling.

"Your rashness was unmatched, Rider," Ariella chided, half-bothered by the reminder of his actions.

"Rashness? Ha! If not for Baelgor's command of the stone, we'd be Dragon fodder," Rider replied, clapping the Dwarf's broad shoulder.

"Speaking of which," Ariella turned to Baelgor with genuine curiosity, "how do you wield such mastery over the earth?"

Baelgor leaned back on his palms "It's a gift passed down through generations. My bloodline hails from Rockbar, kin to the Deceased Queen's brother. For over four centuries, my ancestors have served King Ragnoc Blackhammer."

"Ancestral magic." Ariella murmured. "So her legends are true."

"Indeed, lass," Baelgor affirmed.

As the fire dwindled to embers, Baelgor rose, stretching his limbs. "I reckon it's time to retire," he grumbled, his keen eyes flicking between Rider and Ariella. "You two share one tent. My snores are louder than a charging ram, best not to prevent your rest." The corner of his mouth twitched into a knowing grin.

Rider caught the implication as Baelgor vanished into his own tent, leaving them alone under the canopy of stars.

Inside their shared shelter, Ariella moved close to Rider, her gentle hands reaching for the clasps of his armor. "Let me help you with that," she whispered, her touch light and lingering on his shoulders. The silken glide of her fingers traced the contours of his arms, causing shivers to race across his skin.

"Thank... you," Rider managed, his voice unsteady as the weight of his armor fell away.

Turning slowly to face her, Rider found himself lost in the depths of Ariella's gaze, emotions swirling between them like the eddies of a stream. He reached out, his hands finding the curve of her waist, drawing her closer until their lips met in a tender, exploratory kiss.

The world outside faded as their passion kindled the beginning of a different kind of flame.

Ariella slowly backed away with a soft moan. "We shouldn't," she sighed. "Too much depends on this mission succeeding."

"I understand," Rider exhaled slowly, attempting to gather himself as withdrew his hands from her waist.

"I want to Rider, I do," Ariella looked down, hesitation warring with desire. "I just..." Ariella began before correcting herself. "We need to stay focused. Perhaps when this is all over we can... entertain other possibilities."

"As you wish... my lady," Rider replied with a devilish smile.

"It is dreadfully cold outside though." Ariella began, with a grin of her own. "Perhaps we should still lay close tonight? To keep each other warm of course."

"Ya know, Ari? I think that would be wise," Rider replied with a soft laugh.

Rider laid down and raised an arm for Ari to cuddle close. They shared the warmth of the leathers, furs, and their budding desires.

Outside, the remnants of the campfire sent smoke and sparks spiraling into the night, joining the glittering expanse of stars above Amakiir Forest, indifferent witnesses to the emotional promise between Human and Elf.

The morning light crept through the canvas of the tent with a gentle insistence, stirring Rider from the night of warmth and intimacy he had shared with Ariella. He dressed quietly, mindful not to wake her, and stepped out into the cool embrace of dawn. The forest was alive with the chirping of birds and the rustling of leaves, as if nature itself was shaking off the vestiges of night.

Baelgor was already up, tending to a small fire that crackled merrily. On a flat stone beside the flames, strips of rabbit meat sizzled alongside slices of lush fruit, their juices caramelizing in the heat.

"Morning," Baelgor grunted with a knowing grin as he flipped the meat with a practiced flick of his wrist. "Sleep well?"

Rider cleared his throat, feeling a flush of warmth that had nothing to do with the fire. "Like a rock," he replied, matching the dwarf's grin with a sheepish one of his own.

"Good, good," Baelgor chuckled, plating the breakfast. "Found a rabbit at the break of dawn. Figured fresh meat beats jerky and hard tack any day."

"Can't argue with that," Rider said, accepting a plate loaded with the fragrant offerings.

A rustle of fabric announced Ariella's emergence from the tent, her cheeks tinged with a blush that rivaled the pink hue of the dawn. Baelgor handed her a plate without comment, though his eyes twinkled with unspoken mirth.

"Thank you, Baelgor," she murmured, taking a tentative bite of the succulent fruit. Its sweetness burst on her tongue, mingling with the savory richness of the rabbit meat.

The meal was a quiet affair, punctuated by the sounds of the forest and the occasional glance exchanged between the two companions now bound by more than duty. Once they finished, they packed their belongings with practiced efficiency and set out deeper into the woods.

The following days melded into one another as they traversed Amakiir Forest. They encountered rabbits darting through underbrush, squirrels chattering from the branches above, and deer that observed them with cautious curiosity before bounding away. Birds sang melodies that wove through the canopy, each tune a unique thread in the tapestry of the forest soundscape.

Ariella paused occasionally to inspect tracks on the forest floor, her trained eyes deciphering the stories left behind by wolves and bears. But it was a set of unfamiliar prints that brought the party to a halt. They were large and oddly shaped, with claw marks that spoke of strength and wildness.

"Never seen anything like these," Rider remarked, crouching beside Ariella for a closer look.

"Nor I," Baelgor added, his brow furrowed. "These woods are ancient. They keep secrets."

"Best we keep moving," Ariella decided, standing gracefully. "But let's remain vigilant. Whatever made these tracks might still be nearby."

With a sense of wary wonder, they pressed on. The mysteries of Amakiir Forest stretching out before them like an uncharted map, its hidden corners waiting to be explored. Colossal trees loomed like the ancient pillars of a forgotten temple, their vast trunks vanishing into the high canopy overhead. The branches, thick as castle ramparts, intertwined to form an emerald roof that could shelter legions. As the adventurers pressed forward through the underbrush, an awed silence fell upon them.

"By the gods," Rider whispered, his voice barely carrying above the hushed forest. "I've never seen trees so massive."

"Like the bones of the earth reaching for the heavens," Baelgor murmured, running a hand along the gnarled bark, feeling the pulse of the forest. "Felled neither by axe nor storm."

Ariella lifted her gaze skyward, her eyes reflecting the greenish twilight filtering through the leaves. "It's as if the sky has abandoned us, enveloped by this eternal canopy."

Their conversation came to an abrupt halt as a distant thunder rolled through the forest, a deep rumble that shook the ground beneath their feet and warned of an impending squall. They exchanged glances, a silent consensus reached without words. Rider began clearing a space for camp, while Baelgor and Ariella gathered fallen branches for a fire amidst the softening light.

As the campfire crackled to life, the storm grew fierce, its anger echoing above them like the drums of war. They huddled close, their faces illuminated intermittently by flashes of lightning that played across the roiling clouds hidden from view.

"Feels like we've been wandering these woods for an age," Baelgor grumbled, prodding the fire with a stick. "Think the Wood Elves are aware of us yet?"

"Without a doubt," Ariella replied, her face cast in firelight. "King Lucian's communion with Sune and Rallathil is said to grant him supernatural insight into their woods. If he so wishes, he knows of every leaf that falls in his domain. There is no way we could have traveled for a week through his woods unnoticed."

A column of white-hot brilliance blinded them, a bolt of lightning that struck just beyond their camp's perimeter. In the afterglow, a tall figure emerged, silhouetted against the fading light.

"Who goes there?" Rider called out, hand on the hilt of his sword, his heart pounding in his chest.

"Peace, travelers," the figure responded, stepping forward into the firelight. He was a Human of modest height, but whose presence commanded attention. His blond hair fell in loose waves around his shoulders, covered by the elegant cape attached to his runed breastplate. His piercing blue eyes seemed to spark with an inner tempest. An aura of arcane energy clung to him, as tangible as the storm filled air that surrounded them.

"Kael Stormbringer bears no ill will," he said with an easy smile and striking eyes. "And whom might I have the fortune of encountering this evening?"

"We are but travelers seeking passage through these woods," Ariella answered, her tone cautious yet courteous.

"Then let us find comfort in shared company," Kael suggested, gesturing towards the fire with a grace that contradicted his formidable presence. "The night is long, and this beautiful storm shows no sign of mercy."

"May I share in your fire's warmth this eve?" Kael's voice rippled through the damp air, carrying both the rumble of thunder and the soothing cadence of a gentle stream.

"Of course," Rider said, after exchanging a look with his companions. "Though I fear our hospitality is as meager as our camp."

"Then let us improve upon it," Kael proposed with a hearty laugh that seemed to challenge the storm itself. He clapped his hands, and with a dramatic flourish, he invoked his magic.

"*Harmoniael Festivion*," Kael said with authority, snapping his fingers.

The very earth responded. Stones rolled together to form elegant benches and a long table, while overhead branches bent low, intertwining to create an overhead lattice where glowing orbs of light flickered to life.

The feast that materialized before them was one of epic proportions. Giant roasts, glistening with juices, lay alongside platters of freshly cooked fish which released steam into the cool night air. Cheeses of various textures and hues, from creamy white to deep amber, tempted the senses with their different sharp and mellow fragrances. Fruits plush with sweetness, their vibrant skins barely containing the lushness within, while vegetables, crisp and colorful, arranged themselves like a painter's palette.

Freshly baked breads, warm and inviting, lay next to pies that promised flaky crusts filled with tart and sweet fillings. Pitchers of wine reflected the flickering firelight, promising notes of oak and berry, while small barrels of ale stood at the ready.

"Join me!" Kael beckoned, slicing through the air with a grandiose gesture that invited them all to partake in the sudden opulence.

As they took their seats, comforted by the rich fare and the camaraderie it inspired, Kael leaned forward with a spark in his eye. "So tell me, what quest brings you to these ancient woods?"

Between mouthfuls of succulent meat and sips of robust wine, the party recounted their tale. They spoke of the cult that threaded its dark influence through the land and the battles fought to thwart its insidious plans.

As Rider leaned in with interest, Kael settled back into his chair and took a slow sip of wine. He gazed thoughtfully at the deep red liquid, swirling it gently in the glass as he began to speak. "There are places," he explained, "where the elements hold a power beyond comprehension. They are realms governed by a single truth such as fire or water."

The party's expressions of disbelief did little to deter him.

"This world is but a single note in the grand scheme of the cosmos," he stated, the shadows dancing across his face and highlighting the intensity with which he spoke of the wonders he had encountered on his travels. Each word seemed to paint a vivid picture in the minds of those gathered around him. The heat from the flames intensified as he delved into his stories, transporting them to far-off lands where nature ruled supreme and magic was alive and well.

"Alas, since arriving here, I've been unable to weave the portals that are my pathways between realms." Kael conceded.

"We've read of the cult's meddling with the leylines. Could that be the cause?" Ariella asked, her curiosity evident even as she struggled with the notion.

"Indeed." Kael's eyes darkened like the clouds above. "They thrum with an unnatural cadence here. That is the disturbance I seek to understand."

As the storm's fury waned, they rose from the table, bellies full, minds alight with wonder and skepticism. "We should tidy up—" Baelgor began, but was quickly interrupted by Kael.

"*Essentiael Verdonar, Luminar Pavilia,*" he spoke as he gave another effortless snap of his fingers. The grandeur vanished, leaving no trace behind save for a lavish tent that hadn't been there before.

Chuckles erupted from the group, a mix of amazement and amusement. "Well, goodnight then," Rider said, still grinning as they retreated to their tents, the memory of the feast lingering like a shared dream.

Morning dawned, casting a pale light through the dense canopy of Amakiir Forest. The heroes stirred from their slumber, the air crisp with the scent of pine and earth after the night's storm. Kael emerged from his luxurious tent, stretching languidly.

"Kael," Rider called out, a steaming mug in hand. "We've discussed it amongst ourselves. We'd like you to join us. Your knowledge of the leylines could prove invaluable."

"Ah, an alliance of necessity then," Kael replied with a smirk, accepting the invitation. "Lead on, my new friends. What a story this will make."

As they trekked deeper into the moss-clad labyrinth, Ariella, graceful as a breeze, paused and crouched beside an odd trail of indents upon the forest floor. "These tracks," she murmured, "they're the same as we saw before..."

Kael knelt beside her, examining the markings. "Owlbear prints," he declared without hesitation. "Two adults and one youngling, if I'm not mistaken." As he spoke, an owlbear feather, dappled brown and floated between them, its descent silent yet ominous.

A low growl vibrated through the undergrowth. A massive, feathered form emerged, eyes ablaze with protective fury—the mother owlbear.

"Slowly, back a–," Kael whispered, but it was too late. A second beast, the male, loomed behind them, cutting off their retreat.

"Stand ready!" Baelgor bellowed, his voice echoing through the trees. He grasped his warhammer tightly, his stance grounding him like the ancient stones of his homeland.

The mother owlbear charged, a wall of feathered power and unbridled rage.

"Rider, with me!" Baelgor cried, summoning the earth to rise at his command, creating barriers that shattered beneath the owlbear's assault.

Rider, gripping his longsword with both hands, met the mother's charge. His weapon clashed against the owlbear's talons—a song of steel against the guttural cries of nature.

Ariella loosed arrows in a deadly dance, each shot whistling through the air, finding purchase in the thick hide of the father who had approached their flank. Moving with Elven grace, she vaulted from tree to tree, her auburn hair a fiery trail behind her.

"That's quite enough. *Aerovien Zephyra, Caelum Arcili*," Kael intoned, his hands weaving intricate patterns as bolts of lightning arced from his fingertips, striking the male with sizzling fury while gusts of wind buffeted the creature, throwing it against a nearby tree.

The mother owlbear fought with relentless ferocity as she threw Rider aside. With a mighty swipe from her other paw, she tore across Baelgor's chest, rending his armor asunder.

"Graaaah," Baelgor grunted, pain flashing across his features.

"Baelgor!" Rider shouted, as he reengaged the mother, only for her to snap her powerful beak around his blade, shattering the steel like brittle glass.

Ariella, now approaching from above, released her bow. Dropping from the canopy, she drew her blades and she drove them deep in the back of the beast's neck.

The final growl of the mother owlbear echoed through the Amakiir Forest, a lingering testament to the ferocity of nature. With the great beasts slain, the party stood amidst the savagery they unleashed, the scent of blood and earth heavy in the air. Baelgor, leaning heavily against his warhammer, bore a grimace of agony as a dark stain spread across his torn armor.

"By the depths," he rasped, touching his hand against his chest, feeling the crimson liquid starting to pool.

Ariella hurried to his side, her violet eyes wide with concern. She fumbled with the last healing scroll, her fingers trembling as she unfurled the delicate parchment. The ancient script shimmered with a pale light as she chanted the incantations, her voice a melodic whisper that swelled with desperation.

"By the Queen's light, heal this flesh, bind this soul," she implored, but the magic flickered like a dying flame and then extinguished, leaving Baelgor's wound untouched.

"Damned be your queen, and her magic!" Baelgor spat, his face ashen.

"Stay still, you stubborn Dwarf," Rider ordered, kneeling beside him. "We'll figure something out."

"We're not alone, friends." Kael murmured as a rustling above heralded an ethereal descent.

Wood Elves, garbed in leaf-green tunics, dropped soundlessly from the towering branches, landing with the grace of leaves touching down upon the forest floor.

"Quite the spectacle," one Elf remarked, his gaze traveling over the fallen owlbears. "Your bravery shines brightly in these shadows."

"Help him," Ariella pleaded, gesturing to the wounded Baelgor.

"Of course," another Elf said, stepping forward, his hands aglow with a soft green light. "I am Elandir, and our healers can tend to your friend. Come, we shall escort you to Amakiir Castle."

"Castle?" Baelgor grunted, skepticism etched into his furrowed brow. "What need have I for castles? My fate is here, in the wilds."

"Nonsense," Elandir chided gently. "No noble warrior should fall to wounds when aid is near. Allow us the honor of hospitality."

"Very well," Baelgor conceded with a nod, gritting his teeth as two elves carefully removed his sundered armor and bound his wound. Once he was stable, they hoisted him onto a makeshift stretcher woven from living vines.

"Impressive," Ariella commented at the swift and effective techniques used by the Wood Elves.

"We take nothing for granted in Amakiir," one Elf whispered to Ariella as they began to move. "The forest provides all we need. She will care for your friend."

"Lead the way," Rider said, his voice carrying a note of respect for their unexpected saviors as the forest began to swallow them whole, its secrets kept close to its heart.

As the dense expanse of Amakiir Forest gave way to a clearing, the grandeur of Amakiir Castle unfurled before their eyes. Towering fortresses spiraled upwards, cradled within the arms of colossal trees whose ancient roots wove through stone and bark alike. A testament to Wood Elf artistry, each structure boasted elaborate carvings depicting the storied past of the woodland realm—scenes of battles won and lost with grace, alliances forged and chains broken beneath starlit skies, and the serene march of seasons across uncountable years.

"By the forge..." Baelgor's voice trailed off as his consciousness waned, his usual stoic demeanor momentarily eclipsed by awe as they crossed an invisible threshold into history made manifest.

"Welcome to the living heart of our people," a Wood Elf murmured.

The group tread upon mossy paths that felt like clouds underfoot, the air rich with the scent of ancient wood and blooming flowers. Light filtered through archways, refracting into prismatic cascades that cast the castle in a perpetual twilight glow.

Elandir gestured towards an opulent doorway. "Behold the healing chambers of the Amakiir."

A priestess emerged, her robes the color of dawn, and approached Baelgor with a delicate touch. She cradled a bloom in her hands—the sacred Amakiir flower, its petals shimmering with an inner light. As she pressed it to Baelgor's chest, the Dwarf's grimace softened, his wounds visibly knitting together amidst the luminous motions of the petal's magic.

"Thank you," he rasped, reverence lacing his words.

"Rest now, Stoneheart of Rockbar," the priestess replied, her voice like wind through leaves. "You are safe within these walls."

"How did you . . .?" Baelgor managed a questioning sigh before falling to slumber.

Rider watched in silence as his comrade found solace in the Elven ministrations, before turning to follow Ariella, Kael, and Elandir towards the heart of the castle.

Amakiir Castle was a living, breathing wonder unlike anything the party had ever seen. They ascended an external spiral staircase carved into the bark of a massive tree-tower, and with each winding step, the true scale of the Elven stronghold became apparent. Each structure, from the sprawling halls to the soaring keeps, was an integral part of the ancient trees themselves. The trunks were so immense that they seemed to hold up the sky itself, their emerald canopies stretching out like green clouds. The fading sunlight filtered through the dense foliage, casting dappled shadows that swayed across their path. The forest floor fell away beneath them, revealing a sprawling city nestled amidst the roots and boughs.

Elegant bridges, woven from living vines, connected the

various tree-towers, creating a vast network of walkways that hummed with the pulse of Wood Elf life. Far below, the party could see winding pathways lined with luminescent flowers, their soft glow lending a gentle ambiance to the castle and city grounds. Graceful spires, carved to mimic the twisting branches, rose from the depths of the forest, their peaks disappearing into the green expanse above.

Ariella paused to catch her breath, her eyes wide with wonder. "I've heard tales of Amakiir's grandeur," she whispered, "but I never imagined such a sight."

Rider nodded, equally struck by the natural beauty. The castle seemed to vibrate with life, as if the very trees were infused with the wisdom of countless generations.

The wind picked up as they climbed higher, carrying with it the scent of blooming flowers and fresh leaves. The breeze played through Ariella's auburn hair, whipping strands across her face. Rider felt his heart skip a beat as he watched her, marveling at the way she seemed to belong amidst the timeless beauty of this Elven realm.

Elandir glanced back at them, a knowing smile playing across his lips. "The heart of Amakiir awaits," he said, gesturing towards a grand archway carved into the trunk of the tree-tower.

The throne room awaited—a vast expanse embraced by the forest itself, roots curving to form pillars that reached for the heavens.

Upon a platform woven from living vines, stood High Priest King Lucian Amakiir. His golden hair cascaded over his shoulders, like sunlight filtering through the forest canopy. His green eyes, deep pools of wisdom, surveyed them with an intensity that seemed to peer into their very souls.

"Travelers from… distant lands," Lucian paused as his

gaze passed from Ariella and Rider to Kael. His voice carried through the chamber, melodious yet commanding. "I bid you welcome to my court."

"Your Majesty," Ariella began, her voice a melodic thread in the tapestry of the audience. "We are honored by your hospitality and seek..."

"Alliance," Lucian finished for her, a knowing smile touching his lips. "Yes, I have listened to the tremors of your journey upon the winds. Speak freely here, beneath the watchful gaze of Sune and Rallathil."

Their tale unfolded before the king, the fragrance of ancient incense wrapping around them. The heroes' journey, fraught with peril and bound by fate, found a sympathetic ear in the regal presence of the High Priest King.

"Your path is woven tightly with the threads of destiny," Lucian observed after a pause, his gaze lingering on each of them. "And this castle, my home, shall be your sanctuary as long as need be."

"Thank you, Your Grace," Rider replied, bowing deeply. "Your kindness is as vast as the forest that shelters us."

"Come," Lucian beckoned, rising to his feet. "Let us share in the evening's repose. Tomorrow, we may discuss what fate has in store for you all."

As the audience concluded, the heroes were led away to quarters that resonated with the tranquility of the woods. Yet even as they retired, the echoes of their conversation with the king lingered in their minds, like the gentle rustle of leaves whispering secrets of the world beyond.

The great hall of Amakiir Castle, with its soaring arches and light-dappled walls, echoed with an unusual stillness.

The scent of pine and ancient bark mingled in the air as the party, still weary from their travels, found solace in the refuge offered by the Wood Elves. Baelgor, his stout frame still hunched over from both fatigue and the healing wound received from the talons of an owlbear, leaned heavily on a sturdy table. His breaths were ragged and matched the flicker of torchlight against the walls.

"By Moradin's beard," he grumbled, wincing as a kind Elven healer applied another poultice with gentle hands. "That beast had claws like forged daggers."

Kael, his blond hair now matted with sweat, slumped beside him. "Rest now, my friend. We've earned the peace of these halls." His voice was a soft murmur, a stark contrast to the usual confident timbre that commanded attention.

Elandir approached, his movements a graceful contrast to the heavy languor that hung upon the others. His gaze held the weight of unspoken stories as he placed a comforting hand on Baelgor's broad shoulder. "Your resilience is admirable, Baelgor," he said softly. "But even the mightiest oak must occasionally bend to the storm to avoid breaking."

"Speaking of storms," Kael interjected, his curiosity piqued despite his exhaustion, "I find myself wondering about the tempests your people have weathered here in Etonya. How did you come to be so… harmonious amidst such history?"

Elandir paused, his eyes darkening with memories long passed. "It is a tale steeped in sorrow," he began, the cadence of his voice weaving an almost tangible tapestry in the air. "During the Great War, our ancestors were shackled in chains, their spirits caged as much as their bodies. Enslaved by the Orcs, they were forced to abandon their bond with the land, to forsake the very essence of what it means to be an Elf of the Woods."

"Generations of knowledge, lost," Kael murmured, the blue in his eyes dimming with empathy. "Such a wound to the collective spirit does not easily heal."

"Indeed," Elandir confirmed, his gaze lingering on the shadows dancing across the wall. "The scars remain, etched into the heartwood of our culture. We may have reclaimed our freedom, but the fear... It lingers like the last note of a mournful song. And though we have strived to catch up with the world once again, the specters of our past haunt us still."

"Yet, here you stand," Kael said, gesturing to the castle around them, "a testament to endurance and strength."

"Strength, yes," Elandir agreed, a small smile playing on his lips. "But more importantly, a testament to hope. For though our past may be dark and full of horror, the dawn of a new day always carries the promise of new beginnings."

Baelgor nodded slowly, his eyes reflecting the orange glow of the fire. "A promise worth fightin' for," he rasped, clenching his fist with renewed resolve.

Their conversation, a blend of somber reflection and burgeoning determination, filled the room, swirling amidst the ancient branches that had bore witness to countless such exchanges throughout the ages. The heroes sat together, united by their shared burdens and the unspoken understanding that their journey was far from over.

The morning sun filtered through the canopy, casting dappled light upon the royal garden where Elandir led his weary companions. In the heart of Amakiir Castle's grounds, nature thrived in an orchestrated wildness that spoke of meticulous care and respect.

"Behold," Elandir gestured with a sweeping hand, "the essence of our pact with the forest."

Kael stepped forward, his eyes tracing the seamless blend of flora and architecture. Vines crept lovingly over stone, flowering shrubs nestled against walls as if they were born from the masonry itself. He watched, enraptured, as a giant elk sauntered towards them, its antlers a majestic crown of living wood.

"Lovely," Kael whispered, reaching out tentatively. The elk nuzzled his palm with a gentleness that contradicted its size.

"Here, there are no masters, only kindred spirits," Elandir's voice was low, reverent. "We ask and listen. If an animal chooses to accompany us, it is by their own will."

Baelgor, observing a pair of squirrels playfully chasing each other, grunted in approval. "Aye, 'tis a bond not forged by chains but by mutual respect."

"Indeed," Elandir smiled, watching a woodpecker flit from tree to tree without fear. "Our homes, like this castle, rise alongside nature, not over it. We live as one with the woods, taking only what we need, giving back twofold."

Their senses were enveloped by the harmony of this place—the scent of jasmine and pine, the soft rustling of leaves, the taste of fresh air mingling with the sweetness of blooming flowers.

This tranquil moment, however, was short-lived. A clarion call echoed through the trees, summoning them to the heart of the castle. With a final appreciative glance at the garden, the group made their way to the royal court.

King Laucian Amakiir awaited them, his golden hair a radiant contrast against the deep greens and browns of his throne room. His face, a bastion of serenity just a night ago, was etched with lines of concern.

"Friends," he began, his voice carrying the weight of

the impending conversation, "troubling news has reached my ears. Our scouts report that the Orc Clans have begun to unite under a single banner, one belonging to a 'Drogor Thunderfist'."

Murmurs rippled through the court like wind through leaves. King Laucian raised a hand, silencing the whispers.

"My scouts report that this Orc is known for his savagery and cunning. This, combined with the news you brought to our lands, has us fearing he seeks to reforge an alliance with the Dragon Lord—an alliance that could once again spell doom for my people."

Ariella felt the gravity of the king's words settle upon her like a leaden cloak. Beside her, Baelgor's hand instinctively went to the hilt of his hammer, his jaw set in grim determination.

"We have long cherished peace," King Laucian continued, his gaze scanning the faces of his subjects around the room, "but we must ready ourselves for the possibility of war. The safety of our realm, the sanctity of our woods, hangs by a thread."

In the heavy silence that followed, the heroes exchanged somber glances. They understood the stakes and felt the pressing urgency that now charged the very air around them.

"Your majesty," Ariella said, respectfully stepping forward with a bow, "We stand with you. Whatever threatens Amakiir, threatens us all."

King Laucian nodded solemnly, meeting Ariella's gaze with one of profound gratitude. "Then ready yourselves, brave ones. Dark times loom on the horizon, and we must meet them with courage and unity in the coming days."

As they left the court, the scent of rain pervaded the air—nature herself seemed to brace for the coming change.

CHAPTER XI
BLOOD AND TRADITION

The morning mist clung to the Amakiir woods like a delicate shroud as the heroes gathered in the courtyard, their armor glinting with beads of dew. King Laucian stood before them, serene yet quietly urgent.

"Brave adventurers," he began, his voice resonating through the crisp air, "I have sent news to Brightspire informing them of our decision to stand united against the cult. However, a united Orcish horde is a threat not just to Amakiir, but to all free peoples. You must uncover the intentions of this Drogor and thwart any dark designs they harbor."

Baelgor's deep voice rumbled in assent. "You saved my life, for that, my hammer and heart are at your service in this."

King Laucian nodded, his eyes reflecting pride and concern. "You have told us of your valor tested by fire and fang. But remember, these Orcs are not mere Goblins. You will need cunning as much as strength."

"The Human lands are far to the east, and your quest requires speed." King Laucian gestured toward the towering oak gates, which creaked open to reveal majestic Griffins. Their golden feathers shimmered in the morning light, fierce eyes surveying the gathering. "These noble creatures have pledged to ferry you to the edge of our realm. May their wings carry you swiftly and safely."

Ariella approached the nearest Griffin, her hand outstretched. The beast lowered its head, allowing her touch, a silent accord between them. She turned to her companions, her face alight with determination. "Let us ride these winds of fate then, and may they hasten our return with tidings of peace."

One by one, the heroes mounted the magnificent beasts, feeling the raw power of their muscled forms beneath them.

"*Telathrin Caelinor Velorian,*" Kael whispered in appreciation as he settled behind the proud arch of his Griffin's neck.

The Griffin let out a piercing cry as if in acknowledgment, as they all took to the skies.

The world below transformed into a tapestry of green, rivers and clearings threading through its vastness. Wind whipped past their faces as wings beat rhythmically, the scent of pine and the crispness of the altitude filling their senses.

"What a sight!" Rider exclaimed, his voice barely carrying over the rush of wind.

"Indeed," Elandir agreed, his gaze sweeping across the landscape. "The Great Mother's embrace is boundless."

Ariella leaned forward, her hand gently caressing her mount's feathered crest. "We are but specks upon her vast canvas," she said, a note of reverence in her tone.

As hours passed, the edge of the forest approached, revealing the golden hills of the plains. From their aerial vantage, the party observed the earth's quilted pattern, where the shadows of clouds roamed freely over the rolling terrain.

"Behold," Elandir whispered, pointing towards the horizon. "The Great Plains."

Baelgor grunted in approval, his eyes tracing the lines that roads made, etched upon the plains like ancient runes. "A sight to stir even a Dwarf's heart," he admitted, a rare smile touching his lips.

Finally, the Griffins began their descent, powerful legs outstretched as they touched down upon the soft grass. The heroes dismounted, each taking a moment to bow deeply before their majestic steeds.

"Your service has been a gift, noble creatures," Rider said, his words earnest. "We are in your debt."

"May the winds carry you swift and true," Ariella added, her voice laced with gratitude.

"Go now, back to the skies that are your rightful domain," Kael intoned, watching as the Griffins took to the air once more. As twilight approached, the party chose a site for camp and began readying their tents. The evening air was crisp, carrying the scent of wildflowers and the distant echo of the Griffins' departing cries.

"Let us raise shelter and rest," Elandir suggested. "The journey ahead will test our resolve."

"Agreed," Baelgor said, his hands already at work setting up a secure perimeter. "Tonight we sleep under stars and open sky. Tomorrow, we face whatever fates have in store."

With a shared nod, the heroes set about their tasks. As night fell upon the plains, they settled close to the fire, its warmth a small comfort against the chill of uncertainty that lay ahead.

Dawn unfurled across the plains, casting a golden hue over the undulating hills. They broke camp as they had many mornings before, Baelgor cinching his pack with a grunt. His owlbear wound ached but did not slow him.

"Let's be off," he said gruffly, leading the way as the party trekked into the vast plainlands.

The sun climbed higher, its rays breathing life into the expanse. A herd of wild horses galloped in the distance, their manes catching the light like flickering flames. Above, hawks circled languidly, sharp eyes piercing the grass sea for unsuspecting prey.

"Nature's dance is ever captivating," Elandir murmured, his gaze following the graceful arc of a diving bird.

"Indeed," Kael agreed, though his mind seemed elsewhere, likely unraveling the tapestry of history that had brought them to this point.

As the day waned, a column of smoke caught Rider's attention. "There," he pointed, and the party adjusted their course toward the rising gray plume. As the hours passed, they made their way to the first tribal camp they came across.

A makeshift barricade loomed ahead, tree trunks and hay forming a primitive yet imposing wall. The group slowed, their steps cautious as they neared the wooden pike fence encircling an unseen camp.

"State your business!" a booming voice demanded. Two Orc guards emerged, muscles bulging beneath weather-worn leather, their jagged swords gleaming dangerously in the fading light.

"We seek food and refreshment," Ariella called out, her tone steady despite the imposing figures before them.

"Ha! You'll find no Elven delicacies here!" one guard scoffed, eyeing them with barely concealed amusement.

"Fine by me," Baelgor countered, puffing out his barrel chest defiantly. "I've got a taste for stronger stuff than forest brews."

"Your Dwarven swill?" the second guard chuckled, running a hand along the jagged edge of his sword. "Our ale would knock you to your knees."

"Try me," Baelgor shot back, his red eyes glinting with challenge.

The guards exchanged a look, then stepped aside, gesturing for the group to pass.

"Enter, then. But be warned, this isn't your home." The warning was clear; they were watched, judged, but for now, allowed within the heart of this Orcish domain. Dust and the iron tang of blood hung thick in the air as the party made their way through the Orc encampment. Suspicious Orcs watched them with challenge in their eyes. Ariella's nostrils flared in distaste, her eyes scanning the rough structures that rose haphazardly like jagged teeth.

Orcs, burly and scarred, milled about with an air of aggression that seemed to seep from their very pores. Challenges were issued with growls over the smallest slights—over a spilled drink, a bumped shoulder, or a coveted piece of gristly meat. In this harsh land where the earth yielded little bounty, the Orcs' warrior culture thrived on might and dominance. Neither a stream nor lush hunting grounds graced this barren expanse. They feasted on what meager creatures the arid plains offered, and their relentless sparring honed them into creatures of survival.

"Notice how they settle every dispute," Elandir murmured, his gaze following two orcs grappling over a piece of salted jerky.

"Strength is currency here," Rider added, his voice low.

At the center of the camp, roars and cheers erupted from a fighting pit carved into the earth. The party edged closer, drawn not just by the spectacle of raw violence that unfolded before them, but by opportunity.

Two behemoth orcs clashed within the pit, their jagged swords sparking as they met with the force of thunderclaps. Leather hides swayed and strained across their massive forms, providing scant protection from the brutality of their blows.

The crowd jeered and whooped, their fervor reaching a fever pitch as one Orc landed a vicious strike, severing his opponent's arm at the elbow. A sickening squelch resonated as the limb hit the dirt, blood spurting in a grotesque fountain. Without pause, the victor pressed the advantage, his sword arcing high before descending in a grim finality that cleaved through neck and spine. The defeated gladiator's head rolled listlessly to the edge of the pit, eyes wide in eternal lifeless surprise.

"Barbaric," Ariella whispered, her face pale beneath the fiery cascade of her hair. Her violet eyes shimmered with revulsion, yet she could not tear her gaze from the carnage.

"Bloodsport," Kael said softly, though the analytical glint in his eye did not mask the unease that knotted his brow. "A brutal necessity for them, but a sport nonetheless."

The victorious Orc bellowed triumphantly, hoisting his bloodied weapon skyward as his chest heaved with ragged breaths. The crowd's elation swelled, a living entity that fed on the spectacle of death and glory.

The Orc victor, muscles slick with exertion, stooped to lift a fallen pike. A banner, black as midnight, fluttered like a raven's wing as he thrust it aloft. Emblazoned on its surface was a clenched fist wreathed in lightning.

"That's gotta be our mark," Baelgor muttered, as he

assumed the banner's emblem belonged to Drogor Thunderfist.

With the throng of orcs cheering wildly, their roars echoing off the crude wooden palisades, the party edged closer to the gladiator's egress. Rider, dwarfed by the towering figures around him, approached the massive Orc champion with an appreciative nod.

"Strong arm, fierce heart," Rider said, raising his voice to be heard above the horde. "A might worthy of sagas."

The Orc grunted, a guttural sound of acknowledgment, his gaze lingering on Rider's smaller stature with a smirk etched into his battle-hardened face.

"Your prowess honors your lineage, good sir. I might say a splendid display of macabre technique!" Kael interjected, attempting to bridge the gap with diplomacy.

Confusion clouded the brute's features, followed swiftly by irritation. He stood taller, muscles tensing, as if the words were a veiled insult.

"Enough!" boomed a voice from behind them. They turned to see another Orc, decked in furs and bone jewelry that spoke of status, emerging from the shadow of the tents. His eyes held a cunning that set him apart. "Hrungnir, stand down."

The chieftain cast a measured glance over the group before speaking further, "I am Grashnak. Why are you here?"

Before Rider could speak, Ariella stepped forward, her voice firm despite the disdain in the chieftain's eyes. "We come seeking information about—"

"Silence, Elf!" Grashnak snapped, his interruption as sharp as a cleaver's chop. "Women do not speak for men, especially Elvish women."

Her cheeks flushed with anger, but before she could retort, Baelgor leaned in close. "You'd give their finest warrior pause in combat," he murmured, his voice a low rumble.

Ariella's lips curled into a half-smile, touched by the compliment.

Rider took a step forward, meeting Grashnak's gaze squarely. "We come seeking information about an Orc called Drogor Thunderfist," he said, "one we hear is uniting your clans."

Grashnak's expression remained unreadable as he listened, the weight of his gaze measuring their intent. His scowl deepened as he regarded the heroes before him. The air was thick with tension, the scent of blood and sweat from the fighting pits still mingling with the earthy aroma of the camp.

"Thunderfist," Grashnak spat the name like a curse, his voice low and edged with a growl. "That one... is not uniting, he is conquering."

Around them, the Orcish camp buzzed with a restless energy, the recent battle's echoes still vibrating through the throngs of orcs who murmured amongst themselves. The defeated gladiator's blood and body was left to stain the dirt, a stark reminder of the dangers that awaited any who dared challenge Drogor Thunderfist's emissary.

"Every chief who faces him falls," Grashnak continued, his gaze distant as if lost in thought. "And with each fall, his ranks grow. We are warriors, but he... he is something else. He challenges us by the ancient laws, but dishonors our kin. His strength cannot be purely of blood and bone."

"Enhanced by magic, quite the cunning strategy," Kael mused aloud, eyes narrowing in thought. "But why not challenge his right after he betrays the laws?"

"Who is left to challenge him?" Grashnak retorted as his brow furrowed. "The champions lay defeated by his emissaries, then Drogor arrives to challenge and slay the chief. Only the weaker clansmen survive, those left must submit for survival."

"Your champion fought bravely today," Rider said, nodding towards the pit where the crowd had begun to disperse.

"If Drogor takes my clan, many more will follow," the chieftain stated gravely. "We are one of the last clans still resisting. Thunderfist banners will fly over every hearth, and our old ways will be lost."

"Allow us to stay until Drogor arrives," Rider proposed, taking a calculated risk. "Let us see him. Let us understand what we're facing."

Grashnak's eyes narrowed as he calculated the outcomes, his decision hanging like a guillotine above their heads.

"Stay. There." he consented at last, his voice a low rumble as he pointed to a vacant pitched tent in the distance. "But one of you must face him in Gor'makh Ghash*. If you win... we can talk more. If you lose, your lives are forfeit."

"Agreed," Baelgor said stoutly, his chest puffing out as if already relishing the challenge as the others exchanged looks of quiet determination.

"Good," Grashnak growled. "Ready yourselves. Thunderfist is no tale to frighten children. You will need all your strength come morning."

With a curt nod, the party turned, leaving the chieftain behind as they made their way through the camp. The smell of dust and guttural Orcish songs filled the air, painting a vivid tapestry of life within the clan.

---

*   *"Gor'makh Ghash - "Gor" signifies purity or essence, "makh" represents combat or battle, and "ghash" embodies strength or power. Together, "Gor'makh Ghash" encapsulates the raw, unbridled essence of combat in Orc culture, emphasizing the unforgiving nature of battle and the indomitable strength required to emerge victorious."*

The heavy canvas of the tent whispered with the sighs of night air as the party huddled within, their figures casting long shadows by the flicker of a single candle. The air was thick with anticipation and the musky scent of worn leather.

"The clans fear him, so he won't go down easily," Rider began, breaking the silence. "But my speed has felled greater foes. I could outpace him, wear him down until he's ripe for the killing blow."

"Speed is nothing without power, and your blade is broken" Elandir countered, his voice dismissive. "My blows can break stone and bone alike. If I could just reach the cage of his heart."

"Magic may be our key," Kael interjected, steepling his fingers as the light played across his thoughtful face. "A well-placed spell could disrupt any enchantments he has, open his defenses. My knowledge of the arcane gives us that edge."

"Your spells and his fists have merit, but this calls for brute force and fortitude. I possess both," Baelgor's voice rumbled like distant thunder. "Dwarven steel and earthen might should crack that Orcish skull."

Ariella's voice cut through the tension. "Underestimating one's opponent is folly. We must see him, study his movements. Only then can we truly know which of us is best suited to the challenge."

They all nodded, the weight of her wisdom settling over them like a cloak. They would wait, watch, and learn. Tomorrow's dawn would reveal much about Drogor Thunderfist.

As the first light of dawn crept into the tent, they emerged to find the camp abuzz with whispers.

Drogor had arrived.

He rode at a commanding pace, his giant black wolf cutting a swath through the crowd like a scythe through wheat. The beast's fur was as dark as a moonless night, its eyes glowing embers in the daylight. The colossal frame of Drogor loomed above, an unyielding mass of muscle and scars, his tusks catching glints of sunlight as if in warning of the danger they posed.

The trio of guards flanking Drogor were no less impressive, astride their own formidable grey wolves, each a mirror of disciplined ferocity to the master they served. The air seemed to thrum with their combined presence, a palpable force that drew the eyes and stilled the tongues of all who watched.

"His aura... he's been enchanted," Kael whispered, feeling the prickling of magic at his fingertips.

"Looks like more than just an enchantment," Ariella murmured, her Elven eyes narrowing as she took in every detail, from the way Drogor's wolf moved to the grip he had on his reins.

"Magic or not, he'll bleed like any other," Baelgor grunted, but even his bravado couldn't mask the tightness in his jaw.

"Watch closely," Elandir cautioned, the tension in his stance belying his usual serenity.

As Drogor dismounted, the ground buckled under his weight. He moved with a predator's grace, unnaturally fluid for his size, as he surveyed the gathered crowd with piercing eyes. Not a word was spoken, yet his command was absolute. Every Orc stepped back, giving him space. Respect, or perhaps fear, evident in their faces.

"Such power..." Ariella breathed, her fingers twitching as she studied their future foe.

"Power we can match," Rider declared, his gaze locked on the formidable warlord. "We'll find his weakness. We have to."

The heroes' eyes met, a silent vow passing between them. In the shadow of Drogor Thunderfist's towering figure, they stood united, ready to face the challenge that lay ahead.

The sun continued to rise, casting long shadows that stretched across the dusty expanse of the Orc camp as Drogor Thunderfist made his presence known. His entrance was a spectacle of intimidation. Each thunderous step made the ground tremble, and the murmurs of the gathered Orcs rose to an excited clamor.

"I am here!" Drogor's voice boomed. "I challenge any warrior among you to face me. Prove your strength or bow to my rule."

A behemoth of an Orc stepped forward, rippling with muscle and rage. He roared, accepting the challenge, and charged with a ferocious battle cry. But Drogor's reaction was swift and brutal—a single, dismissive backhand sent the challenger careening through the air, crashing into a makeshift forge as scraps of metal and hide clanged about. The fallen Orc lay motionless, the silence that followed interrupted by the crackling of the fire he'd disturbed.

"Is this what passes for warriors?" Drogor sneered, his voice dripping with contempt. "I seek blooded combatants, not pretenders!"

With contemptuous ease, he thrust a pike bearing his banner into the hardened earth, its black fabric unfurling in the wind. Without another word, he turned on his heel and strode toward what passed as a tavern, his guards flanking him like a moving fortress.

"His strength is monstrous," Ariella sighed. "But brute force can be outmaneuvered. Precision, speed... those could be our keys."

"Indeed," Elandir nodded sagely. "One must look beyond sheer power. The mind is a weapon just as lethal."

"His arrogance may yet be his downfall," Kael added thoughtfully, tracing arcane symbols in the air with a slender finger. "Overconfidence breeds mistakes."

"Where's Baelgor?" Rider asked suddenly, glancing around. They all turned, realizing the Dwarf's absence.

"Stoneheart?" Kael questioned, his voice laced with concern.

The raucous laughter and guttural chants of the Orcish patrons drinking near Drogor hushed as Baelgor Stoneheart, The Enchanted Smith, marched through the throng. Each step thudded with the weight of his intent, drawing the eyes and ears of all present. His broad shoulders brushed past the rough-hewn wooden tables, the stench of sweat and spilled ale mingling in the thick air.

Baelgor growled at the behemoth across from him, slamming a hefty drinking horn before Drogor Thunderfist with such force that it rattled the table and splashed its contents. The remaining heroes, sensing an impending clash, surged forward with wide eyes and hands ready at their weapons.

Drogor remained seated. He craned his neck downward, his gaze piercing from beneath a furrowed brow. He was massive, a dark mountain in Orc form. Even seated, he loomed over the stout Dwarf, a sneer playing across his scarred face.

"Looking to die, Dwarf?" Drogo's voice boomed, his words laced with mockery.

"Lookin' to prove a Dwarf can outdrink an Orc," Baelgor retorted, his red eyes glinting with cunning.

Murmurs and snickers broke out among the crowd as they encircled the unlikely pair. Drogo's expression shifted from anger to amusement. With a grunt of acceptance, he seized his own drinking horn, embossed with the symbols of his lineage.

"Begin!" shouted an onlooker, and thus the contest commenced.

Round after round, the two competitors matched each other, swilling the potent Orcish brew that flowed like liquid fire down their throats. Baelgor's cheeks reddened, but his grip remained steady, each quaff met with cheers and jeers alike.

"Your belly's as deep as a forge, Dwarf!" someone bellowed, clapping Baelgor on the back.

"Put him in his place!" another Orc roared toward Drogor, though concern creased in their forehead.

By the fifth round, beads of sweat glistened on Drogo's brow, his usual sneer replaced by a grimace of determination. The crowd roared with anticipation, many had not expected the Dwarf to last this long.

"Last one, Dwarf," Drogor grunted, raising his horn in a final salute. The concoction within sloshed ominously, promising oblivion.

With a nod, Baelgor lifted his horn, and together they drank. With a thunderous slam, Drogo's horn hit the table first, a hair's breadth before Baelgor's.

"Victory is mine," Drogor declared as he started to sway in his stance, his voice a low fumbling rumble.

Baelgor swayed heavily, his vision blurring as he acknowledged defeat with a belch that shook his very bones. "So it be true," he conceded, though his pride remained unscathed.

The crowd erupted into cacophonous applause. Some out of genuine respect, others out of relief that blood had not been spilled. The party gathered around Baelgor, steadying him with firm hands and glances that spoke volumes of their admiration, though equally mixed with confusion and disbelief.

"What was that, Baelgor?" Rider questioned, offering a supportive arm.

"That otta,'" Baelgor hiccuped as he began to lose consciousness, "help one of y'all in the ring."

A grin formed on Rider's face as he looked up from the drunken Dwarf and caught eyes with Ariella.

"You promised me, Rider." Ariella stated in anger. She knew what Rider was thinking.

"We've got an edge now… if we act quickly," Rider confidently stated through his grin as he eyed his companions.

CHAPTER XII
GOR'MAKH GHASH

Amidst the flickering shadows cast by the great fire pit, the air was thick with tension and the stench of sweat. Chieftain Grashnak, his massive frame a dark silhouette against the leaping flames, pounded a meaty fist on the rough-hewn table before them.

"You must decide! Who will challenge Drogor? He's drunk, but not for long!," Grashnak bellowed, his eyes scanning the firelit faces.

Elandir stepped forward, his slender form standing proud and his eyes alight with a warrior's fervor. "I will face him. It would be a pleasure to end one who serves the Dragon Lord. Never again shall my kind be slaves."

Grashnak's laughter boomed, harsh and mocking. "You? An Elf?" His disdain hung heavy in the air. "Yes, your kind served as slaves to my ancestors. Thus, no Elf may claim the right of Gor'makh Ghash. None would follow you into battle."

Ariella's lips tightened—a mixture of anger and disappointment—but she held her tongue, recognizing the futility of argument.

"Then I shall confront this brute," Kael interjected confidently, magic crackling faintly in the air around him. "Magic flows through my veins stronger than anything that brute's muscle can muster."

"Silence, mage!" Grashnak's voice sliced through the air like a cleaver. "Sorcery defiles the sacred duel. Only steel and flesh may speak in the arena." The chieftain's patience was wearing thin.

Rider, silent until now, exchanged a look with Ariella—a silent conversation passing between their sapphire and violet gazes. She nodded begrudgingly, conceding the inevitable.

"Fine," Rider declared, his voice resolute. "I'll do it."

He turned away from the group, his dark raven hair brushing against his ears as it had grown over the past few months. He began strapping on his leather armor with methodical precision, each piece conforming snugly to his athletic build. His hands were steady, but his mind raced with strategy, envisioning the fight to come. The worn soles of his boots scraped against the stone floor, echoing in the stillness as he readied himself. Finally, he reached for his blades and wrapped his fingers around the hilt of his magic dagger as he inspected the blade, its presence reassuring yet insufficient against the might of Drogor Thunderfist.

As Rider tested the weapon's balance, he could feel the heat of the nearby fire teasing his skin. His eyes hardened, reflecting the dancing flames—a silent oath to emerge victorious or die with honor in the attempt.

Chieftain Grashnak stood towering over him, a grim expression etched into his scarred visage as he examined Rider with a critical eye.

"Your blade, small though it may be," Grashnak rumbled in his deep voice, "holds no honor in our pit. You will need a true weapon to face Drogor."

With a hefty grunt, the chieftain drew an old sword from its scabbard on the wall—a relic of times long past—and offered it hilt-first to Rider. The sword's blade was dulled by age, its edge nicked by generations of clashing steel, yet it carried the weight of tradition and lineage.

"Passed from chieftain to chieftain," Grashnak announced solemnly. "Let it serve you well in the Gor'-makh Ghash."

Rider hesitated, his hand hovering before the weathered hilt. With a measured breath, he grasped the sword and reluctantly acknowledged the gift.

"Keep Baelgor and Elandir safe," Grashnak commanded, nodding towards two imposing Orc warriors who gently ushered the inebriated Dwarf and the silent Elf away from the center of attention.

As the party neared the fighting pit, the noise swelled. The ground vibrated with the stomp of heavy boots and the clamor of the crowd, hungry for the spectacle of combat. The scent of sweat mingled with the coppery tang of spilt blood, while the jeers and cheers of the orcs filled the air like a war drum's call.

Rider's boots crunched on loose stones as he approached the edge of the pit. Orc eyes watched around him—sneering, excited, bloodthirsty. His fingers tightened around the hilt of the Orcish blade, the metal cold and unforgiving against his skin.

"Challenger!" Drogor's booming laughter echoed off the pit's walls as he acknowledged Rider's approach. "You come to claim leadership with Human tricks and frailty?"

The Orc warrior stood resolute, his ebony skin gleaming beneath the sun, his tusks sharp and ready.

Drogor's contemptuous gaze swept over Rider, taking in the foreign sword at his hip with a mixture of amusement and disdain.

"Let us see if you understand the depths of Gor'makh Ghash," Drogor taunted, drawing his own massive blade. It sang a deadly note as it left the sheath, a promise of pain and finality.

Rider squared his shoulders, stepping into the circle of packed earth that served as the arena. "I challenge you, Drogor Thunderfist, to Gor'makh Ghash! Single combat. Leadership by right of strength." The cry rose up, a single voice amidst the chaos battering against the arena, yet it cut through the noise, silencing the throng as they awaited Drogor's response.

The orc's laugh rumbled once more, a harbinger of the clash to come. "So be it, Human. May your blood feed the soil and your spirit find no rest!"

The iron gates of the fighting pit clanged shut. Drogor stood across from Rider, a smirk playing on his lips.

"Did you truly believe I would be so easily bested by swill?" Drogor's voice boomed, cutting through the din of the jeering crowd. "I wanted your challenge, Human. I planned for it."

Ariella's sharp intake of breath was barely audible over the crowd's clamor, but to those who knew her, her shock was as clear as a thunderclap. Her violet eyes widened with fear as she realized the grave misstep. Beside her, Kael's lips began to move silently, weaving an arcane whisper beneath his breath.

"Rider, be swift!" Ariella called out, urgency cracking her usually calm voice.

Drogor charged forward, each step shaking the ground like a war drum, and Rider met him head-on. The Orc's movements were deceptively quick for his size, his strikes carrying the wrath of a giant. Rider, though surprised by deceit, danced around each blow with speed and finesse.

Swords clashed in a song of metal, sparks flying as if they were stars birthed from the fury of their battle. Rider feinted left and leaned back under a sweeping arc aimed to cleave him in two. He slashed upward, the ancient Orcish sword singing a desperate tune, only to meet the immovable force of Drogor's hide.

"Your blade lacks conviction, Human," Drogor taunted, barreling forward with a vicious uppercut that Rider narrowly avoided.

"Conviction isn't forged in steel," Rider retorted, his confidence unwavering even as he parried another deadly overhead swing.

But fate is a fickle mistress. The ancestral sword shattered under Drogor's relentless assault, its fractured remnants falling to the bloodstained earth. The follow-through of the Orc's strike bore down upon Rider, slashing deep into his right shoulder. A scream tore from his lips as blood painted the dirt beneath him.

With a swift motion borne of desperation, Rider tumbled away, his right arm now useless, putting distance between himself and the looming shadow of death.

"Die, Human!" Drogor bellowed, advancing with the certainty of victory in his stride.

"Come on," Rider hissed through gritted teeth, his left hand drawing the magic dagger concealed at his side. It glowed faintly with an ethereal light, a stark contrast to the darkening sky above.

Rider struck—slashes quick and precise, targeting the behemoth's tendons, this time his magic blade finding the flesh beneath the Orc's hide. Drogor roared in both rage and pain as his stance faltered, his knees buckling beneath the cunning assault.

"Yield, or die!" Rider commanded, pressing the glowing edge of the dagger to Drogor's exposed throat. "Reveal the cult's plans, or meet your end!"

The crowd fell silent, the tension so thick it could suffocate. Below, the combatants remained locked in their deadly tableau, two warriors bound by blood and blade.

Kael's incantation ceased abruptly, the ethereal glow dimming from his eyes until they resumed their natural stormy blue. His heart thundered in his chest, a harbinger of dread spreading through him like wildfire. He met Ariella's gaze, her eyes wide with trepidation, and without a word, he pushed through the throng of Orcs, shoving aside the mass of sinewy bodies with an urgency that betrayed the grave premonition stirring within him.

"Grashnak!" Kael bellowed, his voice lost amidst the guttural roars of the crowd, but Ariella was swift to follow, her lithe form weaving behind him with practiced grace.

Drogor's mocking laughter echoed above the din, cutting their frantic path short. "Grashnak, now is the time! Honor our pact—save me and claim your rightful place beside our Lord!"

All eyes turned as Chieftain Grashnak rose from his throne, his brute presence commanding silence. The two Orc guards appearing from behind their Chieftain presented Baelgor and Elandir, forcing them to kneel before him, the former still swaying in a drunken haze, the latter now appearing bloodied and beaten, barely clinging to consciousness.

Concern and confusion rushed over Rider as he pressed the dagger harder against Drogor's exposed neck, its blade now releasing the crimson liquid beneath his hide. "Grashnak! I swear if you–"

"Your filthy Wood Elf steeds could not shield you from the Dragon Lord's gaze," Grashnock sneered interrupting, his tone dripping with contempt. "His spirit has watched you, pitiful pawns. And you," he spat the words at Elandir with venomous disdain, "you dared to disgrace my camp with your presence."

With a sudden, brutal motion, Grashnak's fist crashed down upon Elandir's temple, sending him sprawling backward, his lifeblood seeping into the earth as if feeding it with his essence. The guards dragged his limp form away, leaving a dark trail in the soil.

"Disgusting creatures," Grashnak growled, turning his hateful glare towards Baelgor. "But what's more revolting are those who would fraternize with such lesser beings."

Rider's jaw clenched tight as he gripped his dagger, while Ariella's hands trembled at her sides, her breath caught in her throat.

As realization dawned on Kael, a memory flashed—a shadow of another time, another ally's desperate eyes as he failed to reach them in time. He had seen this betrayal in fragments, whispers of magic that taunted him with the truth too late.

"Grashnak, don't do this!" Kael's plea was swallowed by the chaos, his outstretched hand futile against the inevitable.

In one swift, ruthless act, Grashnak unsheathed a jagged blade and plunged it into Baelgor's chest. The Dwarf gasped, a sound wrenched from the depths of his being, as the weapon tore through flesh and bone with a sickening crunch. Baelgor's eyes, once bright as rubies, dulled as the life fled from him, his body collapsing to the ground with a heavy thud.

"Baelgor!" Rider screamed as he stepped forward, his voice raw with grief and fury, even as his wounds bled profusely.

A collective gasp rippled through the spectators, and

then all was pandemonium. Orcs surged forward, some eager for a glimpse of the kill, others shouting in confusion or baying for more blood.

Ariella stood frozen, horror etched into every delicate feature as she stared at the fallen Baelgor, her mind reeling from the brutality of the moment.

Kael's expression twisted into a mask of rage and sorrow, a tempest brewing behind his eyes that threatened to engulf him whole. "With me," he snarled, grasping Ariella's arm and pulling her away from the burgeoning nightmare that surrounded them. They were trapped in the very jaws of treachery, their mission unraveling with each passing heartbeat.

Rider, consumed by a seething cauldron of rage, barely registered the blood soaking his arm and the ground beneath him as he turned back towards Drogor. The Orc chieftain's mocking laughter reverberated in the pit, but Rider's focus was singular—vengeance for Baelgor's murder.

"Die, you filth!" Rider bellowed, lunging his magic dagger at the brute's skull.

But Drogor was not so easily bested. His reflexes contradicted his massive frame. With a sneer, he caught Rider's wrist mid-strike, halting the blade inches from his skin. His grip was iron, unyielding, but it was not enough to contain the tempest within Rider.

"AHHHH!" Rider's scream tore through the arena. A raw, primal sound that echoed the depths of his pain and fury. Power surged within him, magic sparked and crackled around his hand like a living thing, seeking an outlet for its wrath.

The air itself seemed to pulse with the force of his scream, and in a blinding flash of arcane energy, the dagger flew from his hand and drove through Drogor's skull. Bone shattered, brain matter splattered, and the once-mighty Orc crumpled to the dirt, lifeless.

Above, Kael's own anger manifested as a storm incarnate. The skies darkened as clouds formed and a maelstrom of magical energy swirled overhead. Lightning danced across the heavens, a symphony of destruction orchestrated by one man's fury.

"To me!" Kael commanded, his voice barely audible over the howl of the wind. He extended his hands downward, palms open, and the gales responded, lifting him and Ariella off their feet. With a rush of air, they soared across the battlefield towards Rider, who stood stunned, his chest heaving from exertion and emotion.

"Rider, we must go!" Ariella cried, her bow now clutched tightly in her hands. "Now!"

"Go? But—" Rider began, disoriented, but Kael cut him off.

"Move, or we die here with our vengcance," Kael's eyes blazed as he spoke, lightning cracking from their depths.

As they ran towards the gate, Ariella's arrows felled oncoming Orcs, while Kael's body crackled with pent-up energy, his cloak torn away by the ferocious winds. Enemies fell before them, struck down by bolts that answered Kael's silent commands.

"Left, there's a break in their ranks!" Ariella shouted, her senses keen even amidst the bedlam.

"Keep close!" Kael yelled back, arcs of electricity jumping between his fingers as they sprinted past charred and paralyzed foes.

Rider, his right arm hanging limp and uscless, fought with the ferocity of a cornered beast. His left hand wielded the remnants of the magic dagger, its power diminished but no less deadly as he helped carved a path through any of the horde that dared approach.

They were a whirlwind of desperation and determination, defying the odds with every step they took. The clash of steel, the stench of scorched flesh, and the cries of the fallen filled their air as they fought their way to freedom.

"Almost there..." Kael gasped, his power waning but still potent as they neared the camp's boundary.

"Rider, can you stand?" Ariella asked, her voice laced with concern as she fired another arrow into an advancing Orc, its body collapsing mere inches from them.

"Let's finish this," Rider rasped through gritted teeth and a wavering breath, as he struggled to regain his footing.

As they rounded the last bend, the gates of freedom finally in sight, a formidable figure blocked their path. Grashnak, flanked by a horde of Drogor's warriors, stood with an air of superiority. The remnants of Drogor's army lay just beyond, ready to strike from outside the camp's boundary.

"You dare to defy us, you weak and wounded creatures!" Grashnak bellowed, his voice carrying the weight of his Orcish rage. "You are nothing but insects compared to the might of the Horde!" he screamed, veins bulging on his neck.

But Kael, undeterred by the looming threat, continued down his path towards the gate with determined steps. Each footfall was accompanied by a deafening crack of thunder from above. With each step, bolts of lightning struck his body as he felt the power within him building.

"You may call yourselves the Horde," Kael began, his voice rising above the chaos around them. "But I... I am the Storm!"

And with those words, he unleashed the full fury of the energy stored within him upon the enemy forces beyond the gate, a cataclysmic barrage of lightning that obliterated all in its path.

With the way cleared and the screams of their enemies fading into the night behind them, the trio staggered forward into the vastness of the open plains, seeking refuge from the chaos and destruction of the Orc camp.

————

As the plains stretched before them, an eerie silence settled over the trio, a stark contrast to the chaos of battle they just left behind them. The cool night air nipped at their weary bodies as they trudged along, the adrenaline that once fueled their escape now fading into exhaustion.

Ariella's keen eyes scanned the horizon, vigilant for any signs of pursuit, while her hands worked deftly, aiding Rider with his injured arm. She could see the pain etched on his face with every step, yet she also saw the steel in his gaze, the unyielding spirit that refused to be broken.

"Rider," Ariella said softly, breaking the silence that hung heavily between them.

"Bravery is worth little if it costs us our friends," Rider replied, his voice barely above a whisper, laden with a weight far heavier than his wounds.

Kael walked ahead, the storm within him subsided, but his aura still crackling with residual energy. His eyes, once aglow with power, now reflected a storm of a different kind —a tempest of sorrow churning in the depths of his soul.

"Kael," Ariella called out, her voice tinged with concern, "talk to us. Please."

The mage stopped, turning to face them. His features were drawn, haunted by the events that had unfolded. "It's the same in every world," he murmured, the words catching in his throat. "Those who seek power, paying for it by the blood of others. Baelgor's laughter... Elandir's wisdom... Gone," he sighed through ragged breaths and tears now forming in his eyes.

"We will carry them with us," Ariella insisted, reaching out to grasp Kael's hand. "We fight on, for them."

They moved like shadows under the moonlight, the weight of loss a silent companion on their journey. Each step was an act of resistance, a vow whispered against the dark.

"We will bring justice to Baelgor and Elandir. We press on," his voice steady despite his pain.

Their hearts heavy, their bodies spent, they pressed onward, driven by the memories of those they had lost and the unwavering determination to ensure their sacrifices were not in vain.

The sun had just begun its ascent when the silhouette of the Fortress cut a formidable shape against the pale morning light. Its towering spires and fortified walls stood like a guardian, stark and proud against the pale light.

"Look," Ariella said, her voice carrying fatigue and loss, yet edged with a steely resolve, "a sanctuary, for now."

Rider nodded, his injured shoulder a constant throb of pain, but his eyes mirrored the determination in Ariella's violet gaze. Kael moved beside them, his cloak still carrying the scent of charred Orc from the battle, they moved forward.

As they neared the fortress, the thunderous beat of hooves broke the silence. Nine knights clad in gleaming armor rode out to meet them, lances raised high—a protective barrier between the refugees and their home.

"Halt! State your purpose with House Bloodmane!" the lead knight commanded, his voice booming across the plains.

"We seek sanctuary, " Rider replied, his voice hoarse but unwavering. "We bring dire news and plea for aid."

After a tense moment, where the knights scrutinized them with suspicion, they lowered their lances and one gestured towards the open gates of the fortress.

"Come. We will escort you," he said gruffly.

Bloodmane Fortress loomed closer, its imposing stone walls offering a stark reprieve to the endless plains they had traversed. Within its confines, the air held the warmth of hearths and the tang of iron from the forges.

Royal physicians ushered them through the halls, their footsteps echoing against the cold stone floors, to a chamber where Human doctors and mages were waiting for their arrival.

"It's a miracle he's still alive." One of the healers sighed in disbelief as the team began cutting away the remnants of Rider's armor to access his wounds.

"Is he going to be alright? How can I help?" Ariella asked through the tears trailing down her delicate face.

"Guards, get these people out of here. We need the room," the lead physician shouted.

Ariella's gaze hardened as two guards began to approach. "Not happening," Ariella declared with finality as she gripped the blades at her hip.

Jarl Bloodmane entered the room in urgency, flanked by a large man in ornate armor. "You can stay as long as you tell me everything. What's happened and who are you?" he demanded.

Ariella and Kael recounted their visit to the Orc encampment and the harrowing escape that followed, each word painting the blood-soaked betrayal in sharp detail.

"Baelgor and Elandir..." Ariella whispered, her hands still clenched around the hilts of her blades.

"The Orc leader, Chief Grashnak, struck them down without honor." Kael added.

Jarl Bloodmane listened intently, his rugged face etched with concern and anger. "These are dark times indeed," he agreed solemnly. "But you'll find no treachery here. Rest now, recover. We will stand with you. General, dispatch ravens to each of the great kingdoms bearing the news of their losses as well as a call to arms to House Kor and House Reshu. Urge them to honor their oaths as members of the Human Trinity and join us in retaliatory attacks against the Orc Clans."

"As you command, my liege." the large man behind him responded before departing from the room.

CHAPTER XIII
THE THREE HOUSES

In the days that followed, the fortress became a hive of preparation. Ariella, Rider, and House Bloodmane scholars, enlightened Kael on the Human kingdom's past. What was once a symbol of unity, now lay shattered like shards of glass. Three great houses, each tracing their lineage back to heroes of old, now existed in an uneasy truce upon the plains with varying beliefs. House Bloodmane, with their mighty Lancer Corps, believe it their duty to ride about the plains and keep the Orcish tribes in check. House Reshu, home to the Human Arcane Academy, continue their study of the mystical arts for answers about Etonya's past and future. Lastly, house Kor, and its fanatical church, attempted to lead a crusade against magic shortly after The Great War. Failing miserably, they turned reclusive and now often refuse communication with outsiders. The Human banners now flutter in the wind, their clashing colors and creeds on display for all to see.

The smithy rang with the rhythmic clanging of iron, and strategy meetings consumed the war chambers. The team, along with House Bloodmane's military leaders, poured over maps, their fingers tracing potential paths of retaliation.

"Orc raids grow bolder," one commander reported. "Caravans decimated, villages razed. House Reshu and House Koric have sent ravens—they too share the losses from these attacks."

"Then let us be the ones to end them," Kael stated, his deep voice resonating with a power that seemed to crackle in the air around him.

"We will." Ariella added, her Elven eyes fierce. "We will avenge our fallen and halt this menace."

The chambers of Bloodmane Fortress echoed with their pledges of vengeance, and the clinking of armor as they readied themselves for the battles to come. Their unity was unspoken but palpable—a bond forged in the fires of loss and the shared fervor to protect their world from the encroaching darkness.

The clatter of steel and the rhythmic thud of boots against stone filled the air as Rider, Ariella, and Kael gathered in the armory of Bloodmane Fortress preparing for the next counterattack to the Orc's raids. With meticulous care, they strapped on layers of leather and mail, each piece a silent promise to withstand the fury of the Orcish Horde.

"Remember, aim for their joints and underarms," Rider instructed, adjusting the straps on his bracers. "Their hides are thick, but it's there that we'll bleed them."

Ariella nodded, her fingers deftly checking the fletching on her arrows. "And keep moving. They're strong, but we're faster." Kael was silent, his focus inward as he infused his magical breastplate with protective enchantments. The sigils etched into the metal glowed briefly before settling into a soft hum of power. He glanced at his companions, his blue eyes alight with an intensity that made the air sizzle.

"Let's not forget," Kael said, voice steady, "the cult will have tricks up their sleeves. Be ready for anything."

Their preparations complete, the trio made their way to the war council room, where Jarl Bloodmane and his commanders were assembled around a grand table littered with maps and missives. The chamber buzzed with tension, and the scent of oiled leather mingled with the faint odor of burning candles.

"Are we all set?" Jarl Bloodmane asked, his gaze sweeping over them.

"Ready as we'll ever be," Rider replied, his hand resting on the hilt of another newly acquired sword.

"Good," said the Jarl, turning to address the room. "We face not just the Orcish horde, but the darkness they serve that seeks to engulf Etonya. Stand together. Fight as one. We shall prevail."

A chorus of affirmations rose from the gathering. Before another word could be spoken, a young page burst into the room, his chest heaving with urgency.

"Ravens, my lord," he gasped, extending two sealed scrolls towards Jarl Bloodmane. The seal of the Stonefire kingdom was stamped on one, the emblem of the Amakiir on the other.

The Jarl's expression darkened as he broke the seals and scanned the contents. A heavy silence fell upon the room, punctuated only by the sound of the nearby hearth.

"By the gods..." he muttered, his knuckles whitening around the parchment.

"What news, Jarl?" Ariella pressed, stepping forward, her instincts telling her that their trials were far from over.

Jarl Bloodmane lifted his eyes to meet hers, his jaw

tight. "It seems that both the Stonefire and Amakiir king-doms suspect a Brightspire conspiracy."

"They suspect us!?," Rider questioned angrily, his jaw tightening.

"Because you stand unscathed, while both of their champions fell" the Jarl added grimly, addressing Ariella.

"Unscathed!?" Rider shouted, as he motioned to his shoulder.

"They question why death follows all but the Bright-spire envoy and her outsiders."

Ariella's face paled, but her stance remained unwaver-ing. "I understand their suspicion," she admitted, though the hurt was evident in her tone. "But I swear, we've played no part in such treachery."

Rider stepped beside her, placing a reassuring hand on her shoulder. "We know the truth," he said firmly. "And we'll prove our innocence."

"Indeed, we must," Kael interjected, his voice rising above. "For now, though, our priority remains the same: stop the Orcish threat, save this Trinity, gather our new allies against the cult that orchestrates this chaos."

As the implications of the ravens' messages sank in, the room seemed to constrict with tension. Accusations from powerful kingdoms, once strong allies, were the last thing they needed with a battle on the horizon.

"Prepare yourselves," Jarl Bloodmane commanded, his voice cutting through the uncertainty. "The coming days will test us all. House Kor and House Reshu plead for our aid against the Orcs," he continued, redirecting the focus to the letters still clutched in the commanders' hands. "Our enemies unite while we stand divided."

"Help that we must provide," declared General Darian, his fingers resting on the crossed lances emblazoned on the

Bloodmane banner nearby. "The raids grow bolder, and our people suffer."

"Indeed," added Rider, his gaze sweeping over the assembled leaders. "We cannot allow fear to dictate our actions. We must rise united against this common foe."

Ariella's expression hardened, her determination rekindling like a blade forged anew. "Then let us answer their calls," she said, her voice now clear and commanding. "Let us show them the strength of House Bloodmane and quell these insidious rumors."

As the gathering dispersed, Rider lingered by Ariella's side, their shared glance speaking volumes. In the trials they faced, their love bloomed like the rarest of flowers—resilient, vibrant, and undeterred by the shadows that sought to envelop them. They would face the coming storm, united in heart and purpose.

The next morning, the war room of House Bloodmane's fortress was steeped in the scent of oiled leather and the musty odor of ancient maps. Rider leaned over a table strewn with scrolls and tokens representing troops, his fingers tracing the contours of the Great Plains that sprawled across the parchment. The sound of steel-clad warriors shifting restlessly echoed off the stone walls as they awaited his command.

"Orcs are creatures of brute force," Rider declared, breaking the silence. "They favor frontal assaults, relying on their monstrous goliaths to break our lines. But their strategy is as crude as their craftsmanship." He glanced at the gathered leaders, eyes alight with strategic fervor. "We must be cunning, strike swiftly, and exploit their lack of coordination."

"House Bloodmane's lancers can outmaneuver them on the open field," Jarl Bloodmane added, his voice resonating in the chamber like a drumbeat, firm and absolute. "Our cavalry will harry their flanks, keep them disorganized."

"Indeed," Rider nodded. "And let us not forget House Reshu's magi. Their arcane prowess could devastate Orc ranks from afar. We need them on our side."

"Reshu's mages are powerful, but their numbers are few," interjected Varek, his brow furrowed with concern. "The Orcish Horde has grown bold, and if their university falls, we lose a vital ally."

"Then it's settled," Ariella said, her voice full of conviction. "First, we ride east to bolster Reshu's defenses. If we secure the university, we gain access to spells that could turn back the tide against these raids."

Rider met her gaze, seeing the same fire burning in her that stirred within him. "With the mages secured," he continued, "we'll have both the muscle and the magic to confront the Orcs head-on. Bloodmane's lancers, alongside Reshu's sorcery, will present a front too formidable for even the boldest warbands."

"Time is against us," Varek interjected, his hand gripping the hilt of his sword. "We should dispatch scouts immediately, find weaknesses in the Orc patrols before they realize our intent."

"Agreed," Rider said with a decisive nod. "Stealth and speed are essential. We strike before the enemy can reinforce their positions around Reshu's lands."

"Let us raise our banners then," Jarl Bloodmane proclaimed, standing tall among his peers. "For honor, for the trinity of Humanity, for Etonya!"

"Tonight, we dine, we plan, we sharpen our blades," Rider added, his voice carrying the weight of impending battle. "At dawn, we ride with the fury of the storm and the strength of our steeds. To House Reshu. To victory!"

On the third night on their journey to House Reshu, the night was as silent as a crypt, the campfire's embers glowing like the dying heart of day. Ariella Moonwhisper lay restless on her bedroll, her senses extended beyond the canvas of tents and the snores of weary soldiers. Then, a soft rustling not carried by the wind, a series of gentle snaps of twig and leaf far too rhythmic for mindless nature.

"Rider," she whispered urgently, shaking the slumbering form beside her. "Wake up. Something is amiss."

Groggily, Rider's eyes opened, meeting hers. He saw the alarm in them and reached instinctively for his sword. In the span of a breath, chaos. The camp was suddenly ablaze with screams of terror and confusion. Ariella's ears were assaulted by the crackling of fire and the pungent smell of smoke as tents became pyres.

"Orcs!" someone shouted, their voice cutting through the clamor.

Ariella loosed an arrow into the dark, guided by her Elvish intuition. A pained roar confirmed its target. They fought back to back, the ambiance of battle casting shadows upon their determined faces. Rider's blade danced with lethal precision as he parried a blow from a towering Orc, whose muscles bulged beneath its grimy skin.

"Bloodmane! To arms!" bellowed Jarl Bloodmane, rallying his lancers amidst the chaos. But as the Orcs freed horses and torched supplies, the calculated savagery of their ambush became apparent. The stench of burning grain filled the air, a bitter taste on the tongue that signified the loss of much-needed provisions.

"Kael! We need your lightning!" Rider called out as he felt the heat of the flames licking his skin.

"Already on it!" came Kael's reply, and with it, a sky-shattering bolt that sizzled through the Orc ranks.

But even magic seemed frail against the brute force of the Orc goliaths who stormed through the camp, sending men tumbling like ragdolls. They wielded swords that were more like slabs of iron than refined weaponry.

"Fall back!" commanded Ariella, her voice cutting through the inferno as she let another arrow fly, finding its mark between the eyes of an advancing behemoth. "Protect what's left!"

When dawn broke over the smoldering ruins of their camp, the survivors took stock. The losses were considerable. The once-proud lancer corps had been reduced to a shadow of its might.

"Perhaps we should reconsider our strategy," Jarl Bloodmane's jaw clenched as the words left his lips, scanning the burnt remnants of their provisions.

"Jarl," Kael approached, his cape singed but his spirit unbroken. "I have journeyed through realms where honor was forsaken, and it led only to ruin. Here, now, you have the chance to uphold your vows—to defend those who rely on us."

"Kael speaks truth," Ariella affirmed, her steely gaze meeting Jarl Bloodmane's. "Even in darkness, we must be the light."

The Jarl's eyes softened, and a new resolve kindled within him. "Then let us ride forth. House Reshu awaits our aid, and we shall not fail them."

"House Bloodmane will not see defeat this day," Rider vowed.

"Nor any day," Ariella added, bow in hand, ready to face whatever trials lay ahead. Together, they mounted their steeds, the sun cresting the horizon, heralding their continued march eastward toward destiny.

The stench of brimstone and charred earth assaulted their nostrils as the Heroes and the remnants of House Bloodmane's Lancer Corps crested the rise to witness Reshu Fortress besieged. The magical barrier shimmered like a mirage under the relentless elemental onslaught, holding fast against fireballs that exploded against it like volcanic anger made manifest. Giant icicles, sharp as Dragon's teeth, shattered upon impact, while boulders hurtled through the air, trailing dust clouds before crashing into the barrier with the sound of thunder.

"By the gods," Rider gasped, his eyes wide at the sight of cult mages lining up in formation, their hands weaving intricate patterns as they summoned their devastating spells.

"Steady," Ariella intoned, placing her hand on his arm. Her keen eyes scanned for weaknesses among the enemy ranks.

"Form up!" Jarl Bloodmane's voice boomed, punching through the chaos. "Lancers to the front!" The sound of hooves stampeded forward.

Rider drew his longsword, the steel glinting coldly. Arcane energy crackled at his fingertips, eager for release. "Ariella, find me a target!"

"Left flank!" she called out, notching an arrow to her bowstring. "The one with the twisted staff!"

"Got it." Rider spurred his mount forward, the

powerful steed pounding towards the Orcish lines with the Bloodmane Lancers thundering beside him.

"Bloodmane! For Reshu!" Jarl Bloodmane roared, leading the charge.

"Shield wall!" shouted Kael over the din, pointing to the right where another contingent of Orcs prepared to counter.

"Let no beast pass!" a knight echoed, rallying his comrades as they braced their lances.

"Here they come!" Rider yelled as he closed the distance to the cult mages. With a surge of power, he unleashed a blast of magic directly at the mage, who grunted in surprise as the spell tore through his defenses.

"Ha!" Rider crowed triumphantly, slashing down with his sword. The blade sang a deadly arc, cutting deep into the mage's flesh.

"More incoming!" Ariella warned, her arrows flying true, felling Orc after Orc as she rode between the lines with lethal grace.

"Focus on their leaders!" Rider called out, spotting an Orc chieftain rallying his forces with guttural commands. "Cut off the head!"

"Follow Rider!" a lancer cried out, pivoting his horse to join the fray, his lance skewering foes with disciplined precision.

"Kael, anytime, friend!" Rider shouted, ducking under a sweeping Orcish club.

Kael replied with outstretched hands as bolts of electricity leaped from his fingers, chaining through the Orcs and reducing them to ash.

"Push through!" Jarl Bloodmane ordered, his voice a clarion call amidst the chaos of war. His lance punctured armor and flesh with ruthless efficiency, leaving a trail of destruction in his wake.

"Stay together!" Ariella commanded, her presence a rallying beacon as she moved from atop her steed like a phantom, each shot finding its mark.

"Protect the Spellsword!" one of the knights urged, referring to Rider, as he continued to weave magic and steel into a formidable offense.

"Keep pressure on their mages!" Rider hollered, his vision narrowing as he focused on the next target, the taste of battle metallic and exhilarating on his tongue.

"Drive them back!" Jarl Bloodmane bellowed, his horse rearing as he delivered a crushing blow to an advancing Orc warlord.

"Stand firm!" Kael shouted, his voice bolstered by the arcane, as he cast protective wards around his allies.

"Watch your backs!" Ariella warned, her senses attuned to every shift in the tide of battle.

"Advance!" Rider rallied, sensing victory within their grasp as the Orcs faltered under their coordinated strikes.

The combined cries of the heroes and the Lancer Corps rose above the clamor, the promise of victory spurring them ever onward.

As the last of the Orc and cult forces fell, the shimmering barrier encasing Reshu Fortress began to dissipate, the air crackling with residual magic. The great gates creaked open, revealing the resplendent Jarl Reshu, her robes aglow with ethereal light, her gaze sweeping over the weary but victorious forces.

"Brave warriors of House Bloodmane, noble allies," Jarl Reshu's voice rang out, imbued with power and grace. "Your valor this day has preserved not just these ancient walls but the very essence of our knowledge. For that, you have my eternal gratitude."

Rider, his clothes singed and armor dented, stepped forward, offering a respectful nod. "Jarl Reshu, we are honored to stand with you against the darkness that threatens Etonya."

"Yet I see fewer lancers than legend speaks of," she observed, eyes narrowing slightly as they rested upon the remnants of the Lancer Corps.

Jarl Bloodmane, his own armor marred by battle, moved beside Rider. "We suffered great losses. An ambush by Orc guerilla forces thinned our ranks before we could reach your fortress."

The headmistress's expression softened, and a touch of sorrow graced her features. "Such is the cost of war. Come, let us tend to your wounded, and may this be the dawn of unity between our houses once more."

Inside the fortress, the scent of healing salves and the soft glow of magical lights filled the infirmary. Jarl Bloodmane stood shoulder to shoulder with Jarl Reshu, their conversation low and earnest.

"House Kor's reluctance to embrace the arcane is... problematic," Jarl Reshu confided, her gaze locked with his.

"Indeed, but we shall ensure your magi's safety," Jarl Bloodmane vowed. "Their prowess is needed now more than ever."

"Then it is agreed. We stand with you, to the very end," Jarl Reshu declared, a spark igniting in her eyes.

"May our unity endure beyond these dark times," Jarl Bloodmane replied, a sense of camaraderie burgeoning between them.

At dawn, a cavalcade of mages and soldiers assembled at the fortress gates. The magi of House Reshu had summoned an array of fantastical creatures: winged serpents gliding gracefully through the air, earth elementals striding with seismic steps, and water nymphs riding on streams that flowed at their command.

"Behold the might of Reshu's conjurations!" Jarl Reshu proclaimed, pride evident in her voice as she mounted a majestic Griffin, its feathers shimmering in the morning light.

"Truly, it is a sight to behold," Jarl Bloodmane agreed, admiration clear in his tone. He swung onto his steed, the horse's barding glinting in the sun.

"Let us ride forth with hope in our hearts," he called to the gathering crowd. "Together, we carry the future of Etonya!"

"Forward!" Rider shouted, spurring his mount onward.

Ariella, her quiver restocked and bow at the ready, exchanged a glance with Rider. "To witness such unity, it gives me faith."

"Faith that even in the shadow of the cult's reach, we find new allies," Rider responded, his eyes reflecting the burgeoning partnership between the two great houses.

With the combined force of House Bloodmane cavalry and House Reshu Magi, the horizon beckoned them southward, toward destiny and the uncertain battles that awaited.

The once-golden fields of the great plainlands now lay in ruin, trampled underfoot by the relentless march of the Orc Horde. Scorched earth and shattered homesteads bore witness to their passage, as blackened timbers reached skyward like the skeletal fingers of the dead. The sickly-sweet stench of decay clung to the air, mingling with the copper tang of spilled blood as the alliance of House Bloodmane and House Reshu traversed the desolated landscape.

"By the gods," Ariella murmured, her hand tightening

around the grip of her bow as they passed a ruined farmstead. The cries of the wounded and the bereft echoed in her Elven ears, more haunting than any banshee's wail.

Rider had seen death before, but the wholesale slaughter of innocents carved a hollow pit in his stomach. "This ends with us," he vowed, his words slicing through the heavy silence that hung over the procession like a shroud.

"Indeed," Jarl Bloodmane replied, his voice a low rumble. His lance bore the scars of recent combat, yet it remained ever at his side, a symbol of his unyielding commitment to protect.

Ahead, the imposing silhouette of House Kor's Cathedral Fortress loomed on the horizon, its spires casting long shadows across the plains. As the allied forces drew closer, a sea of figures coalesced at the edge of vision, forming ranks outside the fortress walls.

"Prepare yourselves," Kael announced, lightning crackling at his fingertips—a warning of the storm to come. His gaze was distant, focused on the massing armies that seemed to merge into one formidable entity.

"Something is amiss," Ariella said, squinting against the glare of the setting sun. Her heart quickened as the banners of House Kor billowed alongside those of the Orc Horde. Not two armies poised for battle, but one.

"Betrayal..." Rider's whisper was barely audible over the thunderous beat of hooves and the restless murmur of the magi's mounts.

"House Kor sides with the cult!" shouted a Bloodmane knight, his voice filled with disbelief and outrage.

"Then we fight not only for our survival but for the very soul of the plains," Jarl Reshu declared, her eyes ablaze with arcane fire. "To arms, for honor and for justice!"

"Formations!" Jarl Bloodmane commanded. Lancers lowered their weapons, and the magi began incantations, weaving protective spells around their ranks.

"Let them come," Rider growled, unsheathing his sword, its blade glinting with an otherworldly light. Beside him, Ariella nocked an arrow, her presence serene yet deadly, the embodiment of Brightspire's wrath.

"Stay close, focus on the leaders," Kael advised, his voice steady despite the rising tide of enemies. "Just as before, cut off the head, and the body will falter."

"May our weapons strike true," Jarl Bloodmane intoned as he raised his lance high, signaling the impending clash of steel against steel, magic against malice.

"Today, we are one," Jarl Reshu added, her words bolstering the spirits of all who heard.

With a roar that shook the earth, the combined forces of Bloodmane and Reshu surged forward, their resolve as unbreakable as the bonds forged in the heat of battle. They were ready for the onslaught, ready to face whatever twisted sorcery or brute strength the traitorous alliance could muster. And through the din of war, a singular thought united them: this would be a day remembered in songs, a day when the fate of kingdoms was decided.

The clamor of war erupted across the plains, steel clashed against steel, drowned by the guttural cries of the Orc Horde and the defiant shouts of the Human armies. The scent of blood mingled with the acrid stench of scorched earth as elemental spells from the Reshu Magi rained fire and ice upon the battlefield. The ground shook under the charge of the Bloodmane Lancers, their horses' hooves pounding rhythmically like the heartbeats of the warriors they carried.

Ariella Moonwhisper moved through the chaos with a

dancer's grace, her bowstring humming as arrows found their marks with deadly precision. Her violet eyes, mirrors of the storm above, flashed with determination as she wove between fallen combatants.

"Keep them at bay!" she called out, her voice cutting through the din as she loosed another volley.

Rider stood firm amidst the fray, his sword and dagger flashing in tandem, arcs of magic force blasting from his fingertips to send Orcs reeling. His blue eyes locked onto an advancing Goliath, the electric tension of battle singing in his veins.

"Kael, now would be good!" Rider yelled, ducking under a wild swing.

"Patience," Kael Stormbringer replied with a smirk, lightning crackling along his arms before he unleashed it in a devastating chain that leapt from one adversary to another.

On the periphery, Jarl Bloodmane's armored form was a beacon of might, his lance skewering enemies as easily as a farmer might harvest wheat. His mighty steed reared, its neigh piercing the tumult as he spotted Jarl Reshu, her back against a rock, her magical shield flickering under the onslaught of Orcish brute force.

"Reshu!" he bellowed, spurring his mount forward, driving his lance through multiple foes in a spray of gore. But the tide was relentless, and an errant club struck his steed, sending both rider and horse tumbling to the earth.

Jarl Bloodmane rolled to his feet, the taste of dust and fear bitter in his mouth. He drew his sword, moving to stand with Jarl Reshu. Their blades sang a desperate duet as they fought back-to-back against the encroaching horde.

"Bloodmane!" Ariella's shout cut through the noise as she raced toward them, her movements swift and sure.

Rider was close behind, his sword cleaving Orc and crusader alike as he approached the two Jarls.

"Fall back!" Rider commanded, parrying a vicious blow meant for Bloodmane. "We have you!"

"United we stand!" Jarl Reshu chanted, her hands igniting with leyborn energy that surged forth in a wave, clearing a path for their retreat.

The clatter of steel and the roar of combat dwindled as the Orc forces, leaderless and broken, scattered across the trampled plains. The Heroes and Jarls, their armor stained and dented, watched with a wary mixture of relief and exhaustion. Rider wiped a smear of blood from his brow, his eyes fixed on the imposing silhouette of House Kor's Fortress.

"Let's see what treachery lies behind those walls," Ariella said, her voice carrying the weight of betrayal.

The fortress stood like a monument to corruption—a stark, gothic structure with spires that clawed at the sky. Its once-proud banners, now a tattered mix of white, blue, and the black of Orcish clans, fluttered in the wind. The great doors, carved with scenes of holy wars and crusades, hung open, revealing a royal court where two worlds had collided in uneasy coexistence.

"Look at this place," Kael muttered, stepping over an ornate rug frayed at the edges. "A blend of Human piety and Orc savagery."

"Once, these halls resounded with hymns, not war chants," Bloodmane said, surveying the high-vaulted space where statues of saints stood defaced by crude Orcish glyphs.

They found Jarl Kor on the throne—a grotesque fusion of Human and Orc, his features both regal and brutish. His crown, a jagged thing of iron and bone, sat askew atop tangled locks.

"By the gods, what has your house become?" Jarl Bloodmane demanded, his voice echoing through the chamber.

"Survival demanded evolution," the half-Orc sneered.

"Your 'evolution' has brought ruin upon your people," Jarl Reshu snapped, her eyes blazing with fury.

Without ceremony, they stripped him of his crown and bound his hands, leading him away from the throne he had defiled. "We will decide your fate," Ariella proclaimed, "but the Human Trinity is no more."

In the days that followed, the heroes and Jarls rested within the cold stone walls of Castle Kor. The echoes of battle faded, replaced by the sounds of recovery and contemplation.

"Your bravery turned the tide," Jarl Bloodmane said, addressing the trio. "House Bloodmane owes you a debt."

"As does House Reshu," Jarl Reshu added, nodding to Kael.

"Then I ask for access to the university and its libraries," Kael said, his eyes alight with anticipation. "There is much I seek to learn."

"Granted," Jarl Reshu smiled. "May our archives quench your thirst for knowledge."

Ariella stepped forward. "From House Bloodmane, I request a steed—"

"Say no more," Jarl Bloodmane interjected, offering a scroll sealed with wax. "For you and your lineage, our finest mounts."

Rider listened, his thoughts adrift. When the Jarls turned to him, questioning eyes awaiting his desire, he hesitated.

"I mean no disrespect Jarl Bloodmane, but I already have a faithful steed back at Stonefire. One I would have trusted my life to in these battles." Rider confessed. "I also do not know if my travels will return me to your archives, Jarl Reshu."

"Then it shall be so," Jarl Bloodmane declared, sharing a knowing glance with Jarl Reshu. "We bestow on you the title of Jarl and the keys to this fortress. So your travels will always lead you back to the land you helped save."

"Kor Fortress," Rider mused aloud, amusement dancing in his eyes as he looked around. "Perhaps it's time for a new name."

"Indeed," Jarl Bloodmane chuckled. "One befitting its new master."

"Let it be a beacon," Jarl Reshu said, "a symbol of unity in these fractured lands."

"Unity," Rider echoed, feeling the weight of responsibility settle upon his shoulders. "To protect the plainlands and all who dwell within."

"Then we are agreed," Jarl Bloodmane concluded, clasping Rider's shoulder. "Rest now, Jarl Rider, for tomorrow we rebuild."

Banners fluttered in the twilight breeze, the once stark white of House Kor now mingling with vibrant reds and golds, dancing alongside the black and silver of House Bloodmane. The air was sweet with the scent of roasting meat and fragrant spices as tables groaned under the weight of a celebratory feast. Rider stood amidst it all, taking in the scene with a mix of pride and disbelief.

"Never thought I'd see such revelry," Rider remarked, accepting a goblet of rich wine from a passing server. He chuckled, swirling the dark liquid. "Especially not in my honor."

"Jarl Rider, it has quite the ring to it," Ariella said, her eyes twinkling mischievously in the firelight. She raised her goblet in a toast. "To new beginnings!"

"New beginnings," Kael echoed, clinking his goblet against theirs. "And perhaps a new name for Kor Fortress?"

"Ah, yes," Rider replied with a grin, watching as the gathered warriors, mages, and citizens alike indulged in the festivities. "How does 'Spellsword Stronghold' sound? A place where magic and might meet hand in hand, rather than conflict."

Laughter erupted around them, the jest easing the gravity of their recent trials.

"Spellsword Stronghold," Jarl Bloodmane boomed, striding over with Jarl Reshu at his side. "A fitting title for a stronghold reborn."

"May it stand long as a symbol of our combined strength," Jarl Reshu added, her gaze sweeping over the assembly with pride.

As night fully descended upon them, musicians struck up a lively tune, inviting all to partake in dance and song. The aroma of spiced dishes wafted through the air, mingling with the smell of fresh pine garlands that adorned the hall. Rider savored the taste of sweet honeyed pastries, his senses alive with the warmth of the fire and the soft textures of silk banners beneath his fingertips.

Yet, amid the jubilation, there was an undercurrent of resolve. Rider's laughter faded as he scanned the horizon beyond the fortress walls, where stars began to peek through the darkening sky.

"Tomorrow we ride at dawn," he declared, his voice carrying the weight of duty. "The fate of Etonya is far from secure, and the Stonefire and Amakiir Kingdoms remain estranged allies at best."

"Indeed, Rider," Kael agreed somberly, his hand

resting on the hilt of his sword. "We must mend those bonds, lest the Cult seize upon our discord."

"Stonefire's mountains hold strong, but they need to know we stand with them," Ariella added, her Elven ears catching the distant call of a night bird—a reminder of the wild lands that lay beyond their celebration.

"Then let us drink to alliances yet unbroken and futures still bright," Jarl Bloodmane said, raising his goblet high. The others followed suit, their voices joining in a chorus of hopeful determination.

"May our unity light the way through the darkest of times," Rider proclaimed, feeling the fiery spirit of the gathering bolstering his courage.

"May it be so," echoed the crowd, their cheers ringing out into the night.

CHAPTER XIV
SHADYVALE

The grand hall of Spellsword Stronghold echoed with the weighty discourse of war and allegiance. Once a monument to House Kor's might, the cathedral-fortress now stood as Rider's bastion against the encroaching darkness. Its white stones, etched in blue, absorbed the morning light that spilled through the stained glass, casting an ethereal glow on the gathering leaders within.

"Stonefire and Amakiir must hear the truth from our lips first," Rider said, pacing before the hearth where flames crackled and spit, the scent of burning pine filling the air. "We cannot allow rumors of our involvement in Baelgor's death fester into distrust."

Ariella Moonwhisper leaned against the cool granite of a window sill. "Rider, my heart grieves for swift action too, but Queen Vyshaan's influence is not to be underestimated. Her words can soothe suspicions far more effectively than ours alone."

"Indeed," Kael chimed in, his fingers tracing the intricate carvings of his wrist guards, "but we tread a razor's edge. Each moment squandered brings the cult closer to their heinous goal."

A silence fell upon them, punctuated only by the distant clanging of metal as the stronghold's defenses were bolstered. The great banners of their united houses fluttered softly above—a symbol of the fragile unity they sought to forge across Etonya.

"Her magic, her authority... It's paramount," Ariella stepped away from the window to join Rider by the fire. "Queen Vyshaan's voice could bridge the divide, mend the wounds inflicted by treachery."

"Time waits for no monarch," Kael interjected, leaning casually against the wall, his blue eyes sharp beneath blond locks. "While we debate, the cult moves unchallenged. Our path is fraught either way."

"Indeed, it is." Jarl Bloodmane's deep, resonant voice filled the chamber as he stepped through the doorway, his military bearing unmistakable. His black and silver attire shimmered with martial grace born of his Lancer Corps's prowess. "But you need not walk it alone."

"Jarl Bloodmane," Ariella acknowledged with a nod, her posture easing.

"Your cause is just, and my lancers are at your service," he declared, surveying the group. "Let us ride out together and face whatever awaits with steel and valor."

"An offer most generous, but I bring an alternative," said a new voice, as Jarl Reshu emerged from the dim corridor, her red and gold robes flowing behind her like molten metal. She approached the gathering with a serene confidence, the sigils on her garb shimmering subtly.

"Teleportation, my friends," she continued, her articulate tone carrying the promise of swift aid. "My magic can whisk us to House Reshu in mere moments, saving precious time."

Bloodmane chuckled, the sound rich and warm. "Swift indeed, Jarl Reshu. Should you ever long to see our side of the plains, our gates are open to you—and a taste of Bloodmane hospitality awaits." His eyes twinkled with mischief and something more, a shared secret on the cusp of revelation.

"Perhaps sooner than you think," Reshu replied, her lips curving into a sly smile. "I believe a permanent tele-portation circle within Fortress Bloodmane would benefit us both—for frequent... consultations."

"Consultations," echoed Rider, a smirk breaking through his earlier intensity. "A worthy investment for the future."

"Then it's settled," Ariella said, her expression soft-ening as she looked at Rider. "To Brightspire we go. With speed granted by House Reshu's magic."

"Agreed," Kael added, pushing away from the wall. "Brightspire shall be our next chapter, and let us hope it reads in our favor."

The air of Spellsword Stronghold crackled with newfound purpose, the alliance between them strength-ened by shared visions of victory and whispers of intimacy yet to come. They turned towards preparations, knowing that the road ahead, though now swifter, remained fraught with danger and darkness.

Rider strode through the cobblestoned corridors of the stronghold, his boots echoing against the ancient floors. The fortress, once a bastion of stoic might and hate, now teemed with life and arcane energy. He gathered supplies for their journey: potent healing salves, pouches of dried herbs, and scrolls etched with battle spells. Each item was meticulously chosen, essential for the treacherous path that lay before them.

Ariella moved gracefully beside him, her keen Elven

eyes scanning for anything they might have overlooked. Her quiver brimmed with newly fletched arrows, her bow polished to a gleam. She had always been the more practical of the two, her foresight a guiding light in the shadowy uncertainty of their quest.

"Are we nearly ready?" she asked, her voice a soft melody amidst the bustle.

"Almost," Rider replied. "Just a few more pieces of equipment."

"Good." Ariella nodded, her gaze lingering on the wrapped bundle of her ranger's cloak. "We cannot afford delays."

Kael, hands aglow with preternatural blue light, hovered over an assortment of crystals and arcane instruments laid out on a heavy oak table. His focus was absolute as he charged each object with magical energy, ensuring they would be ready for whatever trials awaited them.

"Remember, Rider," Kael said without looking up, "the weight of your new title carries with it not just honor, but responsibility. The stronghold must stand as a beacon of hope, even in our absence."

"Indeed," Rider acknowledged, feeling the gravity of his role as Jarl settle upon his shoulders like a mantle. "And it will."

At that moment, Jarl Bloodmane and Jarl Reshu entered, flanked by their respective retinues. The two nobles exuded authority and camaraderie, their alliance palpable in the respectful nods they exchanged.

"Everything is prepared on our end," Bloodmane announced, his voice echoing off the high-vaulted ceilings. "My best engineers and masons will remain here to fortify Spellsword Stronghold. It shall stand impregnable, a testament to our unity."

"Thank you, Jarl Bloodmane," Rider said, offering a grateful nod. "Your support is invaluable to us."

Jarl Reshu stepped forward, her magi already beginning to weave their enchantments. "Let us attend to the matter of the teleportation circle. This way, please."

The dedicated chamber was a masterpiece of stonework, its walls inscribed with runes and sigils that thrummed with latent power. Reshu led her magi in delicate incantations, their voices harmonizing in an ethereal chant. Their gestures infused the air with magic until the very stones seemed to pulse with anticipation.

"Watch closely," Reshu instructed Rider and Kael. "The operation of this circle will be crucial for swift travel between our strongholds. Should you require aid or wish to confer, you need only step within and call upon its power."

"An impressive feat," Kael murmured, admiration evident in his gaze.

"Indeed," Rider agreed, studying the intricate patterns that glowed beneath Reshu's touch.

"Secure alliances, indeed," Kael whispered wryly to Rider a smirk playing at the edge of his lips. The earlier flirtations between the two Jarls had not escaped his notice.

Rider chuckled softly, shaking his head. "Let's hope their... diplomacy remains as fervent as their spellcraft."

With a final incantation, the room hummed with completion, the teleportation circle etched permanently into the stone floor. It shimmered in golden radiance, awaiting its first journey.

"Step forth," Jarl Reshu beckoned, her eyes alight with triumph.

The heroes took their places within the circle, their hearts pounding in unison as the magi raised their arms. A dome of magic enveloped the room, the air crackling with power. Scenes of the plainlands, vivid and swift, painted themselves upon the walls, images flashing by in a dizzying cascade of colors and shapes.

"Remember your purpose," Reshu's voice echoed, strong and clear above the crescendo of magic.

Then, as quickly as it had begun, the vision stilled, the lights flared, and the world shifted. Silence fell, and the dome dissipated, leaving behind only the faint scent of ozone.

They opened their eyes to find themselves within the grandeur of Reshu University's teleportation circle, the journey completed in the span of a breath. Relief flooded through them, mingled with awe at the marvels of arcane travel.

"Steeds await you outside," Jarl Reshu said, gesturing toward the exit. "Shadyvale lies to the northwest, a day's ride from here."

"Thank you, Jarl Reshu," Ariella said, her heart still racing with the exhilaration of the spell.

"May fortune favor your path," Reshu replied, a hint of warmth softening the formality of her words.

With a shared glance, the team stepped out into the crisp air, their resolve hardened. The road to Shadyvale—and Brightspire beyond—beckoned, and they would answer its call.

Dust curled around the hooves of their steeds as they approached Shadyvale, the golden light of the setting sun casting long shadows across the road. The town sprawled before them, alive with the clamor of commerce and the vibrant melding of cultures. Stonefire Dwarves haggled over sparkling gemstones, while Amakiir Elves traded silken cloths that shimmered like the surface of a still pond.

"Never thought I'd find relief in the sound of bargaining merchants," Rider mused, his voice tinged with fatigue and wonder. "It's a welcome change from the clash of steel and Orcish war cries."

"Indeed," Ariella agreed, her keen eyes scanning the crowds. "Look at the flags—every kingdom represented, every race mingling. Shadyvale truly is the crossroads of Etonya."

Kael leaned forward in his saddle, absorbing the babble of languages and the rich tapestry of attire. "This place... it's a testament to what Etonya could be without the shadow of war looming over it."

As they tethered their horses and approached the entrance, the mood shifted palpably. A crowd had gathered around a man on the street standing atop a wooden box. "Are you afraid to go out at night? Do you fear that you lack the strength to protect those you love? I too once shared your fears, but through trust in our Lord I have been granted strength beyond my wildest dreams."

"Makes sense they'd have a more public presence here." Rider commented as he overheard the zealot's preaching.

"Freedom of speech cuts both ways, Rider." Ariella began. "He has a right to share his beliefs whether we agree with them or not."

Their conversation turned to practical matters as the Wolves' Den tavern came into view. The timber and stone establishment towered over the town, its multiple stories teeming with life. Laughter spilled from open windows, accompanied by the lively tunes of unseen minstrels. The aroma of roasting meats and exotic dishes wafted through the air, enticing their senses.

"Let's secure a room for the night," Ariella suggested,

dismounting with graceful ease. "And perhaps a meal that doesn't taste of travel rations and haste."

"Agreed," Kael said, patting his stomach. "I wouldn't mind sampling the local fare."

A cluster of Stonefire Dwarves eyed them suspiciously, whispering amongst themselves, while a group of Amakiir Elves narrowed their eyes in silent accusation. The team exchanged a glance, the weight of misgivings pressing upon them.

"Remember," Rider said firmly, his gaze sweeping over the crowd, "we're here to get back to Brightspire and mend alliances, not fray them further."

Ariella nodded, stepping forward with poise. "We'll face their doubts with the truth of our deeds. Let's show them our honor."

"Let the Humans herald our arrival then," Kael chimed in, a wry smile playing on his lips. "For today, we dine as heroes among allies."

With that, the trio entered the boisterous fray of the Wolves' Den, the footsteps of their armored boots resounding with purpose on the wooden floors. The scent of ale and hearty stew greeted them, mingling with the smoky undertones of the tavern's hearth. They moved through the throng, ignoring the mixed reception, focused solely on the task at hand: to find solace in rest and sustenance, and prepare for the journey to Brightspire come morning.

Thrust into the raucous heart of the Wolves' Den, the trio was enveloped by the sounds of revelry. Bards, perched precariously atop tables and bar edges, serenaded patrons with tales of heroic deeds set to melody. The clatter of dice on wooden surfaces blended with the boisterous laughter and bawdy cheers of gamblers.

"Barkeep!" Rider called out, his voice barely cutting

through the din as he signaled for service. "A table, if you please!"

"Over there, by the hearth," the barkeep gestured gruffly, wiping his hands on an apron stained with the day's work. "I'll send someone to tend to ya."

They wove through the throngs, finding solace at a sturdy oak table. As a barmaid approached, Rider ordered a robust tankard of Brightspire barleywine and a plate piled high with roast beef and root vegetables. Ariella requested a delicate crystal goblet filled with a fragrant Elvish wine, paired with a platter of forest mushrooms and wild greens. Kael, ever the eclectic, asked for an assortment of small plates—a fusion of flavors from across Etonya—alongside a sampler of exotic liquors.

"Strange to be amidst such life after all we've seen," Ariella mused, as she delicately forked a tender mushroom.

"Indeed," Rider agreed, tearing into his meal with gusto. "Yet, I can't help but notice the wary glances cast our way."

"Let them look," Kael said with a dismissive wave, relishing a sip of a spicy spirit that sent warmth cascading down his throat. "Their curiosity is as piqued as their stomachs are full."

"Curiosity is one thing, but hostility is another." Ariella's gaze had sharpened, catching the disdainful sneer of an Amakiir patron. "We bear the brunt of unjust suspicion."

"Unjust it may be," Rider interjected, his brows knitting together. "But we will clear our names. Our actions will speak louder than any rumor or lie."

"Actions indeed," Kael added, swirling his drink. "Though it seems our valor is misconstrued as villainy in these parts."

"Perhaps," Ariella sighed, taking a measured sip of her

wine. "But let us not forget why we fight—to restore peace to Etonya and thwart those who'd see it burn."

"True enough," Rider conceded, raising his tankard in a toast to their resolve. "To peace and the truth that shall prevail!"

As the raucous din of The Wolves' Den reverberated around them, Rider approached the barkeep to secure lodgings for the night. The middle-aged man, with his graying beard and steadfast gaze, nodded in understanding as he slid a ledger across the worn wooden countertop.

"Rooms are plenty, but I'd advise you keep to the inn after dark," the barkeep muttered, his voice almost lost amid the noise of merriment and clinking tankards.

"Is the night not kind here in Shadyvale?" Ariella inquired as she leaned against the bar.

Before the barkeep could reply, a slurred voice piped up from behind them. "Smart to stay indoors! Night's got teeth, and it bites deep," warned a drunken patron, who swayed precariously on his stool, his bloodshot eyes wide with earnest fear.

Rider turned. "What do you mean?"

"Ah, the wolves," the barkeep interjected, taking over the conversation with a weary sigh. "Been a problem of late. Found some travelers torn apart, their carriage splintered like kindling. Militia says it's just wolves, angered by something or other."

"Yet whispers speak of larger shadows prowling the outskirts," the drunk added ominously, his finger tracing an erratic path through the air.

"Whispers often grow into screams if left unchecked," Kael noted, eyeing the barkeep for further details.

"True enough," the barkeep conceded. "But we've had no shortage of strange tales since the attacks. Hard to separate fact from frightened fancy."

"Perhaps we should lend our aid," Ariella suggested, her gaze meeting Rider's. "Word of our deeds might travel far, quelling misconceptions about us."

"Agreed," Rider said. "We'll look into this matter come morning."

***

The following day, with the fresh sunlight casting long shadows between the buildings of Shadyvale, the team made their way to the local militia office. The chill in the air did little to cool their determination as they stepped inside the modest building, where the scent of leather and steel mingled with stale ink.

"Good morn," greeted Rider, his tone formal as he approached the burly officer seated at a desk littered with reports and maps.

"Heroes of Spellsword Stronghold, what brings you to our door?" the Human militia officer asked, his voice gruff, his attention only half-pulled from the parchment before him.

"News reached us of recent...wolf troubles," Kael stated, his voice layered with a hint of reproach. "We offer our assistance in the matter."

"Ah, that." The officer waved a dismissive hand. "A few deaths, tragic though they may be, hardly warrant concern amidst the multitude of travelers."

"Yet precautions have been taken?" Ariella pressed, her eyebrows arching in silent challenge.

"Signs posted 'round town, warning folk to avoid the woods come nightfall," the officer replied, his attention already drifting back to his work. "It's enough."

"Enough until another tragedy strikes under your watch," Rider countered sharply, his frustration clear.

"Look," the officer said, finally locking eyes with Rider. "We appreciate the offer, but Shadyvale can handle its own. Besides, with the amount of travelers we see, a handful of lost souls is—"

"Unacceptable," Rider interrupted, his clenched fists betrayed his barely contained rage as he leaned across the worn oak table that separated him from the indifferent militia officer.

"Tell me more about these travelers," Rider demanded, his voice low but sharp, like a drawn sword at dusk. "Were they from the plainlands?"

"Couldn't say," the officer muttered, barely glancing up. "They were Human, that much I remember. No belongings to speak of—looters saw to that."

Rider exhaled slowly, trying to control the fury simmering within him. "It matters. Those could've been my people trading through Shadyvale. This neglect stains the honor of your militia."

The officer shrugged, unfazed by the biting reproach. "Honor doesn't clean the streets, nor does it put coin in our purses."

"Perhaps not," interjected Ariella, her lilting voice cutting through the tension. "But it preserves the soul of a town. And without it, what are you left with?"

"Enough," Kael chimed in, his calming presence like a balm. "We'll find the answers ourselves." His gaze drifted towards the verdant horizon visible through the grimy window. "To the north then."

"Suit yourself," the officer shrugged, returning to his papers. "Just don't get yourselves killed."

The road to Brightspire beckoned, its grassy path a stark contrast to the scorched and desolate plains they had traversed. The vibrant greens of the Emerald Forest on one side of the road blurred into the richer hues of the Jade Forest on the right, nature's palette on full display.

"Such diversity in landscape," mused Kael, his eyes sweeping over the myriad colors around them. "Like the cosmos itself, every world unique, every path untold."

"Yet some paths bear scars deeper than others," Ariella added softly, her gaze fixed on the disturbed earth ahead.

Ahead, the shattered carriage told its violent tale, the remains strewn chaotically, splinters mingling with torn fabric and dark stains upon the ground.

"Look here," Ariella pointed out, crouching beside an imposing claw mark etched into the wood. "These are no ordinary wolves' work."

Rider joined her, noting the size and ferocity of the gashes. "Lycans?" he questioned.

"Too ragged for Lycans," Ariella concluded after a moment's scrutiny. A frown creased her delicate features as she searched her memory. "I've seen such marks... but where?"

"Let's follow the trail," Rider decided. "Answers lie within the forest, not in the past."

As they ventured to the northeast and deeper into the Jade, the air grew thick with the scent of pine and earth, their passage disturbing the quietude of the woods. Whatever secrets lay hidden beneath the canopy, they would unearth them together, bound by their mission of safeguarding the realms they loved.

The tendrils of the Jade Forest grew ever more insistent, clawing at the travelers' cloaks and boots as they ventured deeper into its heart. Ariella, who had once danced through these woods with the grace of a falling leaf, now slashed at the bramble with her curved Elven blade. "I've hunted by the lake's northern edge near Brightspire many a time," she said, slicing through a particularly stubborn vine, "but never have I seen it choke on such wild growth."

"Well, we'll make our own way," Rider noted, his own sword carving a path forward. He wiped sweat from his brow; the air was dense and humid, and each breath felt like drawing in a mouthful of moss. Magic sparked at his fingertips, incinerating obstructive foliage that dared to bar their way.

"Even the very earth rebels against us," Kael muttered, keeping pace behind them. In one hand, he held a glowing orb that hovered just above his palm—a source of light and a beacon for any spells he might need to weave swiftly.

"Or against something else," Ariella proposed, her violet eyes scanning the tangled overgrowth. "This is no natural occurrence. Some magic stirs at its core, and we must tread warily."

"Could this be related to the cultists?" Rider pondered aloud, taking a moment to peer into the dense canopy where sunlight struggled to penetrate.

"Perhaps," Kael said, his voice tinged with unease. "Their dark rituals could corrupt more than just hearts."

"Then let us hope our blades are swift enough to uproot such corruption," Ariella declared, setting back to work with renewed vigor.

As the sun began its descent, casting the forest in a golden hue filtered through emerald leaves, the trio found a small clearing suffocated less by the intrusive greenery. They agreed, with collective exhaustion etched into their features, that this would be where they made camp.

"Let us rest," Kael announced, waving his hand. A feast appeared before them, conjured from the ether—a reminder of their first shared meal and of the bond that had since grown.

They settled around the spread, the aroma of roasted meats and freshly-baked bread mingling with the damp scent of the forest floor. Each flavor was a comfort, a brief respite from the dangers that lurked unseen.

"Remember how Baelgor devoured this feast," Ariella mused, her laughter tinged with sorrow as she lifted a leg of fowl. "He always appreciated your culinary magic, Kael."

"His appetite for life was as large as his belly," Rider added with a wistful smile. "We carry his spirit with us. His memory sharpens our resolve."

"Indeed," Kael raised his goblet, the liquid inside shimmering with its own inner light. "To Baelgor, whose forge burns bright in the halls of our hearts."

"To Baelgor," they echoed, clinking their cups together in solemn remembrance.

As twilight settled and the stars began their silent vigil overhead, they shared tales of Baelgor's hospitality and resolve within the mountain—of hostility and hospitality intertwined like the vines around them. Their conversation wove a tapestry of determination and duty, each thread a promise to continue fighting, to honor those lost, and to protect the realms they called home, though Ariella's Elven senses couldn't help but feel something pressing against her mind.

"Tomorrow, we find what makes the wood's overgrowth so fierce," Ariella vowed as they finished their meal.

"Agreed," Rider affirmed. "Time to retire for the night."

Kael Stormbringer began to finish his drink in solitude, his eyes pacing the woods as he swirled a goblet of arcane wine in his hand. His mind occupied elsewhere as he seemed to be looking for something or someone.

"Bah, the wine's getting to my head tonight. See you both in the morning." he dismissed and with a wave of his hand the feast returned to the ether and his tent magically opened before him.

Their words hung in the air, a pact sealed beneath the watchful gaze of the Jade Forest. With heavy limbs and hearts full of purpose, they retreated to their tents, the echoes of their resolve fading into the whispers of the night.

Inside their shared tent, Ariella exhaled softly, her auburn tresses spilling across her bare shoulders like liquid fire as she slowly undressed herself. Rider followed suit, his agile muscular frame flexing beneath his armor as it melted away. Eyes locked on one another, they moved closer, their bodies yearning for each other's warmth. His hands trailed down her back and encircled her waist, pulling her against him. She nestled her head into his chest with a sigh of contentment and licked her lips hungrily. Their followed kiss was slow but deep; an offering of love that had grown over time spent together. He grasped fistfuls of silken hair and held her still while deepening the kiss further; tasting her became an obsession he could ignore no longer. This moment was all they had - a stolen moment between battles and danger - so they would make it count.

Moans escaped both their throats as their tongues tangled. Her slender fingers traced along strong jawlines and explored hard planes before trailing lower down towards his bulging manhood straining against his leather breeches. With skill only honed by necessity and desire, she freed him with gentle nudges at studded buckles and pliable metal rings holding him captive. Once freed, Ariella gazed as Rider's girth pulsed with eager anticipation for what came next. Ariella knelt down before him, her velvety smooth hands wrapped around his rigid length—and she stroked him gently in encouragement while she took him into her mouth. Those captivating violet eyes looking up at him seemed to glow even more brightly in this light.

Tasting his dripping desire sent shivers down her spine as she slowly worked him deeper along her tongue, sucking on him like he was an elusive treat she's been craving for days. His hands found her luscious red locks, tangling them between his fingers as he guided her head up and down his shaft in time with each deep stroke. The act left him no choice but to moan out loudly from the pleasure overtaking him. The sensation was erotic and invigorating as they shared this intimate moment born of their desire, rarely spoken, yet palpable. His hips began to rock slightly forward involuntarily meeting every delicate swirl of Ariella's tongue, sending shudders through his core signaling his impending climax long before the moment finally overtook him. Eagerly, Ariella swallowed each powerful surge as she took him down to his root, greedily enjoying each shot of his hot pleasureful release. She continued gazing up at him adoringly until the warm liquid finished releasing. Gently and hungrily she continued to slowly suck and stroke him with her warm mouth, until they both slowly crumbled to the furs beneath them.

As they slipped beneath the soft furs, Rider pulled Ariella close, his strong arms cradling her supple frame like a treasure. He nuzzled her neck, breath hot against her cool skin as she shivered with anticipation. His rough hands traveled down her sides, tracing patterns on her soft stomach, before moving to cup her perfect rear. She sighed, arching into his touch as he parted her thighs slightly.

The world outside continued to melt away as their

mouths met in another passionate kiss, tasting of wine and desire. His fingers delved deeper, exploring her Elven skin teasingly before sliding inside her. She moaned into his mouth, pushing back against him as he continued to pleasure her. With a soft gasp, she broke the kiss and laid back on the warm fur. Her breath came in ragged gasps now as his fingers relentlessly danced inside her. Ariella buried one hand in his dark hair and led his eager tongue downward towards her waistline while the other clutched at the fur beneath them.

"Rider," she panted between gasps for air.

He paused the gentle, yet firm stroking of his tongue against her and lifted himself from between her thighs until their face met once more. He could see the pleasure swirling within her eyes, their gaze now locked in the heated moment that spoke volumes between them. With a slow grin spreading across his face, he leaned down once more and swirled his tongue around one of her nipples while moving his other hand between her thighs allowing him to slide two fingers deep inside her core once more. She cried out softly at this dual sensation which only seemed to fuel his hunger as he suckled harder on her breast while thrusting his fingers faster inside of her.

"You are so beautiful," he murmured against her skin before trailing open-mouthed kisses along the side of her breast all the way down once more between her thighs.

"Rider," she whispered again, pushing herself up to meet him halfway as she rolled him onto his back. She pulled herself atop him so that she straddled his hips while continuing to ride his fingers deep within herself. She groaned at the sweet friction created by their meeting bodies; feeling every muscle in her abdomen contract around his fingers embedded inside her. It was time for something more. She wanted nothing more than to feel herself wrapped around his hard cock as he released his seed deep within her; she craved it with an intensity that surprised even herself.

With one swift motion she took control and positioned him at her entrance; she guided him inside slowly as her warm wet pussy surrounded him until he was buried completely within her. She continued to ride him like one of the many animals she'd conquered through her long Elven life, basking in the ecstasy with each sway of her hips. Her heart pounded faster with the heat of their passion. Rider began to rise as she locked her arms outward against his shoulders, pinning him to the furs beneath them. She was a huntress, and tonight he was her prey, and she would have what her body desired. Violently she rode him faster and faster, she could feel him rhythmically swelling deep within her. His breaths quickened as he fought against his looming climax. In this moment, she was no longer his lover, she was his conqueror, and she would have the reward her body craved. Ariella's violet eyes gazed deeply into Rider's, pools of sapphire, their hearts raced together as he vigorously erupted deep within her. She slowed the sways of her hips to match his throbs of pleasure pulsing inside her as she milked every drop he had to offer.

"Ariella" Rider whispered out.

"I know my love," she responded in his ear as she lay her head against his collarbone. "But I'm not done with you yet." a devilish smile crossed her lips as she embraced the man beside her.

Was it their denied love built up until this final release or was there simply something here deep within the forest's confines that unleashed their inner desires. Either way, the pair lost themselves in similar passion-filled moments throughout the night until exhaustion forced them both to sleep.

CHAPTER XV
VORATHOR

Rider stirred, the soft warmth of Ariella's body against his own slowly drawing him from the depths of slumber. Eyelids parted to reveal the dappled light of dawn playing across their intertwined forms. He inhaled deeply the scent of her auburn hair—an intoxicating blend of wildflowers and adventure—intertwining with the crisp morning air.

"Good morning," he murmured, voice rough with sleep, as his sapphire eyes locked onto her jeweled gaze.

"Morning," Ariella replied, her voice a gentle melody that resonated within him. The memory of the night they shared sent a shiver of delight down his spine.

With tender reluctance, they untangled from each other and rose, donning their garments piece by piece—the soft rustle of fabric a gentle counterpoint to the urgency of their awakening euphoria. Rider laced up his boots, the worn leather familiar and grounding, while Ariella tied back her hair, movements graceful and practiced.

Something was off. They stepped out of the tent side by side, expecting the usual comforts of Kael's morning ritual. But the aroma of grilled meats and the robust scent of fresh brew did not greet them. Instead, silence hung heavy in the air—a void where the comforting sounds and smells of their comrade should have been.

"Kael?" Rider called out, his brows furrowing as he scanned the clearing. "That's odd... He's always up before us."

Ariella's hand drifted to the hilt of her blades, instinct sharpening her senses. "This isn't right, Rider. Where is his tent?"

"Where is anything familiar?" Rider added, taking in the surroundings that bore no resemblance to the dense Jade Forest they'd bedded down in the night prior. His mind, still foggy from the remnants of last night's passion, struggled to piece together the unfolding mystery.

"His magic could have transported us elsewhere... but why would he leave without a word?" Ariella said, though uncertainty laced her voice.

"More importantly, how do we find him if his magic is what's missing?" Rider's hand instinctively went to his sword. The weight settled him, but not enough to quell the unease crawling beneath his skin.

"First things first," Ariella said with resolve, her Elven eyes scanning the alien landscape. "We need to understand where we are—and why."

Rider arched a brow, his gaze sweeping across the expanse where tangled brambles had been their last obstacle before sleep claimed them. Now, verdant undergrowth sprawled out like a welcoming carpet, dotted with fruits glimmering like jewels in the morning sun. "Ari, look at this," he murmured, crouching to pluck a raspberry, its ripe fragrance teasing his senses.

"Impossible," Ariella whispered, her violet eyes wide with wonder as she joined him, their fingers brushing in the soft grass. She plucked a fruit herself, examining it with a mixture of awe and suspicion. "This isn't native to the Jade Forest."

"Then whose?" Rider questioned, popping the berry into his mouth, the sweet juice bursting over his tongue. He watched Ariella's lips part slightly, tasting the air that was rich with floral scents.

"Magic," she replied, though her voice seemed distant, caught on the edges of enchantment as birdsong wove around them.

"Kael's?" Rider probed, but even he could taste the difference in the air. It was as if the very essence of life hummed within it, vibrant and untamed.

"No," Ariella shook her head slowly, tendrils of her fiery hair catching the light. "This feels older...wilder."

"Could it be a gift then? From the forest itself?" Rider suggested, trying to piece together the puzzle that unfurled around them.

"Or a trap," Ariella countered softly, her hunter's intuition a flickering shadow behind her mesmerizing gaze. But even as she spoke, her attention drifted to the canopy above, where sunlight dappled through leaves of emerald and gold.

"Let's find out," Rider said, determination lacing his words. He offered her his hand, and together they ventured deeper, the beauty of their surroundings a stark contrast to their mounting unease.

They passed trees laden with fruits neither had seen nor named, each more tantalizing than the last. Flowers bloomed in impossible vibrancy, petals unfurling with seductive grace as if inviting them to lose themselves in this paradise. Ariella's breath hitched, her senses ensnared by the symphony of nature's allure around them.

"By the stars, Rider... It's like a dream," she breathed,

her hand tightening in his. Her touch was warm, grounding amidst the ethereal splendor they traversed.

"Stay sharp," Rider reminded her, but even his voice held a note of fascination. "Dreams can quickly turn to nightmares."

"Indeed," Ariella agreed, her eyes scanning their path, ever the vigilant huntress despite the enchantment that tugged at the edge of her consciousness. "But for now, let us see where this dream leads."

A silver rabbit darted across their trail, followed by foxes locked in playful, primal pursuit. . Ariella's gaze followed the creatures, a smile tugging at her lips."Beautiful, isn't it?" Ariella murmured. Her eyes lingered on the creatures and lushness of the forest. The heat of the previous night rekindled beneath her skin, an ember fanned by each fervent display around them.

"Wild," Rider replied, his voice a low rumble. He watched the animals, but his sapphire eyes held a deeper hunger as he turned to face the woman at his side. Her presence, an intoxicating blend of strength and sensuality, drew him in, and he found himself leaning closer to her.

"Rider..." Ariella's breath hitched as she reached for him, her fingers trailing along his jawline. She pulled him into her, sealing their lips in a kiss that tasted of longing and echoes of a night spent together. The world seemed to fade, leaving only the heat of her touch and the taste of her desire.

But as their kiss deepened, a sharp intrusion cleaved through the haze of passion. Kael's terrified voice tore through the enchantment. The warmth between them shattered. The forest dimmed. "Rider!" Kael's voice fractured the tranquility, jolting Rider back to reality.

"Kael?" Rider's heart hammered against his ribs, his

instincts now fully alert. He felt a tightness in his chest, the weight of impending peril pressing down upon him.

"Sorry, love," he whispered against Ariella's lips, wrenching himself from the seductive pull of her pursuit. With a swift motion, regret lacing his actions, he pinched the delicate tips of her Elven ears with a firm grip.

"Ouch, Rider! You know I hate that!" Ariella's scream shattered the serenity, her eyes flaring with pain and indignation.

"I know, I'm sorry," Rider stammered, his hands already retreating. "But something's wrong, Ariella. We're in danger." His words fell between them like stones, stark against the forest's allure.

"Kael?" she questioned, shaking off the lingering fog of enchantment, her eyes sharpening with the clarity of pain. "What did he say?"

"Only my name, but it was a warning... he sounded fearful," Rider confessed, scanning the treacherous beauty that surrounded them. "We need to stay alert. The magic here is potent, and it's not just the flora bewitching us."

"Then let's move," Ariella said, her tone steel wrapped in velvet, the huntress within her awakened once more. She nocked an arrow to her bow, the string taut with tension as they edged forward, the playful antics of the forest creatures now a backdrop to their grim resolve.

"Kael's voice, it was like a thunderclap in the void," Rider murmured, his sapphire eyes darting through the emerald canopy of the once-familiar forest. "He screamed my name with such terror."

"An illusion then," Ariella concluded, her violet eyes narrowing as she surveyed the enchanting grove, her senses sharpened by the huntress training of her youth. "We must tread carefully. Something else is working against us." She swept a lock of fiery auburn hair from her forehead, her lithe frame tensed for action.

"Where could Kael be?" Rider said, frustration lacing his words as they ventured deeper into the woods, the absence of their companion gnawing at him.

"Nothing," Ariella confirmed, after a thorough search yielded no sign of their ally or his magical abode. "Not a trace of his magic remains."

"Then we're truly on our own," Rider sighed, gripping the hilt of his sword with unease.

"Look there," Ariella pointed out, stopping before a majestic tree with bark as rough as an ogre's hide. "I'm sure we've passed this very tree thrice already." She drew her dagger, its blade glinting in the dappled sunlight, and carved an intricate symbol into the trunk—a crescent moon cradling a star.

"Let's keep moving," she suggested, leading the way as they meandered through fantastical terrain that seemed to defy logic. They traversed under arches formed by intertwining branches where luminescent flowers bloomed with vibrant hues, casting an ethereal glow upon their path.

The air was alive with birdsongs, melodies so pure they seemed woven from threads of magic itself. The aroma of untouched wilderness intermingled with the sweet scent of blooming jasmine, tantalizing their senses, inviting them to forget their dire situation.

"Could this be the work of Pixies or Dryads?" Rider pondered out loud, recalling stories of Fae who delighted in leading travelers astray.

"Or something far more cunning," Ariella replied, her gaze distant, as if piecing together an unseen puzzle.

Time stretched and folded upon itself until, an hour later, Ariella halted abruptly. "There!" she exclaimed, pointing toward a figure in the distance—her unique symbol staring back at them from the tree's broad trunk.

Rider breathed heavily, realization dawning. "A maze... or a potent illusion."

"Either way, we're within its snare," Ariella stated, her voice steady despite the gravity of their plight.

"Then we break it," Rider declared, his charismatic tone edged with steel. "Together."

Ariella's slender fingers brushed the bark where her symbol mocked them, a crescent moon enwrapping a star. A flicker of frustration sparked in her violet eyes, and she turned away from the damning sign.

"Tracking beasts and bandits is one thing," she muttered, "but this enchantment... it's beyond me."

Rider stepped closer, placing a comforting hand on her shoulder. "You helped lead us through the shadows of Stonefire, laid waste to Goblin and Orc alike. I've personally watched you end horrors in the dark with nothing more than your instinct. Without you, Ariella, we'd be naught but bones scattered in the underbrush."

She looked up at him, the steel in her gaze softening. "It's just... I'm supposed to know these lands, these tricks," she confessed, her voice a whisper lost among the songs of the forest.

"Perhaps your knowledge can still guide us," Rider suggested, hope glinting in his eyes."The arcane secrets you've studied, the tales of Fae—could they hold the key?"

Ariella closed her eyes, delving into the depths of her memory. "There are Pixies," she explained, her words painting images in the air, "small, winged sprites with a penchant for mischief. They lead travelers astray with flickers of light and laughter, luring them into endless chases."

"Then there are the Dryads, spirits of the trees. Their

presence is soothing, their whispers woven with the wind. But they guard their groves fiercely, ensnaring those who would harm their woodland sanctum with roots that rise like serpents from the earth."

"Ah, and Leprechauns—the tricksters little folk. They hide their gold and conjure illusions to protect their treasures. A mind caught in their riddles can wander for an eternity, always seeking, never finding."

"Satyrs, though..." Ariella's voice trailed off as the very air around them seemed to pulse with untamed magic. The forest shimmered, colors bleeding and blending into new, impossible hues. A figure leaned lazily against a nearby tree, its goat legs crossed at the ankles, a bushel of grapes cradled in its arms.

"Ah, you speak of me, do you?" The Satyr's grin revealed pointed teeth as he popped a grape into his mouth, juice dribbling down his chin. His laughter was rich and warm, like honey poured over hot stones. "Curious creatures, aren't you? So keen on unraveling the threads of my realm."

"Oh, the sweet agony of love unconfessed," he crooned, his mocking eyes glinting with mischief as they rested on Ariella and Rider. "Why resist such delectable yearning when last night you indulged in every whim and whisper of desire?"

Ariella stiffened, her vibrant eyes darkening like a stormy sky. "Did you weave that enchantment upon us?" she demanded, her words edged with frustration and a hint of fear for their loss of control.

"Merely removed the shackles of hesitation, my dear," the Satyr replied with a nonchalant shrug, tossing another grape into his mouth. "The passion, the fervor... all your own creation. I am but a facilitator of joy."

Rider clenched his fists, feeling the Satyr's words coil

around him like thorny vines. Before he could speak, a whisper fluttered inside his mind, urgent and familiar. "Rider, are you there? Are you ok? Can you hear me? Do not give in, resist! I know you can do it, break free!"

"Kael?" Rider thought back, his mental voice tinged with desperation. "I'm not as powerful as you in the arcane. I can summon a few tricks when the time is right, but this…this is different."

"Damn it, Rider!" Kael's voice returned, stern yet encouraging. "I've fought countless foes alongside you. The Spark within you is fierce. Light your flame, fight this creature!"*

He turned toward Ariella. The Satyr's laughter dancing through the air, and prepared to reclaim his will from the depths of enchantment.

"Light my flame? What do you…" Rider thought in response.

A sharp snap echoed through the glade, pulling Rider's gaze back to the Satyr with a force that severed the ethereal tether to Kael's voice. The creature before them wore a smirk, twisting the air with its fingers and mischief as it spoke.

"Now, now, Human," the Satyr chided, locking eyes with Rider. "We'll be having no interruptions from that outsider."

The connection was lost.

Rider's mind groped in silence for Kael's guidance. Beside him, Ariella exhaled a seething breath, her violet eyes ablaze with indignation. They were alone—just the

---

*   *The Astralan believe magic resides in everything and everyone. Some ignite their Spark through lengthy study and determination. Others find themselves in moments of dire need, causing their Spark to either ignite or be snuffed out by darkness. A Spark, once ignited, can grow into a raging source of arcane power.*

two of them and this capricious entity within what seemed like an endless labyrinth.

"Choose then," the Satyr continued, gesturing lazily at the surroundings. "Succumb to the delights as I aided you two last night or..."

Ariella had reached her limit. With a scream that tore through the deceptive calm and interrupted his offer, she snatched her bow, the sinewy pull of the string singing defiance. She nocked an arrow with fluid grace, her voice slicing the air like a blade.

"*Ferastel!*" The Astralan word Kael taught them for "be gone".

Ariella had summoned arcane arrows before, but this was different. The command was born from celestial knowledge as it left her lips charged with Astralan potency. Light exploded from the arrowhead as it leapt toward its target, bathing the clearing in a radiance that rivaled Etonya's own celestial beacon.

As sight returned, squinting against the lingering brilliance, they found emptiness where the Satyr had preened. Rider stumbled over his astonishment, words tumbling out. "How did you...?"

He looked upon her, seeing not just the High Elf huntress but a conduit of cosmic wrath. Before Ariella could claim her triumph, the grove itself replied with a growl that clawed up from the depths of its nightmare.

"I offered you pleasure in these dark times," boomed the voice, rising from somewhere deep, ancient, and angry. "And instead, you choose death!"

Their hearts pounded a feral rhythm, responding to the threat woven into each syllable. The warning hung heavy, laden with the scent of impending doom, a promise from the unseen speaker that their defiance would bear dire consequences.

The verdant splendor of the grove twisted grotesquely, serenity succumbing to corruption before their very eyes. Vibrant greens withered into sickly hues as life-giving trees warped into decaying husks, their once proud branches now clawing towards the heavens like skeletal hands begging release from an unseen tormentor. The air turned thick and heavy; an oppressive blanket woven from the musty stench of rot and the acrid bite of decay. Ariella's nose wrinkled in disgust as she raised her bow, ever vigilant.

"By the spirits," Rider hissed, the scent of putrefaction clawing at his throat. He unsheathed his sword with a rasp of metal, the sound unnaturally loud in the silence that had befallen the mutating landscape.

"Can you smell that?" Ariella's voice was tense, barely above a whisper as if afraid to disturb the perverse tranquility of their new surroundings.

"Smell it? I can almost taste it." Rider spat, his gaze darting to the bubbling muck where clear waters had been. The ponds, now cauldrons of dark sludge, seemed eager to swallow any who dared come too close.

"Kael..." Rider muttered under his breath, his eyes closing as he sought the mental connection that had been severed. "Damn it! Come on, Kael where are you!?" His voice trembled with desperation within the confines of his skull, each plea for contact echoing unanswered against the walls of his mind.

Ariella reached out, placing a reassuring hand on his arm, her touch grounding him amidst the chaos. Her fingers clung tightly, betraying her own fear, yet her eyes remained fixated on the shifting shadows, searching for threats yet unseen.

Without warning, the forest shook with a deep, thunderous beat. The ground vibrated beneath their boots, sending ripples through the mire. Rider opened his eyes just as the sky birthed a terror the likes of which tales could scarcely contain. Wings unfurled, blocking the scant moonlight, casting the bog into deeper darkness.

"Look out!" Ariella shouted, pulling Rider aside as a monstrous green Dragon descended upon them, its arrival heralded by the crackling destruction of a once-majestic tree trunk as the beast settled upon the shattered wood, splinters raining down around its taloned feet like offerings to its might.

"Your call for help is misplaced, Human," the Dragon sneered, its voice a guttural symphony of contempt.

Rider gripped his sword tighter, knuckles white, as Ariella nocked another arrow, her jeweled eyes reflecting the fierce determination that burned within her soul. "We'll see about that," she retorted, the bowstring taut with promise.

"Indeed, we shall," the Dragon rumbled, and the night held its breath.

"Your feeble attempts to intimidate and escape are as futile as an insect's struggle in a spider's web," the Dragon's voice boomed, full of pride and self-righteousness. "You are within Vorathor's domain now, Human. Your celestial companion cannot see you here."

Rider's jaw clenched as he stood defiantly before the immense Dragon. The creature's words were like venom, but they sparked an ember of hope within him. "Celestial traveler... he's blocking Kael from seeing us," he murmured under his breath.

"... the sky!" With a sudden surge of desperation, Rider thrust his left hand upwards, fingers splayed wide, reaching for the obscured heavens. His heart pounded, each beat a silent plea for the arcane energies to heed his call and clear the darkness and clouds above.

But nothing happened.

Vorathor's laughter rumbled through the bog, deep and mocking. "Your spark is but a flicker here, young one. Let me show you what true power looks like!"

The Dragon inhaled deeply, its massive chest swelling with the anticipation of release. Ariella tensed beside Rider, her bowstring strained against the pull of her fingers.

With a roar that tore at the fabric of the night, Vorathor unleashed a sonic tempest. The sound was primal, a raw force that resonated through bone and soul. Rider stumbled, grappling with the overwhelming pressure that thrummed in his ears, his vision blurring.

Beside him, Ariella swayed, her lithe form battered by the invisible onslaught.

As the reverberations of the Dragon's roar faded, a sinister churn rose from beneath them. The muck began to roil and bubble, dark ripples of liquid churning as if to claim the land itself.

"Something stirs," Ariella hissed, her eyes scanning the shifting pools.

"Stay close," Rider replied, his voice barely a whisper over the stirring chaos of the bog's newfound life. He tightened his grip on his sword, ready to defend against whatever Vorathor had summoned from the depths.

Ariella's violet eyes widened as the macabre spectacle unfolded before them. Skeletal remains, clad in rusting armor and tattered banners of long-forgotten houses, clawed their way out of the bubbling muck, their movements jerky yet relentless. Green eldritch flames flickered within their hollow eye sockets, casting an otherworldly glow upon the dark waters that birthed them.

"Rider, steel yourself!" Ariella shouted. Her bowstring sang as she loosed a shaft into the advancing horde. The arrow found its mark, piercing through a skull with a crack.

"These creatures too had hope, had a Spark, and look at them now. Puppets for my amusement," Vorathor's voice boomed, sure of its impending victory.

Rider grunted in response, his sword flashing silver arcs in the dim light as he severed the grasping limbs of the undead. "I'll not be your meal this night, Dragon!" The sound of steel cleaving bone and the scent of ancient decay filled his nostrils.

Ariella moved like a shadow, dancing between the groping hands of the undead, her bow a constant blur. Each swift step was measured, every deft turn avoiding a swipe that sought to drag her into death's embrace. Her arrows flew true, piercing one warrior after another, but still, they came, an endless tide of death.

"They don't stop!" Rider's frustration mounted as he hacked through another wave of armored corpses. The cold bite of fear gnawed at him as he realized the futility of their efforts.

"Focus on the present, Rider!" Ariella called out "We fight until our last breath!"

The dank air of the bog clung to them, heavy with the stench of rot and the metallic tang of blood. The sounds of battle rang out as the heroes fought back against the relentless press of undead.

"Damn these cursed things!" Rider shouted, his blade slicing through a ribcage with a satisfying crunch. He could feel the fatigue creeping into his muscles, the weight of his arms growing with every swing. Yet, his resolve did not waver; he would not let this be their end.

With each fallen foe, Ariella's determination grew, her spirit unbroken despite the odds.

"Back to the abyss that spawned you!" she yelled, her

voice fierce as she dispatched another skeleton with a well-placed shot.

The ground beneath them squelched with each step, the once lush paradise now a grotesque tableau painted with violence and despair. The moon, shrouded by the dense canopy above, offered no solace, its light unable to pierce the gloom of Vorathor's lair.

"Keep fighting, Ariella! We're not done yet!" Rider's voice carried over the din of battle, his sword arm relentless as he carved a path through the encroaching dead.

Their world had narrowed to the space between breaths, the gap between life and undeath. Every sense was heightened—the clash of metal, the caress of the mist, the sight of relentless foes, the taste of fear, and the touch of fate hanging in the balance.

"Your struggles are but the flailing of newborns against my might," Vorathor's voice thundered, a taunt of malice that pierced through the clangor of battle. "You could have bathed in endless ecstasy, unknowingly surrendering to the rapture I offered. Instead, you chose this futile resistance."

Ariella loosed another arrow, its shaft slicing through the dank air before it shattered against the skull of an advancing undead. The creature barely staggered, its eldritch flames flickering like the mockery of life within its hollow gaze. She glanced at Rider, his sword a blur of steel as he fought with the desperation of a man possessed.

"Rider!" she called out, her voice rising above the tumult. "The enchantment... it wasn't just that! I wanted—you and I—"

"Save your breath, Ari!" Rider grunted, cleaving through bone and decay. "Our moments together, they were real. Beyond any spell or illusion!"

Their eyes met in a fleeting moment of shared understanding amidst the chaos—a spark of connection that defied the darkness encroaching upon them.

"Then let us fight for those moments!" Ariella shouted, her bow now a burden rather than a boon. With swift grace, she dropped her bow and drew her dual short swords, their edges gleaming with a lethal promise. Each step she took was measured, her blades dancing in her hands as she cut down one skeletal warrior after another.

"Look at them. My puppets," Vorathor sneered, the sound vibrating through the fetid air. "They cling to their mortal desires even as they face oblivion. How quaint."

Rider felt the burn in his muscles, the wet slick of blood on his skin, not all of it his own. His longsword swept through the ranks of undead, each stroke fueled by the urgency to reach Ariella's side. They had become separated by the waves of undead they dodged and parried.

"Watch your left!" Rider yelled, as he parried a strike of his own, watching a blow aimed at Ariella's flank.

"Got it!" she replied, spinning to dispatch the threat with a lethal thrust. Her auburn hair, now matted with sweat and grime, clung to her cheeks, her eyes still burning with undiminished ferocity.

"Your courage is commendable," the Dragon's voice oozed sarcasm, "but ultimately pointless. Embrace each other in death, as you did in life's fleeting pleasure."

"Never!" Rider spat, driving his blade through the ribcage of an attacker.

The stench of rot and the sickening squelch of undead flesh were unrelenting, yet their resolve held firm. Rider fought his way towards Ariella, their connection a silent vow to withstand the nightmarish onslaught together, until their final breath or victory's sweet embrace.

Ariella's scream, a sound that sliced through Rider's heart with more precision than any blade could manage.

The undead horde, relentless in their assault, clawed and bit at her, the gnashing of their teeth finding purchase on her once-pristine armor. Blood seeped from new wounds, mixing with the dirt and grime that marred her skin. Strands of her fiery auburn hair clung to her face, pulled free from its usual grace by the grasping hands of death itself.

"ARIELLA!" Rider's voice was raw as he cleaved another skeletal abomination in twain, his path towards her littered with dismembered remnants. He moved not with finesse but with brutal necessity, driven by a singular need: to reach her.

"Your struggles entertain me," Vorathor taunted, his eldritch eyes aglow with malice. Green vapors of poison curled around his fangs like serpents dancing to the tune of despair. "The more you bleed for one another, the sweeter your surrender shall taste."

Rider's reply was a guttural shout as his blade found the ribcage of a particularly tenacious foe, the steel sinking deep into bone. With a grunt, he wrestled to free it, muscles straining against the unyielding grip of death itself. But the sinew held fast, trapping both steel and hope together in a macabre embrace.

"No..." Rider's breath came in ragged gasps as he tugged futilely at the hilt. Panic clawed at his chest, a primal fear that threatened to consume him whole. Ariella—his beacon in this darkened world—was fading behind a wall of decay, her form obscured by the shambling masses. He heard her release another scream from behind the horde seeking to claim her light.

"NO!" Rider's body shook with a powerful surge of emotion, a mix of fear and determination. His eyes blazed with a brilliant cerulean light as the raw energy within him was unleashed. He could feel something change within him, ancient magic coursing through his veins, stronger than anything he had previously summoned. The air around him crackled with sparks and tendrils of blue energy that danced around his body in a beautiful, yet dangerous, display of power. In that moment, he knew what Kael meant.

His hair rose as if the atmosphere around him defied gravity, strands illuminating as if touched by dawn's first light. He let out a primal roar as he unleashed an explosion of energy. The sheer force of his wrath was strong enough to dissipate even the toughest bones and sinew, leaving nothing but a trail of ash carried away on the gust of wind it created.

Through the clearing haze, he saw Ariella laid upon the ground, her body battered and bloody. Her spirit besieged, those violet eyes dimmed in the darkness, as she lay still and bleeding in a fleeting denial of being extinguished.

Rider, furious with his smoky blue aura pulsing rapidly in time with his heartbeat, changed his gaze toward Vorathor.

The battlefield was silent now, save for the Dragon's angry and shocked growl. It slowly began to step down from the shattering tree trunk beneath it.

Without hesitation and with vengeance fueling his soul, Rider stepped toward the monstrosity before him, his Spark ignited.

CHAPTER XVI
AETHERION ASCENDANCE

The bog squelched beneath Rider's boots with each step he took toward the looming figure of Vorathor. The acrid stench of decaying vegetation and magical corruption filled his nostrils, but it was nothing compared to the coppery tang of blood that permeated the air from Ariella's prone form. Her once-radiant face, now ashen beneath streaks of grime and blood, flickered weakly with what remained of her Elven essence.

"Your time ends here, Vorathor," Rider growled through gritted teeth, his voice rough with pain and resolve. His longsword, once simple steel, now pulsed with a smoky blue brilliance that mirrored the power igniting within him.

Vorathor's response was a guttural snarl, a sound that seemed to warp the air around them. From the cavernous depth of its maw erupted a torrent of green eldritch flame meant to incinerate flesh and bone.

Rider thrust his left hand forward, his fingers splayed in silent fury. A shimmering veil materialized, slicing through the Dragon's fiery breath, dispersing it into harmless embers that drifted around the bog like fallen stars.

"Is this your might?" Rider spat, the barrier dissipating as quickly as it had formed.

The Dragon's eyes, pools of malevolent green, narrowed. Its wings unfurled, casting an oppressive shadow over the battlefield. With a roar that shook the heavens, Vorathor launched itself skyward, its massive bulk defying gravity with an unnatural grace.

"You are nothing!" Vorathor bellowed, descending upon Rider like a vengeful god.

But Rider was no mere mortal to be swept away. The arcane energy roiling around him sharpened his senses, heightened his reflexes. He sidestepped the assault with effortless grace, his sword arching through the air in a blur of cobalt light.

"Nothing? I am your destruction!" Rider's blade found its mark, carving through sinew and scale with shocking ease. The Dragon's anguished roar reverberated through the forest as it crashed to the earth. One wing hung limply, shredded and useless.

"My vengeance will be your downfall," Rider breathed, his chest heaving as he watched Vorathor struggle to regain its footing. The scent of fresh Dragon's blood mingled with the swamp's fetid smell, a pungent reminder of the battle's reality.

"Vengeance?" The Dragon's laugh was a rasping choke as it righted itself, glaring daggers at Rider. "No, little insect. That is but a taste of my wrath!"

Rider tightened his grip on the hilt of his sword, ready for the next clash. "Then come, beast. Show me the depths of your so-called power."

Vorathor towered above, swathed in eldritch shadows that coiled around it like mocking specters. From his gaping maw came a torrent of green flames. But the swordsman was no longer bound to mere flesh and blood. He was the tempest, an untamed force of raw fury.

"Your fire is but an ember to my wrath!" Rider bellowed, his voice warped with the crackling energy that enveloped him. With a flick of his wrist, a barrier of shimmering blue light coalesced from the aether, splitting the inferno around him. His boots squished through the mud as he advanced through the bog, the heat of the Dragon's breath warm against his cheek.

The ancient beast recoiled, its malicious eyes widening in disbelief as Rider closed in. Vorathor retaliated with a shadowy bolt, a spear of pure darkness hurling towards the swordsman with the speed of thought. Yet Rider's body moved on its own accord, twisting with preternatural agility as he sidestepped the deadly missile.

"Die, insect!" Vorathor spat, its claws scraping against the earth, tearing up clumps of moss and mud as it prepared another assault. A cloud of poison crept across the ground, seeking to envelop Rider in its toxic embrace.

With a roar that echoed his newfound might, Rider leapt through the haze, his longsword trailing arcs of electric blue. Each swing cut through the venomous fog as if it were mere silk. "What are you?" Vorathor's query was almost drowned out by the clash of steel against scale, the sizzle of magic biting flesh. Rider did not answer with words. His movements were an extension of his will, as natural as breathing yet as devastating as the fiercest tempest. Blue energy crackled along the edge of his sword, echoing his inner turmoil that transformed into raw destructive force. Vorathor's defenses crumbled beneath the relentless tide. Each parry became an opportunity for Rider to weave another spell into his barrage. Its scales, once impenetrable, yielded like parchment under the relentless onslaught of Rider's blade.

"I'm the Spellsword!" Rider shouted. Sparks flew with each contact, illuminating the darkened bog with flashes of lightning, painting stark shadows on the twisted trees. His sword, now a beacon of azure fury, found its way again and again through chinks in the Dragon's's armor, searing flesh and bone.

Vorathor reeled under the unrelenting assault, pain and shock etched into every line of its monstrous visage. The Dragon had lived eons, had seen the rise and fall of empires. Never had it faced a mortal who wields the very essence of magic itself. Each strike from Rider's sword was a revelation, a testament to the power of the arcane, a power that Vorathor could no longer deny.

"Die!" Rider commanded, his voice carrying the weight of his newfound authority. "Meet your end upon my blade!"

This was a battle for the ages, a duel between ancient might and rising fury—a tale that would be sung through the annals of time.

Vorathor's emerald gaze burned with malice as he gathered a miasma of eldritch power within his cavernous maw. With a guttural incantation that rippled through the bog, the Dragon unleashed another torrent of green energy, serpentine flames writhing with the hunger to devour flesh. Rider braced and shouldered the weight of the blast against his steel, absorbing the arcane energy into his blade with ethereal light. The inferno crashed against it and Rider flurried his blade as the assault ended, dissipating the gathered energy harmlessly as sparks danced away into the night.

"Is that your best?" Rider taunted, feeling the pulsating energy coursing through his veins, emboldening him.

Enraged, Vorathor shifted tactics again, expelling another choking cloud of poisonous gas, this time so potent it turned the air around them acrid and thick. Rider's lungs seared as he couldn't help but breathe it in, but his Spark raged within, purifying the toxins from his bloodstream. He coughed, eyes watering, yet he pressed on, his longsword cutting swathes of clarity through the haze.

"Your tricks are feeble, Dragon" Rider hissed between gritted teeth, slicing through the venomous fog.

With a roar that shook leaves from trees, Vorathor summoned the undead once more. Skeletal warriors clawed back to life once out of the bog, their eye sockets ablaze with that unholy fire. Rider met them head-on, the blue glow of his blade a stark contrast to the sickly green that enveloped his foes. Each swing of his sword cleaved bone and banished spirits back to their eternal rest. His movements were a blur, each slash burning away the taint of necromancy.

"You will fall before me!" he cried, his voice echoing with the ring of steel and the crackle of dissipating phantasms.

The Dragon watched, incredulous, as his minions fell one by one. In desperation, Vorathor focused his ancient will, attempting to leech away Rider's newfound strength with tendrils of dark magic. But the moment they touched him, they recoiled as if scalded. Rider's body was a conduit of raw, untamable power, rejecting the Dragon's vile attempt at thievery.

"Your darkness cannot quench my flame!" Rider bellowed, deflecting the eldritch strands with a sweep of his glowing hand.

Fatigue gnawed at Vorathor. He felt the strain of combat, his breaths coming in ragged bursts, scales smoldering from countless arcane-infused wounds. Rider's muscles, still showing arcs of crackling energy throughout the intensity of the battle, taunted Vorathor further. Neither would yield, their clash a crescendo of primal fury and magical prowess.

Their battle raged, the bog a witness to the relentless fury of man and Dragon, locked in a duel where only one could claim victory.

At the battle's zenith of chaos and fury, Rider launched another salvo of blue arcane blasts from a flurry of his blade that shattered against Vorathor's battered hide, each impact a promise of the end. The smoky blue aura that wreathed the blade collided against the shadowy green eldritch light from beneath the Dragon's scales. Vorathor's monstrous form loomed, great wings beating the air, his eldritch eyes wide with a mix of rage and disbelief.

"*Vor'ethra.*" Rider snarled, his sword arcing in a vicious trajectory aimed for the beast's neck.

Vorathor bellowed, a sound that shook the earth beneath them, but it was too late. Rider's blade, aglow with arcane energy, sliced through the ancient hide as a gush of dark ichor sprayed into the air, drops sizzling where they met the charged aura surrounding Rider. With a sickening severance, Vorathor's head tumbled from its elongated neck, the horror of his defeat etched forever on his lifeless face.

The Dragon's body, massive and terrible even in defeat, stumbled forward before crashing to the ground with an earth-shuddering thud. For a moment, it seemed as though the creature refused to acknowledge its beheading, legs twitching, tail thrashing weakly against the mire.

Then, the transfer began.

Arcane sparks spiraled from Vorathor's severed neck, drawn to Rider like moths to a flame. The sparks collided with him, each impact resonating deep within his soul. His confusion was palpable, brows furrowed as he attempted to comprehend the torrent of pain surging into him.

"Wha—?" he gasped, voice laced with a mixture of awe and terror.

Rider's smoky blue aura flared wildly, burgeoning outwards in waves of kinetic energy. The ground cracked and split, vines and brambles withering as though touched by winter's harshest frost. Nearby trees groaned, their branches snapping to the floor, as if trying to flee the unleashed magic.

He could feel the essence of the Dragon melding with his own, a tempestuous storm of wills clashing within his being. Rider cried out, not in pain but with overwhelming sensation, as arcane power erupted from him, a nova of azure luminescence that turned night into day.

And then, as suddenly as it had begun, the flood ceased.

Rider's aura collapsed inward, collapsing back into him with a sigh of spent energy. His sword dimmed, its once-vibrant glow fading to a dull sheen. His strength gave way, and Rider crumpled to the damp earth, consciousness slipping away like sand through fingers.

In the aftermath, the bog reclaimed its silence. Vorathor's dark Eldritch power, once a malignant shroud over the land, now faded like mist under the sun's caress. Moonlight filtered through the canopy, casting the battlefield in a serene glow, stars winking above as sentinels of the eternal night.

Ariella lay nearby, her chest rising and falling with shallow breaths, violet eyes closed against the world. Around them, the bog transformed, no longer a place of foreboding and death, but a tranquil haven under a moonlit sky, embracing the fallen heroes in its newfound peace.

The stillness of the serene was suddenly shattered by a violent crackle of energy, as a bolt of pure arcane lightning split the sky. Where it struck, the earth trembled, and from the epicenter of the disturbance emerged Kael Storm-bringer—his form wreathed in electric tendrils that danced across his magical armor and cape like living things.

"By the stars above," he exclaimed, his voice a melodic thunder that resonated through the clearing. His piercing blue eyes, now alight with an inner glow, scanned the surroundings with urgency and precision. The elegant, controlled gestures of his hands wove intricate patterns in the air, preparing spells, should there be need for immediate combat.

He'd expected a battlefield, but not this. Not Ariella prone and pale amidst the tangled roots, not Rider collapsed and unmoving. And certainly not the headless form of a Dragon, its body still emanating wisps of dark smoke that curled lazily into the night air.

"Merciful cosmos..." Kael whispered, dread hollowing out the momentary relief of his arrival.. He recognized the severed head of Vorathor, its fanged maw agape in eternal silence, eyes dulled in death—a visage straight from the nightmares and legends of the Astralan people.

"Rider! Ariella!" Kael called out, each footfall deliberate, echoing softly in the transformed sanctuary. No response came, only the faint rustling of leaves that served as a cruel reminder of the desolate abandon they were in.

Turning his gaze upon Vorathor's remains, Kael couldn't help but marvel at the power required to fell such a beast. Rider's newly awakened power was raw and untamed—the very same power that now left him uncon-scious and vulnerable on the soft earth of the bog.

Kael's heart thundered in his chest, his eyes locked onto Ariella's crumpled form. Her once-vibrant aura was now a faint, flickering wisp amid the gloom. The residual eldritch energy that hung thick in the air like a shroud of despair clawed at his senses, but he pushed forward, stepping past the ghastly tableau of undead carnage strewn across the bog.

"Stay with me, Ariella," Kael pleaded as he knelt beside her, his hands radiating the soft, electric blue glow of his arcane power. He reached out, fingers trembling slightly, to brush a lock of auburn hair from her pallid face. Her skin was cold, and her shallow breaths whispered of a life teetering on the edge of oblivion.

Kael's mind raced through incantations and spells, each one falling from his lips in a torrent of desperation. Yet, for all his command of lightning and tempest, the healing arts eluded him. Beads of sweat formed upon his brow as he conjured currents of energy, attempting to jump-start her failing systems.

He growled, frustration mounting as each spell fizzled out, absorbed by the miasma of death that lingered in the air. His gaze flickered between Ariella and Rider—two friends, two souls he refused to lose to the dark embrace of the void.

The taste of iron and earth filled his mouth, the scent of charred flesh and damp moss assaulting his nostrils. Kael's ears rang with the silence of the aftermath, broken only by the distant call and crackling of his thwarted magic.

"Hold on, my friends," he whispered, a woeful mixture of acceptance and determination etching lines upon his face as he stood, positioning himself between his fallen comrades. His arms stretched out towards them, palms facing their still bodies, and he closed his eyes, drawing deep into his reserves.

"Let this be enough," he intoned, a raw plea resonating with the weight of his sacrifice. Lightning arced from his hands, not violent and chaotic, but steady and controlled, weaving a triad of life-giving energy between them.

The soft hum of power grew to a crescendo as Kael became the conduit, his own vitality flowing into Rider and Ariella. The blue light enveloped them, pulsating with each beat of Kael's heart, until, with a blinding flash that lit the night sky, the spell reached its zenith.

Kael's knees buckled, and he collapsed, each breath a labored gasp as darkness crept into the edges of his vision. Drained beyond measure, he kneeled among the remnants of battle, his final conscious thought a simple hope—that his friends would awaken from this nightmare.

Consciousness crept back into Rider like a slow thaw, his senses sharpening with each laborious breath. The bog's damp earthiness filled his nostrils, and the distant croak of frogs provided a somber backdrop to his awakening. His eyelids fluttered open to reveal Kael kneeling before him, an exhausted sentinel whose once-vibrant armor was now dulled and lightless.

"Kael..." Rider's voice was a hoarse whisper, barely carrying over the night's whispers. Memories flooded back —the clash of magic and steel, Ariella's broken form—and panic clawed at his chest. He turned his head, frantically searching, until he saw her. Ariella, still as death, lying on the cold ground bathed in moonlight.

"Ar... Ariella!" he choked out, pointing towards her with a trembling hand. Adrenaline surged through his veins, propelling him to unsteady feet. Each step was a battle against his own body, but fear for his lover lent him strength. He staggered, then broke into a desperate run toward Kael.

"Rider, wait," Kael's voice anchored him, calm and certain. "She will be well. I've made sure of it."

Relief washed over Rider, cooling the fire of his panic. He reached Kael and extended an arm, helping his friend rise from his penitent kneel. Together they approached Ariella, who lay between them like a fallen star.

"Can you hear me, Ariella?" Rider called softly, kneeling beside her. His fingers brushed her cheek, which carried the warmth of life rather than the chill of the grave.

Ariella's eyes fluttered open, revealing pools of violet that shimmered with unshed tears. She gasped, drawing in a ragged breath, and flung herself forward into their embrace. Her arms encircled them both, her touch tentative as if they could shatter like glass.

"Rider... Kael..." she murmured, her voice laced with disbelief. They held her, a trio united by bonds deeper than blood.

"How are we... alive?" Ariella's hands roamed over where fatal wounds had been, now finding only unmarred skin. Her gaze bounced between her friends, seeking an anchor in the surreal peace that followed the storm of violence.

"Kael," Rider explained, his tone thick with gratitude.

Their eyes met in silent acknowledgement as they looked at Kael's changed state, each aware of an untold price the mage must have paid. The bog around them, once a stage for carnage, now cradled them under a tapestry of stars, its serenity a stark contrast to the horrors they had faced.

"Thank you," Ariella whispered, her voice trembling in the hush of the aftermath. "For everything."

They remained there, locked in an embrace, the weight of survival pressing upon them. In the aftermath of terror and triumph, they found solace in each other's presence, the quiet understanding that they had overcome the darkness together.

Kael's eyes, once alight with the luster of storm clouds ready to burst, now carried a hazy softness—a calm after the tempest had raged and expended its fury. Rider and Ariella, still entwined in their embrace, turned to him, their faces etched with concern.

"Kael," Rider began, his voice unsteady, "how did you...?" The question hung between them, laden with the gravity of the unsaid.

The blond mage offered a rueful smile, his pale hand raising to rest upon a nearby stone, slick with the residue of arcane discharge. "The Spark that fueled my magic, it's nearly extinguished," he confessed, the words heavy like stones in his throat. "To save you both, I had to let most of it go."

"Most of it?" Ariella echoed, her jeweled eyes searching Kael's face as if trying to see past the surface, to gauge the depth of his loss.

"Aye." His nod was slow, almost imperceptible. "I retain but a whisper of the power I once commanded. My spells will be little more than... fancy tricks."

Rider's brows knitted together, a frown marring his features. He stepped forward, clasping Kael's shoulder firmly. "But is it permanent? Will the strength of your magic return?"

Kael exhaled, a wistful gaze cast towards the heavens where stars blinked into existence, as if whispering secrets of ancient magics from the void. "According to the teachings of the Astrala," he broke the silence, his voice gaining a timbre of reverence, "magic resides within all things—the rock beneath our boots, the air we breathe, even the marrow of our bones."

Ariella drew closer, her curiosity piqued by the promise of ancient wisdom. The bog that had witnessed their darkest hour now seemed to listen, its very essence holding its breath.

"Those few among us who can touch it directly—we Astralan call this connection our *'Spark.'* It can be ignited through rigorous study or in a crucible of dire need." Kael's hand gestured towards the firmament, tracing patterns only he could discern. "Once kindled, it can grow prodigiously, much like nurturing a flame into a roaring fire."

"Then there might be hope for you yet," Rider said, a note of optimism threading through his words.

"Indeed," Kael agreed, though his smile held a twinge of melancholy. "Our Spark can be fortified in many ways. One may claim the power of another through conquest, as a warrior might take up the weapon of a fallen foe."

"Or through diligence and practice," Ariella added softly, recalling the countless hours she had seen Kael immersed in his studies.

Kael nodded. "And finally, there exists the path I chose—sacrifice. To willingly pass one's essence to another, to bolster their flame at the cost of your own."

"Kael..." Ariella whispered, her heart swelling with the enormity of his gift.

"It is a weighty one," Kael finished, his voice barely above a murmur. "But know this, my friends, the Astralan believe not in endings, but in cycles. Today, I am diminished so that you may rise. Tomorrow, who can say what the weave of magic will bring?"

Rider clasped Kael's other shoulder, mirroring Ariella's gesture, drawing him into their circle of solace. "We'll face that tomorrow together," he vowed, his sapphire eyes glinting with unspoken promises.

"United," Ariella affirmed, her voice steadfast.

"United," Kael echoed, his spirit buoyed by their bond, even as the remnants of his Spark flickered dimly within him. Together they stood in the moonlit bog, surrounded by the whispers of life renewed, their shared resolve an unbreakable chain forged in the crucible of sacrifice.

Rider stood, his gaze fixed on the darkened sky above, where stars seemed to twinkle with a knowing light. He breathed deeply, the damp earthy scent of the bog filling his lungs as he recalled the chaotic whirlwind of magic and might that had culminated in Vorathor's demise.

"Kael," Rider began, his voice steady despite the adrenaline that still pulsed through his veins, "when I faced the Dragon, something... changed me. It was like a storm had awakened, and I could feel this intense power coursing through my body."

Ariella, her own Elven senses keenly attuned to the shifts in energy, nodded silently, encouraging him to continue.

"As Vorathor's head fell," Rider continued, "a surge of arcane energy flooded into me. It was wild, untamed—the raw essence of an ancient evil that refused to be snuffed out even in death."

Kael, who had been listening intently, interjected with a knowing look in his shimmering blue eyes. "You entered Aetherion Ascendance, Rider. It's a rare state, one that marks the true bonding between an Astralan warrior and their Arcane Spark. What you describe happened after-ward—that moment of overwhelming power—it's precisely what happens when one tends to their Spark by conquering another."

Rider furrowed his brow, concern etched onto his features. "How much of Vorathor's power do you think I've gained?"

"Power is not a mere commodity to be measured," Kael replied. "Vorathor was indeed powerful, a creature steeped in darkness and malice. But absorbing an Arcane Spark isn't straightforward. The capacity for magic varies from one individual to another, and it seems your own reservoir is vast if you were able to withstand his might and harness a force to fell him."

"Your potential is immense, Rider," Kael added, a soft smile playing on his lips. "With proper guidance, you could master this Aetherion Ascendance. If you'll have me, I would offer my teachings."

"Nothing would honor me more," Rider said, clasping Kael's shoulder in gratitude.

With their bond strengthened and their purpose renewed, the trio made the unanimous decision to return to Shadyvale. The need for rest gnawed at their weary bodies, and the importance of their findings weighed heavily on their minds. As they set off towards the town at the crossroads of kingdoms, the early tendrils of dawn brushed the horizon, painting the sky with hues of promise.

"We'll find respite in Shadyvale," Ariella said, her voice hopeful. "And then, we'll continue our journey to Brightspire."

"Rest and preparation are needed before we face what lies ahead," Kael agreed, his eyes reflecting the first light of day. "We have much to ponder, and our mission is far from over."

Their path back to Shadyvale was quiet, each lost in thoughts of the battles fought and the sacrifices made. The town slowly emerged in the distance, its familiar silhouette a welcome sight against the backdrop of a world still filled with mysteries yet to unravel.

The gates of Shadyvale loomed ahead as the sun dipped low once again, casting long shadows over the cobblestone path. Rider's boots clacked against the stones, as a glimmer of triumph sparked in his eyes. Kael strode beside him, his gaze scanning the ramparts, while Ariella walked with a grace that contradicted her recent brush with death.

"Captain Harrow," Rider called out as they approached the town guards, "we bring news regarding the disappearances."

The captain, a burly man with a grizzled beard and a scar tracing down his cheek, nodded gravely. "Speak, Rider. What have you found?"

"Vorathor, the green terror of the Great War," Ariella interjected, her voice steady and clear. "He has fallen by Rider's hand. No longer will he prey upon your travelers."

Murmurs rustled through the assembled militia like dry leaves in a breeze. Captain Harrow's eyes widened, and he stepped forward to clap Rider on the shoulder. "That's news worth celebrating! But come, tell us everything inside The Wolves' Den."

The tavern's raucous energy enveloped them as they entered, the comforting smell of roasted meat and spiced ale mingling in the air. Patrons turned their heads, curiosity etched on faces both Human and otherwise, as the heroes recounted their tale. With each word, the atmosphere shifted, respect replacing skepticism in the eyes of the listeners.

Over the following days, Rider felt the weight of

glances filled with awe and whispers of gratitude. He watched as merchants hawked their wares with renewed vigor, no longer fearful of the shadows the forest casted upon their routes.

"Seems you've become quite the legend," Kael remarked one evening, sipping at a mug of frothy ale.

"Legends don't fill bellies or mend wounds," Rider replied, though a smile tugged at his lips.

"True," Ariella chimed in. "But they inspire hearts and forge bonds. We've done good here."

As the moon rose high, casting silvery light through the tavern windows, Rider savored the taste of spiced venison, the warmth of companionship, and the soft hum of lutes playing in the background. His body healed, his spirit rejuvenated, he knew it was nearly time to leave.

"Tell us Kael, how is it that the Astralan not only knew about Vorathor, but had legends about him?" Rider asked.

"That's simple, Rider," Kael responded. "Vorathor, like me, was a traveler of the cosmos. My people have encountered him across numerous worlds. As I suspected since my stranded arrival here, there's a larger story unfolding here in Etonya," he finished.

On the morning of their departure, the trio stood at the crossroads, the scent of fresh pine and earth beneath their feet. They shouldered their packs, the leather straps worn but sturdy, and set their sights on the winding road to Brightspire.

"Ready for what comes next?" Kael asked, mounting his horse.

"Always," Rider responded, the blue smoky aura of his power a mere whisper behind his eyes.

"Then let's not keep fate waiting," Ariella said, her eyes sparkling with determination as she gazed at Rider.

"Toward destiny, then," Rider responded to her, remembering the first time they left Brightspire together.

"Toward destiny," Ariella smiled, as she responded in her own remembrance.

ACT III

CHAPTER XVII
TROUBLE AT COURT

The sun hung high above the well-traveled road, its golden light filtering through the foliage of the Emerald Forest to the west, casting dappled shadows on the path ahead. The verdant canopy whispered secrets in the gentle breeze, a stark contrast to the quiet majesty of the Jade Forest on the right, where the ancient trees stood tall like silent guardians.

Ariella Moonwhisper rode beside her companions, her violet eyes reflecting the lush landscape that had once been her training ground. They were not alone on the road; travelers passed them by, each with their own burdens and tales etched upon their weary faces. A merchant, his carriage laden with exotic wares, nodded courteously as he rolled past. A family on horseback, children's laughter mingling with the jingle of tack, offered friendly smiles. And solitary wanderers, cloaks billowing behind them, gave brief nods before continuing on their solitary paths.

"Tell us, Ariella," Rider said, breaking the companionable silence. "These woods seem close to your heart."

"Indeed, they are." Ariella's voice was rich with nostalgia. "My journey began in these forests. As a child of Brightspire's aristocracy, I was fortunate to receive tutelage in both archery and the arcane. My family, though not drowning in riches, provided a life of privilege and learning."

Kael, intrigued, urged his mount closer. "Your mastery of the bow is unrivaled, Ariella. How did such an affinity develop?"

"From the first time I nocked an arrow, I felt a kinship with the bow," she replied, her gaze tracing the familiar terrain. "These woods were my sanctuary. I practiced here, often until the moon claimed the sky. Over time, my instructors realized my potential—not just in marksmanship, but also in weaving magic into my arrows. Arcane arrow spells became my signature, a blend of heritage and personal pursuit."

"You speak of privilege, yet there's steel beneath your words," Kael observed, a note of respect threading his tone.

"Privilege can be a gilded cage," Ariella mused, her expression distant. "Brightspire's noble courts are rife with intrigue—a game I learned to navigate early. But it is out here, in the untamed wilds, where I truly honed my skills and learned what truly mattered. Resourcefulness and adaptability became my allies, for the forest cares not for titles or bloodlines."

The clip-clop of hooves against the cobblestone road provided a steady rhythm as Ariella, Rider, and Kael made their way northward. Travelers continued to flitter past them in the opposite direction—merchants driving loaded wagons bound for Shadyvale, weary pilgrims seeking solace in the Emerald Forest's embrace, and sprightly troubadours whose lilting melodies lingered long after they disappeared from sight.

"Those woods," Ariella continued, her voice carrying over the din of passing caravans, "were both my refuge and my schoolroom. It was there I learned to track and hunt. To trust my instincts."

Rider leaned forward, "And yet, you also mentioned the court's intrigue."

Ariella nodded, her gaze darkening. "I was but a child when it happened. A whisper here, a rumor there, and suddenly my family found itself entangled in a web of deceit spun by those we had considered friends and allies. Our coffers drained like wine at a festival, and our influence waned like the crescent moon. We remained nobles in name only, not in standing."

Kael frowned, his gaze fixed on the horizon. "Such treachery."

"Imagine being raised amidst opulence, only to watch it crumble through fingers like fine sand," she replied, her tone edged with steel. "It taught me that loyalty is often a masquerade, and that true power lies not in wealth, but in cunning and skill. So I honed those skills, blending courtly graces with the primal instincts of a huntress. I forged myself into something the courts couldn't manipulate. In doing so, I became an adept of both realms—able to parry with words or arrows."

"Adversity forged your spirit into something formidable," Rider said, admiration clear in his expression. "A rare combination."

"Lady Moonwhisper," Kael began. "Let me assure you, I have met countless warriors during my travels and your light shines brighter than most. It is an honor to walk beside you."

"Fortune favors the bold, or so the saying goes," Ariella quipped, a hint of a smile tugging at the corner of her mouth. "But let's speak of something else—the adventures that awaited us upon our meeting in Brightspire."

"Ah, the early days," Rider chuckled, recalling the exploits. "Do you remember how we scoured the bounty board at the Silver Harp?

"Indeed," Ariella said, her eyes gleaming with the thrill of nostalgia. "There was the time we tracked down that bandit camp nestled in the foothills—barely more than miscreants hiding in the shadows. We returned the stolen goods to the merchants, their gratitude filled our pockets modestly."

"Modestly, but enough to keep us fed and eager for more work," Rider interjected, his tone playful. "Then there were those cutpurses along the Queen's Road. You should have seen their faces when Ari loosed an arrow that burst into a net ensnaring them."

"An effective spell," Ariella admitted, her cheeks blushing slightly. "Though it was teamwork that truly ended their reign of mischief, Rider. Each task, no matter how small, brought us closer and tightened our coordination."

"Such praise," Rider mused, his gaze affectionate as he regarded Ariella. "We've come far since those days, haven't we? And yet, it seems our journey has only just begun."

"Indeed, it has," she agreed, her voice firm and filled with purpose.

"Truly, you two, to think my journey through the cosmos would lead me to witness such kinship. It's like a tale woven by the stars," Kael proclaimed, his voice tinged with the wisdom of one who had traveled far beyond this world.

"Don't sell yourself short, Kael," Rider countered, flashing a reassuring grin. "Your prowess has saved our skins more than once. You're more than a mere chronicler in our saga. You're a big part of it."

"Indeed," Ariella chimed in, her eyes softening as she regarded Kael. "You possess a rare spirit—one that will not be dimmed. We shall seek the counsel of High Queen Vyshaan. Her command of magic is rivaled only by her vast knowledge. She may hold the key to restoring your power."

"Vyshaan..." Kael murmured, the name sparking a hope within him that had lain dormant. "To harness the ether once more, to feel the raw energy coursing through my veins..."

"Then let us hasten!" Ariella declared, her hair catching the sunlight in fiery cascades as she spurred her mount forward. "For every moon we tarry, the forces against us grow stronger."

The hooves of their steeds pounded against the well-trodden path in a cadence of urgency. The tang of sweat from their exertion mingled with the fresh greenery around them, as the road to Brightspire unfurled beneath their determined charge.

The horizon shimmered with a brilliance unmatched in all Etonya as the distant silhouette of Brightspire began to carve itself into the azure canvas of the sky. The setting sun cast its golden glow, igniting the precious metals that adorned the Elven city's walls and foundations, transforming it into a living mosaic of light. From the well-trodden road, the kingdom appeared as a constellation of floating islands, each tethered to the other by elegant bridges seemingly spun from dreams.

"By the stars," Kael breathed, his voice catching on the sight. "I've traversed realms aplenty, but nothing...nothing quite like this."

"Wait until you see it up close," Ariella said, pride

shining in her voice as she glanced over at him, her hair a flame against the dying light.

Waterfalls of magic cascaded from the main castle, pouring into the Crystal Sea below, their luminescence rivaling the celestial bodies above. Platforms moved between islands, carrying cloaked figures whose silhouettes danced in the enchantment of the falls. Below, the massive port buzzed with life, nearly a city unto itself, echoing the vitality of Shadyvale but with a grace unique to Elvenkind.

"It rivals even the best Astralan cities," Kael admitted, his gaze transfixed.

"Feel that?" Rider asked, motioning towards the cityscape with an open palm. "The air thrums with power here."

Kael nodded, closing his eyes for a moment to let the atmosphere wash over him. Energy pulsed in layers, a living current beneath every cobblestone, every sigh of the wind. It stirred something in his soul. They pressed forward, hooves thundering rhythmically, each beat drawing them nearer to the heart of Brightspire.

As they approached the lower port, the scents of saltwater mingled with exotic spices carried on the breeze, teasing their senses. The clamor of dockworkers and the creaking of ships' timbers became the soundtrack to their entry, while mages haggled over artifacts imbued with ancient spells. It was a convergence of commerce and sorcery, an intoxicating blend that made Kael's heart race with anticipation and familiarity.

"Feels like home, doesn't it?" Ariella remarked, her eyes reflecting the myriad sparks of light that danced around them.

"Yes," Kael replied softly, a smile of genuine contentment spreading across his face. "A different resonance, yet akin to the heartbeat of my own world."

"Then let's ride," Rider declared with determined cheer. "Brightspire's splendor is only matched by its secrets, and we have much to uncover before dusk falls."

The bustling port of Brightspire teemed with life as the trio waded through a tide of travelers. Merchants hawked their shimmering wares, and the air was thick with the scents of roasting meats and spiced wines. A sea of voices and dialects blended with the calls of seabirds, creating a vibrant tapestry of sound that was unique to this magical metropolis.

"Keep close," Ariella murmured, her eyes scanning the throngs. "The guards here are vigilant."

Rider nodded, his hand eager for his sheathed sword, its presence unspoken but unmistakable. Kael's gaze lingered on a stall displaying scrolls etched with arcane symbols, but at Ariella's prompting, he tore his attention away and followed.

They skirted the queue for entry, the privilege of notoriety escorting them past weary faces and impatient grumbles. It wasn't long before a quartet of guards, clad in gleaming armor embossed with the crest of Brightspire, parted the crowd like a ship's bow cutting through water.

"By the stars, it's Ariella Moonwhisper!" one guard exclaimed, his voice carrying over the din. "And Rider too!"

"Indeed," Ariella began, her tone measured. "We bring urgent—"

But her words were cut short as the guard stepped forward, urgency creasing his brow. "You'll need to come with us. The Queen desires an audience."

Rider and Kael exchanged a look, unspoken words passing between them. Something about the guards' haste tingled the edges of caution within their seasoned minds.

"Lead on," Ariella said, masking her surprise with

poise. She motioned to her companions. "Let's not keep her majesty waiting."

As they navigated the city's winding avenues, the fragrance of blooming night jasmine mingled with the more mundane odors of city life. Magic-fed lamps bathed the streets in soft luminescence, casting elongated shadows that seemed to dance upon the cobbled stones.

"Notice anything... off?" Kael whispered, leaning toward Rider. His keen eyes spotted additional guards merging into their escort from intersecting alleys.

"Too many guards," Rider replied tersely and with a slight nod, his sapphire gaze sharp.

Ariella, meanwhile, attempted to engage the lead guard in conversation. "What news of Brightspire? Any changes since our departure?"

"Many things, Lady Moonwhisper," the guard responded, though his voice was clipped, his steps never faltering. "Best saved for the Queen's telling."

Her attempt thwarted, Ariella fell silent. Her mind churned with curiosity and an unease coiled within her. They continued their march, passing beneath archways of living vines and traversing bridges suspended by nothing but spells, the city's grandeur undiminished by the creeping sense of foreboding.

At last, the royal gates loomed before them, their towering presence both welcoming and imposing. It was here, on the threshold of the court, where destiny awaited —with whispers of intrigue carried on the wind.

The royal gates, gilded and grandiose, swung open with a silence that contradicted their massive form. The guards motioned them inside, their gestures sharp and rushed. Kael's eyes narrowed as he took in the sight—too many glances exchanged, too swift a welcome for comfort. Beside him, Rider's hand twitched as he adjusted his fingers, a subtle readiness that spoke volumes.

"Something is amiss," Kael murmured, just loud enough for Rider to hear.

"Agreed. But let's not show our hand just yet," Rider replied, his voice low.

They stepped into the grandeur of the courtroom, high ceilings arched like the very heavens above, adorned with frescoes that depicted the storied history of Brightspire. Despite the opulence, a chill hung in the air, a tension that prickled at the skin. Ariella, however, strode forward with the confidence of one returning home, her violet eyes bright with the anticipation of reunion.

"Your Majesty," she began, her voice carrying clearly through the chamber. "We have returned with—"

But Queen Vyshaan, imposing in her regality, raised a slender hand adorned with rings that sparkled with arcane energy. With a flick of her wrist, a silent wave rolled forth that stifled Ariella's words in her throat. From across the room, Ariella's bow—an extension of her soul—soared into the Queen's waiting grasp.

"Wha—" Ariella's shock was palpable, her mouth moving wordlessly as her cherished weapon found a new master.

Rider stepped forward, his charm momentarily forgotten in the face of this unexpected hostility. "Your Grace, we—"

"Silence!" The Queen's snapped, voice as sharp as a blade's edge. "You were warned, Rider. Failure was not an option. My wrath is as fearsome as my generosity is great."

"Queen Vyshaan, please, allow me to introduce Kael Stormbringer," Rider attempted, hoping to salvage the situation.

"Kael Stormbringer?" The Queen's lips curled into a

sneer. "I need no introduction to trespassers. Your audacity wounds me, Rider."

"Please, forgive the slight," Rider began, but his apology was swept aside by the tempest of the Queen's ire.

"Enough! I see all within my realm, and beyond." Her gaze, piercing as ice, fixed upon each of them in turn.

"Your Majesty, we have not faltered. Our mission against the cult thrives," Rider said, his tone earnest. "Less than a fortnight past, I struck down Vorathor, one of the ancient servants..."

His words hung between them, the gravity of their deeds heavy in the air. The Queen's expression, unreadable for a moment, promised a storm on the horizon—one that could change the fate of Brightspire and its champions forever.

"Vorathor?" The Queen's voice trembled with a rage that seemed to shake the very foundations of the throne room. "You dare slay one of Drakzeneth Maleficarum's servants!" As her anger boiled over, a slip of the tongue revealed a truth that chilled the air. "One of my greatest generals!"

The atmosphere congealed into something thick and foreboding. Rider's eyes narrowed as he caught the implication. He shook his head almost imperceptibly at Kael, a silent warning that the entity before them was no ally but an ancient nemesis clad in the guise of the queen.

Understanding dawned upon Kael, with hope as his catalyst, he secretly wove an incantation with the slightest movement of his fingertips—the Astralan runes shimmering into existence around his fingers. With more of a plea to the cosmos itself than a proper spell, he spoke out, "The light of the stars commands you to reveal yourself," his voice clear and resonant.

The Queen raised her hand in a swift motion,

expecting to quash Kael's defiance as easily as snuffing out a candle flame. But the words hung in the air, untouched by her magic, protected by Kael's Astralan spellwork.

A silence descended, broken only by the crackling energy that now emanated from the Queen's form. Her visage, once regal, began to contort. Not from rage, but as though something beneath the surface clawed its way free. A spectral figure rose like smoke from a pyre—a towering presence wrapped in tendrils of shadow and mist.

Drakzeneth Maleficarum's spirit unveiled itself, engulfing the courtroom in a penumbra of dread. His eyes were orbs of infernal fire, casting a baleful glow that sliced through the gloom. Ethereal scales, like the remnants of an ancient armor, adorned his ghostly frame—faint glimmers of his draconic majesty.

"Behold," Kael breathed, "your queen's possessor."

Rider's hand instinctively went to his sword hilt, though he knew steel would be of little use against such a foe. Yet it was not just fear that gripped him; it was the betrayal of seeing Ariella's once-beloved queen reduced to a vessel for such darkness.

"Drakzeneth," Ariella whispered, now able to speak, the name tasting of ash upon her lips.

The specter that had been their queen, now fully revealed, loomed over them all. His presence felt like a suffocating weight upon their souls. They stood, united in their resolve yet divided by the creeping tendrils of despair, facing an enemy whose malice had transcended time itself.

"Fight!" Rider's voice cut through the silence, a rallying cry as he drew his longsword with a metallic song. The blade shimmered in his grip, and he lunged forward, striking at the guards to his right with precise, practiced slashes. Desperation and skill wove through his motions, each strike an arc of silver against the once loyal queen's guard.

Ariella, bereft of her bow and the familiar weight of her arrows, called upon the dual blades in her hands. Not her preferred tools, but she wielded them with practiced grace. She spun, her twin blades whirling a deadly pattern around her, striking at one of the eight corrupted courtiers now advancing upon them.

"*Vistara el'lythos amin'karyn!*" Kael incanted, his voice strained but determined as he summoned what magic he could muster. Pockets of light erupted among the shadows, disorienting the possessed guards who shielded their eyes from the sudden brilliance. From the folds of his cloak, he produced a glowing orb, hurling the trinket into the fray where it exploded into writhing tendrils of binding energy, ensnaring their foes in a web of arcane restraint for Rider and Ariella to finish.

The throne room of Brightspire became a maelstrom of clashing energies and flesh, its once hallowed ground marred by the dark incantations the Queen's corrupted court now launched at the heroes. The stone walls, etched with the noble histories of old, now bore witness to betrayal and murderous intent.

"Steel yourself!" Rider bellowed, his voice a warhorn amidst the fray. He could feel the thrum of Vorathor's Arcane Spark within him, lending a preternatural swiftness to his blade. An ice spike hurled toward him, he parried it with a deft maneuver and countered with a devastating arc of his longsword, severing the mage that dared challenge him.

Ariella's twin blades sang through the melee, a deadly dance of steel and shadow. "You disgrace our great kingdom," she snarled, twirling beneath a fireball and skewering her assailant upon her shimmering blades. Acrobatics were her verse, each leap and lunge a stanza in the symphony of combat. A backflip onto a table sent scrolls and tomes scattering; she used the momentum to launch herself at another mage.

The Queen, a silent sentinel amidst the chaos, radiated a darkness that threatened to engulf the room. Kael's wards around her flickered like candle flames in a tempest, barely containing the Dragon Lord's spirit clawing at its prison with ethereal tendrils. It writhed behind her lifeless eyes, a storm of malevolence waiting to break free.

As Rider slashed through the last challenger standing before them, a crack like thunder echoed through the throne room. The wards shattered, sending shards of light fading into oblivion. "No!" Kael gasped, his heart sinking as Drakzeneth's essence recoiled into the Iron Sorceress.

Her eyes turned a soulless black. With an ear-splitting scream, she unleashed a torrent of soul-scouring force. Ariella and Kael flew like ragdolls, as they slammed into the walls with bone-jarring force. Only a smoky blue aura stood stalwart against the eldritch onslaught. The Aetherion Ascendance had transformed Rider once more into a bastion against darkness.

Rider had braced himself, his glowing longsword absorbing the brunt of the blast. The force had slid him backward, his boots carving lines in the marble floor, but he did not falter. Surprised by his instinctive and sudden transformation, he roared defiantly, "Is that all the great Dragon Lord can muster?" His voice changed and reverberated by the power of the Astralan.

Rider's muscles thrummed with newfound power, the smoky blue aura cascading up his frame like a celestial flame. He stared at his opponent, luminous energy crackling between his fingertips, an electric symphony playing upon his very skin. With the Aetherion Ascendance coursing through him, he felt invincible, unbound by the laws of man and magic.

"Time to dance, your malevolence," Rider called out, his voice carrying the weight of the cosmos, vibrant and alive with Astralan might. His feet propelled him forward like a comet across the night sky, each step leaving a faint afterimage as he charged the possessed Sorceress. The air sizzled around him, his longsword trailing arcs of arcane brilliance that hungered for the darkness before him.

Queen Vyshaan, her eyes abyssal voids, ceased her eldritch scream. Her focus shifted solely to the radiant warrior barreling towards her. She raised a hand, the air thickening around it, conjuring a smoking obsidian barrier to intercept Rider's assault.

Rider's blade met the barrier in a clash of light and shadow, as vibrant hues of azure battling against the consuming darkness of her defenses.

As Rider's blade pressed against the force of darkness before him, Drakzeneth's spectral form loomed over him.

"Such insolence!" Drakzeneth roared, his voice booming through the chamber. As if on command, the barrier erupted, sending Rider flying backwards. He crashed against a stone column and crumpled to the ground.

As Rider struggled to stand, a blend of voices began to echo in his head, filled with disdain and hatred.

"The filth of the Astralan spreads," they spat, watching Rider's ascension flicker and fade.

"Draining the leylines was supposed to keep your kind out," Drakzeneth's voices continued, their tone dark and menacing.

"But no matter, your Spark and the power you stole from Vorathor will soon be mine."

CHAPTER XVIII
THE BANSHEE'S WAIL

The courtroom of the spectral Drakzeneth was a maelstrom of fear and fury. Shadows churned like smoke in a gale, thick with the scent of impending death. The towering figure, wreathed in shadows and malice, summoned forth a scythe of eldritch darkness which hummed with a thirst for Rider's soul. Its blade, a slice of void itself, poised to sever head from shoulders, to steal both life and the Spark that crackled within.

"Kael, we need to leave—now!" Ariella called out, watching the scene unfold before her. She knew they could not win this fight, not against the Iron Queen possessed by the essence of the Dragon Lord himself.

"Agreed," Kael grunted, his eyes scanning for an escape amidst the chaos. Whispering an ancient prayer to himself, a plea for his arcane powers to heed his call just this once, Kael extended his arms forward, palms outward. The symbols tattooed onto his skin flickered to life, channeling the latent energies that permeated Brightspire's enchanted grounds. With a defiant shout, he released a burst of pure magical essence toward Drakzeneth.

The blast of light struck Drakzeneth like lightning cleaving the sky. The spectral entity roared in agony as the magical assault fractured his shadowy shell, revealing glimpses of the tortured soul trapped within.

"Window!" Rider bellowed, pointing towards the stained glass that depicted the history of Brightspire in vibrant hues. It was a masterpiece of artistry, but now, it would serve as their portal to freedom.

"Go!" Ariella shouted, slicing through an approaching guard's armor and kicking another in the chest to clear a path.

With their enemies momentarily staggered, the trio sprinted towards the window. Rider swung his sword, the blade singing as it shattered the glass into a thousand shards falling to the city below. Without hesitation, Rider launched himself through the fragmented aperture, feeling the rush of wind and the sting of glass as he tumbled into the unknown. Ariella followed, agile as ever, leaping through the jagged opening with grace despite her heart pounding against her ribs.

"Stars, guide us," Kael murmured, with a final glance at the throne room turned battlefield before hurling himself through the window into the open air beyond.

The fall was dizzying, the world a blur of color and sound as they plummeted towards the city below.

Ariella's auburn hair whipped around her as she dove, increasing her speed to pass Rider. With an acrobat's precision, she angled her body, her cloak billowing like wings. As the city rushed up to meet her, she spotted a series of overhanging canopies and protruding balconies—stepping stones in the sky. The Elven reflexes honed in the very forests she had spoken of earlier now saved her. Twisting mid-air, she skimmed a canopy that rippled violently under her weight. Pushing off with the balls of her feet, she leaped onto another, rolled, and sprang off again. Each movement was fluid, a dance against death as she descended, until finally, her boots kissed the cobblestone with barely a sound.

"Rider!" Ariella's call was sharp as she searched the dark sky.

There, silhouetted against the moon, Rider plummeted, power swirling around him. Yet it wasn't terror that dominated—it was exhilaration, the thrill of newfound power coursing through his veins. With a defiant cry, he thrust his left hand downward, a torrent of azure energy pouring forth. The stream of magic collided with the stone, creating a cushion that slowed his descent to a mere drift.

"Ha! Would you look at that?" Rider's laugh was a wild thing, untamed as he landed with a flourish, the sapphire glow fading from his palm. "I'm starting to enjoy this magic business."

"Enjoy it later. We must move," Ariella said, her ears picking up the distant shouts and clanging of armor of those on the hunt for them.

"Your turn, mage!" she called up to Kael, her voice tinged with concern.

Kael's descent was less graceful, but no less calculated. His fingers attempted to draw sigils that glowed faintly before releasing puffs of wind. He winced when his shoulder scraped against a stone gargoyle as he ricocheted from another wall with a small burst of air, tumbling towards a merchant's awning. A brush against stone slowed his fall, until he slid down the last few feet, landing with a roll that carried him into an alleyway. He rose, dusting off his armored vest and tattered cape, his heart racing yet his body mostly unscathed.

"Kael, you all right?" Rider called out, scanning the chaos for his companions.

"Present," Kael announced, stepping from the shadows of the alley, his gaze lingering on the towering spires of Brightspire above them.

The trio dashed through the narrow alleyways, their boots splashing in murky puddles as they evaded the clutches of darkness. The city was alive with chaos—whether from the throne room's devastation or whispers of treachery, they didn't know. But the scent of blood was on the air, and the rhythm of pursuit echoed behind them.

"We can't keep running in circles," Ariella hissed, her Elven eyes darting to every shadow that moved.

"Agreed," Rider panted, sword still drawn. "We need to get out of Brightspire, warn the others."

"Without being seen," Kael added, a hint of desperation in his tone.

"Like shadows," Ariella murmured, her gaze fixed on the treacherous skyline of the city they once called home.

"Shadows, indeed," came a gruff voice from behind them.

They spun around, weapons raised, but what greeted them wasn't an enemy. It was an opportunity.

"Who are you?" Rider demanded, eyeing the newcomer warily.

"Name's Hawke," the sailor said with a crooked grin, tipping his captain's hat slightly. His trench coat shifted, revealing the gleam of pistols and the curve of a sea-worn scimitar. "I'm the one offering you a way out."

"Lead the way," Rider said after a tense moment of glances between his allies. The city was closing in around them.

They slipped through the labyrinthine backstreets, the tang of saltwater growing stronger with each step. Hawke led them to a nondescript door tucked away beneath a tangle of overgrown ivy. Inside, the musty smell of old wood and the creak of the floorboards underfoot accompanied their descent into the bowels of the city. The air grew cooler as they descended into a grotto, their footsteps echoing off the cavern walls adorned with luminescent fungi that painted the space in ethereal blues and greens.

"Welcome to our humble abode," Hawke declared, sweeping an arm across the expansive cave that unfolded before them. "Hidden right under their noses," he quipped.

Ariella's breath caught at the sight. The hideout was alive with activity—pirates sharpening blades, cleaning flintlocks, or sharing stories over mugs of ale. Ropes and wooden planks criss-crossed above, connecting platforms that served as lookouts and perches. Chests overflowing with glittering coins and jewels hinted at their plunderous ventures.

"Remarkable," she whispered, taking in the scent of brine mixed with tobacco and the unmistakable tang of adventure.

"Indeed," Kael agreed, his eyes reflecting the flicker of torchlight that danced upon the walls.

"Here, you're out of sight and out of reach," Hawke said, leading them past barrels of gunpowder and crates stamped with foreign seals. "And if you're inclined to help us with a certain... acquisition, we might just consider smuggling you out of the kingdom."

"An acquisition?" Rider arched an eyebrow but kept quiet, knowing that any port in a storm was a chance worth taking.

Hawke leaned against a sturdy oak table, strewn with nautical charts and flickering candles. "Gentlefolk," he began, his voice as smooth as aged rum, "we've got a mutual interest in seeing you free from Vyshaan's iron grip."

Rider nodded, his sapphire eyes sharp with anticipation. "Go on," he urged, his fingers absentmindedly tracing the hilt of his sheathed dagger.

"The Banshee's Wail," Hawke said, tapping the parchment where the silhouette of a grand vessel was sketched. "Vyshaan's prized flagship, and by fortune's favor, it docks tonight for supplies. Help us take it, and you've got your escape—and we gain a ship that'll turn the tides of our fortune."

Ariella's violet eyes widened, her surprise mirroring the gasp that escaped her lips. "Steal the Banshee's Wail? That's... ambitious." She paced around the table, her Elven grace evident in every step. "What madness drives this plan? The security will be impenetrable!"

"Ah, but chaos is a ladder, my fair Elf," Hawke retorted with a roguish wink. "And there's enough chaos on the streets. The guards are scattered, searching for you lot. Our window is open, but it won't stay so."

Rider's gaze bounced between his companions, weighing options and risks. "It's bold, I'll give you that. But what assurance do we have that you'll hold to your word?"

"Assurance?" Hawke chuckled, pushing off the table to pour himself a drink from a nearby decanter. "My dear fellow, in times like these, our word is all we have. Besides, we're not so different, you and I—seekers of fortune, lovers of freedom."

Kael, who had been quietly observing, abruptly stood from the stool, his eyes scanning the grotto's recesses. Shadows seemed to play just beyond the reach of the torchlight, whispering secrets only he could hear.

"Something wrong, Kael?" Rider asked, rising to his feet, his tone laced with concern.

"Shadows," Kael murmured, more to himself than to his comrades. "They're restless tonight." His hand hovered above his magical breastplate, feeling the thrum of arcane energy at his fingertips. "We must remain vigilant."

"Restless shadows or not," Ariella interjected, returning to the matter at hand, "we need a plan that accounts for every variable. The Banshee's Wail is no mere merchant vessel—it's enchanted, bound to the Queen herself. How do you intend to break such spells?"

Hawke took a slow sip of his drink, savoring the burn before setting the glass down with a decisive click. "That, my friends, is where magic meets guile. We have ways of dealing with enchantments. And with your help, we'll have ways of dealing with whatever else the night throws our way."

They huddled closer, conspiring under the watchful eyes of the grotto's luminescent fungi. They were united by necessity, bonded by a shared enemy, and driven by the very essence of adventure that pulsed through the veins of the Crystal Sea.

"We're not alone, Rider," Kael warned as he flooded the pirate grotto with radiant light. Kael's hands were trembling, not from fear but from the sheer exertion of conjuring the massive amount of light. The shadows that had crept along the walls like sinister specters recoiled as if burned by the intense, gleaming aura that radiated from him. Cascading waves of light rippled outward, bathing the cavern in a brilliance that made the luminescent fungi lining the walls pale in comparison. The luminescent aura seemed to shrink back into Kael as the shadows pushed back the magelight seeking to repel their darkness before being pushed out once again.

"Kael! How long can you hold it?" Ariella shouted over the din of battle between darkness and light.

Rider, with a swift motion, unsheathed his sword—the metallic ring of blade against scabbard seemed to sing in defiance of the encroaching gloom. His eyes scanned the edges of the room for any breach where darkness might seep through, his body tensed and ready for whatever emerged.

"I... can't... stop it," Kael gasped, his voice ragged as he fought to maintain the spell. "I... don't... have enough... magic." His words were punctuated by a flicker, then a glow, then the shadows as they gnashed at the edges of his faltering barrier, as his light died out.

Zara Nightshadow appeared, stepping gracefully out of a shadow on the wall. Her entrance was silent, yet her presence commanded attention, the stark contrast between her dark attire and the golden laced mirror beside her on the wall, creating an almost ethereal silhouette.

"Close one," she quipped, brushing off imaginary dust from her leather bracers. "The shadows are thicker than usual tonight. I nearly got lost in between them."

"Zara!" Rider exclaimed, a mix of relief and shock etched across his face, as he slid his sword back into its sheath.

"By the ancients," Ariella breathed, her eyes wide with astonishment. "We believed you lost to us."

"Lost? Never," Zara replied, her smirk barely visible. "Merely... shadow-walking."

"Where did you learn such magic?" Kael inquired, his tone laden with both intrigue and deep concern. He knew the dangers that came with delving too deeply into the arcane, especially when it bordered on forbidden arts.

"I take it I have you to thank for my delayed arrival?" Zara responded snidely. "Let's just say I've walked through more than my share of darkness," Zara said cryptically, her gaze meeting Kael's with an intensity that suggested untold stories.

The room filled with a charged silence, every eye fixed on the enigmatic figure who had returned from the shadows—Zara Nightshadow, the mentor and spy, whose sudden arrival promised new hope against the tides of encroaching darkness.

Zara's gaze lingered on Kael, a certain solemnity replacing the earlier mischief in her eyes. "In service to Queen Vyshaan, I infiltrated the cult," she explained, her voice low and steady, as if each word was being pulled from a deep well of secrecy. "During that mission, I encountered an artifact meant for our monarch."

Ariella leaned in, curiosity etched into her fine features. Rider, too, appeared captivated by Zara's confession.

"Upon touching the relic, its power surged through me, unbidden," Zara continued, her fingers reflexively curling. "It granted me dominion over shadows, allowing me to traverse their depths at will." She moved her hand through the air, and for a moment, it seemed as if the darkness itself caressed her skin.

"Shadow magic," Kael murmured, a frown creasing his brow. "It is a perilous path you tread, Zara. Many Astralan have delved into those veiled arts only to lose themselves to madness."

"Your concern is noted, mage." Zara waved a hand dismissively. "But the shadows have whispered no secrets to me, nor led me astray. They are but a tool, like any other arcane force."

"Even the most disciplined mind can be eroded by such forces," Kael pressed, his blue eyes reflecting the flickering torchlight that danced around the grotto. The scent of seaweed and brine wafted from the hidden waterways nearby, mingling with the earthen musk of the cave.

"Enough, Kael," Ariella interjected softly, placing a gentle hand on his armored forearm. "Zara has proven herself time and again."

"Indeed," Zara said, stepping forward. "But there's more pressing news. Queen Vyshaan... she's been ensnared by cultist trickery."

"Far worse," Ariella whispered, her gaze falling. "She's possessed by Drakzeneth himself."

"Drakzeneth?" The name fell from Zara's lips like a stone into still waters, sending ripples of shock across her normally composed demeanor. Her breath caught, and she faltered back a step, her hand finding support against the rough cavern wall. "The Dragon Lord... in Vyshaan?"

"His darkness threatened to consume us all within the queen's very court," Rider explained, his voice tinged with the weight of the encounter. "We almost didn't escape, Zara."

"My Queen..." Zara's voice was barely audible above the distant sound of lapping waves. She closed her eyes, taking in a shuddering breath. When she opened them again, the resolve had returned to her stare. "I failed her. And now, Etonya teeters on the brink once more."

"You did what you could," Ariella reassured her, reaching out to clasp Zara's shoulder. "We all bear the weight of this battle, not just you."

"Indeed," Kael agreed, nodularity returning to his tone. "Together, we must kindle hope against this evil. Your skills, your knowledge—they may be the very keys we need."

"Then stay by your side, I shall," Zara vowed, her voice firm, unwavering. "Until Drakzeneth's hold is broken, or until the light fades from my soul."

"Let it be so," Rider intoned solemnly, meeting each of their gazes in turn.

The sea-salt air intermingled with the mustiness of the pirate grotto as Hawke's boisterous laugh cut through the tension knotted between the heroes. "Well, this is a fortuitous twist of fate!" he exclaimed, clapping his hands together with ill-concealed glee. "An extra pair of stealthy hands to help liberate *my* boat." His grin was wide, eyes gleaming like the polished flintlocks that adorned his leather-clad chest.

"Your... boat?" Zara inquired, one eyebrow arched in amusement.

"Ah, The Banshee's Wail," Hawke corrected with mock propriety, stretching the words out like the unfurling of a sail. "Tonight, she sets off on a maiden voyage under new command." He paced before them, the click of his boots against stone setting a rhythm to his words. "Our beloved Queen's navy jewel, docking tonight for resupply—a rare and secret occasion."

"Which you know because…?" Rider prodded, leaning forward.

"Let's just say, some schedules are best shared among friends," Hawke winked, producing a worn parchment from his coat. "We've been eyeing this heist for months."

"Then the chaos we've sown has only sweetened your pot," Kael surmised, arms folded across his chest.

"Exactly," Hawke agreed, pointing a finger skyward. "While the city's guard scours Brightspire for you lot, we'll be pilfering their prize vessel right under their noses."

"Tell us your plan," Ariella demanded, her tone leaving no room for further antics.

Hawke nodded, the corner of his mouth twitching upwards. "Simple elegance. We split into two teams—one to silence the docks, another to board The Banshee's Wail undetected. I have my men stationed already, eager for the signal. You four—" he gestured to each in turn, "—will grace the ship with your unique... talents."

"Assassinations? Incapacitations?" Zara pressed, shadows dancing at the edge of her vision.

"Whatever ensures silence," Hawke replied with a shrug. "We take the night—and the ship."

The harbor lay drenched in moonlight, a canvas of shadows and silver. The team moved with quiet precision, each step a whisper against the cobblestone. Rider's hand crackled faintly with arcane energy, ready to burst forth. Kael's breaths were measured, his focus attuned to the slightest disturbance. Ariella's Elven senses cut through the darkness, every rustle of fabric or creak of wood amplified in her ears. And Zara was the shadow itself, slipping in and out of visibility with grace.

"Two guards ahead, by the main gate," Ariella murmured, her eyes narrowing.

"Leave them to me," Zara breathed, melding into the darkness.

There was no sound, not even a struggle, just the soft thud of bodies collapsing into unconsciousness, hidden from view beneath an overhang.

"Clear," Zara's voice came, almost from nowhere.

"Nicely done," Rider whispered back, leading them onward.

Hawke's pirates, cloaked in obscurity, dispatched dock workers and loitering sailors with swift, silent strokes. Not a cry escaped; not an alarm was raised.

"Rider, with me," Kael signaled, pointing to a scaffold. "We ascend."

"Zara, Ariella, the stern," Hawke directed, his tone low but commanding.

As Rider and Kael scaled the wall with the aid of conjured gusts, Ariella leaped, agile as a cat, onto the deck where a pair of guards stood watch. They barely had time to register her presence before she struck, twin blades finding their marks with lethal efficiency.

"Deck's ours," she called softly, scanning for more threats.

Zara emerged from the bowels of the ship, her handiwork evident in the trail of incapacitated guards left in her wake. "Below decks are clear."

"Good. Now, to work," Hawke said, joining them aboard. "Positions, everyone. Cut lines, raise anchor. This beauty sails with us tonight."

"Smooth as silk," Rider commented, unable to suppress a smile.

"Like she was always meant to be ours," Hawke boasted, his hand resting affectionately on the ship's wheel.

"Let's not celebrate just yet," Zara warned, her eyes reflecting the stars above. "The hardest part comes after our escape."

"Agreed," Kael added solemnly. "But for now, we sail. And Brightspire's tyranny wanes with each wave we leave behind."

They set about their tasks with renewed vigor, each action bringing them closer to freedom, their unity binding them tighter than the strongest ship's rope. The Banshee's Wail, once the pride of a corrupted crown, would now bear the weight of their rebellion and the hope of all Etonya.

Hawke's whistle cut through the air, piercing and clear—a signal to his crew lurking in the shadows. Within moments, dark figures emerged from their hiding places along the docks and swarmed aboard The Banshee's Wail. Their movements were swift and practiced, each one knowing their role in this finely-tuned choreography of piracy.

"Like clockwork," Hawke said, a smug grin on his weathered face as he watched his crew scurry about the deck with pride. "Each one of you is worth your weight in gold."

"Let's not start counting our coins just yet," Rider cautioned, casting a wary glance over the rail at the distant flicker of torches along the harbor.

"Ah, but I've always had a penchant for optimism," Hawke replied breezily, striding confidently around the helm. "Raise the sails! Let us taste the salt on our lips and feel the wind at our backs!"

The crew responded with enthusiastic shouts, hoisting the canvas high above as the ship began to creak and groan, eager to break free from its loosed moorings. Kael stood beside the mainmast, his eyes closed as he whispered an incantation, a gentle breeze picking up to fill the sails with a favorable wind.

Ariella's gaze swept across the bustling deck, her hand resting on the hilt of her sword. She could already feel the freedom of the open sea calling to them.

"Almost too easy, don't you think?" Zara murmured, appearing suddenly beside Ariella like a wraith. Her eyes glistened with the reflection of a distant fire.

"Easy or not, it's done. We're away," Ariella replied, her voice tinged with relief.

As The Banshee's Wail began to drift away from its berth, Hawke sauntered over near where Rider stood, his expression unreadable beneath the shadow of his captain's hat. Without warning, he drew one of his many flintlock pistols and aimed it squarely at Rider's head.

"Damn your eyes, Hawke!" Ariella gasped, her hand flying to her blade as Kael and Zara tensed, prepared to leap into action.

But before panic could truly take hold, Hawke's smirk broadened, and he squeezed the trigger. The shot whizzed past Rider's ear, so close that the whisper of its passage stirred his hair. It sailed unerring toward a nearby ship, striking a barrel which erupted in a violent explosion. The night sky lit up as flames leaped from vessel to vessel, the harbor thrown into pandemonium.

"Did ye really think I'd turn on our new friends?" Hawke chuckled, twirling the pistol with a flourish before sliding it back into its holster. "No, no. That was simply the grand finale of our little performance—insurance that my ship answers only to me."

"Your sense of humor will be the death of you, Hawke," Zara said, though the hint of a smile played at her lips.

"Or the making of legends," Hawke countered, placing both hands on the wheel and steering them toward the open sea. "Now, let's see what this beauty can do."

The Banshee's Wail surged into open water, its figurehead slicing the waves like a ghostly siren calling them forth. Behind them, Brightspire shrank into the distance, its harbor ablaze with chaos and confusion.

"Next time, let us know the whole plan," Rider said, shaking his head in disbelief yet unable to suppress a relieved laugh.

"Where would be the fun in that?" Hawke retorted, his gaze fixed upon the horizon.

The Banshee's Wail cut through the night, its sails billowing like the wings of a dark angel as it fled from the inferno that had once been Brightspire's pride. From the deck, the distant explosions and crackling flames played a symphony to the chaos they left behind. The pirates hooted and hollered around them, the thrill of conquest and destruction igniting their wild hearts.

"By the gods," Ariella murmured, her violet eyes reflecting the distant fires, "the city looks like a Dragon's maw."

"The city will survive," Zara replied, her voice low, "but our souls may bear the soot of this night forever."

"Ah, me beauties!" Hawke bellowed above the din, raising his mug high. Salt spray mingled with the taste of ash on the wind. "Ye've done more than earn yer share of plunder tonight! Look at 'em run! No navy'll dare cross swords with us now!"

"Indeed," Rider said, clapping Kael on the back, "we've not only clipped Drakzeneth's claws, but gained the mightiest ally on these waves."

Kael nodded, his blond hair flickering in the glow of destruction.

"And we sail under no banner but our own. That, my friends, is true freedom. Yo ho!" Hawke roared in approval, then turned his gaze to the group with a sly grin.

"So, shall we chart a course for Stonefire, then?"

CHAPTER XIX
THE RETURN TO STONE

The Banshee's Wail cleaved through the crystalline waves with a prow as sharp as destiny, her sails billowing like the breath of tempests past. The ship's deck thrummed beneath Rider's boots, a constant vibration that hummed of urgency and escape. Above, the stars pierced the night's veil, indifferent to the turmoil below. Salt hung heavy in the air, mingling with the scent of charred timber carried from the distant Brightspire Port, now nothing more than a smoldering memory in their wake.

"Stonefire Mountain will hear of Vyshaan before the next moon," Rider muttered, his sapphire eyes reflecting the turmoil that churned within him. The chaos of the recent events had left an emotional imprint as deep as the grooves on the ship's wooden planks.

"Let them try to stop us now," Hawke declared, striding across the deck with the confidence of a man who'd just claimed the sea's most coveted prize. His laughter was a volley of cannon fire, spurring his pirates into another round of raucous celebration. They drank and sang shanties of conquest and future plunder, their joy a stark contrast to the gravity settling into the heroes' bones.

"Rest would do us good," Zara observed, her eyes turned upward, eyes tracing the glittering sprawl of constellations.

"But I find solace in these constellations," Kael responded, his voice soft.

"Then watch over us, Stormbringer," Rider said, clapping him on the shoulder. "I've no doubt the stars speak to you."

As the rest of the party began dispersing, seeking quiet in the ship's belly, Ariella's fingers brushed against Rider's, her touch electric. With a coy glance, she led him down the timber corridors, the creaks of the ship whispering secrets only they could hear.

One by one, doors closed behind their companions, until the hallway echoed with the solitary footsteps of two hearts pulsing in unison. Alone at last, they exchanged glances charged with desire and shared memories. Ahead, the dark hallway loomed, inviting and unknown—a haven for what was to come.

With a surge of passion, Rider pressed Ariella against the wall as they reached the end of the hallway. His strong hand held both of hers above her head, their fingers laced as their eyes locked, heat blooming in the space between them. He leaned in, claiming her lips with an intensity that spoke of longing and need. Their tongues danced together, a remembered language from nights beneath the stars of the Jade Forest.

Ariella's body trembled beneath his touch, her heart pounding. She struggled to contain her desire, pushing back against him with all the strength her small frame could muster. The sensation of his fingers exploring the contours of her body sent shivers down her spine, igniting a burning hunger deep within her core.

"Rider," she whispered breathlessly, "I need you."

They moved as one down the hallway, hands fumbling for unlocked doors, their yearning growing stronger with each passing moment. They ached for the connection they had shared in the Jade Forest, a memory now etched into their souls like a sacred vow.

At last, they found an unlocked door leading to private quarters fit for royalty. As the waves of the sea crashed outside, rising and falling in sync with their racing hearts, Ariella and Rider lost themselves in a whirlwind of passion and ecstasy. Their emotions burned like wildfire, consuming them entirely as they explored each other's bodies with newfound fervor. The taste of their lips, the feel of their skin, the heat of their breath against one another – it was a symphony of desire and longing that they had only begun to understand.

The moment they crossed the threshold into the lavish quarters, they were greeted by furniture adorned with gold and intricate carvings. A grand bed, draped in rich velvet, was positioned before a towering window offering a breath-taking view of the ocean beyond. Here, they would satiate their desires, surrendering to the tempestuous storm within them. The scent of exotic incense heavy in the air, mingling with the unmistakable aroma of desire.

Stumbling further into the room, their fingers traced feverishly over each other's bodies, as if attempting to memorize every curve and contour. The soft glow of enchanted candelabras cast dancing shadows on their lust-hazed faces. The royal bed before them beckoned entic-ingly, its plush velvet sheets and mountains of silk pillows promising a world of sensual delights.

"Please," Ariella gasped, her eyes filled with unbridled need. "I need you inside me."

Her words sent a shiver down Rider's spine, his manhood throbbing with anticipation. He grinned wickedly, grabbing her by the waist and pulling her flush against him. Their lips crashed together once more, tongues entwining in a passionate dance that left them both breathless.

In a frenzy of lust, they tore at each other's clothes, desperate to feel skin on skin. With each layer that fell away, their hunger intensified, driving them closer and closer to the precipice of ecstasy.

As soon as they were both fully exposed, Ariella dropped to her knees before Rider, her violet eyes smoldering with desire as she gazed up at his throbbing girth. She licked her lips hungrily. Without hesitation, she leaned forward and ran her tongue along the underside of his shaft, tracing the thick vein that pulsed with need. Rider's hips bucked instinctively, a soft hiss falling from his lips at the sensation.

"Fuuuck Ari." Rider let loose in a slow breath.

"Mmm, you taste divine," she purred, before taking the swollen head between her lips. Her mouth was hot and wet, enveloping him in exquisite sensation. She swirled her tongue around the sensitive crown, lapping up the pearly beads of desire that leaked from his tip.

Rider groaned, his fingers tangling in her silken hair as she took him deeper. Ariella hollowed her cheeks, and began sucking him feverishly. She reveled in the weight and heat of him on her tongue, her own desire pooling between her thighs.

Slowly, she bobbed her head, taking in more of him with each stroke. Saliva dripped down her chin as she worshiped his cock with needy slurps and licks. The sounds of her passionate mouth filled the room, mingling with Rider's grunts of pleasure.

"Fuck, Ariella," he rasped, his grip on her hair tightening. She merely moaned in response, the vibrations sending jolts of ecstasy through his body.

Ariella's eyes watered as she pushed forward, relaxing her throat to engulf him completely. Her nose nestled in the dark curls at the base as she throated him with sensual determination. She swallowed around his length, her throat massaging him in ripples of blissful sensation.

Rider's hips jerked involuntarily, trying to drive himself impossibly further into her eager mouth. Lost in her own hunger to taste and please him, she drew back gasping for air, strands of saliva and his desire connecting her swollen lips to his glistening shaft.

"I want to taste your cum," she whispered huskily, pumping him with her hand. "I've been craving this," she purred.

With a growl of surrender, Rider surrendered as she thrust him into her mouth once more. Ariella welcomed him readily, sucking and slurping with desperation. She could feel him pulsing on her tongue, his climax was building like a raging storm.

Rider groaned, his fingers tangling in her fiery hair as she eagerly devoured him. The sensation was exquisite, her warm tongue swirling around his length, teasing him mercilessly. He watched, entranced, as she continued to slide her mouth up and down his manhood eagerly as she swallowed him deeper, her eyes never leaving his.

"Gods, Ariella..." he managed to choke out, feeling his climax about to release. And when it finally came, she took it all, drinking down every last drop.

Finally, she released him, licking her lips to savor the taste of his pleasure. Her eyes glimmered with mischief and satisfaction. "Your taste..." Ariella whispered, rising to her feet with a smile and pressing her body against his. "I need more."

Rider couldn't deny her. With a growl of desire, he lifted her up and tossed her onto the bed, pinning her beneath him. He kissed his way down her lithe body until his mouth descended upon her glistening warmth, his tongue eagerly tasting her wetness. Her moans grew louder, her body writhing beneath him as he brought her closer and closer to the edge.

Her nails dug into the sheets, her body arching off the bed as he found her swollen nub. Her taste was ambrosia, and he knew he could feast on her forever. His tongue teased and flicked, sending waves of pleasure coursing through her body.

"Fuck… how are you so good at that," she panted, her breath catching in her throat. That was all the encouragement he needed. Her intoxicating taste filled his senses, spurring him onward in his relentless quest to bring her to the pinnacle of pleasure. As his tongue swirled and flicked against her sensitive clit, he slowly slid two fingers into her dripping entrance.

Ariella cried out, her body trembling as Rider's skilled fingers began pumping in and out, curling upwards to stroke the secret spot deep within her. The dual sensations of his fingers and tongue were exactly what she needed. Sparks of ecstasy danced along her nerve endings, building towards an explosive crescendo.

"Oh gods, Rider, don't stop," she panted, her fingers tangling in his dark hair, holding him firmly against her swollen lips.

He had no intention of relenting. Rider's fingers thrust faster, plunging deep before withdrawing with an upward curl, only to surge forward again. All the while, his tongue maintained its maddening rhythm against her, circling and flicking until Ariella was writhing beneath him.

Her walls clenched around his fingers as the first wave of ecstasy crashed over her. Ariella's back arched off the bed, a strangled cry tearing from her throat as the orgasm consumed her, but Rider refused to grant her respite. As the aftershocks coursed through her body, he continued his efforts, tongue lashing mercilessly against her.

"I can't...it's too much," Ariella whimpered, trying to squirm away from the intense stimulation. Rider's free arm snaked around her hips, holding her in place as he continued his sweet torment.

In one final, powerful lick, Ariella shattered beneath him again, her body convulsing in ecstasy. She cried out, her back arching off the bed as wave after wave of pleasure coursed through her body. As her orgasm ripped through her, Rider devoured her with fervor, not wanting to miss a single moment.

Ariella looked down at him, body trembling, panting and wild-eyed. "Now, Rider... fuck me."

He needed no further encouragement. He positioned himself between her creamy thighs as she lay sprawled across the edge of the lavish bed. With a slow, deliberate thrust, he sheathed himself inside her. They both moaned at the exquisite sensation, their bodies joining as one.

Ariella cried out in pleasure as she reached up, her nails now digging into his back as they moved together, their rhythm growing more frantic by the second. The primal sound of flesh slapping against flesh filled the room, punctuated by their impassioned cries of ecstasy.

"More, Rider!" she screamed. "Harder!"

With a feral growl, Rider flipped Ariella over, her creamy skin and perfect breasts pressed against the soft sheets. He positioned himself behind her, admiring the arch of her back and the curve of her ass as she eagerly pushed it towards him. His hands gripped her hips tightly as he entered her with a primal need, each subsequent thrust causing her to moan in pleasure.

"Yes, just like that!" she screamed, fisting the velvet sheets.

"Tell me you want it," Rider demanded, his voice gravelly with lust. "Tell me you want my cum inside you."

"Please, Rider!" Ariella cried out, her body trembling with need and anticipation. "I want your cum!"

And with one final powerful thrust, Rider gave her what she craved, emptying himself deep within her Elven body. Their cries of passion echoed through the luxurious chamber as they collapsed together in a passionate embrace.

As they lay in the aftermath, the world beyond the walls of their sanctuary seemed nonexistent, leaving only the sound of their racing hearts and the warmth of their passion.

Exhausted and sated, Ariella's limbs entwined with Rider's, her chest heaving against his as they both struggled to catch their breath. Her fingers traced idle patterns on his sweat-slicked skin, the soft touch eliciting a contented sigh from him.

"Rider," she murmured, her voice barely above a whisper. "Stay with me."

"Always," he replied, his arm tightening around her.

As the rhythm of Ariella's breathing deepened, Rider's consciousness began to drift, and the familiar tendrils of dreams wove into his mind. A shadow loomed over Stonefire Mountain, a figure wreathed in darkness wielded a warhammer that crashed against the earth with such might that it unleashed a blaze across the landscape. Flames licked hungrily at the mountain's base, as if attempting to devour the stone itself.

The inferno receded to reveal two majestic Dragons soaring above, their wings cutting through the smoke, claiming the peak as their dominion. A shiver ran through Rider's dream-self, filling him with a sense of impending doom.

Then the vision shifted, and he stood alongside his comrades, a bastion against the fiery onslaught of Queen Vyshaan, now a vessel for unspeakable dark power. Together, they pushed back against the encroaching flames, their determination unyielding. It was a battle for the future of Stonefire, for the very soul of Etonya.

An urgent knocking pulled Rider from the depths of slumber with a jolt. Hawke's voice, muffled but insistent, filtered through the door.

"Rider! We've made landfall in a hidden cove. Safe and secure, just shy of Stonefire Kingdom."

Rider blinked away the remnants of the dream, the images still seared into his mind. With gentle care not to disturb Ariella too abruptly, he whispered her name, his hand softly brushing her shoulder.

"Ariella... wake, my love. We have arrived."

Her violet eyes fluttered open, meeting his gaze with a sleepy smile that slowly transformed into alertness as she registered his words.

"Already?" she asked, her voice tinged with reluctance as she clung to the last threads of their shared intimacy.

"Time and tide wait for no one, not even for those entwined in passion," Rider said with a smile, pressing a tender kiss to her forehead. They rose together, limbs still languid but minds sharpened by the urgency of their quest.

Together, they dressed and prepared to face the world

once more, the memory of their night a talisman against the challenges that awaited them beyond the safety of The Banshee's Wail.

Rider emerged onto the top deck, Ariella by his side, just as the first rays of dawn cast a golden hue over the sails of The Banshee's Wail. The cool sea breeze was crisp with salt and pine, while the distant cries of gulls carried over the soft lap of waves. Hawke, leaning against the helm with casual authority, greeted them with a knowing smirk.

"Hope the night's rest did you both good," he said, his eyes glinting with unspoken jest.

"Better than good," Rider replied, matching the pirate captain's grin with a roguish twinkle of his own.

"Good to hear," Hawke chuckled, then he turned serious as he addressed the gathered heroes. "The Banshee's Wail has served us well, but she needs some... enhancements. My crew and I will stay behind to see to her needs."

"Your dedication to our cause is appreciated, Captain," Ariella responded, her voice laced with genuine respect that contradicted her cautious nature.

"Think nothing of it, my Elven lady," Hawke winked before turning away, barking orders to his crew.

Ariella and Rider exchanged glances, a silent understanding passing between them. They were allies with Hawke now, but whether Hawke's newfound commitment would hold remained to be seen.

Stepping onto the gangplank, the party descended into the hidden cove. Their boots crunched on the gravelly shore, the air rich with the musk of seaweed and wet rocks. The grotto loomed around them, its walls draped in moss and the drip-drip of condensation echoing like a quiet serenade. Sunlight filtered through the canopy above, dappling the ground with patches of light that danced to the rhythm of the swaying leaves.

"Quite the secret haven," murmured Kael, his voice hushed in reverence.

"Let's not linger," Rider urged, his hand resting on the hilt of his longsword. "Stonefire won't come any closer on its own."

The path ahead was rough-hewn, winding upwards into the mountains that towered over the cove. Stones skittered beneath their feet as they ascended, the smell of pine resin growing stronger with every step. A hawk cried overhead, its sharp call slicing through the rustle of the trees. Flashes of color caught their eyes as butterflies flitted by, their wings iridescent in the sunlight.

The way was steep and unyielding, testing their resolve. The heat of the day began to assert itself, sweat beading on brows and soaking through tunics. The taste of salt lingered on their lips, a reminder of the sea they had left behind.

"Water?" Ariella offered, extending a skin to Rider. He nodded gratefully, taking a deep draught of the cool liquid before handing it back.

"Thank you," he said, wiping his mouth with the back of his hand.

"Always," she returned softly, securing the water skin at her side.

As they climbed higher, the sound of the ocean receded, replaced by the occasional rumble from Stonefire Mountain. It was a constant, low growl, like the snoring of some great beast deep within the earth. The smell of sulfur tinged the air, a pungent reminder of the fire that lay at the heart of the kingdom they sought.

"Stay alert," Rider muttered, scanning the path ahead.

"The mountain has many secrets, some best left undisturbed."

"Agreed," Ariella added, her gaze wary as they surveyed the rocky terrain.

Together, the band of heroes pressed on, driven by their mission and bound by the shared memory of last night's revelations—revelations that fueled their determination to face whatever awaited them at Stonefire Kingdom.

The journey through the mountainous terrain was arduous, but the party pressed on with determination. As they rounded a bend in the path, they were met with the steely gazes of a group of Stonefire scouts, their crossbows aimed at the party's hearts. The tension in the air was palpable, it was clear that the scouts viewed them with suspicion.

"Who goes there?" barked the lead scout, his eyes narrowing as he assessed the party.

"Hail friends, it is I, Rider, and my companions," Rider replied cautiously, raising his hands to show he meant no harm. "We come bearing urgent news for King Ragnoc Blackhammer."

"News? Or more trouble like you've already brought upon us?" the scout retorted, clearly unconvinced. "Our kingdom still mourns the loss of Baelgor. How dare you show your face here again?"

"Believe me, we would have given anything to save Baelgor," Rider said earnestly. "But fate did not grant us that choice. Please, let us speak with the king. Time is of the essence, and the entire realm is at stake."

The scouts exchanged glances, their stony expressions unreadable. Finally, the lead scout nodded curtly. "We'll escort you and Lady Moonwhisper, but your other companions will remain in custody while Blackhammer decides what to do with you lot. Know this: any false move will be met with steel."

As they were led through the gates of Stonefire Kingdom, wary eyes followed their every step. The guards' hands rested on weapon hilts, and murmurs of distrust filtered through the ranks. Rider could feel the sting of accusation in each glance, the silent judgment for their perceived past transgressions, for the absence of Baelgor— an absence that left a void no words could fill.

"Rider, stay your heart," Ariella whispered, sensing his unease. "Only truth can light our path now."

He gave her a terse nod, grateful for her presence, as they were ushered into the throne room of King Ragnoc Blackhammer.

"King Ragnoc Blackhammer," Rider announced as they entered the throne room, "we come to warn of a peril that threatens every realm."

Ragnoc loomed before them, his armor gleaming dully in the torchlight, his warhammer resting beside the throne like a silent guardian. The smell of old leather and oil wafted from his presence, mingling with the subtle hint of ale on his breath.

"Why have you returned? To face judgment perhaps," Ragnoc questioned, his voice rumbling through the chamber.

"Queen Vyshaan is no longer herself," Ariella said, stepping forward. "Drakzeneth's soul has ensnared her being, plotting resurrection through the cult's dark magic."

"Drakzeneth?" Ragnoc's nostrils flared, the name sparking a fire in his gray eyes. "That vile wraith should remain in the abyss."

"He doesn't intend to stay there. It endangers your kin, our lands," Rider interjected, his voice tinged with the strain of their journey.

"Vyshaan's deceit runs deep," Ragnoc spat, "and Brightspire's shadow has long darkened my door. Why not let it fall?"

"Blackhammer!" Rider shouted back, putting all of Blackhammer's guards at the ready. "I came before you once warning of the darkness threatening your kingdom and you swore to join our alliance," Rider continued, meeting Ragnoc's gaze squarely.

King Ragnoc stood from his throne slowly, grabbing his warhammer as he rose, never taking his eyes off Rider.

"Baelgor's memory, I swear, I would have died in his stead if given the chance," Rider said in a lower and more respectful tone.

"So there is fire in your Human heart," Ragnoc bellowed as he laughed. "Let it be known," Ragnoc declared, rising to his full, imposing height, warhammer held high. "Stonefire Mountain honors its oath and stands against the coming darkness!"

"Thank you, King Ragnoc," Ariella breathed, relief washing over her features.

"Go now," King Ragnoc instructed, gesturing broadly with a hand that had swung his hammer in countless battles. "Prepare yourselves for the trials ahead. You will find all that Stonefire can offer at your disposal."

The heroes bowed deeply, their resolve bolstered by the renewed commitment of the Dwarven king.

The deep hum of Stonefire Mountain's forges had dimmed to a respectful silence as Rider and his companions trudged through the stone-laden streets toward Baelgor's home. Each step echoed off the carved walls, resonating with the weight of their intentions. Warm light spilled from the windows of the sturdy stone house, casting a welcoming glow onto the cobblestone path.

"Remember, we're here to honor his life," Ariella whispered, her violet eyes shimmering with unshed tears, the usual poise in her voice wavering slightly.

Upon reaching the stout door carved with intricate runes, they hesitated, a collective breath held between them. Baelgor's widow opened the door before they could knock, revealing the warmth of a hearth and the rich aroma of spiced mead. Her soft smile was like a balm to their heavy hearts.

"Come in, come in," she urged, stepping aside. The scent of freshly baked bread and spiced stew wrapped around them as they entered the warm embrace of the household.

"Thank you, Hilda," Rider said, removing his cloak and draping it over his arm. "We wish to express our deepest condolences."

"Your presence honors him," she replied, guiding them into the sitting room where Baelgor's children played quietly on a woven rug.

"Your father... he was a true hero," Kael added, kneeling to be at eye level with the children, his voice tender.

"Indeed, he forged bonds stronger than the steel of his anvil," Ariella chimed in, joining Kael on the floor, her eloquent tone soothing the somber atmosphere.

Hilda gestured toward a pair of items resting atop the hearth. "Before he left, Baelgor crafted these for you two. Said they were to aid your journey if he couldn't return."

Ariella approached the bow first, its limbs adorned with intricate gemstones that sparkled under the firelight, and a mithril bowstring that hummed with potential. "It's beautiful," she breathed, running her fingers along the smooth surface.

"And this," Hilda picked up a longsword, offering it to

Rider, "carries the runes of protection and courage. Just like Baelgor."

Rider accepted the weapon reverently, feeling the balance and craftsmanship in his hands. The gemstones in the hilt caught the fire's light, reflecting it back tenfold. "I'll wield it with honor, in his memory."

Their mission weighed heavily upon them, even in the warmth of the Stoneheart home. But for the time they were there, sharing stories of Baelgor's valor and laughter, the burden lifted.

"His spirit marches with you," Hilda assured, her eyes glinting with pride.

"Thank you, Hilda. And thank you, Baelgor," Rider said, his heart swelling with gratitude and determination.

With hearts heavy yet filled with purpose, the heroes left the warmth of the smith's home and stepped into the brisk air of the Stonefire stables. The earthy smell of hay and the sound of hooves against stone greeted them as they entered. Rider's gaze swept through the stable, searching for one familiar face amid the sturdy Dwarven steeds.

"Looking for someone?" a gruff stablehand asked, noting Rider's impatient surveying of the stalls.

"My steed, Eve. It's been months since we've seen each other," Rider explained, his eyes not leaving the line of horses.

"Ah, the chestnut mare? Follow me."

The stablehand led Rider down the aisle, where the clamber of hooves and snorts of equine breaths filled the air. Finally, they stopped at a stall where a muscular chestnut mare stood, her dark mane braided with metal bands glinting in the dim light.

"Eve," Rider called softly, stepping forward.

The mare's ears perked up, and she let out a gentle

whinny, recognizing her master's voice. As Rider approached, Eve nuzzled into his palm, her warm breath sending puffs of steam into the cool air. Her calm brown eyes held a look of recognition, and a softness spread through Rider's chest.

"Missed you, girl," he murmured, running a hand along her sleek neck, feeling the strength beneath her skin.

Eve responded with a contented snort, leaning into his touch. For a moment, the world outside—the looming threats, the urgent quests—faded away as Rider reveled in the simple joy of reunion.

"Looks like she's missed you too," the stablehand commented, a smile cracking his weathered face.

"More than can be said," Rider replied, still focused on Eve. He slipped her a sugar cube he had pocketed earlier, which she accepted with a delighted crunch.

Across the stable, the rest of the party was selecting their mounts. They would need the sturdy steeds to navigate the treacherous mountain paths back to The Banshee's Wail. Even amidst preparation, there were moments of laughter and light-hearted banter, a brief respite from the weight of their mission.

"Ready to ride out?" Ariella asked, approaching with her own mount, a spirited mare with a coat as dark as the night sky.

"Always," Rider grinned, swinging himself up onto Eve's broad back with practiced ease.

One by one, the heroes mounted up, the clinking of tack and the creak of leather filling the stable as they prepared to depart. With a final pat to Eve's neck, Rider led the way out, the sunlight of the mountain's dawn casting long shadows behind them.

Together, the party rode out from the embrace of Stonefire Mountain, the beats of their steeds' hooves echoing like a drumbeat of hope against the stone. They carried with them not just the weapons of a fallen friend, but the determination to see their quest through to its end.

The crisp mountain air whipped through Rider's hair as he leaned forward, pressing his cheek against Eve's warm mane. The sky stretched above them, a canvas of brilliant blues and the whisper of clouds, as if painting their path with strokes of freedom and urgency. The steady rhythm of her gallop was a song he remembered by heart.

"Stonefire's heart beats strong in you, my friend," Rider murmured to his steed. Eve responded with an eager snort, her powerful muscles bunching beneath him as they descended the rugged path towards the hidden cove where The Banshee's Wail awaited.

Ariella rode alongside, the mare's hooves finding purchase on the loose stones with astounding grace. She caught Rider's gaze and nodded, her eyes gleaming with unspoken resolve.

"Drakzeneth will not prevail," she said, her voice carrying over the wind. "We carry with us the strength of Baelgor's craft, the renewed promise of Stonefire."

"Indeed, we do," Kael added from behind, his words punctuated by the clinking of his arcane-imbued armor. He rode a robust dun stallion, its coat shimmering like burnished copper in the sunlight filtering through the clouds.

Rider felt a smile tug at his lips.

Laughter rippled through the group, easing the tension that gripped their hearts, if only for a moment. They reached the crest of a hill, and the hidden cove unveiled itself before them—a secluded basin of tranquility where The Banshee's Wail lay moored, its newly blackened sails and paint furled, awaiting their return.

"Look at her," Hawke called out, emerging from the

cove. "She's ready to sail the Crystal Sea! This time, we'll steer her straight into legend."

"Or infamy," Rider chimed back, a grin splitting his stubbled face. "Either way, history will remember us," he declared, taking in the sight of the ship—their symbol of rebellion against an encroaching darkness.

"Tonight, we make our plans. At dawn, we set sail," Rider announced, casting his voice across the gathered heroes. "We have allies yet to rally, battles yet to fight, and a world to save from the grip of Drakzeneth. But together, there is nothing we cannot overcome."

The party dismounted, their boots crunching on the gravelly shore. With every step toward the Banshee's Wail, their resolve hardened—shared purpose forging a bond stronger than steel.

As Rider helped Ariella onto the deck, their hands lingering for a heartbeat longer than necessary, he knew the road ahead would test them all. But in her eyes, he saw not fear, but fiery defiance—the same fire that burned within him.

"Let's end this," he whispered, more vow than statement.

"Let's end this," she echoed.

CHAPTER XX
THE EMERALD SEA

The shimmering silver hull of the Banshee's Wail mirrored the dance of sunlight on water, creating a spectacle of light that would have been mesmerizing if not for the urgency gripping those aboard. At the bow, Rider's sapphire eyes fixed on the receding coastline of Stonefire, a solemn vow to return etched in his gaze.

"Steady as she goes!" Hawke's command sliced through the salt-laden air, his presence an unyielding force against the vastness of the sea. The pirate captain's orders were met with the hustle of boots and the creak of rope as his crew scurried to obey, their silhouettes stark against the billowing obsidian canvas above.

"Rider," Kael's voice drew him back from his thoughts, the mage's blue eyes glittering with a knowledge that spanned worlds. "The journey ahead is long, and the seas are known for their treachery. Perhaps this is the opportune moment to delve into the lore of Astrala."

Rider turned, his dark hair fluttering in the sea breeze, and found Ariella already nodding in agreement. Her violet eyes held a scholar's curiosity, the kind that hungered for ancient tales and forbidden secrets. They shared a silent understanding before descending below deck, seeking refuge from the briny winds in the belly of the vessel.

The low thrum of the ship's heart greeted them, a comforting cadence amidst the wooden embrace of the Banshee's Wail. Kael led them to a secluded corner where the world of Etonya seemed nothing more than a distant memory, and the scent of old timber and wax mingled with the ever-present aroma of the ocean.

"Tell us everything," Ariella urged, her lilting voice rich with anticipation as she took her seat on a worn barrel, her posture regal despite the humble setting.

Kael began, his words weaving the tapestry of Astrala's past as Rider listened intently, the mage's narrative painting vivid images in his mind. He spoke of a people who looked like any other yet bore the weight of eons within their souls, of a land where magic was as natural as breathing, and of the harrowing tale of Aetherion Ascendance.

Rider's own power stirred within him, a dormant beast awakened by the resonance of Kael's storytelling. It was a connection he couldn't yet fathom, a legacy that whispered of destiny and battle, of freedom fought and won. As the ship plowed onward, forging its path toward Amakiir, the trio delved deeper into the secrets of an ancient race.

In the confines of the Banshee's Wail, surrounded by the muffled sounds of the crew above, Kael's voice was a guiding light through the darkness of history. The Astralans' discovery of magic, he explained, was not merely an accident but a destined awakening, as if the very stars had aligned to bestow upon them the knowledge of the arcane. With each word spoken in the ancient language, the Astralans shaped their reality, bending the elements to their will and nurturing a society where scarcity was unknown, and harmony reigned.

"Imagine," Kael said, his eyes glinting with memory, "a world so attuned to its inhabitants that seasons changed with a shared desire for growth or rest. Food sprung from the earth at the mere suggestion, rich with flavor and sustenance."

Ariella's eyes widened, her senses ignited by the thought of such abundance. Even Rider, whose early life had known little of wonder, felt a longing stir within him— a yearning to witness such a place where magic flowed like water, boundless and pure.

According to Kael's tale, the Astralans' curiosity grew, their gaze turning skyward, toward the vast expanse that stretched beyond their utopia. They sought not conquest but knowledge, extending their reach across the heavens to touch other realms, to learn, to grow. Each portal opened was a doorway to new worlds, new allies, and the treasure of experiencing the unknown.

"Such was the might of my people," Kael murmured, pride lacing his tone, "that we traversed the cosmos itself, sowing seeds of wisdom and gathering the fruits of the universe's endless bounty."

Below deck, the air seemed to vibrate with the power of his words, and for a moment, it appeared as though the ship sailed not on water but on the currents of arcane energy that Kael conjured with his narrative. The past was alive again, breathing through him, and both Rider and Ariella were captivated, transported to an era long gone, where magic was the key to unlocking the celestial rhythm of existence.

Kael's voice grew somber as he delved into the darkest chapter of Astralan history, his eyes reflecting the pain of a wound that still ached within the collective memory of his people. "Our greatest mistake," he began, "was born from our greatest virtue—the desire to share our knowledge and uplift those in need. The Draconin were a race on the brink of collapse, their world ravaged by famine and strife. The Astralans, in our infinite compassion, saw a chance to heal, to guide a struggling civilization towards the light of prosperity. We shared our secrets of magic, teaching the Draconin to harness the power of leylines, to restore balance to their dying world. We thought we were saving them," Kael whispered, his voice heavy with regret. "But in truth, we were sowing the seeds of our own downfall."

As the Draconin's world blossomed under the guidance of Astralan wisdom, so too did their hunger for power. The once humble race grew arrogant, their forms twisting and changing as they delved deeper into the arcane arts. Scales replaced their skin, wings sprouted from their backs, and their eyes gleamed with an insatiable lust for dominion.

"They became Dragons!" Ariella breathed, her voice tinged with a mix of awe and horror.

Kael nodded solemnly. "The very ones that plagued your world. They craved power, coveted the greatest secret of the Astralans, our ability to traverse the cosmos."

The ship creaked around them, as if bearing witness to the unfolding tragedy. Kael's voice painted a vivid picture of the Draconin's betrayal, of Astralan envoys captured and tortured, their minds and bodies broken until they yielded the key to the stars.

Rider's fists clenched, his knuckles white with rage. He could almost hear the screams of the Astralan people, could almost feel the searing agony of their suffering as the Draconin ripped the knowledge from their very souls.

"They came for Astrala," Kael continued, his eyes distant, seeing not the wooden walls of the ship but the once-proud spires of his homeland crumbling under the onslaught of draconic might. "Our peaceful world became a battlefield, our people enslaved by the very race we had sought to save."

The weight of centuries pressed down upon them, the echoes of a civilization's fall reverberating through the silence that followed Kael's words. Ariella reached out, her slender hand resting on the mage's arm in a gesture of comfort, a silent acknowledgment of the pain he carried within him.

Rider's mind raced, piecing together the fragments of Kael's tale, understanding dawning like the sun cresting the horizon. "But you fought back," he said, his voice eager to know more.

Kael's gaze fell to the floor, a heavy sigh escaping his lips as he shook his head. "No, Rider. We didn't fight back. Not at first." His voice was barely audible above the gentle creaking of the ship, yet it carried the weight of a thousand sorrows. "The Astralan people were scholars and explorers. We had never needed the kind of offensive magic it would have taken to defeat the Dragons. Our spells were meant to explore, to create, not to destroy."

He lifted his eyes, meeting Rider's intense stare with a look of profound sadness. "For generations, we were slaves to the Dragons. They used our knowledge, our connection to the arcane, to drain the leylines of countless worlds, siphoning the very lifeblood of magic to fuel their own power."

Kael's words painted a bleak picture, each syllable a brushstroke of despair. Rider could almost see it: the once-vibrant lands of Astrala, now desolate and gray, the sky above choked with the smoke of draconic fires. He imagined the Astralan people, their luminous eyes dulled by the weight of their chains, their voices raised in a chorus of anguish as they were forced to watch their oppressors grow stronger with each passing day.

Ariella gripped Kael's arm, her delicate features etched with a mix of horror and compassion. "How did you survive?" she whispered, her voice trembling with the force of her empathy.

A flicker of something—pride, perhaps, or defiance—danced in Kael's eyes. "We endured," he said, his tone hardening with resolve. "Even in our darkest hour, the spirit of the Astralan people refused to be extinguished. We clung to hope, to the belief that one day, we would be free."

He leaned forward, his gaze intense as he locked eyes with Rider and Ariella in turn. "And then, when all seemed lost, a miracle happened. One of our own, an Astralan whose name has been lost to history, developed a power beyond anything we had ever seen before. A power that could challenge the might of the Dragons themselves."

Rider's heart raced, his breath catching in his throat as he leaned in, hanging on Kael's every word. "Aetherion Ascendance," he breathed, the name rolling off his tongue like a prayer.

Kael nodded, a smile ghosting across his lips. "Yes. With this power, born of desperation and forged in the fires of our people's suffering, the Astralan were finally able to fight back. Our champion led a rebellion that shook the very foundations of Astrala, shattering the chains that had bound us for so long."

Kael's eyes shone fiercely as he recounted the final chapters of the Astralan struggle. "Our champion, imbued with the raw, untamed power of Aetherion Ascendance, became an unstoppable force. He sundered the bonds that had held our people in thrall for so long. The Dragons, once so mighty and fearsome, trembled before his onslaught."

Rider and Ariella sat transfixed, their hearts pounding in sync in rhythm of Kael's tale. They could almost feel the heat of the battle, could almost hear the roar of the Dragons as they fell before the Astralan hero's might.

He paused, his gaze distant, as if seeing the events unfold before his very eyes. "In the end, our champion stood victorious atop the ruin of Dragons. The Astralan people were free at last, our homeland reclaimed from the clutches of our tormentors."

Ariella let out a breath she hadn't realized she'd been holding, her eyes glistening with unshed tears. "But it wasn't over, was it?" she whispered, her voice barely audible above the creaking of the ship.

Kael shook his head, a grim smile playing across his lips. "No. Our champion knew that as long as the Dragons possessed the secrets of our magic, they would always pose a threat. And so he embarked on one final mission, a journey to the heart of Draconis itself."

Rider leaned forward, his elbows resting on his knees as he hung on Kael's every word. He could almost picture it: a lone Astralan warrior, armor gleaming in the other-worldly light of Draconis, striding towards his destiny with unwavering resolve.

"What he found there was a world on the brink of collapse," Kael said, his voice heavy with the weight of memory. "The Dragons had drained Draconis's leylines to the point of near extinction, leaving the once-vibrant planet a husk of its former self. The very air reeked of decay, and the ground was cracked and barren beneath his feet."

Kael took a deep breath, as if steeling himself for what came next. "Our champion knew what he had to do. With a heavy heart, he unleashed the full might of Aetherion Ascendance upon the leylines themselves, severing the Draconis' connection to the arcane forever."

A somber silence hung in the air, broken only by the gentle creaking of the ship as Kael's tale drew to a close. He spoke softly, his voice carrying the weight of centuries. "It was a decision that haunted our champion until his dying day. To sever an entire world from the lifeblood of magic, to leave its people adrift in a sea of uncertainty... it was not a choice made lightly."

Kael's eyes glimmered with a distant hope, a flicker of light amidst the shadows of the past. "But in his heart, he held fast to the belief that the Draconin could find a better way. That in the absence of arcane power, they might turn their gaze inward, seeking strength not in conquest, but in the bonds of community and the pursuit of wisdom."

Ariella listened intently, her violet eyes luminous with wonder. "And what of the Astralan?" she asked, her voice soft as a whisper. "What became of your people, after so much had been lost?"

A wistful smile played across Kael's lips. "We thrived, as we always have. With our homeland freed from draconic rule, we set about the task of healing, of mending the wounds that centuries of enslavement had inflicted upon our society. It was a time of great sorrow, but also of great joy, as families were reunited and ancient traditions were reborn from the ashes of oppression."

He straightened, a glimmer of pride shining in his eyes. "In time, we returned to the stars, our hearts filled with the same unquenchable thirst for knowledge that had defined us since the dawn of our civilization. But we were changed, tempered by the fires of our ordeal. No longer would we share the secrets of our magic with those who might abuse its power. Instead, we would walk among the younger races as guides and mentors, offering wisdom and compassion, but never the keys to our most potent arcane arts."

Rider leaned back, his mind reeling with the weight of Kael's revelations. The tale of the Astralan people, their rise, their fall, and their ultimate triumph, was a story that resonated deep within his soul. He could feel the echoes of their struggle, the whispers of their ancient magic, thrumming in his veins like a distant heartbeat.

As he sat there, lost in thought, a question began to form in his mind, a nagging uncertainty that refused to be silenced. He looked up, meeting Kael's gaze with a furrowed brow. "Kael," he began, his voice hesitant, "before the Draconin, before Draconis... did Dragons exist on other worlds?"

Kael paused, his eyes distant as he pondered the question. The gentle rocking of the ship seemed to fade away, replaced by the weight of centuries, the knowledge of countless worlds and civilizations. When he spoke, his voice was soft, almost reverent. "The Astralan have walked among the stars for over 10,000 years, Rider. We have seen wonders beyond imagining, and worlds torn asunder. But in all our travels, in all the realms we have touched... we have never encountered Dragons like those of Draconis."

He leaned forward, his hands clasped before him as he met Rider's gaze. "We believed that the Dragons were unique to that world, a product of the Draconin's twisted experiments with our magic. When our champion severed the leylines of Draconis, we thought that the Dragons had been wiped out, their power broken forever."

Ariella's eyes widened, a sudden realization dawning on her face. "But Vorathor..." she whispered, her voice trembling with a mix of fear and awe. "The Dragon that Rider defeated in the forest. You knew of him, Kael and he was here, on Etonya."

Kael nodded slowly, his expression grim. "I know. When I saw his corpse, saw the terrible majesty of his form even in death... it was like a nightmare come to life. The Dragons of Etonya's past, the ones that terrorized this world centuries ago... I believe they were remnants of Draconis, survivors of our champion's purge."

He stood, pacing the length of the cabin as he spoke, his voice rising with each step. "The more I think about it, the more it fits. The Dragons appeared on Etonya, following a powerful magic user, sowing chaos and destruction wherever they went. They were a scourge upon this world, just as they had been on countless others; and their leader promised power through transformation."

Rider's heart raced, his mind reeling with the implications of Kael's words. If the Dragons of Etonya were indeed of the Draconin, then they must have found a way to travel the cosmos again.

Kael's voice grew heavy with the weight of revelation, his eyes shimmering with a mix of dread and determination. "... Drakzeneth must have learned the secrets of Astralan magic, rekindled the leylines of Draconis, and restored the Dragons to their former power. We can't let him spread his influence. Make no mistake, he will enslave this world."

The cabin seemed to shrink around them, the walls closing in as the enormity of the threat loomed ever larger. Rider could feel the weight of destiny pressing down upon his shoulders, the power of Aetherion Ascendance, a tool he needed to learn to control now more than ever.

Ariella's hand found his, her slender fingers intertwining with his own in a gesture of solidarity. "We won't let that happen," she said, her voice steady against the rising fear. "Etonya has suffered enough at the hands of the Dragons. We will stop them, before it's too late."

Kael nodded, his gaze hardening with a warrior's resolve. "We will."

He turned to Rider, his eyes alight with a fierce intensity. "You, Rider, are the key. The power of Aetherion Ascendance flows through you, a legacy of my people's greatest champion… and I'm starting to believe that legacy may be yours as well."

Rider felt the power stirring within him, a wellspring of ancient power that thrummed in harmony with the beating of his heart. He knew with a certainty that defied explanation that this was his destiny, his calling. To stand against the tide of shadow, to be a beacon of hope in a world besieged by fear.

"But what of the leylines?" he asked, his mind racing with the countless challenges that lay ahead. "If our enemy has found a way to drain them, to drain the magic from other worlds..."

Kael's expression grew somber, the weight of centuries etched into the lines of his face. "Then we must find them and sever his connection to them. It will not be easy, Rider. The secrets of the Astralan are ancient and powerful, but with your Ascendance and my guidance, the power of our combined might... I believe we can prevail."

He placed a hand on Rider's shoulder, his touch a silent gesture of unwavering support. "We will scour the corners of this world and save it."

Just then, the Banshee's Wail plunged through a towering wave, its black sails billowing like the wings of a night specter. Salt-laden winds lashed against the ship's shimmering silver hull as it cut a stark silhouette against the churning sea. Rider gripped the table, Kael at his side, both exchanging a worrisome look.

Zara appeared through the door of their shared room, her face set in grim resolve. "A storm brews on the horizon," she announced, her dark eyes carrying a hint of fear. "It is no ordinary tempest."

The party followed her topside as they moved through the ship's innards, the vessel groaning and creaking as if protesting the impending assault. The wooden planks beneath their feet buckled and shifted, sending them stumbling against the walls. As they reached the deck of the ship, they gazed upward, witnessing the ominous clouds that gathered with unnatural speed, blotting out the sun.

"Brace yourselves!" Hawke shouted, his voice barely audible over the howling winds that surrounded them as they emerged on deck.

The world had transformed into a realm of fury. Dark storm clouds roiled overhead, gale winds whipped the ocean into a frenzy, and lightning cracked the sky with electric veins. Hawke stood resolute at the helm, his coat flapping wildly, his eyes alight with the thrill of the challenge.

"Back below deck, all of you! Now!" he yelled, but his command was met with hesitance from Rider, who could see the strain etched on Hawke's face.

"Let me help," Rider called out, moving closer despite the tilting deck.

"Ha! A true pirate!" Hawke grinned, a mix of respect and concern in his eyes. He directed Rider to the riggings. "Tighten those lines! Keep 'em taut!"

Together with the rest of Hawke's crew, they worked to keep the Banshee's Wail on course, muscles straining against the pull of the ropes as they tried to outmaneuver each wave. But the storm was a beast beyond taming, and Hawke's confident demeanor waned, replaced by furrowed brows of worry.

"Something's wrong," he muttered, fighting with the wheel. "These winds... they're not natural. Every time we correct course, they change with us. It's forcing us to go where it wants."

Above them, the sky unleashed a torrent of rain, pelting their skin with icy needles. Thunder rolled, a deep rumble that resonated in their chests. The Banshee's Wail groaned under the onslaught, her crew scrambling to secure sails and lash down anything that could become a deadly projectile.

"That's enough, get below, damn it!" Hawke ordered again, but this time there was an edge of desperation to his voice. The storm was more than a match even for his seasoned skills, and the danger to his ship and crew had never been clearer.

Rider nodded, casting one last glance at the maelstrom that raged around them. With a heavy heart, he turned and fought his way back towards the stairs, each step a battle against the relentless force of nature that sought to claim them all.

"Rider! Get that blasted mage up here now!" Hawke roared above the gale, his voice barely carrying over the storm's roar. Rider's boots skidded on the slick wood as he lunged towards the door leading below deck. Thunder cracked overhead like celestial cannons firing, and a monstrous tornado, its funnel a swirling abyss encased in a spiraling tomb of water, bore down upon the Banshee's Wail.

The chaos was instantaneous. Men shouted, ropes snapped taut, and the ship creaked ominously under the tempest's wrath. The once formidable vessel now seemed as fragile as parchment caught in the fury of the elements. Sails whipped violently, torn between the commands of their masters and the wild dance orchestrated by the storm.

"Secure yourselves!" Hawke bellowed, the salt-crusted

strands of his hair whipping around his face. His crew scrambled, their hands flying over ropes and riggings, securing their bodies to the ship with hastily-made knots. With every violent tilt, the Banshee's Wail threatened to cast them into the ravenous sea.

"Rider, to the railing!" Hawke pointed to a coil of rope near the helm. Rider didn't hesitate, grabbing the lifeline and tethering himself amidst the roiling winds. The ship groaned, her hull lifting from the ocean's surface as if she aimed to join the clouds in their frenzied waltz.

Sweat and rain mingled on Rider's brow as he watched the crew fight for their lives. Then, disaster struck—the rigging snapped. Sailors slid across the pitching deck, their screams lost in the howl of the wind. Hawke abandoned the wheel, which spun uselessly, its purpose nullified as they became passengers of the sky.

"Men overboard!" Hawke's voice was thick with fear and determination, his eyes scanning the crew with fervent protectiveness. He lunged toward the nearest sailor, arms straining to reach him. Debris, turned lethal in the maelstrom's grip, flew past, one piece—a barrel of gunpowder—hurling directly at Hawke. It collided with a sickening thud, pinning him against the mast, his grunt of pain almost inaudible.

"Captain!" Rider cried out, unsheathing his dagger. With a swift cut, he freed himself from his own tether and plunged into the fray. The ship pitched and yawed, a broken toy in the hands of an angry god. Adrenaline surged through him as he leaped from beam to beam, his eyes fixed on his imperiled comrades.

One by one, he reached them, his rope a lifeline in the literal sense. Three men he secured to the railing, their expressions a mixture of terror and gratitude as they clung to their salvation. But the storm was not finished. It spun the ship faster, a carousel of nightmares, as Rider stretched his hand towards the fourth sailor.

"Take my hand!" Rider screamed, his voice almost lost to the wind. Their fingers clasped, but the storm's ferocity was relentless. The man's grip slipped, his body flung outward like a ragdoll into the heart of the tempest.

"NO!" Rider's cry was a raw shred of anguish.

He turned just in time to meet the unforgiving wooden mast, the impact sending shocks of pain through his body before darkness claimed him. Unconscious, his form became ensnared by the sail, wrapping him like a cocoon as the Banshee's Wail continued her hellish dance within the wall of the hurricane.

* * *

The merciless sun beat down on the wreckage-strewn beach where the Banshee's Wail lay marooned, her once proud sails tattered and her hull littered with cracked planks. The ship lay rested atop the sand at an unnatural angle, debris scattered like the lost treasures of a fallen empire.

The tropical paradise paid no heed to the carnage, weaving itself calmly around the remnants of the crash.. Gigantic palm trees swayed gently in a mocking breeze, their fronds whispering secrets to thick vines and brightly colored flowers that bloomed with wild abandon.

"Over here!" Hawke's voice cut through the stillness as he stumbled upon a mound of sailcloth, beneath which lay Rider. His body was limp, his dark hair matted with sea brine, bruises blooming across his skin. Ariella, Zara, and Kael rushed over, their faces etched with concern for their fallen comrade.

Hawke fished out a pouch from his coat, the leather

worn by countless adventures. He spilled gunpowder onto the ground and ignited it with a snap of his gloves—flint-lined fingertips sparking to life. The sudden crackle and acrid scent of smoke assaulted the senses, pulling Rider back to consciousness.

Rider coughed, sputtering, his eyes fluttering open to the sight of worried faces. "You're one hell of a storm rider," Hawke said, his tone a mix of reprimand and respect. "Could've gotten yourself killed."

"Someone had to save your sorry skins," Rider retorted with a weak grin, pushing himself up on his elbows.

"Easy now," Hawke chided, extending a hand to help Rider stand. Their forearms locked in a solid grip, and they pulled each other into a brief, fierce embrace—a silent acknowledgment of the bond forged in the tempest.

As the group turned their attention to the Banshee's Wail, a sense of purpose united them. Together, they assessed the damage, the enormity of the task ahead not enough to dampen their spirits. They moved with determination, salvaging what could be used, savagely chopping trees with their various blades, and gathering vines that would bind the wounds of their vessel.

Amidst the clatter of activity, Kael paused, a distant look in his eyes as he stared toward the dense heart of the island. Rider approached, noting the shift in the mage's demeanor. "What is it, Kael? What do you feel?"

"Power... Ancient, faint, but it's here," Kael murmured, almost to himself. "There's a leyline access point here. I can sense it."

Rider nodded, understanding the gravity of Kael's words. It was decided—they would venture into the unknown, seeking the source, hoping to restore Kael's power and interrupt Drakzeneth's plan.

"That may be so, but we still need to inform the other

kingdoms of what transpired. That news cannot wait." Zara interrupted. "You are all more than capable of handling the situation here, I'm going to travel the shadows and inform the other kingdoms."

"First mate!" Hawke barked, almost in response to Zara's decisiveness. A burly man who would assume command in his stead stiffened to attention. "Get her seaworthy again. And make it quick. We'll be back before ya' know it."

His first mate shifted uneasily, the doubt in his eyes as clear as the crystal waters lapping at their makeshift camp. "Cap'n," he started, "the hull's been split, the sails torn to tatters. And all we've got are coconuts and palm leaves."

"Listen up!" Hawke's voice cut through the murmur of the sea, commanding attention. "We've been through worse than this—storms, sea monsters, and ships nipping at our heels!"

Hawke's laugh was a hearty guffaw that seemed too confident for their dire situation. He clapped the man on the shoulder, shaking his head. "You think a few scratches and splinters will keep The Wail from dancing on the waves again? Not by a long shot."

The crew exchanged skeptical glances, their hands callused and their shirts sticking to their backs with sweat. They could taste the salt on their lips and feel the sting of it in the cuts they'd acquired while salvaging what they could from the wreckage.

"Look around you, mates! This island's given us wood for planks, vines for ropes. We're pirates, aren't we?" He swept a hand towards the lush greenery that bordered the beach. "Everything we need is right here."

"But cap'n," another piped up, "even if we fix her, what then? We don't even know where we are."

"Ah, but that's where you're wrong." Hawke's brown

eyes sparkled with mischief. "We're exactly where we need to be, with each other," he tapped his chest with a gloved hand, "and I've never steered us wrong… yet," he half-joked with a grin.

A murmur of agreement began to rise, fueled by the infectious energy of their captain. He paced before them, boots leaving deep impressions in the sand, his trench coat billowing behind him like the sails they would soon mend.

"Remember when we outgunned that galleon with just six cannons and a barrel of rum?" he asked, a grin spreading across his face. "Or the fact that we stole the damn capital ship of the Queen's navy? Now fix her up!" The crew chuckled, the memories igniting a fire in their bellies. They were survivors, fighters, and above all else, they were Hawke's crew—the luckiest damned pirates to sail the Crystal Sea.

"Alright, cap'n. We'll patch her up," the first mate conceded, his voice firm and resolute now.

"Damn right, you will," Hawke said, clapping his hands together. "And when we set sail, we'll raise a toast to that damn storm."

The pirate crew hooted and hollered, slapping each other on the back. They dispersed to their tasks with renewed vigor, scavenging materials from the island's generous bounty. Hawke watched them begin to work, a proud smile on his face, the setting sun casting his shadow long and triumphant across the sands.

CHAPTER XXI
SHIPWRECKED

The scorching sun beat down as they hacked their way through the dense, overgrown jungle. Sweat glistened on their brows, the stifling heat turning even the simplest task into a grueling endeavor. Hawke led them with the assured strides of a man who had braved far worse than this tropical crucible.

"Keep close, mates," he called back, his scimitar hacking away the thick vines and dense underbrush.

Before long, the twisted green gave way to reveal a sight both breathtaking and somber. Ancient ruins loomed before them, a dilapidated square pyramid-shaped building, its weather-worn stones scorched by the ravages of time and war stood as a monument to a forgotten civilization.

"Would ya' look at that," Hawke muttered under his breath, admiration lacing his words.

As they ventured closer, the vibrant chatter of the jungle faded, replaced by a heavy silence that settled over the ruins like a shroud. The air felt charged, the echoes of ancient magics still clinging to the crumbled stone.

It was then that Hawke's boot crunched on something brittle. He paused, the sound jarring in the quiet. Beneath the foliage—a skull, charred and splintered under his weight.

"What the…" he swore softly, nudging aside the brush with the tip of his scimitar. As the leaves were swept away, a grim scene of skeletal remains revealed itself, chained together in eternal captivity. Some were unmistakably Human, their skulls blunt and sturdy. Others were more delicate, with elongated craniums and slender bone structures, graceful even in death.

"Elven," Hawke murmured, recognizing the subtle differences.

His eyes followed the chains, trailing through the underbrush to a broken stone pillar, pocked with scorch marks that spoke of magical fire. It was a scar upon the earth, a dark memorial to lives taken by unfathomable power.

"Oi!" Hawke's voice sliced through the quiet, commanding the attention of his comrades. "Come have a look at this!"

He stood back, allowing them to take in the full scope of the sacrificial pit that unfolded around him. The air hung heavy with the weight of untold stories, the whispers of spirits long gone. The ruin bore witness to a history written in blood and magic, a legacy of pain etched into every blackened stone.

Ariella approached the edge of the pit, her violet eyes scanning the horror before her. She breathed a sign of shock, a hand covering her mouth as if to ward off any possible stench of death that might still linger like a curse. "We must tread with caution. Whatever executed these horrid rites could still haunt this place."

The party nodded in somber agreement, their steps

careful and reverent as they crossed to the other side of the sacrificial ground. They spoke little, each lost in contemplation of the lives snuffed out so cruelly.

"Look here," Ariella suddenly called out, her tone shifting as she crouched to brush away a curtain of creeping vines. Beneath the dense layer of greenery was not the dark soil they had expected, but a pathway paved with ancient stones, worn by time yet unmistakable in their purpose. "A path," she said, more to herself than the others, "leading towards the mountain."

With a mix of trepidation and resolve, the group followed their Elven huntress deeper into the tropical forest. The lush foliage thrived in the undisturbed jungle, an emerald maze that clung to their clothes and hindered their progress. Roots snaked across their path like slumbering serpents, and thick vines dangled from above, brushing their faces with leafy fingers.

Hours passed as they hacked away the stubborn undergrowth, revealing small stepping stones and faded trail markings that guided them along the ancient route. Kael, who had been unusually quiet, suddenly stopped in his tracks. He closed his eyes in concentration as he tilted his head back towards the sky and took in a deep, chest-filling breath before slowly exhaling. "Wait," he said softly, almost in reverence, as his arms stretched outwards at his sides.

A gentle hum filled the air, a vibration that only those attuned to the arcane could perceive. Kael turned his palms upwards, fingers dancing gracefully through the invisible currents of energy that flowed around them.

His tattoos, those intricate symbols of power etched across his skin, began to shimmer with a soft luminescence. Trails of azure and gold snaked up his forearms, the magic coursing through him like a dry riverbed flowing openly after a fresh rain. With each pulse of energy, the tattoos glowed brighter, until they reached his elbows and dissipated into the humid air as he sighed.

Kael's eyes fluttered open, a crackle of lightning danced across each of his blue irises. A smile played upon his lips—a smile of pure exhilaration. "The leyline," he announced, his voice infused with a newfound vigor. "It's growing stronger. We're close."

"It's gotta be in that mountain, I'm sure of it," Kael continued, his gaze fixed on the towering silhouette that loomed ahead.

"Then let's not waste another moment," Ariella said, her voice cutting through with the sharpness of a blade.

"Indeed," Kael agreed, a sense of urgency propelling him forward. "Onward, my friends."

The party hastened their pace, driven by hope and the promise of the power that lay hidden within the heart of the mountain.

The dense canopy above whispered secrets in the language of rustling leaves as the party pressed on, their boots treading upon a path long reclaimed by nature's embrace. The mountain loomed ever closer, an imposing sentinel against the darkening sky.

"Look here," Rider called out, his voice filled with awe. He brushed away a curtain of ivy to reveal the solemn face of a stone warrior, its visage marred by time and violence. "These were once guardians, perhaps."

"Or oppressors," Hawke added grimly, his hand resting on the pommel of his scimitar as he surveyed a mage statue whose face had been obliterated. He scanned the forest, his senses alert for any hint of danger that may still linger.

"Elves, Humans... they all fell before something," Ariella noted, her jeweled gaze somber. She traced a delicate finger along the base of a crumbled statue.

"An entire civilization lost to power or fear," Kael mused, sorrow flickering in his expression for the forgotten souls who once walked these lands.

They continued their silent vigil among the statues until Hawke's sharp intake of breath drew their attention to him. "Over here," he beckoned, revealing a solitary figure untouched by the wrath that claimed the others. Its face bore horns and scales—a visage both majestic and haunting.

"By the gods..." Ariella whispered.

Kael stepped forward, recognition lighting his features. "Draconin," he said, his voice hushed. "This is what they looked like before they became Dragons. Before greed consumed them."

The party exchanged glances, a silent understanding passing between them.

They fanned out, their eyes scanning the dense foliage for any sign of a path or entrance hidden among the vines and ancient stone.

"Well, that's as far as I think we'll get tonight," Hawke announced.

The sun began its final descent, bathing the ruins in a warm amber glow. Rider and Hawke worked in tandem, gathering dried branches and vines to build a modest campfire. Ariella scouted the perimeter, her Elven senses alert for any signs of danger lurking in the shadows.

Kael stood before the Draconin statue, his fingers tracing the intricate scales etched into the stone. His mind raced with the implications of their discovery. "This island must have been one of the first places the Draconin conquered," he remarked aloud, his voice carrying a mix of fascination and dread.

Ariella returned, a bundle of tropical birds in hand. "The area seems secure for now," she reported, setting about preparing their evening meal. The aroma of roasting meat soon mingled with the earthy scents of the jungle, a comforting familiarity amidst the eerie ruins.

As darkness settled over the camp, the flickering firelight cast shadows across the ancient stones. The party huddled close, their faces illuminated by the warm glow as they discussed the day's revelations.

"If the Draconin were here, there must be more to this place than meets the eye," Hawke said, his gaze fixed on the crackling flames. "Drakzeneth wouldn't have wasted his time on some backwater island."

Kael nodded, his brow furrowed in thought. "I suspect this was merely the first stepping stone in his grand plan. A place to experiment, to perfect his twisted magic before unleashing himself upon the rest of Etonya."

Ariella shuddered, her eyes reflecting the firelight. "The suffering that must have taken place here... it's unimaginable."

Rider remained silent, his thoughts drifting to the chains and charred remains they had discovered. The weight of those lost souls hung in the air, a cold presence that the warmth of the fire couldn't entirely dispel.

As the night wore on, exhaustion began to take its toll. One by one, they settled into their bedrolls, the softness of the moss and ferns providing a welcome respite from the day's hardships.

Rider's dreams were anything but restful.

Visions flooded his mind once again, the island's grim history played out behind his closed eyelids—shackled figures herded like cattle, their screams echoing through his mind. Bloodstained altars pulsed with dark magic that twisted flesh and bone into monstrous forms.

The faces of the sacrificed morphed and shifted, scales erupting from skin as they contorted. Wings unfurled, talons tore through fingers, and their horns enlarged and twisted as they sprouted further from their brows. The Draconin rose as Dragons from the ashes of their victims, eyes ablaze with an insatiable hunger for power.

In the depths of Rider's dream, the blood-soaked altars faded into the mists. A new vision took shape, with vivid clarity.

A magnificent blue Dragon soared above the island, its scales glinting like sapphires in the sun. It moved with wings outstretched as it rode the warm currents rising from the jungle below.

Suddenly, the Dragon's head snapped downwards, its eyes locking onto a flurry of movement in the underbrush. Humans and Elves, faces painted in terror, burst from the foliage. They ran in desperate, wild patterns, seeking to evade the predator above.

The Dragon's maw twisted into a cruel smile. It folded its wings as it plummeted from the sky. The fleeing figures scattered, their screams rending the air as the Dragon's shadow engulfed them.

With a sickening crunch, the Dragon's talons closed around an Elf, the unfortunate soul's spine snapping like a twig. The Dragon lifted off again, dangling its prize as it scanned for its next victim.

A Human male, his face streaked with tears and sweat, stumbled and fell. In an instant, the Dragon was upon him. Its jaws open wide, rows of dagger-like teeth glistening. The man's scream was abruptly silenced as the Dragon's maw closed around his torso, shearing him in half. Blood sprayed across the Dragon's snout as it gulped down its grisly meal.

The remaining survivors raced to the mountains, desperate for shelter. The Dragon gave chase, its hunger far from sated.

The scene shifted again as the remaining huddle of Elves and men squeezed against a large ornate door in what appeared to be a temple, pressing themselves against the damp cold metal. The Dragon landed behind them, and with a roar that shook the mountain, unleashed a torrent of lightning from its maw. The room lit up with a blinding blue-white light, the screams of the Elf and Human drowned out by the crackling of electricity.

When the light faded, all that remained were charred corpses.

With a gentle touch, Kael placed his hand on Rider's shoulder, giving him a firm shake. "Rider, wake up," he urged, his voice low yet insistent. "It's morning."

Rider's eyes snapped open, a gasp escaping his lips as he bolted upright. His chest heaved as he gulped in the humid jungle air, his gaze darting wildly before settling on Kael's concerned face. Recognition slowly dawned in his eyes, and he ran a trembling hand through his sweat-dampened hair.

"I... I saw it, Kael," Rider rasped, his voice hoarse from the night's terrors. "The Dragon, the sacrifices... I saw it all."

Kael's eyes widened, his grip on Rider's shoulder tightening. "Tell me everything," he said, his tone laced with urgency.

As Rider recounted his vivid dream, the others began to stir, drawn by the hushed voices. Ariella and Hawke gathered around, their expressions growing more somber with each grim detail. The weight of Rider's visions hung heavy in the air.

"A blue Dragon," Kael mused, his brow furrowed in thought. "It must be one of the Ancient Draconin, a survivor of the Great War."

Ariella shuddered, her violet eyes dark with concern. "If Rider's dream is a warning, we must be prepared for the worst. This creature will not take kindly to us."

Hawke nodded grimly, his hand resting on the pommel of his scimitar. "That leyline temple holds the key to stopping Drakzeneth and saving Etonya."

With collective resolve, the party set about breaking camp. The ancient ruins seemed to watch them, the stone faces of the forgotten guardians bearing silent witness to their determination.

The team trekked through the dense jungle, the mountain looming ever closer, its craggy face cloaked in a veil of mist. Each step brought them closer to the source of the arcane energy that thrummed through the island.

The tree line began to thin as the party finally reached the base of the mountain. Kael led the way, rushing to the side of the mountain. His eyes were alight with anticipation as he ran his hands along the stone face of the mountain, searching for a way inside. He could feel the powerful energy emanating from within the mountain, a promise of his power restored.

Rider followed close behind, his hand resting on the hilt of his longsword, ready to draw at a moment's notice. The visions of the Dragon still haunted him, the screams of the sacrificed echoing in his mind. He scanned the jungle. Every shadow, every rustle of leaves was a possible danger lurking just out of sight.

As he turned back, he noticed Kael's desperation, his movements growing more desperate as he searched. He was driven to complete their quest, but there was something more, it was as if his very soul depended on finding a way into the mountain's depths.

"Kael, we'll find a way in," Rider reassured him, resting a steady hand on his shoulder. His touch seemed to ground him, if only for a moment. "We won't leave until we do."

Kael turned to face Rider as he nodded, his eyes glistening with unshed tears. "Thank you," he whispered, his voice thick with emotion. "I... It's hard, Rider. I've never been without it; it's like I lost a part of myself."

"We're going to get it back, Kael. I promise," Rider said firmly as Ariella and Hawke split off from the duo and began searching a small distance apart.

Ariella's Elven eyes scanned the stone for anything irregular. It was then that she noticed it—a piece of an image peeking out from beneath a curtain of moss. With careful hands, she began peeling back the green blanket, revealing a large stone mosaic.

The image was breathtaking, a masterpiece of intricate runes and celestial bodies. Stars and planets danced across the stone, their paths woven together by the delicate lines.

"Over here!" Ariella's voice sliced through the thick air of the tropical forest. The others converged where she stood, awestruck before the ancient carvings.

Kael wasted no time, his fingers dancing lightly over the engraved runes, recognition playing in his eyes. "These are words of power," he murmured, "in the Astralan tongue... and these," he gestured towards the celestial bodies with an outstretched arm, "are the Astralan and Draconin home worlds."

"Can you make them work?" Rider asked, peering at the unfamiliar script with a mix of curiosity and impatience.

"Perhaps," Kael replied. "Rider, speak the phrase *'Avelor en'dur'*. It is a call to open, to reveal."

Rider's first attempt was clumsy, the words tumbling out like stones in a landslide. "*Av-eh-lor on-dour?*"

"Close," Kael corrected gently. "With conviction, Rider. Let the words flow like water. *Avelor en'dur.*"

Inhaling deeply, Rider's chest swelled. His voice rang loud, pure, and clear, "*Avelor en'dur.*"

The mosaic reacted instantly. From left to right, the runes sparked to life, glowing a fierce gold against the stone. The ground trembled beneath their feet, and dust cascaded from the edges of the mural.

"Look!" Hawke exclaimed as the stars began to rotate, clicking into new alignments. It was as if they were watching the night sky fast forward through countless seasons.

"By the gods," whispered Ariella, her eyes reflecting the luminous dance.

The mural reconfigured, segments of the mosaic moving independently, creating a song of stone grinding against stone. It was a puzzle rearranging itself, the solution unfolding before their very eyes.

"Stand back," Kael warned, as the last piece slid away with a thunderous groan, revealing a gaping threshold.

A rush of frigid air greeted the adventurers, a stark contrast to the sweltering tropical heat behind them. As they stood before the mountain's newly revealed passage, the cold seemed to seep into their bones, an invisible barrier between the known and the unknown.

Rider stood proud, grinning from ear to ear, his teeth a flash of white against his tanned skin.

Kael's response was affectionate but teasing. "Now, Rider, let's not have your head swell. You still have much to learn." His voice carried the weight of wisdom, even as his hand clapped reassuringly on Rider's shoulder.

Rider chuckled, rubbing the back of his neck sheepishly.

"Shall we?" Ariella asked, her Elven eyes already adjusting to the dim light within. She drew her bow, its string humming softly with latent power.

"Let's tread carefully," Kael advised, stepping over the threshold with a cautious grace. He raised a hand, and faint light emanated from his fingers, illuminating the rough-hewn walls of the tunnel. Their shadows danced eerily on the stone, elongating and contracting as they moved forward.

The sound of their boots against the ground reverberated in the confined space, the occasional drip of water from the ceiling adding a rhythmic punctuation to their advance.

"Can you feel it, Rider?" Kael whispered. "The leyline's pulse, the access point is in here."

Ariella nodded silently, her High Elf senses attuned to the shift in the arcane energies surrounding them. The very air seemed to thrum, charged with ancient magic waiting to be awakened.

"Aye, whatever lies ahead," Rider murmured, "we'll face it together." His voice was steady, but his grip on the hilt of his sword betrayed a hint of tension.

With each step, the anticipation built, a crescendo of excitement and fear that pushed them deeper into the belly of the mountain. They could feel the weight of the earth above them, the age of the stone around them, the secrets of the past beckoning just beyond their reach.

The heroes' silhouettes vanished into the darkness, leaving behind the lush greenery of the island and the oppressive heat.

CHAPTER XXII
SYL'VADREN

The mountain passage yawned before them like the mouth of an ancient behemoth. As the team crossed the threshold, what unfolded before their eyes was no mere cavern but a sanctum draped in once-fine cloths, now webbed and dusted. The walls, floor, and columns were sheathed in stone so smooth they looked like polished glass.

"By the stars," Rider whispered, his voice a reverent hush amidst the stillness.

"Only magic could forge such perfection," Kael commented, his gaze sweeping across the seamless surfaces. His fingers hovered inches from the wall, sensing rather than touching. "This place was carved by a master in the arts of transmutation. Observe, Rider—feel not with your flesh but with your Spark."

Rider watched, entranced, as Kael closed his eyes and extended his hands, palms outstretched. "The leylines stir around us like currents in the deep. Can you sense it? The pulsing energy woven into the fabric of this temple?"

Tentatively, Rider emulated Kael's stance, his brow furrowed in concentration. A moment passed, then another.

At first, there was only the echo of his own heartbeat, but slowly, a gentle thrumming began to resonate within him. It vibrated in his chest and swept through his limbs like sunlight over water. "Yes," he breathed," I feel it. "It's like... like warm air blowing across my skin, but deeper, more intimate."

"Good. Now follow that sensation to its source," Kael instructed, a note of pride in his words. "Lead us through these hallowed halls."

With newfound purpose, Rider stepped forward, the energy tugging at his core like an invisible thread, pulling him onward. Hawke and Ariella trailed behind, their expressions a mingling of curiosity and awe as they witnessed Rider's burgeoning connection to the Astralan legacy.

"Careful, everyone," Rider called back, his voice laced with the gravity of their undertaking. They descended further, winding along the smooth corridor until the interior of the mountain unfurled before them. It was a hollow expanse, vast and echoing, carved away by the island's previous inhabitants.

"By the Ancients," Ariella whispered, her violet eyes wide with wonder. Her hand rested lightly on the quiver slung across her hip.

Before them lay a colossal stairway that clung to the mountain's wall, spiraling down into the abyss. Its design was both majestic and harrowing, for one side was absent, leaving open air and death to those not mindful. The party aligned in a single file as they began their cautious descent.

As Rider set foot upon the first step, sconces embedded in the walls flared to life. Each subsequent step downward brought forth another burst of flame, illuminating their descent like a constellation of stars leading into the depths of the island.

"Remarkable," murmured Kael, his eyes reflecting the flickering torchlight. "But it is not merely showmanship. These energies suggest that the leyline access point is remarkably potent."

Rider nodded, focusing on the rhythmic pulse of magic that resonated through his hands.

Kael continued, "The leyline here is overactive, perhaps compensating for others that have been tampered with. It's caused an imbalance, but also an opportunity." His voice was steady, but an undercurrent of urgency hinted beneath.

"An opportunity?" ask Rider, his eyes narrowing.

"Long ago, our ancestors learned to channel the leyline directly into their Arcane Sparks. The process is arduous, requiring at least three magic wielders to act in unison." Kael's gaze swept from Rider to Ariella and back again. "We must perform this ritual with caution. If we draw too much energy, we risk further harm to Etonya's magical veins."

Ariella's brow furrowed. "And if we succeed?" She asked.

"Then I can restore some of my power... and perhaps fortify our chances against what lies ahead." Kael's words were lined with an undeniable mixture of desperation and hope.

"Well, then let's ensure we leave enough for Etonya, yeah?" Hawke chimed in. He didn't fully understand the conversation, but he knew anything involving Etonya's veins had to require caution.

The stairs finally tapered off, revealing an immense hall that spanned the chasm's width. The sides of the hall plunged into darkness below, a void stretching down to the island's core. With each step the party took into the chamber, braziers ignited in sequence along ancient pillars, banishing shadows to unveil its ancient design.

"Hands at the ready," Hawk muttered, his hand resting on the hilts of his pistols.

"Always," Ariella affirmed, her fingers brushing the fletching of an arrow.

As the last of the braziers sparked to life, their luminosity revealed a grand doorway marking the passage's next room.

"Looks like we've made it," said Rider, gesturing towards the imposing door with a mix of awe and determination.

"Come," Kael replied, his blue eyes alight with the fire of anticipation. "Let's not waste time here."

The air hummed with tension, charged with the unspoken agreement among them: they would face the unknown, united by their shared destiny and the ancient magic coursing through their veins.

As the team hastened their pace across the room, their footsteps echoed in the vastness of the grand hall. Their eyes were drawn toward the doorway at the far end, where the true horrors of the past lay.

Ancient corpses, their bones fused and melted together in grotesque sculptures of death, were piled against the grandiose entrance. The sight stole the breath from Rider's lungs as a flash of memories surged through his brain—the very scene he'd witnessed in his troubling dream. These were the people running desperately for escape, only to meet their doom by Dragon breath. But this far beneath the surface, a new, chilling thought took root. Perhaps they had been trying to contain something down here with them.

"Rider." Kael's voice, muffled by the vision, broke

through Rider's consciousness. "Focus. The phrase, remember?"

Rider shook his head in an attempt to dispel the haunting images. He steadied his breath, finding solace in the task at hand. He closed his eyes momentarily, reaching out to feel the arcane energy pulsing around them.

"*Avelor...*" His voice was clear, reverberating off the smooth walls, but it was quickly drowned out by a roar that seemed to rise from the very bowels of the island's core. The ground began to shake in rhythmic convulsions, each tremor like the heartbeat of some colossal beast awakening from an ageless slumber.

Kael's blond hair swayed with the force of the vibrations, his blue eyes sharpening as he processed the imminent threat. Ariella's gaze darted about, seeking the source, her fingers closing tighter around her bow. Hawke's pistols were already drawn, the metal glinting ominously in the firelight.

"Steady," Kael commanded, his presence a calming force amidst the chaos. "We knew we were likely not alone."

"Company I can handle," Hawke said, his voice betraying none of the fear that clenched his gut. "It's the waiting I'm not fond of."

"I don't think we'll have to wait for long," Ariella murmured, her eyes locked on the shadows that danced menacingly around them.

Rider gripped the hilt of his sword and unsheathed it over his shoulder, ready to confront whatever emerged from the abyss. They stood side by side, ready to face the unknown horror crawling from the darkness below.

The concussive thuds grew louder, accompanied by the rumble of crumbling stone as the source ascended toward them. Rider's eyes narrowed, his grip on the sword tightening. Ariella nocked an arrow, the string of her bow pulled tight against her slender fingers. Hawke readjusted his shoulders one last time, a smirk playing upon his lips despite the tension that knotted in his chest.

"Whatever it is," Hawke muttered, "it's big."

"Big is an understatement," Ariella whispered back, her eyes reflecting the flickering flames of the braziers.

Out of the darkness, a colossal shape emerged, its presence commanding and absolute. The figure materialized in the baleful glow of the firelight, a blue Dragon of immense proportions, scales shimmering with an ethereal hue as energy crackled around her grand form. She was a relic of The Great War, a general of the Dragon Lord, now standing before them as a testament to the horrors of the past.

With a voice that boomed through the hall and sent shivers down their spines, she announced, "What morsels have found their way into Syl'vadren's lair?"

"Your lair?" Hawke retorted, bravado masking his inner alarm. "Looks more like a tomb to me."

"Quiet, Hawke," Kael hissed under his breath, but the Dragon's gaze had already fixed upon them with predatory intensity.

"Ah," Syl'vadren purred, her tongue flicking over her cracked lips. "It has been so long since I've tasted the flesh of Etonians. Far too long."

Rider stepped forward, sword raised, determination etched into his features. "We're not here to be anyone's meal," he declared, though his heart raced at the sight of the Dragon's formidable might.

"Nor are we strangers to battle," Ariella added, her posture radiating defiance.

Syl'vadren let out a low, guttural chuckle, a sound that seemed to echo from deep within her belly. "We shall see," she said, eyeing them hungrily, her massive form blocking the only path forward. "We shall indeed see."

As Syl'vadren's snout flared, she inhaled deeply through her nostrils, the air quivering with power. Kael and Rider stood firm, though their hearts hammered against their ribs like war drums. With a slow, deliberate exhale, Syl'vadren grinned, revealing rows of sharp teeth. "Ah, Astralans," she mused, "what a rare delicacy indeed! How my stomach has ached for a proper meal."

Rider felt the Dragon's words vibrate through the very air, carrying with them her ancient hunger that chilled his blood. He tightened his grip on the hilt of his newly-forged blade, its edge glinting with anticipation.

"You must be the ones my master's telepathic messages have described," she stated, her twisted smile widening. "The meal before me is sure to bring favor from Drakzeneth after your demise."

Behind them, Hawke's fingers twitched nervously over the triggers of his pistols, the leather of the handles growing slick with sweat. The pirate captain's eyes darted between the Dragon and his weapons, calculating the odds. His normally roguish demeanor was frayed at the edges, giving way to a primal fear as the enormity of their adversary truly sank in.

"Your master ain't gettin word of nothin'," Hawke spat defiantly, the bravado returning to his voice. "Eat this!" he shouted in defiance.

With a swift motion, Hawke raised two of his pistols and fired directly into Syl'vadren's gaping maw. The bullets streaked through the air, accompanied by the smell of gunpowder. One ricocheted off the Dragon's bared teeth in a flurry of sparks while the other, more fortunate—or perhaps guided by fate—struck true, chipping away at a fang, eliciting a roar of pain and shock from the mighty beast.

"Move!" Kael shouted, as the party dispersed in all directions, seeking refuge behind the massive pillars that dotted the hall. Their footsteps echoed as they ran, the sound mingling with the crackle of the awakened sconces.

Syl'vadren's wrath materialized into a breath of blue lightning as she arced it across the room, chasing the fleeing figures. The blinding blue-white light filled the air with static, causing the hairs on their arms to stand on end as the electric current sought its prey. Pillars exploded upon impact, sending stone fragments flying and filling the room with dust and debris.

"Keep moving!" Ariella called out, her voice barely audible over the deafening roar.

They dove for cover, the heat of the Dragon's breath scorching the stones beneath their feet as it scattered by. They knew they had but moments before the creature would unleash another torrent of destruction. It was now a battle not just of steel and magic, but of wits and will.

Hawke's fingers danced across the hilts of his pistols, drawing and firing in rapid succession. The percussive reports of the gunshots joined the cacophony of battle as he emptied one pistol after the other. With each pull of the trigger, a round screamed towards the Dragon, some glancing off her scales, others finding purchase in the gaps between them.

"I ain't gonna be that thing's next meal," Hawke muttered under his breath. His hands were a blur, holstering spent pistols and drawing fresh ones.

Meanwhile, Ariella took a deep breath, steadying herself against the pillar as she notched an arrow to her bow. She released the string, sending the projectile hurtling through the air with a force that contradicted its silent flight. The arrow struck Syl'vadren square in the chest, the magical projectile glowing upon impact. A scale shattered like glass as the tip penetrated the tough hide, eliciting a pained screech from the Dragon.

"Well done, Baelgor," Ariella whispered, admiring her new bow's enchanted strength.

Kael, eyes glowing with arcane energy, extended his hands forward, casting bursts of blinding light at Syl'vadren. The flashes served their purpose, disorienting the Dragon, providing precious seconds for his comrades to maneuver. "Rider, focus! Ascend!" He yelled, trying to guide Rider amidst the chaos.

Rider gripped his longsword, the metal cool and light in his grasp. Its edge shimmered with a faint hue. He rushed forward from behind his pillar, slashing at Syl'vadren's underbelly as he darted past her colossal form. The sword cut through scale and hide easier than should be possible, leaving a trail of dark draconic blood in its wake.

"Keep firing!" Rider called out as he circled around for another pass.

Ariella dove forward, firing multiple arrows at the great beast. Syl'vadren, however, was no stranger to battle. The Dragon fought with savage grace, even wounded, as she swung around and knocked Ariella's arrows away with her wings. The force created by her movements buffeted Ariella back, knocking her against a pillar and onto the ground.

Hawke pressed forward towards Ariella as he fired two more rounds into the Dragon's neck, attempting to draw its attention away from Ariella.

Syl'vadren was relentless, the Dragon's tail crashed down towards Hawke like a battering ram, cracking the foundations. Hawke dove towards Ariella as the force of the impact caused him to lose his footing.

Electric blue arcs of energy swarmed in Syl'vadren's maw, threatening to unleash another devastating blast.

It was then that Kael made his move, rushing toward Hawke and Ariella with a chant and a sweeping gesture.

"*Luminar'eth!*" Kael shouted, as he conjured a dome of shimmering light above them, a protective barrier against Syl'vadren's elemental fury.

"Stay down!" Kael ordered his companions, his voice strained with effort as the shield flickered, weakened by his dwindling power.

The shield held, just barely, as Syl'vadren's lightning breath cascaded upon them. The air crackled and hissed, the stone beneath their feet vibrating with raw power.

"Kael… please…" Ariella urged, her eyes wide with concern as she watched the barrier waver.

"Working on it," Kael grunted out, pouring the last vestiges of his magic into maintaining their only defense.

Rider's chest heaved, his breath ragged with exertion as he approached for another strike of sword. Every attempt to move closer was met by the beast's mighty tail. He couldn't get through, he couldn't stop her.

All he could see were flashes between the furious swipes of the Syl'vadren's tail. Ariella's pained expression. Hawke's grim resolve. Kael's faltering magic. Their impending doom looming. The thought of losing them, of losing Ari made his heart thunder, not with fear, but with an unyielding determination.

"Come on!" Rider growled to himself, and the Arcane Spark in his core responded. It surged, thrived on his heightened emotions, fed on his desperation. The air around him shimmered as if the fabric of reality itself acknowledged his need for ascension.

"Rider?" Hawke's voice was laced with concern, but it seemed distant, almost lost amid the chaos.

Electricity danced across Rider's skin, crackling up his arms, weaving through his hair. Tiny fragments of shattered stone and dust orbited him as though caught in the gravity of a star.

"Well done, my boy..." Kael breathed out, witnessing the transformation.

The blue flames of Rider's Ascendance enveloped him, casting an ethereal light which battled against the darkness of the cavern. The aura pulsed, mirroring the beat of his racing heart, and then exploded outward in a forceful shockwave.

Syl'vadren halted her attack abruptly, her silver eyes widening. She reared back, the scales along her spine rising as she sensed the shift in power. "No," she hissed. "How... only Drakzeneth—"

"Believe it, you piece of shit!" Rider cut her off, his voice booming with a resonance amplified by the Spark within.

He dashed forward in a blur of motion and light. The Dragon swiped furiously with her claws, but Rider was no longer there. Each strike met empty air, the blurry afterimage of his movements the only trace left behind.

"Raahh!" Rider raged with each slice, his sword arcing through the charged atmosphere, leaving trails of incandescent energy. Sparks flew where the enchanted blade met Syl'vadren's scales, each hit a note in the symphony of battle.

"Impossible!" Syl'vadren shrieked, confusion and terror in her draconic snarl. Her confidence waned, the predator had become prey to a force she had never anticipated. She snapped at him with deadly fangs, but could never hit her mark.

"Oh, it's possible, scaly bitch!" Rider yelled back, his sword a streak of blue fire cutting through the air. He was everywhere and nowhere, a tempest incarnate, the embodiment of Astralan fury and might.

The echoes of their conflict resounded like thunder, a primal drumbeat signifying the turn of the tide.

Syl'vadren's form grew more erratic, her massive body teetering dangerously towards the edge of the platform, Hawke and Ariella seized their moment. They emerged from beneath the flickering remnants of Kael's barrier.

"Time to dance, you oversized lizard!" Hawke barked, drawing his next set of pistols. He fired rapidly, his shots a deadly cadence that punctuated the air. *BOOM! BOOM!* – each pistol expelled its flintlock fury before being holstered, only for another to be drawn in seamless succession.

Ariella arose, her bowstring pulled with the promise of destruction. The magical bow crafted by Baelgor thrummed as she released arrow after arrow. Each projectile sang through the air, a whistle of impending doom that found its mark in the Dragon's hide.

The arrows burrowed deep into Syl'vadren's flesh where scales had been already torn asunder by Rider's relentless assault. With each hit, Syl'vadren's mighty roar turned into a pained whine. The once indomitable beast was being undone.

"End it, Rider!" Kael's authoritative voice sliced through the cacophony. "Behead her! Claim the Spark!"

Rider nodded, his eyes ablaze with a fierce light. With a surge of Aetherion energy pulsing around him, he leaped high above Syl'vadren. Time seemed to slow as he hovered in midair, the world holding its breath. Then he descended like justice itself, his glowing blade raised for the final blow. His sword came down in a graceful arc, cleaving through scale, sinew and bone with supernatural ease.

Syl'vadren's head separated from her neck, a fountain of dark blood erupting from the wound. Her body, now a lifeless husk, coiled reflexively before slumping to the ground. The severed head slammed against the floor before sliding away, eyes dimming as the last vestiges of life faded.

The chamber fell silent but for the echo of clattering teeth and the heavy thuds of a Dragon's corpse settling onto the stone floor. Blood spread across the platform, glinting in the brazier lights.

"Is... is it over?" Hawke murmured, holstering his last smoking pistols, his chest heaving with exertion and relief.

"Not quite," Kael answered softly, his gaze on Rider, who stood amidst the carnage, the weight of victory and its toll etched upon his features.

"Rider," Ariella breathed, her voice a mix of concern and wonder as she took a tentative step towards him. Her violet eyes were wide, reflecting the flickering light that played across the scene.

"Stay back!" Kael's command cut through their moment of respite. His stern gaze was still fixed on Rider, who stood panting, his shoulders rising and falling with the effort of each ragged breath.

As if in response to Kael's warning, the air around Rider began to crackle. Chaotic magic, unleashed by Syl'-vadren's demise, erupted violently. Stones from shattered pillars hurtled across the chamber like projectiles caught in a tempest; arcs of blue lightning snaked across the marble floor, igniting the Dragon's blood in brilliant flashes of electric fire.

"What the..." Hawke swore under his breath, grabbing Ariella's arm to halt her advance. They could feel the raw energy even from where they stood—a gust of wind and heat that pushed against them, an unseen force that whispered of power untamed.

Ariella's hand flew to her mouth, her other hand

clutching at the fabric over her heart. Rider stood resolute as the Dragon's life-force spiraled into him. His silhouette was a beacon within the storm, framed by the infernal glow of Syl'vadren's burning blood.

"Rider!" she called out, but her voice was swallowed by the maelstrom.

Hawke felt it too—the pulsing waves of power that thrummed through the air, the scent of scorched earth that filled their nostrils. He kept his grip firm on Ariella, knowing any attempt to reach Rider now could be their end.

"Let the magic do its work," Kael shouted over the din, his eyes never leaving the spectacle before them.

They could only watch as Rider became the eye of the magical storm. His figure was both magnificent and terrifying, a testament to the might of the Astralan and the fearsome legacy he had inherited.

And then, as suddenly as it had begun, the tempest subsided. The last of the surges ebbed away, leaving a charged silence in their wake. Rider's aura faded, the glow dissipating until he was just a man again—exhausted, his strength spent.

With nothing left to hold him upright, Rider's knees buckled. He fell forward, catching himself on the hilt of his sword as it struck the stone with a dull clang, the blade's tip embedding into the floor to prop him up.

"Rider!" This time Ariella's cry pierced the stillness, and she broke free from Hawke, rushing to Rider's side.

"Easy there, lad," Hawke called out, following close behind, his own concern etched into his furrowed brow.

Kael approached more slowly, knowing the burden of their shared Astralan inheritance.

Ariella reached Rider and knelt beside him, her violet eyes wide and wet with concern.

"Is he..." Hawke began, his voice trailing off as he too dropped to a crouch by Rider's side.

"Alive," Kael affirmed, placing a reassuring hand on Ariella's back. "But the transfer... it takes a toll."

Rider's chest heaved with each breath, his dark hair plastered to his forehead with sweat and Dragon blood.

"Look at him," Ariella whispered in awe, her gaze following the faint traces of residual magic that clung to Rider's face. "He's magnificent."

"Indeed," Hawke muttered, though his eyes betrayed his grudging respect. "Never seen anything like it. Not sure I want to again."

Kael nodded solemnly, observing Rider with an inscrutable expression. "The power he wields... It's both a gift and a curse. One that he must learn to master, or it will master him."

"Can you help him?" Ariella asked, her hands hovering over Rider as if afraid to touch him, lest she disturb the arcane energies still settling within him.

"In time," Kael replied. "For now, let him rest. He has earned it."

Silently following Kael's wisdom, Ariella and Hawke remained by Rider's side, their presence a silent vigil. The echoes of battle slowly faded, replaced by the hush of breath, of thought, of magic settling once more into stillness.

CHAPTER XXIII
THE LEYLINES

Rider's breath came in ragged gasps, his chest heaving. He leaned heavily on his sword, the steel tip gouged into the stone beneath him. Sweat trailed down his temples, mingling with the grime of battle, and his sapphire eyes, clouded with fatigue, slowly lifted to meet Kael's gaze.

"Steady now, Rider," Kael encouraged, stepping closer with a hand outstretched. The warrior's arm shook as Kael helped him rise, but there was an unyielding look in those weary eyes.

With a grunt of effort, Rider yanked his blade from the floor, the sound echoing in the hallowed chamber. The sword slid home into its sheath upon his back with a satisfying click, and for a moment, he stood tall, his silhouette framed by the flickering torchlight.

From her place on the cold ground, Ariella rose, her movements graceful even in the midst of turmoil. She wrapped her arms around Rider, her embrace encompassing all the emotions that swirled within her: sadness at witnessing the toll the magical exchange took on him, pride for the mighty warrior her lover and friend had become, thankfulness for him having saved them once again, and lastly fear for the trials he must still face as they move onward to stop Drakzeneth.

"Once more you've shielded us from the dark," she whispered against his ear, her voice laced with both gratitude and fear for the unknown path ahead.

"Drakzeneth will fall," Rider murmured back, face pressed against hers, his voice low but fierce.

The party moved together toward the ornate door that barred their way, its surface a tapestry of shadows, carved runes that seemed to slumber in wait.

"Rider, the incantation," Kael prompted.

Rider squared his shoulders, summoning what remained of his strength. "*Avelor en'dur*," he proclaimed, his words resonating in the air.

The door stirred as if waking from an ancient slumber. Runes ignited along its dark expanse, a ripple of light that danced across the intricate carvings. Dust cascaded down, fine particles shimmering in the ethereal glow. The symbols pulsed with life, a heartbeat of magic. With a slight groan of stone against stone, the door began to part.

The door folded inward upon itself, vanishing into the walls. What lay beyond was no ordinary chamber. Statues of draconian mages and warriors stood in a solemn square around the room's perimeter, each gripping a massive crystal obelisk aloft.

Ariella stepped forward, awe blooming across her features. The air thrummed with power, and she could feel the magic coursing through the room. As she looked closer, a chill of realization traced her spine. The crystals... They were identical to those adorning the spires of Brightspire, glinting under the kingdom's sun.

"No," she breathed out, her voice barely above a whisper.

Before them, reality seemed to weave itself anew. From the aether, streams of prismatic magic spiraled toward the crystals, drawn by an invisible force. A kaleidoscope of color burst forth, painting the air with vibrant streaks of energy. Each stream twisted and turned with purpose before coalescing into a triangular device perched regally upon its pedestal at the room's center.

"Look at this," Ariella said, stepping closer to the pedestal, her gaze tracing the flow of magic.

Ariella turned to Rider, her expression laden with concern. "Rider, doesn't this resemble Queen Vyshaan's scrying room? The one we visited after coming back from the Serpent's Lair?"

Rider nodded, his own realization dawning. "It's more than resemblance. It's an exact replication."

"Then the queen..." Ariella's voice trailed off, the implication hanging heavily between them.

Kael, who had been silently observing the flows of magic, finally spoke. "I suspected a connection when I first sensed the energies in Brightspire, but the city's own magic clouded certainty. Now, though, it's apparent." His voice carried the weight of revelation. "Queen Vyshaan's sorcery —it's linked to a leyline."

The foursome stood in silent contemplation, surrounded by the whispers of ancient magic and the echoes of their newfound understanding.

Kael's gaze sharpened as he turned to face Ariella and Rider, his posture commanding despite the softness of his words. "Now is the time to act," he declared, a spark of excitement flaring within his shimmering blue eyes. "We must tap into the leyline's energy, harness it to reignite my Arcane Spark."

Ariella's eyes met Rider's, a silent agreement passing between them. They nodded in unison.

"Teach us the Astralan ritual, Kael," Ariella said with a steely resolve.

"Let's do this," Rider added, his voice carrying an eager edge.

Kael guided them through the intricate complexities of the ritual, ensuring each word, each gesture was understood and memorized. Hours passed as they practiced, repeating the motions and incantations until they flowed as naturally as breath.

At last, they each positioned themselves under separate Draconian statues, each taking their place at a different point surrounding the pyramidic structure.

"Remember," Kael instructed, his voice now a whisper of power. "Let the magic flow through you, and begin the counterspell the moment I tell you." He closed his eyes, lifting his hands skyward in homage to the celestial beings whose language they were about to invoke. His palms faced the heavens, fingers splayed wide as if to embrace the very cosmos.

Ariella and Rider mirrored his stance, their bodies tensing with the responsibility of the moment. Around them, the room pulsed with arcane potential, waiting for the command.

"*Vel'ethrae, Vri'shanar, Leyarin'sol, Ar'kanon!*" Kael's voice boomed with a resonance amplified by the acoustics of the temple's grand heart. The words were ancient and powerful, charged with magic that vibrated the stones beneath their feet.

Ariella felt the air hum around her, the statues seemed to lean in, attentive to the spell woven by Kael's voice. She exchanged a glance with Rider, the same determination mirrored in his eyes. Together, they drew in a deep breath and responded to Kael's call.

"*Vel'ethrae, Vri'shanar, Leyarin'sol, Ar'kanon!*"

Their voices joined as one, harmonizing with Kael's incantation. The syllables rolled off their tongues like liquid silver, each word imbued with centuries of arcane knowledge and celestial power.

The room responded immediately. The crystals atop the Draconian statues began to glow brighter, pulsating with energy. The multicolored streams of magic twined through the air, coalescing into a vibrant tapestry of light. Ariella felt the hairs on her arms stand on end, an electric charge filled her senses.

They repeated the chant, over and over, allowing the rhythm of the Astralan language to guide them. With each repetition, the magic grew more intense, the aether around them crackling with raw, unbridled power.

"Vel'ethrae, Vri'shanar, Leyarin'sol, Ar'kanon!" they called out again, their voices unwavering, strong and clear.

"Vel'ethrae, Vri'shanar, Leyarin'sol, Ar'kanon!" The invocation was a beacon, a summons to the energies hidden within the fabric of reality, a heed to answer the call of those who dared to commune with the stars.

"Vel'ethrae, Vri'shanar, Leyarin'sol, Ar'kanon!" The temple shook with power. Light swirled around them, a celestial storm reaching its zenith

"Stop!" Kael's thunderous voice shattered the rhythmic cadence like a lance through glass.

As Ariella and Rider stopped, the apex of the ritual arrived in a cataclysmic release. Majestic and terrifying, the energy from the device surged forth, an unrestrained river of arcane might. It sought out Kael as its vessel, a maelstrom of power funneling into his chest.

The sight was both awe-inspiring and petrifying. Kael's eyes snapped open, aglow with an otherworldly luminescence that pierced through the dimness of the surroundings. His arms flung wide, embracing the tempest as it lifted him from the ground. He hovered over the ground, suspended by the invisible strings of magic that writhed around him.

Ariella's heart hammered against her ribs, a mixture of fear and wonder seizing her as she beheld Kael transformed into a beacon of pure arcane brilliance. Beside her, Rider tensed in unison.

"Rider, Ariella," Kael's voice cut through the chaos, steady despite the tumultuous energy engulfing him. "The counter chant, now!"

"*Asha'khel, Nol'shivar, An'arae, Spar'kannon!*" Rider and Ariella launched into the counterspell without hesitation. Their voices were clear and resolute across the surging tide of magic.

"*Asha'khel, Nol'shivar, An'arae, Spar'kannon!*" they repeated, their incantation weaving a net to ensnare and tame the wild energy. The air grew thick with resistance against the containment of such raw power.

"*Asha'khel, Nol'shivar, An'arae, Spar'kannon!*" They did not falter, did not cease, even as sweat beaded on their foreheads and their throats grew hoarse. The chant became a mantra, a rallying cry against the storm.

"*Asha'khel, Nol'shivar, An'arae, Spar'kannon!*" Magic rippled and tightened. The leyline pulse slowed, no longer pouring unchecked, but tethered by their will

"*Asha'khel, Nol'shivar, An'arae, Spar'kannon!*" Finally, the last of the energy receded, leaving only a faint glow within the crystalline structures and a sense of profound silence.

Kael remained aloft for a moment longer, the light fading from his eyes, before his feet softly touched the stone floor once again. The danger had passed, their friend was anchored back among them, the tempest of magic quelled by their united stand.

"Thank you, my friends," Kael murmured, his eyes

fluttering open to reveal the serene blue that had been momentarily eclipsed by arcane luminescence. A small smile graced his lips as he snapped his fingers, and from the simple gesture, twin sparks danced into existence, crackling with residual energy.

Ariella and Rider watched, a mixture of relief and fascination coloring their expressions, as Kael's laughter mingled with the soft sound of lightning dancing between his outstretched fingers. With a final flourish, the playful bolts of electricity vanished, and Kael stepped forward. His arms encircled them both—a warm, encompassing embrace that conveyed gratitude deeper than his words could ever relay.

"Never seen anything like it," Hawke admitted, a note of reverence threading his usually boisterous tone. "These past few days... wildest ride of my life, and that's saying something."

Their laughter echoed through the temple, a brief respite of joy in the midst of dire circumstances. As the laughter ebbed, Kael stepped back, his gaze intent on Rider and Ariella.

"Time for your next lesson," Kael declared, the weight of responsibility returning to his voice. "You must learn to commune with the leyline access point, not just harness its power. It will reveal the others."

"All right," Rider said, his eagerness apparent.

"Close your eyes," Kael instructed. "Let your breath steady and feel the magic that permeates this place. The leyline's song is subtle but unmistakable."

Rider and Ariella obeyed, shutting out the visual splendor of the temple to focus inward. They stood still, breathing deeply, reaching out with their senses under Kael's teaching.

"Feel the pulse," Kael continued, his words painting

invisible strokes in the air. "The ebb and flow of power. It's like the heartbeat of the world—steady, rhythmic, eternal."

At first, there was nothing. Then, a hint of vibration tickled their awareness, a whisper of energy that grew steadily clearer. It was as if they had tapped into the very veins of the earth, feeling its lifeblood thrum beneath them.

"When you feel it, grab hold. Open your eyes and don't let go."

As they opened their eyes, the room seemed unchanged, yet everything was different. Their sight shimmered as they shifted their sight around the room.

"Now place your hands upon the device," Kael directed, his voice a calm command that resonated with authority. Rider, Ariella, and Kael each laid their palms on the cold, angular surface of the ancient device.

They closed their eyes once more, delving into the mystical connection they had just forged. A current of energy surged up their arms, flooding their senses with a torrent of images.

The expansive Great Planes unfurled before them, vibrant and serene in their mental vista. Reshu Academy, majestic and imposing, rose from its scholarly solitude, its spires reaching for the heavens. Then the scene shifted to Mount Stonefire, alive with magma, a cradle of elemental creation.

But tranquility shattered when Brightspire Castle loomed into view, its elegance marred by the horrors unfolding within its walls. Citizens and prisoners alike twisted grotesquely, their bodies contorting unsuccessfully into draconic nightmares, only to collapse lifeless under the strain of spells gone wrong. The Queen's face emerged amidst the chaos, her eyes—a chilling, soulless void—fixing onto theirs with recognition.

Abruptly, the connection severed, snapping their consciousness back to the temple with a jolt. They removed their hands from the device, gasping, their faces etched with horror and determination.

"By the gods..." Rider breathed out, his eyes clouded with the dark vision they had all shared.

Ariella's gaze met Rider's, mirroring his dread. "What does this mean?" she whispered, her normally composed tone laced with fear.

Kael's features were set in grim resolve as he answered. "It means Queen Vyshaan has been trying to make Dragons out of her subjects."

Hawke, who had been watching intently, stepped forward, alarm furrowed into his brow. "What did you just say? What did you see?"

"Evil," Ariella replied, her voice barely above a murmur. "We saw the Queen turning her own people into monsters."

"Monsters..." Hawke echoed, aghast.

Kael turned to them all, his piercing blue eyes now alight with a spark of defiance. "We must travel to these locations—the leyline access points—and find the other devices. Only by taking control of the network can we hope to counteract Drakzeneth's plans."

Rider nodded, his jaw set. "Then we haven't a moment to lose."

As they exited the heart of the temple, Hawke cast a glance back at the closing door, its runes dimming until they disappeared completely. It was a silent acknowledgment of their departure, a threshold crossed from which there could be no return.

They traversed the grand hall in silence as they passed the grisly remains of Syl'vadren. The decapitated corpse lay in solemn testament to their victory, its blood now seeped into the cracks of the stone floor.

Kael, without pause and with a fluid motion of his hand, uttered the incantation with practiced ease, "*Vor'ethra.*" The spell burst forth from his palm, an eruption of raw energy that reverberated through the chamber like the clap of thunder following a lightning strike. Rider flinched at the sound, feeling the residual power tingling on his skin as he watched the Dragon's body hurled mercilessly against the mountain wall. It then descended into the abyss below, leaving only the severed head behind—a grim reminder of their encounter and a warning to those who would dare tamper with forces beyond their understanding.

"Filthy," Kael said, his voice carrying the weight of authority and contempt.

With urgency fueling their steps, they retraced their path, the stairway before them now familiar territory. Ariella led the way, her auburn hair catching the dim light filtering through the canopy above. Her grace was evident even in haste, every step deliberate and sure.

The journey back through the forest was expedited by their previous passage: foliage trampled, branches broken and pushed aside, all created a clear trail for them to follow. The scent of crushed leaves and earth filled the air, mingling with the distant saltiness of the sea.

"Feels like we just did this," Hawke remarked jokingly, brushing a hanging vine out of his face.

"Except now, it feels like we're being chased by time itself," Rider replied, casting a glance over his shoulder at Hawke.

"Every second we delay, more innocents may suffer," Ariella added, her voice steady despite her quickened breath. She wiped a bead of sweat from her brow, feeling the humidity of the forest cling to her skin.

"Keep your eyes sharp," Kael instructed, his gaze flitting between the trees. "We may have cleared a path, but the forest may still hold more than we know."

They moved with renewed focus, their feet finding rhythm on the forest floor. The sounds around them—the distant calls of birds, the rustle of small creatures—were a constant reminder of the life that hung dependent upon their quest..

"We gonna stop soon?" Hawke asked, his voice beginning to get ragged under labored breaths.

"Come on Hawke, it's just air," Rider joked. "We can rest aboard The Banshee's Wail."

Ariella nodded in agreement, her thoughts already turning to the challenges ahead. They had battles yet to fight, secrets to uncover, and a Queen to confront. The gravity of their quest weighed heavily upon them all, but together, they pressed forward.

The moon hung like a watchful sentinel by the time they emerged from the forest's embrace, casting its silvery glow over the shoreline. The cool night air was a balm to their sweat-slicked skin, and the sound of gentle waves lapping at the shore played a soothing counterpoint to the urgency that still gripped their hearts.

"Almost there," Rider encouraged, his voice a low rumble in the quietness of the night.

"Rest will come with the tide," Kael whispered, more to Hawke than himself, as he gazed across the dark expanse of sand stretching before them.

Suddenly, a sharp crack disturbed the peace—a warning shot sent a spray of sand into the air just ahead of their weary feet. Instinctively, the party halted, hands going to weapons out of habit rather than intention.

"Who goes there?" a rough voice called out, barely discernible above the sound of the surf.

"The first one of ya to scuff my boots, I swear to the gods I'll make sure the depths claim ya!" Hawke's commanding tone cut through the tension as he stepped forward, recognizing his own men in the dim light.

Laughter and cheers broke out from the shadows as the pirates recognized their Captain, their relief palpable in the salty sea breeze. The figures approached, their outlines becoming clearer under the moon's silver gaze.

"Captain! You've returned!" a burly pirate exclaimed, his teeth gleaming white against his tanned face.

"Bring us any treasure?" another chimed in, half-jesting but hopeful.

Ariella, Rider, and Kael stepped into the moonlight beside Hawke, each carrying the weight of their mission in their gaze. They were ready to face whatever lay ahead.

"Let's gather the crew," Hawke ordered, his voice laced with the promise of action. "We have a world to save."

Hawke's stride was purposeful as he made his way across the sandy beach to a huddled figure slumped near the remnants of a half drank bottle of rum. With a swift kick from his booted foot, he nudged the first mate's leg, rousing the man with a start.

"Cap'n! You're back!" The first mate rubbed his eyes, scrambling to attention.

"Repairs done?" Hawke asked gruffly, his gaze like steel.

"Aye, sir. 'The Wail' awaits your command," replied the first mate, standing up and brushing sand from his trousers.

"Good man," Hawke clapped him firmly on the shoulder with approval. "Now muster the lads. There's news to be shared."

With a nod, the first mate bellowed orders that cut

through the night, the snores and quiet murmurs of sleeping men replaced by the rustling of bodies stirring to life. Pirates emerged from their makeshift shelters, yawning and stretching as they congregated around the flaring bonfire at the heart of their camp. Flames licked the air, crackling as the crew assembled in a ragtag formation before their Captain.

"Listen up, you sorry lot!" Hawke's voice carried above the crackle of the fire. "The tales we'll have after tonight will be worth more than any chest o' gold."

Curiosity sparked in the groggy eyes of his crew, drawing them closer together in anticipation of his words.

"Rider, Ariella, Kael, and I – we've seen what darkness seeks to consume Etonya. This ain't just their battle," he gestured towards his companions, "it's ours too. This ain't some petty kingdom squabble, nor a storm to weather and forget come mornin'. Nay, it's a threat to every free soul in these lands."

Unease shifted through the pirates like a cold wind, the weight of Hawke's declaration settling on their shoulders. The fire popped and hissed, throwing erratic shadows over the faces of men whose lives were spent chasing horizons, not wars.

Hawke stood tall, the firelight casting his shadow over the sands. "Etonya teeters on the brink of a Great War," he bellowed, his voice carrying over the waves and wind. "And mark my words—history will remember us! The Pirates of the Crystal Sea won't be idle tales for drunkards; we'll be legends. We will be the tide that washes away Drakzeneth's return!"

His motley collection of hardened seafarers and brash buccaneers listened, rapt. Some nodded in agreement, eyes alight with the spark of impending adventure. Others exchanged wary glances, their hands instinctively gripping the hilts of cutlasses and daggers.

"Cap'n, what about the spoils?" called out a grizzled quartermaster, one eye squinting skeptically under a weathered brow.

"Ah, me hearties, did ye doubt?" Hawke's laugh was a hearty boom that seemed to blend with the crackle of the bonfire. "The kingdoms will shower gold upon those brave enough to face this scourge!" He spread his arms wide, as if to embrace the promised fortune. "Riches beyond measure await those who help cast down this fiend!"

At the mention of treasure, the pirates' mood shifted like the tides. Cheers erupted from the crowd, hoots of excitement piercing the night air as visions of wealth filled their heads. They clapped each other on the backs, their earlier trepidation drowned out by dreams of riches.

Hawke turned to Rider, Kael, and Ariella, sharing an impish grin. With an exaggerated shrug and a knowing chuckle, he acknowledged their silent understanding: sometimes the promise of coin was the strongest spell of all.

The air around them buzzed with anticipation, the sound of the sea blending with the clamor of eager voices. Tonight, they were not merely pirates—they were the vanguard of Etonya's hope, bonded by the promise of glory and gain.

The raucous commotion began to ebb as Hawke raised a hand for silence, his brow furrowed with the gravity of the task ahead. "Lads! To the ropes! We've got a ship to move," he commanded, gesturing towards The Banshee's Wail, its hull ghostly in the moonlight.

"Allow me a moment, Captain," Kael interjected, his voice a smooth contrast to the gruff calls of the pirates. There was a spark of mischief or magic, perhaps both, as he stepped forward. "Our friends here have labored hard in our absence. Let us lighten their burden."

Hawke gave a surprised nod as he swung an arm in response towards the ship, as if granting permission with a flourish.

Kael closed his eyes, focusing on the energies once again coursing through him. His lips moved silently, shaping the incantation before it spilled forth, clear and resonant. "*Aer'leth Talasen, Vael'shara Solan!*"

As the Astralan words left his lips, the air itself seemed to heed his call. A soft breeze stirred, gentle at first, like a caress. It whispered through the leaves of the palms, carrying the scent of the sea and the heat of the sand.

Then, with growing insistence, the breeze swelled into a wind. Palm trees swayed vigorously as the gusts coalesced into a force that surged toward The Banshee's Wail, circling it in a vortex.

Sands shifted under the might of the spell, creating serpentine swirls that slithered away from the ship's keel. Grains of sand skittered across the deck, blown clean by the burgeoning whirlwind, while the sails unfurled with a snap, billowing outwards filled with the breath of Kael's tempest.

Ropes strained against the masts as they creaked in protest under the invisible hands of the wind as it pulled tight. The whole ship seemed to come alive, imbued with the essence of Kael's spell.

"By the gods..." murmured a young deckhand, his eyes wide with wonder. Others joined in a chorus of awe, their voices dim amidst the roar of the wind.

"Behold the might of Astrala!" Kael's shout cut through the din, his arms raised skyward, channeling the fury of the elements. In those moments, the boundaries between sorcery and nature blurred, and all who witnessed knew they stood in the presence of raw power—the kind that could change the course of the coming war, of histories, of lives.

The ship now creaked and groaned as if taking its first breath in ages. Slowly, almost imperceptibly at first, the ship lifted from its earthen bed. It rose gently, its hull cleansed of its sandy shroud, revealing its battle-scarred, yet still majestic form.

"Look at her go!" someone shouted from the gathering crowd of pirates, their voices a crescendo of excitement over the whirling sands. The ship seemed to defy gravity, buoyed by invisible currents of air. It glided across the top of the beach, a phantom sailing on a sea of swirling dust.

As the Banshee's Wail approached the water's edge, the wind's fury lessened, becoming a guiding breeze that ushered the ship into the shallow lap of the waves. With a gentle splash, the mighty vessel kissed the ocean, its rightful domain. A collective gasp escaped the crew, followed by an eruption of cheers, shouts, and clapping that rivaled the storm conjured by Kael.

"Ha! She floats!" Hawke bellowed with laughter, his voice booming over the joyful din.

"Kael, ye wizard, ye've done it!" another pirate yelled, slapping Kael on the back with gratitude that nearly knocked the air from his lungs.

"Let's get a move on, lads!" Hawke called out, already striding towards the supplies scattered about the camp. "We don't have all night!"

The pirates sprang into action, their previous amazement giving way to practiced efficiency. They hoisted crates, rolled barrels, and gathered every last scrap of provision. They loaded up their rowboats, muscles straining and sweat mingling with the salt spray as they heaved their bounty into the small vessels.

"Goodbye, sandy shores," Ariella whispered, her voice tinged with relief and anticipation.

"Goodbye and good riddance," Rider replied, his eyes fixed on the horizon where new challenges awaited. Kael simply nodded, his gaze lingering on the faint arcs of energy still crackling between his fingertips, a silent reminder of his reclaimed power.

Together, they pushed off from the beach, the rowboats cutting through the surf toward the waiting Banshee's Wail. As the distance closed, the moonlight cast a silver glow upon the ship, its sails full and proud, ready to carry them towards Amakiir and whatever destiny awaited them there.

CHAPTER XXIV
STUBBORN ROOTS

The salt-filled air whipped through Rider's hair as he and Ariella stood firm against the railing of The Banshee's Wail. The ship cut through the crystal sea, its sails stretched taut with a favoring wind.

"Keep your hand steady on the line," Hawke instructed from behind, a note of gruff patience in his voice.

Rider gripped the rope with calloused hands, sensing the ship respond like a living creature. Beside him, Ariella listened intently as a one-eyed sailor named Brack spilled his tale of woe, which led him to this life of piracy.

"Was a fisherman once, 'til I was taxed outta me home," Brack muttered, his voice a low rumble. "Now I take what I can, give nothing back."

Ariella's face softened with empathy. "There are too many stories like yours," she said, her voice clear as the waters below. "Brightspire has turned a blind eye for too long."

Rider, still manning the line, stood watching her. Her conversation flowed easily from one crew member to the next, each story revealing the injustices that plagued Etonya.

Their words carried in the breeze, mingling with the distant aroma of the cook's stew wafting from the galley. The deck beneath their feet hummed with activity. Ropes creaked, timbers groaned, and the occasional shout of command punctuated the ship's song.

"Seems you've got quite the heart, m'lady." One pirate, a young lad, was taken by her Elven beauty.

"Thank you," Ariella replied, trying to softly break away from the conversation.

"Let's not forget why we're here," Rider said, shifting his focus back to the horizon, "to meet with King Amakiir and restore our alliance."

"Indeed," Ariella concurred, casting a lingering glance at the crew. "But we'll carry their stories with us. They deserve more than the hand they've been dealt."

The Banshee's Wail continued its relentless surge forward. The day waned on as the two stood shoulder to shoulder, united by a cause greater than themselves.

"Land ho!" The cry echoed from the crow's nest, stirring the crew into a flurry of activity.

Rider's gaze looked towards the horizon as the approaching Amakiir Forest game faintly into view. "Looks like we've arrived," he said, his voice carrying a hit of relief and anticipation.

Ariella's eyes sparkled with excitement as she watched the sailors leap into action. As they pulled ropes and adjusted sails, a symphony of clanking pulleys and flapping canvas filled the air. The wood beneath her feet vibrated with the hustle of their booted steps.

"Best gather your things, " Hawke called over to them, his voice carrying above the noise. "Not sure how far the castle is from the coast, but I've never seen it, so I'd wager it's not close."

"Aye aye, Captain," Ariella replied, her tone respectful yet playful. She turned to Rider with a determined look. "Let's prepare ourselves."

Descending into the bowels of the ship, they navigated the narrow corridors. Their quarters were a mess, the fine drapery and linens scattered about, pillows thrown onto the floor and in corners from their nights of passion.

"Here," Rider said, handing Ariella her satchel. It contained not just small tools and trinkets, but also unbeknownst to him, a hand-drawn portrait she'd made of him while he slept one night.

"Thank you," she responded, securing her straps. Her fingers then ran along the back of his belt.

"I don't know how far the castle is from where we're landing" Rider started, sheathing his dagger and looking back over his shoulder.

"That's ok," Ariella said, her eyes meeting his with longing. "As long as we're together."

"Indeed," he agreed with a grin, his sapphire eyes glinting with shared admiration.

They made their way back to the deck, the sounds of the sea greeting them.

"Ready?" Rider asked, offering his hand.

"Always," Ariella replied, as she grabbed hold.

"Drop anchor!" Hawke's command pierced the air. A chorus of obedience followed as the crew scrambled. With each turn of the capstan, the gears grated against one another. The sound of metal on metal echoed across the deck as thick steel chains unraveled and slithered over the side until the colossal anchor plunged through the water's surface with a resounding splash.

"Drop the boats," Hawke barked, his eyes already surveying the coastline. "Make for shore, lads."

Rider, Ariella, Kael, and Hawke descended to the smaller vessels tethered alongside the ship. They took their places, oars in hand, and cut through the waves. The salt-laden breeze tousled Rider's dark hair as they rowed. The late afternoon sun lingered overhead as they finally hit shore.

"Land awaits," Hawke grinned, as their boats kissed the sandy shore. A pirate's life had etched its tale upon his features, but Ariella noticed he never looked happier than when at sea.

The hulls kissed the shore with a gentle crunch. Around them, pirates leapt out, fanning into the foliage to gather food and resources.

"Amakiir Castle is our destination," Rider stated, voice steady as he gathered his gear. "We'll need Laucian's forces if we're going to confront Vyshaan."

"Convincing him to rejoin us may not be easy, Rider," Kael remarked, adjusting his cape over his shoulders.

"Laucian will see reason. He has to," Ariella said, her tone full of hope.

"Once we're done here, it's on to the plains," Rider continued. "We can use Jarl Reshu's spell and teleport to my hall and then the other houses."

"Then to Stonefire," Ariella concluded, her determination mirrored in Rider and Kael's nods of agreement.

"Your path is clear," Hawke observed, gazing into the forest with a sharp eye. "May the winds be ever at your backs," he offered, a rare glint of sincerity flashing through as he clasped Rider's forearm in a firm shake. "When the time comes to face Vyshaan, know that our Black Sails will be there."

"Thank you, Captain," Ariella replied, her voice tinged with warmth and gratitude.

"Until then," Hawke agreed with a smirk, tipping his hat before turning back to his crew.

The tranquility of their goodbyes were shattered by screams piercing the air. Instinctively, the trio spun around, hands reaching for weapons as they prepared for the unknown.

Rider gasped, eyes wide as the scene unfolded before them.

A torrent of panicked pirates spilled out from the tree line carrying a series of large eggs, stumbling over each other and falling into the sand as they lost their footing amidst the rapid change in terrain.

"Griffins!" someone shouted—a warning drowned out by the beating of powerful wings.

Three Griffins swooped down from above the trees. Majestic yet terrifying, their feathers were a storm of brown and gold, with wings vast enough to blot out the sun.

The beasts descended upon the crew with relentless ferocity, their sharp talons rending through fabric and flesh. Splatters of crimson stained the sand as the men carrying the eggs were cut down.

"Damn it!" Hawke roared, "whose blasted idea was that!?"

"Leave the eggs!" Rider barked, knowing the Griffins' wrath was tied to the stolen children. His command went unheeded as chaos reigned.

A burly crewman drew a blunderbuss and took aim at one of the assaulting Griffins. The beast's eyes flared with a primal fury as it turned towards the threat.

"NO!" Rider's shout split the air like thunder. With an outstretched hand, he summoned a wave of force that erupted from his palm. The pirate was hurled backward, crashing into the sand as his weapon flew from his grasp.

The Griffin's gaze snapped toward Rider. Its golden eyes met Rider's and recognition sparked within the creature.

With a piercing screech that seemed to acknowledge and thank Rider, the Griffin ceased its attack. It folded its wings gently, then approached him with a regal gait, head bowed in a display of respect.

"Look at that," Kael murmured, watching intently as the Griffin approached.

Rider nodded, understanding dawning in his eyes. This was no ordinary Griffin. It was the same noble creature that granted him passage from Castle Amakiir all those moons ago.

With a cautious hand, Rider reached out and touched the Griffin's head, his fingers tracing its feathers. The creature nudged against his touch, seeking the comfort of affection. He obliged, scratching behind the majestic bird's ear, feeling the softness and strength beneath.

The other Griffins, their aggression waning, landed softly on the sand, aligning themselves with their leader. Their presence commanded the attention of all on the beach, a silent truce falling over the scene.

"Return those eggs, now!" Hawke barked at his men. "Be gentle about it, too, ya' geniuses."

"Majestic ones," Ariella called out, her voice soft and carrying a touch of reverence.

The Griffins turned their heads in unison to regard her. "Would you be willing to assist us in getting back to King Laucian's castle? It's a very long journey and we'd very much appreciate your aid," she implored.

For a moment, the creatures seemed to confer among themselves, exchanging glances and tilting their heads as if in deep discussion. Finally, they kneeled on the dirt, the sand clinging to their feathers, offering their strong backs to the trio.

"Ha!" Hawke laughed. "This band of misfits never ceases to amaze me." He shook his head, his bushy black and brown hair moving beneath his captains hat. "I'm glad I chose to save your sorry a—"

The lead Griffin Rider had mounted let out a sharp screech, a clear warning to mind his tongue.

Rider's lips quirked into a smile as a small laugh forced its way out of his mouth. Ariella's chuckle merged with Kael's deeper laugh, a symphony of camaraderie and friendship spilled forth.

Hawke, momentarily startled, blinked before a wide grin split his weathered face. He threw back his head and joined in the laughter.

With the tension dissolved into laughter, the party prepared to leave.

One by one, the Griffins sprinted off with thunderous beats against the sand. Almost in unison, they leapt into the sky as their wings unfurled, catching the wind.

As they ascended, the evening moon began its climb. Beneath them stretched the endless expanse of Amakiir forest. The scents of pine and moist earth soared up to meet them. Ariella breathed deeply, savoring the fresh aroma.

"Look there," Kael pointed out, his voice barely audible over the rushing wind, "the torchlights of Castle Amakiir." The Griffins knew their destination as they descended toward the lights with familiarity. Their screeches echoed off the canopy, heralding their arrival.

"Griffins approaching!" the cry rang out below, alerting all within earshot of the unexpected guests.

With a display of power and grace, the creatures beat

their wings, slowing their descent before hovering above the high royal balcony outside the High Priest King's courtroom. They dropped to their feet, talons clicking on the stone as they folded their wings against their flanks.

"Remarkable," Ariella murmured as she slid off her mount. Her fingers trailed along the creature's neck in a silent gesture of gratitude.

"Truly," agreed Rider, planting his boots firmly on the balcony. He gave his Griffin a gentle pat on the beak, earning a soft hoot in response.

Kael followed suit, dismounting the majestic beast with words of gratitude.

Guards in forest green and gold livery approached, their metal spears in hand. "The hour is late. Please state your business," one of the guards demanded.

Rider stepped forward, his posture relaxed but confident. "We're here to speak with your majesty, the High Priest King Laucian once again," he declared, his voice resonating with a mix of urgency and respect.

The guard scrutinized them, his gaze lingering on Rider's longsword and then drifting to Ariella and Kael, as he weighed their intentions.

"It is late, and no one speaks to our majesty at this hour. You must return in--" the guard begins, only to be interrupted by Laucian himself.

"Ah, Rider. It seems you and your companions have returned at last," Laucian greeted them.

"Yes, your Highness. We bring--" Rider started before being cut off once more by Laucian.

"Arrest them," Laucian ordered, causing the guards to shift into offensive positions and point their spears at Rider and his party.

"Whoa!" Rider exclaimed in response to the sudden aggression.

"Your Highness," Ariella began calmly. "If you are truly as wise as your reputation suggests, then you know that we are not your enemies."

"I trusted Elandir to be safe in your presence. Instead, he perished in that Orcish hell," Laucian retorted angrily.

"We did not leave him to die," Kael interjected. "We were certain he was--"

"Dead?" a familiar voice interrupts from the shadows. "I'm afraid I am not so easily killed," Elandir interjected, as he revealed himself.

"Elandir!" The trio exclaimed in shock and confusion.

"Please, lower your weapons," Elandir commanded, and all of the guards comply immediately.

"What is going on?" Rider questioned.

"It was actually Kael's display of arcane prowess that helped me survive," Elandir explained. "The initial shock of what took place in their camp distracted the guards long enough for me to make my escape. Granted, I was gravely wounded, but I was able to eventually make it out of that smoldering heap you left in your wake."

"We had no idea," Ariella said regretfully.

"There was no way for you to know. By the time I reached my people in the forest, it was too late. Stonefire had already sent news to my court about mine and Baelgor's deaths," Elandir said, revealing the truth.

"Your court?" Rider repeats, confused.

"Laucian's a decoy," Kael explained. "Clever, Elandir."

"Thank you, Kael," Elandir acknowledged before continuing. "My people believed the false information and broke our alliance with Stonefire and House Bloodmane."

"How did Stonefire learn about what happened before we ever sent word back to Brightspire?" Ariella asked.

"I asked myself the same question," Elandir stated.

"And could only come to one of two conclusions: Either they knew it was going to happen…"

"Or someone who did, told them ahead of schedule," Ariella said, finishing Elandir's sentence while looking to Rider. A tense silence followed as the implication sank in.

"Elandir, there is much we need to discuss about Brightspire and Queen Vyshaan," Rider began.

"I am well aware that she is possessed by Drakzeneth. King Ragnoc and I have been in contact. He will be pleased to hear of your arrival. Come, there is much for me to hear about your journey since you last left Stonefire."

As they walked into the great wooden courtroom, Elandir gestured for them to take a seat. As they settled into the surprisingly comfortable chairs, Rider leaned forward.

"Elandir, we've uncovered a dark truth about Drakzeneth," he began, his voice low and urgent. "He's not of this world. He hails from a place called Draconis."

Elandir's brows furrowed, his expression a mix of surprise and concern. "Draconis? Another world?"

Kael cleared his throat, drawing attention to himself. "There's more," he said, his voice carrying a note of reverence. "Drakzeneth's people, the Draconin, once enslaved my ancestors, the Astralan. We believe Rider may be descended from them as well."

Elandir leaned back in his chair as he took in the information.

Ariella nodded, her eyes shining with determination as she added, "We must stop Drakzeneth from regaining his full power. He seeks to control the leylines, the very lifeblood of magic in Etonya."

Elandir exchanged glances with the trio before

responding, "This is grave news. If Drakzeneth succeeds, the consequences would be catastrophic."

Rider stood, as he began to speak, "We plan to investigate the remaining leyline locations at Reshu Academy and Stonefire. King Ragnoc already stands with us, and with your support as well, we can take the fight to Brightspire and stand a real chance at defeating Drakzeneth one and for all."

Elandir rose, his presence commanding the room. "You have my full support. I will begin gathering the rangers at dawn," he affirmed, his voice carrying the promise of swift and silent arrows. "And I shall commune with our forest kin as well; perhaps they will aid in the coming war as well."

"Thank you, Elandir," Ariella said as she stood. "You do a great service to Etonya. I hope we can continue our friendship after this thread is extinguished as well."

"As do I, milady. Rest now," Elandir advised. "We have much to prepare, and the morrow will come swiftly."

As the dawn's first light crept through the forest canopy, it cast a golden glow upon the ancient trees.

Rider stirred from his slumber, his eyes fluttering open. He stretched his arms above his head, feeling the satisfying pop of his joints. Beside him, Ariella slept peacefully, her auburn hair fanned out across the pillow.

He gently brushed a stray lock from her face. Even in sleep, she radiated grace and beauty. Rider's heart swelled with love for this remarkable woman who had stood by his side through every trial.

A soft knock at the door announced Elandir's arrival.

Rider rose, careful not to disturb Ariella's rest, and entered the main living quarters to greet him.

"Good morning, my friend," Elandir said, his voice rich and melodious. "I trust you slept well?"

"Indeed," Rider confirmed with a nod.

"Good, you'll need it," Elandir said as he readied to discuss their next steps. "I've asked the Griffins and sent ravens to the other races of the forest. Only time will tell who answers."

Rider placed a reassuring hand on Elandir's shoulder. "Thank you, Elandir. We do this for everyone."

"I know, Rider, and all of Amakiir stands with you. I hold no ill will for what happened," Elandir replied assuringly.

Ariella awakened in the other room as she called out to Rider, "Rider, is that Elandir?" she questioned. Their voices were low, but her Elven ears didn't miss much.

Elandir gave Rider a knowing grin as he raised an eyebrow. "You two get ready for the journey ahead. Who knows when you'll have this much peace again?" He turned for the door and called back to Ariella, a hint of mischief on his voice, "It is, milady. I trust you two slept well. Meet me in the courtroom when you're ready to depart."

Rider let out a chuckle as he walked Elandir to the door, locking it behind him as he turned back to meet Ariella as she was closing a black silk robe around her chest in the hallway. He gently brushed strands of auburn hair out of her face and captured her lips with a gentle kiss. They stared into each other's eyes lovingly for a moment before he lifted her by the waist as she wrapped her legs around him. Together, as one, they moved down the hall.

Rider carried Ariella into the bedroom, their lips still locked in a heated kiss. He playfully tossed her onto the plush bed, causing her black silk robe to fall open. The smooth fabric parted, revealing Ariella's full, luscious breasts. They bounced slightly as she landed on the soft mattress, her pink nipples already hardening with arousal.

Rider's sapphire eyes darkened with lust as he drank in the sight of her creamy skin and womanly curves. Ariella looked up at him through thick lashes, her eyes smoldering with desire. She slowly spread her legs, giving Rider a tantalizing view of her glistening entrance.

Unable to resist, Rider lowered himself to his knees on the floor before her. He ran his hands up her smooth thighs, relishing the feel of her soft skin. Leaning in, he placed a tender kiss on her inner thigh, making her gasp. He continued trailing kisses higher and higher until his lips hovered just above her slick folds.

"Rider, please..." Ariella moaned breathlessly, her hips writhing with need.

Heeding her plea, Rider dipped his head and licked a long, slow stripe up her slit. Ariella cried out in pleasure, her back arching off the bed. Spurred on by her reaction, Rider lapped at her sensitive flesh, savoring her sweet essence. He swirled his tongue around her throbbing nub before sucking the sensitive flesh into his mouth.

"Oh gods, yes!" Ariella panted, tangling her fingers in Rider's dark hair.

Rider licked and sucked at her dripping core like a man starved. He slipped two fingers inside her tight channel, groaning at how wet and ready she was for him. Pumping his fingers in and out, he curled them upward stroking that special spot inside her.

Ariella's moans grew louder and more desperate as Rider worked her closer to the edge. Her thighs began to tremble and quivered around his head. With a final flick of his tongue and thrust of his fingers, Ariella came undone.

Her walls clenched around him as a powerful orgasm crashed over her. Rider continued to lap at her, helping her ride out the waves of ecstasy.

Finally, Ariella collapsed back onto the bed, her chest heaving. Rider climbed up her body, placing tender kisses across her flushed skin as he went. He captured her lips in a searing kiss, letting her taste herself on his tongue.

Breaking the kiss, Rider gazed down at Ariella adoringly, his heart full and bursting with love for her. In that perfect, passionate moment, the outside world and threats they faced fell away. All that existed was the two of them.

Ariella gazed down at Rider, her violet eyes still hazy with the afterglow of pleasure. Her gaze trailed down his muscular chest and abs until it landed on his rock hard manhood straining against his trousers. She could see it twitch and throb, mirroring the needy pulsing between her own legs.

Spreading her thighs wide in invitation, Ariella reached down and released him from his trousers before wrapping her legs around his trim waist, pulling him closer. She could feel the heat radiating off his body as he nudged against her slick entrance.

"Please Rider," she moaned, her musical voice dripping with lust. "I need you inside me."

Rider groaned, unable to resist her erotic pleas. In one powerful thrust, he buried himself to the hilt. Ariella's tight walls clenched around him like a velvet vice, squeezing his throbbing shaft.

"Fuck, Ariella..." Rider gasped. "You feel incredible. You're so wet."

He started to move, withdrawing until just the tip remained inside her before slamming back in. Over and over he thrusted his hips, fucking her with deep, powerful strokes.

"Yes, yes, yes!" she chanted breathlessly. "Harder! Fuck!"

Rider obliged, pounding into her with a wild fervor. The wet slapping of flesh echoed through the room. Ariella's breasts bounced with every forceful thrust, her rosy nipples turned into stiff peaks. Rider lowered himself toward her and ducked his head to capture one between his lips, suckling and flicking it with his tongue.

"Rider! Don't stop!" Ariella keened, arching into his touch as jolts of electricity coursing through her.

Rider could feel himself tightening as her silken walls fluttered and spasmed around him.

"Please Rider, don't stop, I need it! I want to feel you cum inside me..."

Those filthy words were Rider's undoing. With a primal roar, he slammed into her one last time, burying himself as deep as possible. His cock jerked and throbbed as he unleashed surge after surge of his hot seed deep inside her.

They collapsed into each other. Laying upon the soft pillowing sheets, they lost themselves in the moment, unsure if fate would allow another intimate moment such as this.

CHAPTER XXV
THE ACADEMY

The sun's rays illuminated the intricate wooden carvings adorning Elandir's royal court as the party gathered.

Rider stood tall, his longsword sturdy at his back, as he nodded to Elandir. "We're ready."

Elandir rose from his throne. "Follow me," he instructed, leading them out of the court and into the royal gardens.

The gardens were a paradise, a testament to the Wood Elves' deep connection to nature. Lush grass cushioned their steps as they walked. Vibrant flowers bloomed in every direction, their petals a canvas of colors - deep purples, vivid reds, and soft pinks nestled against ferns and vines.

In the center of the garden, the grass gave way to a smooth expanse of earth. It was here that Elandir stopped, turning to face the party.

"You can perform the ritual here," he announced. "We don't have a teleportation circle like the ones you describe Jarl Reshu helped you craft, but this should be a large enough clearing to not damage the forest."

Kael stepped forward, his boots sinking slightly into the soft earth. "Rider, join me," he instructed. Together they closed their eyes, recalling the intricate hand movements and ancient words that Jarl Reshu had imparted. Their hands began to move, tracing invisible glyphs in the air as their lips formed the specific syllables of power to arrive at Spellsword Stronghold.

A soft breeze picked up, rustling the leaves of the surrounding trees. It grew in strength, whipping around them in a vortex. The grass flattened beneath the force of the wind. A dome of magic began to appear above them.

"Quickly, Ariella, to us!" Kael called out.

Ariella rushed to Rider's side, ducking quickly to enter the dome before it fully enveloped the trio.

Air crackled with power as familiar scenes of the plainlands began to paint themselves all around them, just as before. Images flashed by in a dizzying cascade of colors and shapes until they stood in silence upon the cold stone floor of Spellsword Stronghold.

As the arcane shimmer of the teleportation dome faded, Rider's boots met the familiar stone of Spellsword Fortress. The clank of metal and the murmurs of greeting swelled around him as guards, clad in the emblems of the great Human houses, formed a motley honor guard. Their faces bore the quiet dignity of loyalty and respect.

"Welcome back, Jarl," said a burly guard, his voice echoing slightly off the cold fortress walls.

"Thank you, all of you," Rider replied, his tone earnest and weighed with gratitude. "What news do we have?"

The guards ushered Rider and his companions into the adjoining throne room. Footsteps echoed, each step resonating through the vast chamber as he approached the large round table that dominated the space. His throne awaited at the far end, an imposing seat carved from dark wood and stone.

He settled into the throne as an odd chill crept up his spine. He was home, wasn't he?

The throne felt different this time. The whispers of the past, of bloodlines and birthrights from realms beyond, gnawed at the edges of his consciousness. A sense of dislocation washed over him, the knowledge that his ancestors hailed from another world casting a shadow across his heart.

Ariella and Kael approached from his side. Ariella's auburn hair cascaded over her shoulders as she took her place to Rider's right.

As she sat, her gaze lingered on Rider, noting the distant look in his eyes. With the practiced subtlety of her time spent at court, her slender hand reached beneath the table, finding Rider's. "Is everything all right?" she asked, her voice a whisper.

Rider's focus snapped back. He squeezed her hand in reassurance before releasing it. "I'm fine," he said firmly. Then, with authority that filled the room he stated, "We have work to do."

Kael nodded, settling into his seat beside Ariella.

"Jarl," began one of the Spellsword guards as he took his seat at the table. His armor bore the clean lines and intricate craftsmanship unique to house Bloodmane. "The repairs to your castle are approaching completion. We've also seen to it to remove all Orcish influence within these walls."

Another emissary, cloaked in the colors of house Reshu, chimed in, "Moreover, there has been a collective decision among the houses to pool our resources. The armory of Spellsword Fortress has been restocked, and our coffers have been evenly distributed."

Rider's eyes widened in astonishment. "Is this customary?" he inquired, his voice edged with curiosity as he addressed the emissaries.

The Reshu representative shook his head. "It is unprecedented," he admitted, his voice tinged with respect. "But your deeds have forged a new path for all. We found it fitting that our alliance should commence on a foundation of equality and shared purpose."

Ariella leaned forward. "Your leaders show remarkable faith," she said warmly. "It speaks volumes of their trust and commitment to what we are building here."

Kael gave an approving nod. "Indeed, it is a grand gesture, one that heralds true unity among your people."

Rider's gaze swept across the faces of his trusted allies, his heart swelled with gratitude for their unwavering support and the sacrifices each had made.

"Your dedication in my absence to Spellsword Fortress, and to our alliance, has not gone unnoticed," Rider began. "Leaving behind your homes and loved ones is no easy task, and for that, you have my deepest thanks."

He paused, allowing the gravity of those words to sink in before continuing. "Yet, I must ask even more from you now. Drakzeneth gathers strength. The coming battle will be fierce, and we'll need every able warrior. I ask you to return to your homelands, tell your Jarls to gather their garrisons, and stand ready to defend Etonya."

Rider locked eyes with them, his gaze resolute. "Join us in this fight if you wish, but should you choose to stay back and protect your loved ones instead, know that no dishonor will fall upon you."

The room fell silent, save for the crackling of torches. Then, the emissaries rose one by one. Steel sang against scabbard as blades were drawn in swift succession. With solemn pride, each weapon was laid upon the table, points converging toward its center.

"By the sword and shield," proclaimed the first emissary, "we shall stand with Rider, the Spellsword, until our dying breath."

"House Reshu's knowledge and might are yours," declared another, her blade gleaming under the flickering light.

The declarations continued, a symphony of allegiance that resonated throughout the chamber, until the wave of oaths reached Kael Stormbringer. With a deliberate motion, he placed his hand upon the stone, fingers splayed wide. A surge of electricity crackled from his palm, searing his handprint into the surface as he proclaimed, "Until Drakzeneth lies vanquished, my storm will not cease, nor my loyalty waver from you, Rider."

Ariella's Elven short blades whispered softly as she unsheathed them, laying them across each other on the table. Her eyes shimmered as unshed tears began to swell. She removed a single arrow from her quiver, placing it delicately among the crossed blades. "I am bound to Brightspire," she spoke, her voice quivering with emotion, "but my path lies with Rider. I shall see this quest through to its end."

Overwhelmed by the gravity of their vows, Rider felt a swell of honor rise within him. He stood as he grabbed his scabbard from where it was resting against the table, and with an almost reverent motion, he drew the weapon, the steel singing a long note as it left its sheath.

"Your trust," Rider's voice broke, "is not given lightly, and I will not break it." He placed his longsword on the table, aligning it with the others. "Return to your lands," he commanded, his voice now steady and resolute. "Deliver the news to your Jarls with all possible haste. Gather your armies and march toward Brightspire."

The emissaries nodded, each one purposefully gripping the handle of their sword before pulling them from the table. The clatter of metal marked their departure. Rider watched them go, the weight of their blades' absence a silent testament to the looming battle that would decide the fate of Etonya.

Rider led Ariella and Kael through the corridors of Spellsword Fortress, the stone walls echoing with the distant clamor of preparations for war. In the armory, rows of weapons gleamed menacingly in the torchlight, but it was the trio of suits of armor that grabbed their attention.

"By the stars," Kael murmured as his gaze swept over the male figure garbed in a breastplate runed with bolts of lightning and starbursts. The blue and gold cape that flowed behind seemed to capture the essence of the stormy sky above the fortress.

Ariella approached the female figure, her eyes tracing the contours of the light leather armor interwoven with chainmail - a fusion of elegance and resilience. She brushed her fingers against the dark brown cape, feeling the cool metal of the Brightspire broach clasping it together. It was more than mere armor; it was a statement of her heritage and her commitment to their cause.

Rider stood before the final mannequin, examining the dark gray suit of light armor etched with golden runes. He ran his fingers along the intricate patterns. The weight of responsibility settled upon his shoulders even as he admired the craftsmanship.

"Let's not waste any time," Rider said, breaking the silence as he began to unstrap his armor.

One by one, they disrobed and donned their new armor.

As Rider fastened the last buckle, a warm glow emanated from the golden etchings on his armor. His breath caught as he felt the metal conform to his body, fitting him like a second skin. Every movement was fluid, every breath effortless.

"Remarkable," he exhaled, flexing his arms and marveling at the sensation of boundless freedom.

"Indeed," Kael agreed, now fully armored, arcane glyphs pulsing with energy across his breastplate. "The magic of this world continues to surpass my expectations. I've seen much, but Etonya?" he sighed, "I shall dedicate volumes to it in the Great Library."

"I'd love to see such a place," Ariella chimed in, her voice hopeful, but uncertain of their future.

"It would be my honor to take you," Kael replied with a soft smile. "But something tells me your path will have far greater tasks than roaming the silent aisles of distant libraries."

Their exchange was interrupted by Rider's authoritative voice, "Are we ready?" He stood tall, the runes on his armor pulsating softly with a power that seemed to echo his newfound resolve.

"Yes," Ariella and Kael responded simultaneously.

"Then let's gather back in the teleportation room. We've much to do, and time isn't our ally." Rider's command was firm, leaving no room for doubt about his role or his commitment to their cause.

The trio moved back through the halls of Spellsword Fortress with purpose. Through the windows and open archways, they could see the rush of activity outside. Rider's guards and emissaries from the allied houses were mounting their steeds, the thunderous clatter of hooves against stone filling the air with urgency.

"See how your leadership has united them?" Kael

observed, nodding toward the riders below. "They believe in you, Rider, as do we."

Together, they strode forward, Rider's cape

billowing like a banner of hope. As they neared the teleportation room, the hum of magic grew stronger, the air crackling with anticipation of the journey ahead.

The teleportation chamber's intricate sigils seemed to pulse with energy. The trio stepped onto the designated circle at the room's center, and Kael began chanting the incantations required to activate the spell.

The words twisted in the air, intertwining with streams of light that transformed into a shimmering dome above them. The magic enveloped the party, its warm glow tingling against their skin as the scenery of Spellsword Fortress blurred into fleeting images of the rolling plains between them and Reshu Academy.

Ariella closed her eyes for a moment, taking a deep breath and listening to the thrumming energy that vibrated around them.

And then, as suddenly as it had begun, the teleportation spell ceased. The dome dissipated, leaving them standing within the confines of Reshu University's teleportation circle. The familiar surroundings of the academy's grand hall greeted them, with its high vaulted ceilings and walls adorned with tapestries.

"Welcome back," greeted a group of mages overseeing the circle. Their robes were the deep crimson of House Reshu, embroidered with golden threads that sparkled in the light. "How fared your journey?"

Rider, still adjusting to the sudden shift in location, stepped forward. "We've no time for small talk," he said curtly. "We must speak with Jarl Reshu immediately."

A flicker of disappointment crossed the faces of the mages, but they nodded in understanding. "I'm afraid Jarl

Reshu is not present," one mage informed him. "She's on one of her... visits to Castle Bloodmane."

Ariella couldn't suppress a giggle, her eyes forced shut in amusement. Her smile was a rare sight, one that softened the sharp angles of concern on Rider's face.

"Then fetch her back at once," demanded Rider, the urgency clear in his stance.

"Of course," replied the mage, bowing slightly before hurrying away.

"Let us retire to the courtroom while we await her return," suggested another mage, gesturing toward the ornate doors leading out of the hall.

The trio followed; the air heavy with the smell of old parchment and wax from the countless candles that lined the walls. As they walked, they could hear the distant murmuring of students and scholars—dedication to the pursuit of knowledge, even in the shadow of war.

They settled into the courtroom, an impressive chamber with high-backed chairs positioned around an oval table carved from dark wood. Kael ran his fingers along the intricately carved symbols, each one a story of law and history etched into the grain.

"Patience has never been my forte," Rider admitted, pacing the length of the room, his boots clicking against the marble floor.

"Yet it is often the companion of wisdom," Kael responded.

Half an hour trickled by, each minute stretching longer than the last. Rider ceased his pacing and settled into a chair, the leather creaking under his weight. Ariella stood by a tall window, her gaze lost in the sprawling campus below, while Kael sat absorbed in a tome he had plucked from a nearby shelf.

A sudden burst of energy preceded the opening of the

doors, and Jarl Reshu entered, her robes whispering across the stone. Beside her, the imposing figure of Jarl Bloodmane moved with purpose, his armor clinking softly.

"Rider!" Reshu's voice echoed through the courtroom, commanding their attention.

"Jarl Reshu, Jarl Bloodmane," Rider began, rising to meet them. "Queen Vyshaan has been transformed, possessed by Drakzeneth," Rider said, his voice steady despite the news.

"We're aware. Zara reached us some time ago, warning us to halt all communication with Brightspire," Reshu interjected with a nod. "She departed some time ago. She felt she could do more good for the realm by informing the people of Etonya. Tell us, what else have you uncovered?"

"After Zara departed from the island," Kael took over, his eyes reflecting the gravity of their findings. "We found a temple housing an ancient leyline access point, revealing the others scattered across Etonya. We believe one lies near this university."

"Indeed," Reshu acknowledged, "We discovered a temple beneath this plateau when we first laid the foundations of our Academy. Its magical significance was clear, yet it never produced anything magical."

"Perhaps it was tampered with, or its energies drained," Kael suggested. "We must inspect this temple. If we're right, it could be vital to our cause."

"Let us waste no more time then," Reshu declared, gesturing decisively towards the chamber's exit. "Follow me."

As they walked through the hallowed halls of the academy, murmurs and stares followed them like shadows. The party's footsteps resonated with determination.

Descending a narrow stone stairway, Jarl Reshu led the

group into the bowels of her fortress. The air grew cooler and more damp with each step they took.

"Many years ago, when we discovered this temple," Reshu began, her voice reverberating against the ancient walls, "its doors stood open, as if inviting us in."

"Or as if someone had left in haste," Rider added, eyeing the dark passage ahead.

"Indeed," Reshu agreed. "We found statues, crystals, and a device all matching your descriptions of the ones on that island."

"Undisturbed since?" Kael asked, with a hint of concern.

"Undisturbed and inactive," Reshu confirmed. "It has been nothing more than an academic curiosity."

They entered a vast cavern, where dim light filtered through cracks in the ceiling, casting eerie shadows across the room. In the center stood a temple, an exact replica of the one previously visited.

"Here it is," Reshu announced, gesturing towards the temple with a mix of pride and trepidation.

Kael approached a statue, running his fingers over the intricately carved stones, eyes narrowing.

"You think Drakzeneth drained the leyline's power?" Rider asked, drawing closer to examine a series of glyphs etched into a crystalline device.

"Yes," Kael replied, turning his attention to the crystals. "It's likely what enabled him to rally the Orc clans."

Rider felt a chill at the implication. "An unguarded source of such power would have been irresistible to him."

"Exactly," Kael said. "This was once a wellspring of arcane force. Now it's barren, which means he knows how to exploit them."

"Why wouldn't he have drained the one on the island?" Ariella asked.

"He likely planned to return to it and use it to travel to another world to continue his conquest," Kael replied.

"Can we restore it?" Rider asked, his jaw set with determination.

Kael's face grew somber, eyes reflecting a storm of internal conflict. "The only way to mend the leyline is by feeding it energy from another being's Spark," he explained slowly, as if dreading the words.

"Another sacrifice," Ariella murmured, understanding the gravity of Kael's implication.

"Exactly," Kael said, his voice barely above a whisper. "And it only makes sense that I once again give—"

"No." Rider's voice cut through the chamber like a blade. "I've gathered more than enough arcane energy, Kael. Teach me how to give some back."

Kael's eyes widened, a mix of admiration and fear. "No, Rider," he argued, his tone urgent. "You need every ounce of your power to defeat Drakzeneth. We can't risk you giving anything away."

"Fine," Rider conceded after a tense pause, "after we defeat Drakzeneth, we come back here. I'll be the one to drain my Spark."

"Rider—" Ariella began, her voice laced with concern.

But Rider raised his hand to silence her before turning back to Kael. "You have to return home, share what you've learned. You can't stay trapped here."

A heavy silence fell upon the group before Kael finally nodded, conceding. "Very well," he agreed reluctantly. "You already know most of the ritual. It just requires a few changed words."

Together, the group ascended from the temple's depths, emerging into the academy. In the hours that followed, Kael instructed Rider, Ariella, and Jarl Reshu in the art of sacrificing one's Spark.

"Remember," Kael said, locking eyes with Rider, "the words are not just sounds. They are the very essence of power. You will be binding part of yourself to the leyline, entwining your life force with the ebb and flow of this world's magic."

Rider listened intently, his eyes never leaving Kael's. Ariella watched, her violet eyes clouded with worry, her heart racing at the thought of what this could mean for Rider.

As Kael spoke, Jarl Reshu took diligent notes, her quill scratching on parchment, while Jarl Bloodmane observed with a stoic expression, arms crossed over his broad chest.

"Once done," Kael finished, "the leyline will begin to draw power again, slowly at first, but it will grow stronger with time."

"Alright," Rider said, offering a nod. "When this is all over, we'll ensure Etonya's leylines pulse with magic once more."

"Let us hope that day comes soon," Kael replied, his gaze lingering on the stars outside a nearby window.

Jarl Bloodmane's voice, gruff and resolute, broke the momentary silence. "It is time I return to my fortress. The Lancer Corps will need to be rallied for an immediate march to Brightspire." His black and silver armor gleamed in the dim light as he stood, the embodiment of martial resolve.

"Thank you for sharing your wisdom, Kael," Jarl Reshu said, her tone full with gratitude. "I vow, your teachings shall remain guarded within these walls, disclosed only if absolutely necessary to mend or shield the leylines."

Kael gave a slight bow, his blond hair catching the light as he moved. "Protecting the leylines is protecting Etonya itself. It is my honor to assist."

Jarl Reshu turned to leave, walking past her gathered

magi. Her robes, rich with the colors of gold and red, swished softly against the stone floor. "Gather our forces and summon the elementals," she commanded without looking back. "We ride for Brightspire with all the force our academy can muster."

The sound of hurried footsteps and the clinking of armor filled the corridors as the magi mobilized, their voices a low murmur of spells and orders.

"Come," Jarl Reshu beckoned to Rider and his companions. "Let us make haste to the stables. Your mounts will be readied for travel."

As they exited the study, the smell of parchment and ink was replaced by the fresh scent of the evening air. The soft glow of lanterns guided their path, casting long shadows on the cobblestone.

Ariella moved alongside Rider, her new armor hugging her form. "Are you certain about this, Rider?" she asked, her voice barely above a whisper, betraying her concern.

"Drakzeneth leaves us no choice," Rider replied, his voice steady, though his mind churned with the weight of what was to come. "I will do what I must to stop him. We… the Astralans created him. It's my responsibility."

They arrived at the stables to find their steeds pawing the ground, restless with anticipation. The stable hands worked quickly, ensuring each mount was well-equipped for the journey ahead.

"Your mounts are ready," one of the magi said, offering a respectful nod.

"Thank you," Rider replied, taking the reins of his horse — a powerful stallion with a coat as dark as midnight. He swung into the saddle with practiced ease.

Ariella's gaze lingered for a moment, watching Rider's hair flow gently against the night breeze, before mounting her own horse. She realized it was the first time Rider ever referred to himself as one of them, the Astralan. She loved him, and if this was his burden, then she would help him ease it.

"Rider, on your mark." Kael stated, securing himself atop a robust gelding.

Rider looked at his companions, their faces set with resolve, and nodded once more. With a flick of the reins, and a stout, "YA!" the trio set off into the night, their destinies intertwined with the fate of the realm.

ACT IV

CHAPTER XXVI
THE DIVIDE

Thunderous hoofbeats echoed through the cobblestone streets of Reshu Academy as Ariella and her companions rode through. Her eyes widened with wonder and trepidation as clusters of robed figures chanted in unison, their hands weaving complex patterns that tore at the fabric of reality.

To their left, a mage commanded the land to obey. Massive chunks of earth and stone wrenched themselves from the ground, spiraling upward to form colossal beasts with limbs like boulders and eyes that glowed with arcane energy. The elementals' imposing forms caused some of the younger students to step back in awe. Yet these titanic constructs wasted no time; they bent their stony knees, allowing their conjurers to mount them with commanded grace.

"We were never taught such spells in Brightspire," Ariella murmured.

"I wouldn't think so," Kael's voice came from her side. "House Reshu's mages wield and study their magic with a raw, unbridled curiosity. If the tomes I read in the

Academy were correct, the Queen has regulated much of what your people can learn in Brightspire."

The party passed under the shadow of the Academy gates, leaving behind the sounds of its students preparing for war. In the relative quiet of their journey, Ariella's thoughts turned inward.

"Perhaps it's time for change," she pondered. "The people of Etonya would benefit from a more open and less rigid view on the study and use of magic."

As they rode on, her mind danced with possibilities. The party made their way down the path leading away from the plateau, the academy shrinking into the distance as the sun dipped below the horizon.

"Should we not seek shelter for the night?" Ariella asked, her voice cutting through the growing darkness.

"Agreed," Rider responded, pulling on the reins to slow his steed. "We will make camp here."

The stars began to pepper the sky as Rider dismounted. He watched as Kael gestured for him to observe the invocation of 'Luminar Pavilia'. With a flourish of his hands and the incantation spoken, Kael called forth his shimmering tent.

"Your turn, Rider," Kael encouraged. "Focus on the words, let them flow through you."

Rider took a deep breath before speaking, *"Luminar Pavilia,"* he uttered, as a duplicate of Kael's magnificent tent sprang forth.

"Exceptional," Kael remarked, his eyes showing a hint of pride as his gaze lingered on his pupil and friend.

"Tell me," Kael said, concern etching his brow, "how do you feel? You've absorbed the Arcane Spark of two very powerful beings."

"Strong," Rider said, flexing an arm, the muscles

beneath the armor plate tightening. "Alive... unstoppable even."

Kael raised an eyebrow, his voice lowering in concern. "Rider, I know the power can be… exciting, intoxicating even. Be patient, smart, please. We can defeat Drakzeneth if we work together."

Rider met Kael's gaze, the awareness of responsibility settling upon his shoulders as the thrill of power receded slightly. "Together," he echoed, nodding in agreement.

"Kael," Ariella interjected, "How exactly, are you planning to stop Drakzeneth?"

Kael's gaze flickered between Rider and his sword, then settled on Ariella with a hint of caution. "Well, as with Syl'v—"

"No, Kael," Ariella cut in sharply, "We can't."

Her glare turned to Rider, piercing and intense. "You can't just behead Queen Vyshaan, Rider!" she yelled firmly.

"Ari, I don't know any other way," Rider exhaled, his heart sinking; his voice was heavy with reluctance.

"NO!" Ariella's protest came louder, more desperate this time. Her gaze darted between the two men. "There has to be a spell, a ritual, some other method to purge her body of Drakzeneth's spirit without killing her!"

"Ari," Kael began, his tone steadier, but heavy with realism. "I've never encountered such magic before. Perhaps if I had more time, if access to the Great Library were possible, there might be another way. But as it stands, I don't know of one. Until he's defeated, and Etonya's leylines are restored, I'm stuck here."

A surge of emotion overtook Ariella's composure, her chest heaving with each breath. "NO," she screamed, the word ripping from her throat. "I refuse to murder my people's Queen!" With that, Ariella spun on her heel and stormed toward Rider's summoned tent.

Rider took a step in her direction, his instinct to comfort clashing with the tension of the moment. Before he could reach the tent, Ariella's voice lashed out from within. "Don't even think about it."

He paused, turning back to face Kael, his expression etched with defeat and confusion. Kael, understanding the delicate predicament, gestured for Rider to follow him. Without another word, the two men made their way into Kael's tent, leaving Ariella to her own space.

Inside the tent, the soft glow of enchanted lamps illuminated their faces as Rider began to brainstorm alternatives.

"Maybe we can trap him, drain his Spark like you did with the leyline," Rider suggested, breaking the silence.

Kael's lips tightened as he shook his head. "No, Rider," he responded firmly. "All that would do is ensure he never leaves her body. His mind and soul would remain trapped within Queen Vyshaan."

"Maybe there's a spell that will purge her body and force him out," Rider suggested again.

"None that I know of, Rider," Kael replied.

"Ok, what about—" Rider began.

Before he could finish, Kael interrupted, stating his words as fact, "There is no other way, Rider. I've been around for centuries, and I've never seen magic like what's possessing the Queen. What I… what we both know, is that you can drain his Spark with a swift strike to the neck."

"Kael," Rider pleaded. "It's her Queen. Ariella's lived her whole life trying to restore her family's honor, now you're asking her to help end her life."

"Rider," Kael continued, his voice getting louder. "I cannot, will not, allow a Draconin to regain power. He's already trying to recreate the Dragons using her body. What do you think is next, hmm? I'll tell you, he's going to enslave my people! Our people, Rider!"

Rider stood, unsure of what to do for the first time since beginning their quest. One option had him risking losing the woman he loves, the other risked Drakzeneth's possible return to power, or at least, his escape into the cosmos. But that wasn't any better. He'd probably just begin the same conquest across any number of other worlds before returning to Astrala… a world he'd never known, but somehow felt so connected to and so responsible for saving.

Rider's frustration erupted into a yell as he tore at the buckles of his scabbard, letting it clatter to the ground. His armor followed, piece by piece he discarded it with a clink and thud onto the tent's floor. Crawling into a bedroll, he closed his eyes, seeking relief in darkness.

Rider's dreams offered no comfort, only a relentless barrage of images that tore at his mind. He was once again consumed by visions of death and destruction, witnessing the carnage wrought by his own hands of both Vorathor and Syl'vadren. Every blast of green eldritch energy, every crackle of electric blue lightning, every vicious bite and claw were all etched into his memory. And with each memory, he felt the hunger, the thirst, the insatiable desire for flesh and power that drove these Dragons to kill. The taste of warm blood coated his throat as he devoured the bodies of his fellow Etonyians. Just when it seemed like he couldn't bear any more, Kael's voice broke through the chaos.

"Rider, Rider wake up!" Kael's voice pierced the nightmare.

His eyes snapped open, and his body lunged forward,

breaths heavy and ragged. Kael's concerned face faded into focus.

"Are you ok, Rider?" Kael asked, "I've never seen your nightmares so intense. Another vision perhaps?"

"No, not exactly," Rider replied, his voice hoarse, the taste of nonexistent blood lingering in his throat. "I think I saw their memories, Kael. But it was more than that. I *was* them. I felt everything, every evil act, their hunger, how much they enjoyed eating our…" Rider began to feel vomit rising up from within.

He shuddered, attempting to dislodge the vile sensations that clung to his consciousness.

"This transference," Kael said gravely. "You're not just gaining their power, Rider. You're inheriting their memories, their knowledge." Kael paused, weighing his next words carefully. "Some Astralans believe the Arcane Spark is the embodiment of a soul. It's a gift and a curse. One must tread carefully—especially when the souls are as dark and as potent as the ones you've taken."

Rider rubbed his temples, feeling the weight of centuries-old malice pressing against his skull.

"You need to be careful, Rider," Kael warned. "I've never seen someone take the Arcane Spark of something so powerful, let alone two Sparks in such a short amount of time."

Rider nodded, his hands trembling slightly as he clutched at the fabric of the bedroll.

"Well," Rider sighed, "Let's get this over with, so I can put some of it back into Etonya and help get you home."

Kael glanced at him, with a mix of admiration and concern in his eyes. "You know, Rider," he replied. "It doesn't have to be just my home. I truly believe Astralan blood flows through your veins. I don't know how yet, but that's something I'm willing to help you discover, if you wish for it."

"Thanks, Kael," Rider replied. "I appreciate it, but for now, let's just focus on stopping Drakzeneth and finding a way to do it without taking the Queen's head."

"Rider," Kael started, frustration lacing his tone.

"I know, I know," Rider cut in dismissively as he rose from the bedroll, gathering his belongings.

Rider left the tent first, catching the morning sky before sunrise. He got to work preparing breakfast for his companions, setting a pan atop the still-warm coals from last night's fire. Thin slices of jerky sizzled as they hit the hot surface, promising comfort and deliciousness to his companions. While waiting for the meat to cook, Rider filled a kettle with water and seasoning before nestling it into the embers. In these quiet moments, he finally found solace. There was no quest, no Dragons, just peace. The kettle boiled and whistled with steam as the aroma of morning brew filled the air.

He pored over their maps to mark what lands and roads they could cut across in hopes of shaving precious time off their travels. Shortly after, Ariella exited Rider's tent, where she had spent the night alone and frustrated, the lack of sleep apparent under her eyes.

"Good morning, Ari," Rider greeted, trying to break the tension still lingering from the night before.

"Morning, Rider," she replied.

Well, at least that's progress, Rider thought to himself. "I've heated some jerky and started a kettle if you're interested?"

"Thank you Rider, I appreciate that," she said, the sleep still clinging to her senses.

She sat down beside him on the left, poured herself some of the steaming brew into an old metal cup, and exhaled. She raised her cup, breathed in the aroma, and took a healthy gulp, her eyes never leaving the horizon.

"I love you, Rider," she said solemnly.

"I love –" Rider tried to respond before being cut off.

"No, just listen," Ari commanded, holding up a hand. "I love you. I know I can never fully comprehend what you're going through, but I can't just kill her. I need you to understand that."

"I do," Rider tried responding once again, but was met with a deathly glare. "Sorry," he said. "Please, continue."

"I don't know how, so don't ask," she continued. "But we're going to stop Drakzeneth without killing the Queen. I have to believe that, or I can't be a part of this. So, please, don't make me choose."

Silence fell between them for what felt like an eternity. Then, without a word, she leaned her head onto his shoulder and they watched the sunrise together, without another word.

Eventually Kael exited his tent and commented on the delightful smell of the morning meal and drink. "Ah, lovely! Thank you, my friends," he complimented. "Good morning, Ariella. Will you be continuing on with us?"

"Yes, Kael," she responded. "Someone has to keep you two accountable," she said jokingly before tossing him a friendly smile.

"Exquisite," he replied smiling. "I'd want it no other way."

The three companions sat and enjoyed their breakfast and the calm morning they were sure would be rare in the coming days.

As the trio finished their morning meal, Rider spread out the map on the ground before them, tracing his finger along the parchment. "I believe I've found a way to shave some time off our journey," he announced.

Ariella and Kael leaned in, their gazes following Rider's finger as it moved across the map. "If we cut across the southern pass below Shadyvale," Rider explained, his voice filled with cautious optimism, "and then take a ferry across the Riverlands, we could save a significant amount of time."

"Assuming" Ariella interjected, "we don't run into any trouble along the way, and that we find a working ferry that can support our horses."

"True," Rider responded. "But, if it works, we'll arrive in Stonefire in a fraction of the time."

"I vote yes," Kael chimed in.

"Ok," Ariella sighed. "No point in wasting more time arguing. Let's get started."

The trio gathered their belongings and doused the remnants of the fire with dirt. Kael, meanwhile, waved his hand, muttering an incantation under his breath, and the two shimmering tents dissolved into motes of light before disappearing.

They saddled their horses and secured their packs before swinging themselves atop their steeds. With a nod, they set out, urging their mounts into a gallop. They rode with the rising sun at their backs, casting long shadows before them.

The trio rode hard, their horses' hooves pounding against the earth as they sped across the southern pass below Shadyvale. The landscape transformed around them, from rolling hills to dense forests filled with towering evergreens.

They encountered no trouble along the way. No bandits lying in wait, no wild beasts stalking them from the shadows. It was as if the stars themselves had cleared a path for their urgent mission.

As they descended from the forested hills, the land flattened out before them, revealing the shimmering expanse of the Riverlands. Its mighty river cut through the landscape like a ribbon of molten silver, its banks lined with reeds and willows that swayed gently in the breeze.

They followed the road tracing the river's edge, scanning the shoreline for any sign of a ferry dock. The sun climbed higher in the sky, its rays dancing on the water's surface and casting a golden glow across the land.

After hours of riding, they finally spotted a rickety old dock barely sitting atop the river, with a large raft tethered to its posts. As they approached, they could see the raft was a crude construction of tree trunks bound together with thick ropes. It creaked and groaned as it bobbed on the gentle current. A tight rope stretched across the river, disappearing into the distance, serving as a guide for the raft's crossing.

Rider pulled up on his reins, bringing his steed to a halt near the dock. Ariella and Kael followed suit.

"Well, it's not exactly The Banshee's Wail," Rider quipped as he dismounted, his boots thudding on the weathered planks of the dock. He approached the raft, testing its sturdiness. The logs shifted slightly under his weight, water lapping at their sides.

Ariella joined him as she assessed the vessel. "It looks like it's seen better days," she remarked, running a hand along one of the frayed ropes. "Do you think it will hold?"

"It appears structurally sound," Rider replied. "But I doubt it will support the weight of all three of us and our horses."

Kael nodded, his gaze drifting across the river. "Then we'll have to cross in pairs," he chimed in.

Rider turned to Ariella. "Ari, why don't you and I cross first? Then we can send the ferry back for Kael and his horse."

Ariella shook her head. "No, Rider. You and Kael should go."

Rider's brow furrowed in confusion. "But, Ari, I thought we agreed to stick together."

Ariella placed a hand on Rider's arm. "We all know that you and Kael need to face Drakzeneth together if we're going to stand a chance. Your combined powers are our best hope of defeating him."

Rider opened his mouth to protest, but Ariella continued, "I want to be there, Rider. I will be there. But we don't have time to waste arguing about this. Every moment we delay, Drakzeneth grows stronger."

She turned to the horses, guiding Rider's and Kael's mounts onto the creaking raft. The animals snorted and stamped their hooves nervously as the logs shifted beneath them.

"Ari..." Rider began, his heart heavy with the thought of leaving her behind, even temporarily.

Ariella spun, looking away to hide the tears evident in her voice. "Rider, please. Trust me on this. Just go."

Kael stepped forward, placing a hand on Rider's shoulder. "She's right, my friend. We must press on."

Rider sighed, reluctantly agreeing. He knew they were right, but it didn't make it any easier. He approached Ariella from behind, attempting to gently spin her around, but she refused.

"Ari," he pleaded, pulling her into a tight embrace from behind. "Please be safe," he whispered into her hair, breathing in her scent before forcing her to turn and meet him.

"Take this with you," he said, unlatching a small slit in

his armor before reaching his fingers inside. Rider produced a single coin from inside.

"I found this the day I entered your city. I know this is going to sound foolish and I can't explain it, but something happened when I picked it up. I believe it changed my fate that day. This quest, meeting you… none of it would have happened if I hadn't picked this up. I've survived more than I should have since embarking on this journey with you, Ari. Take it, please," he said, forcing it into her palms before squeezing them tightly as he rested their foreheads together.

"Rider…" Ari exhaled as her breath began to stagger. "If that is true, then keep it. Let it bring you back to me," she replied as she broke their connection and looked up into his eyes.

"Besides, you're going to need all the help you can get with your foolish need to rush head on into danger," she joked, pulling away slightly. "Now be safe," she choked out between quivering lips. "Both of you."

With a final nod, Rider and Kael boarded the raft, their boots thudding heavily on the logs. Rider grasped the rope's tension rod, his muscles tensing as he began to pull, then it kicked loose. The sound of clicking gears and tensioned pulleys began to sing as the raft began to pull them across the river.

Ariella watched from the shore as the two men and their horses drifted further away, their forms growing smaller against the shimmering expanse of the river. The sun glinted off Rider's dark hair and Kael's blond locks, turning them to burnished copper and gold.

As the raft drifted slowly down the river, propelled by the gentle current and the tension of the guide rope, Rider and Kael found themselves enveloped by the serene beauty of the Riverlands. The sun, now high in the sky, cast a warm glow upon the water, turning it into a shimmering expanse of liquid gold.

"All right," Rider said, in an attempt to shake off his emotions, gesturing towards the distant shore that was slowly coming into view. "Let's chart a path to Stonefire from the other end of the river." Kael pulled out a weathered map from his pack, unfolding it and holding it firm against the air. Rider traced a finger along the map, following the winding path of the river.

"Once we make landfall," Rider explained, "we should head north, towards the foothills. We've seen how the Dwarves have multiple access points hidden about. We may get lucky and find one."

As the day wore on, the two men continued their discussions, poring over the map and discussing Rider's ascension, hoping to unlock the key to summoning it on command.

As the afternoon sun began its descent, the raft finally approached the opposite shore. The distant bank, once a hazy mirage, now came into sharp focus. Towering evergreens lined the water's edge, their branches reaching out over the river.

With a gentle bump, the raft nudged against the shore, settling into the soft, rocky, bank. Rider and Kael led their horses off the makeshift ferry, their hooves sinking into the damp soil. The animals, relieved to be back on solid ground, snorted and shook their manes.

Rider approached the tension gears, his hands working quickly to release the mechanism. With a sharp click and a whirring of pulleys, the raft began its journey back across the river.

"She'll be all right," Kael said softly. "Ariella is strong and resourceful. She'll catch up to us in no time."

Rider nodded, tearing his gaze away from the receding

raft. "You're right," he agreed, his voice tinged with a mix of worry and determination. "We need to focus on the task at hand. Stonefire awaits."

Together, they mounted their steeds. Rider took a deep breath, and with the click of his tongue and a gentle squeeze of his legs, he urged his horse forward.

Kael followed suit, and together they set off at a gallop.

As the sun began to sink lower on the horizon, the hills gradually grew steeper, their gentle slopes giving way to rocky outcroppings and jagged cliffs.

Kale and Rider rode through the night, until they reached the base of one of Stonefire's fingers.

"Allow me a moment," Kael shouted forward toward Rider.

"Whoa, steady now," Rider murmured, patting the neck of his mount as he stopped before the rocky trail leading onward.

Kael raised his hands skyward, and spoke, *"Astra'eth Luminae,"* as arcs of azure light spiraled into the heavens.

"Quite the signal," Rider quipped. "Now let's hope the Stonefire Scouts can see it."

The duo continued their journey through the rocking mountain pass with haste, only stopping for moments at a time so Kael could cast another signal above.

Eventually, two silhouettes emerged atop giant rams, horns curled inward toward their cheeks.

"Rider! Stormbringer! Is that you?" one of the guards shouted from atop their mountain steed.

"Indeed," Rider shouted back. "We bring news of war! We need to speak to King Ragnoc immediately!"

"Quickly, this way!" one of the guards shouted, turning their ram back the way they came.

The scout led them to a hidden cleft in the mountain before dismounting. The scout then cleared the dust and debris from a flattened stone and withdrew a pouch from his belt before placing a series of small marbles upon the stone's indented face. A few moments and whispers later, the mountain gave way, revealing a tunnel large enough for a small force of mounted riders to travel through.

"Secrets upon secrets," Kael noted with a hint of appreciation.

"Stonefire's veins run deep," the scout replied, revealing a prideful smile beneath his bushy beard.

Their descent into the bowels of the mountain was cloaked in shadows, the air growing heavy with the scent of earth and iron. Their guide's lantern cast flickering light against the walls, revealing veins of ore and gemstones embedded in the rock. The passage twisted and turned, opening into wider caverns and narrowing into tight squeezes until finally, a distant rumble announced their arrival. They emerged into the bustle and heat of Stonefire, the city alive as ever, with the clangor of hammers and the glow of forges.

"Welcome back to Stonefire," their guide said, his voice tinged with pride. "This way, to the King."

"Make way!" Kael's voice boomed, amplified by a subtle twist of magic, as they thundered down the cobblestone streets. The crowd parted like a sea around them, Dwarven merchants and miners casting curious glances at the Humans and Dwarves rushing past.

"Move! Outta the way!" Rider called out, his voice laced with urgency.

The royal guards, perched high upon the battlements, observed their frantic approach. Their eyes narrowed, recognizing the signs of urgent impending news. As Rider and Kael reached the gates of the courtroom, the guards wasted no time, throwing open the heavy doors.

Inside the courtroom, King Ragnoc stood like an immovable pillar, his presence commanding even in silence. His piercing gray eyes fixed upon the pair as they dismounted with haste.

"Your Majesty," Rider began, taking a moment to catch his breath. "We come with news."

Ragnoc's gaze lingered on the empty space beside Rider. "Where is Ariella?" he asked, his gravelly voice betraying a hint of concern.

"Separated by circumstance, not by choice," Rider replied, grimacing. "We agreed that Kael and I should ride ahead. She should be on her way from the Riverlands by now."

"Should be?" Ragnoc echoed, his brow furrowing. The king turned to one of his royal guards, a mountain of a Dwarf clad in ornate armor. "Get a regiment of rams, and find her, now," he commanded. "Escort the High Elf directly to me."

"Immediately, sire," the guard responded, bowing deeply before departing.

"Thank you, your Majesty," Rider said, nodding in gratitude. He and Kael both moved to share the details of their journey, but Ragnoc raised a hand to silence them.

"Save your breath. Tales of your endeavors have outpaced your arrival," Ragnoc stated. "King Laucian's ravens arrived a day ago, along with word from the other Human houses. The alliance forces gather, and the Wood Elves should be here by nightfall."

With a respectful bow of his head, Kael responded, "Then time is of the essence. We must—"

"Indeed it is, we have much to discuss," Ragnoc interrupted, turning away from the throne. "Come with me."

They traversed through corridors carved from the mountain itself, their footsteps echoing off the stone. Finally, they arrived at the door to Ragnoc's personal chambers.

Rider and Kael entered behind the Dwarf king. At the center of the chamber was a colossal stone table, its surface intricately carved with a detailed map of the mountain's inner labyrinth.

As the trio began to take seats around the table, Ragnoc began, "Our allies have also informed me that you are seeking ancient sites of arcane power, each with a temple built upon it, if I understand correctly."

"Correct," Rider confirmed.

"Well then, behold," Ragnoc murmured, waving his hand above the etched pathways and secret routes revealed by the table's carvings. "The heart of Stonefire, laid bare."

The duo's eyes circled the table, tracing the veins of the map. Kael leaned closer, his fingers hovering over the stone. "You've already mapped the leyline," he observed, admiration and concern lacing his tone.

"Aye, that I have," Ragnoc replied, his eyes narrowing on a particular point within the network of tunnels. "I'm quite familiar with it."

Rider and Kael exchanged a look of relief. "Then you can show us the way?" Rider's pulse quickened.

"Show you?" Ragnoc leaned back in his chair, the wood creaking under his weight. His gaze was solemn as it met Rider's. "I can take you directly to it, or rather, where it was."

"Was?" Kael brow furrowed.

"Aye." Ragnoc's voice turned grave. "I destroyed it during The Battle of Stonefire."

A heavy silence fell over the chamber. Rider leaned back, his mind racing as he absorbed the revelation.

"Destroyed…" Rider started when he finally found his voice. "That's how you defeated Drakzeneth? You forced the volcano's eruption when you destroyed it."

"Exactly." Ragnoc's eyes were still, hard, unyielding. "Stonefire's royal line has known about the leyline since the days our first kings bore the crown."

"Duragrim and Thranak," Rider added, almost sensing the King's next words. "They found it when they defeated Gorndurakh, didn't they?"

"Indeed," Ragnoc continued. "The Dwarves of old dug deep into this mountain and found Gorndurakh. The creature was ancient, and very protective of this mountain's treasure. However, Duragrim and Thranak outsmarted the beast. Over time, they grew to understand how it became so powerful and how they could defeat it. Once they claimed the site of power, they hid its secrets and built this very kingdom to keep it."

King Ragnoc stood and began to pace the room as he continued. "During The Great War, my father watched Drakzeneth grow in power, and he stood idly by as his advisors told him the threat would pass. As next in line for the throne, and his only heir, it was my duty to know the secret of our kingdom's legacy. By the time my father's advisors realized what Drakzeneth was up to, it was too late. The Dragon Lord had already destroyed and manipulated the people of the planes, enslaved the majority of the Wood Elves, and his armies were marching onto Stonefire. He called to Brightspire for aid, but Queen Vyshaan was too stubborn and proud to admit that any other race could possibly wield so much arcane power. So, he rode out to meet Drakzeneth's forces. It was a fool's gambit. He was struck down without honor, without mercy, and without a chance."

"Ragnoc," Rider sighed.

"I do not tell you this to gain your pity, Rider," Ragnoc went on. "I tell you this so you can understand why I chose the path I did. After my father fell, I once again reached out to Brightspire. I had no choice, my people, my entire race, was dying. I revealed our kingdom's greatest secret, the heart of the mountain. I told them what Drakzeneth would gain if we fell, and only then did Brightspire climb down from its northern peak to lend us aid… under the promise of us giving it to Her. Queen's Vyshaan's people claim to be the arbiters of magic, but it's all lies, Rider. They care only about controlling it."

"Selfishness and greed," Kael chimed in. "This is why we do not share our ways lightly, Rider."

"So," Ragnoc continued. "As I watched Drakzeneth's forces climb the mountain, and his Dragons begin to obliterate Brightspire's *superior* mages above, I was left with only one choice. Instead of watching my people die or become slaves, I destroyed the very prize he sought."

"Show me," Rider implored, the intensity in his voice echoing off the stone walls of the chamber.

Ragnoc exhaled deeply, a sound like distant thunder rumbling through his chest. With deliberate movements, he unlatched the clasps of his ornate chestpiece. The metal fell away with a clank against the stone floor, revealing his torso marred by a web of jagged scars, his flesh resembling one struck by lightning.

"Behold the folly of kings," Ragnoc muttered darkly, his fingertips tracing the ridges of his scars. "It was on that cursed day I chose to risk my own life—and the lives of my kin—rather than surrender our world to that abomination and his twisted faith."

Kael leaned closer, his eyes narrowing as he studied the mangled patterns. "You became the bulwark against annihilation," he murmured, almost reverently.

"Annihilation, indeed," Ragnoc scoffed. "There was no hallowed temple within the mountain's heart, only a crystal cavern filled with beams of light. I stood at the core, hands pressed upon the great stone at its center, attempting to gain, or at least, unleash its fury. When next I woke, the chamber lay in ruins, all our people scattered across the slopes in agony..." He paused, a glimmer of pain flashing behind his eyes.

"Yet here I stand, 500 plus years longer than any Dwarf before me," Ragnoc said, his voice rising with a mix of sadness and anger. "But what of Queen Vyshaan and her kin? They claim dominion over all sorcery. Bah! What sacrifices did they offer to vanquish the Dragon Lord? None! They arrived on their borrowed steeds, Griffins plucked from Amakiir's ashes, in the twilight hours of our struggle!"

"Your bitterness is justified," Kael acknowledged softly.

"Argh," Ragnoc breathed in frustration, as walked towards a nearby mirror. "I'm rambling," he apologized. "Regardless, I doubt that cave will do you any good. I seem to have taken all it has to offer," he paused, stroking his beard while inspecting his face in the mirror.

"That's how you've lived so long," Rider commented.

"I'm afraid you're correct, lad," Ragnoc responded with a slight chuckle. "Cursed to remember the day I nearly destroyed the rest of my people and our allies."

Kael rose from his seat. "You're not cursed, King Ragnoc. You're blessed. I believe you ignited what my people call your Arcane Spark. Not only that, you must have fed it an incredible amount of power. If you take us to that room, we may be able to put some of it back and help Etonya in the process."

Ragnoc turned quickly. "And at what cost?" He questioned.

"Well," Kael answered, "I'm afraid your years will once again become more limited, and some of the might within those muscles of yours is sure to diminish."

"You misunderstand my meaning," Ragnoc replied. "At what cost to my people?" He asks solemnly.

"Oh, great Dwarf, you would be ensuring your people's world will once again thrive, as it should have so long ago. The wonders bestowed upon a world when its leylines flourish undisturbed, it's why my people travel the stars. We seek out worlds and people who have discovered things even we have only dreamed of. I promise you, untold wonders await your people if we succeed, and your world leaves the leylines undisturbed." Kael said softly.

A smile played at the edges of Ragnoc's mouth. "Very well, follow me."

As the last word left his lips, King Ragnoc's entire Kingdom rang with the sound of deep Dwarven horns; one by one, they grew in number and intensity.

"Horns of war," Ragnoc warned as his chamber doors were thrown open by his royal guards.

"Dragons, your majesty! The Dragons have returned! We need to get you to safety!" they yelled, placing themselves between Ragnoc and any possible threat outside his chamber.

Drakzeneth had begun The Second Great War.

Rider, Kael, and Ragnoc all followed the royal guards out of Ragnoc's personal chamber with haste. The sounds of Dwarven horns of war continued to sound warnings throughout the mountain kingdom.

Kael pleaded, "King Ragnoc, please. Tell us where to find this chamber."

King Ragnoc, half listening, continued to issue his war commands to his royal guards and strategic council. "Mount the ballistas, ready the rams, and by the ancients, get me my hammer!"

Rider implored King Ragnoc again. "Please, your majesty, where is the chamber?"

Ragnoc waited until his final councilman rushed off in service before responding with an agitated sigh. "It's beneath our great forge. Quickly now, and be sure to stay close."

Ragnoc led the way, his armored footfalls ringing against the stone as they descended into the heart of Stonefire. The streets around them roiled with chaos, and the sound of fear and steel rang loud against the walls. Children wailed, their faces streaked with tears, as they clung to the skirts of elders who shuffled them toward the safety of their stone homes. Doors slammed shut, and heavy bolts were thrown in haste.

Men and women adorned in battle-ready armor dashed past, some still buckling pieces of armor together and adjusting helmets. Their faces set with grim determination, eyes focused on some distant point where they knew danger waited.

"Make way for the King!" a guard roared, his voice booming over the tumult. The crowd parted like waves before them, revealing the grand forge that lay ahead. It stood as the beating heart of the smithing district, its fires never quenched, forever aflame by the mountain's molten heart.

The trio was rushed inside an old blacksmith's shop, which seemed almost to shrink under the shadow of the forge; it was there that they found a keeper of secrets. The shopkeep, a stout Dwarven man, clad in metal plate mail, looked up from his work at the anvil. In his hands, a greataxe, its blade being honed to a deadly edge.

"Your Majesty," he greeted, his voice muffled behind the visor of his helm.

"Open the heart of the mountain," Ragnoc commanded without delay.

The shopkeep nodded once before he began moving a series of chains hanging above the forge. The sound of gears cranking and wheels turning echoed behind the walls.

As the stone wall receded and slid aside, it revealed a hidden passage that led into darkness. Then Ragnoc turned to Rider and Kael. "Down there lies what you seek. You've been warned, there is no temple and most of the chamber is damaged. I must go and defend my people."

"Thank you, Your Majesty," Rider said, clasping the Dwarf king's gauntleted forearm.

"May your hammer strike true," Kael added, his blue eyes reflecting the urgency of their quest.

With a curt nod, Ragnoc departed, leaving them to the shadows of the descending hall. The cool air of the underground enveloped them as they left behind the clamor of war preparation.

The path wound ever downward, the walls slowly transforming from rough-hewn stone to a rich tapestry of gemstones and crystals. With each step, the corridor grew more resplendent, illuminated by the natural glow of the mountain's treasures.

Finally, they emerged into a vast crystalline chamber, a dome perfectly shaped by nature and magic. Its surfaces, cracked and marred by the ancient violence, still shimmered with the echoes of forgotten power.

"Never have I seen such beauty forged from destruction," Rider said softly, his gaze fixed on the center of the room.

There, rising from the ground like a monument to the world's creation, stood a single grand crystal. It soared upward, its surface etched with a myriad of colors, each hue seared deep into the stone.

"Quite remarkable," Kael noted. "The mountain itself has become a guardian, transmuting its very essence to shield the leyline from the magma's wrath."

"Remarkable," Rider agreed. "But how do we proceed? This is no temple, and there's no central device."

"Indeed," Kael said, snapping back to the urgency of their mission. "This will require more than a mere channeling of Arcane Sparks. The leyline's energy within these scarred minerals is dormant, contained, but not lost. We must awaken it."

"How?" Rider asked, uncertainty threading his tone.

"We need to craft an Astralan focus," Kael answered.

"A what?" Rider asked, bewildered by the term.

"Each of the temples we've located had an arcane focus at the center, the triangular devices," Kael answered. "Those were draconian perversions. Together we can craft a stronger version of Astralan design."

Rider nodded, his resolve sound. "Tell me what to do."

Guided by Kael's arcane wisdom, Rider began to cut away crystals and gemstones from the walls around them, his deft hands steady despite the weight of what was to come.

CHAPTER XXVII
THE SECOND GREAT WAR

Ariella's tears carved silent paths down her cheeks as the ferry carrying Rider dwindled to a speck on the horizon. The raw ache of parting from him was tearing a wound in her chest. She had urged him to go, for the realm and the mission, yet her heart broke under every beat as she began to sob and gasp for air as the ferry put distance between them.

The gentle mare she had been riding approached, sensing Ariella's distress. With a soft snort, the horse nudged her tear-stained face and breath-laden chest, before laying its head against her stomach. Ariella lowered her head as she wrapped her arms around the horse's broad neck, her embrace a silent comfort. The horse stood stoic and patient, providing strength when Ariella's will could not.

"Thank you, my friend," Ariella whispered, her voice barely breaking the hush of the riverside. She planted a tender kiss on the animal's forehead, then pressed her own against it, sharing a moment of mutual solace.

The tranquility was shattered by the distant howl of

Orcish wolves. A snap of alarm shot through Ariella's spine. She straightened up, peering into the tree line from where the guttural cries originated. Three dark forms emerged, mounted upon monstrous wolves.

"Come, we must flee," Ariella spoke firmly, wiping her sleeve across her eyes. She hoisted herself onto her mount with practiced grace. The mare, sensing the urgency, pawed the ground restlessly.

The Orc riders dug their heels into their mounts' flanks as they noticed her rise atop the horse. With a swift kick and flick of the reins, Ariella spurred her mare forward. The thunderous beat of hooves against the earth became a rhythm of escape. The Orcs' war cries grew louder and more frenzied as they gave chase.

"Run, swift as the wind," Ariella urged her mare, leaning forward in hopes to create less resistance. The chase was on.

Ariella's heart pounded in rhythm with the mare's galloping hooves as they raced along the river toward Shadyvale. The hope of reaching the town before the Orcish wolves caught up was thin, but hope nonetheless. Suddenly, an arrow zipped past her, slicing the tip of her left ear, causing blood to drip down her face.

Ducking instinctively, she risked a glance back. One of the wolf riders had drawn his bow, while the others rode low in hopes of increasing their speed. The Orc's muscular forms hunched over the backs of their snarling beasts, urging them on with guttural commands and fierce jerks of the reins.

"Curse you, foul creatures!" Ariella muttered under her breath as she swung her bow from her back, notching an arrow of her own. She twisted in the saddle to let the arrow fly, but the furious pace of her horse made the shot go wide.

The wolf rider returned fire, missing in turn. Twice more she let loose an arrow, twice more they missed their marks. The rough terrain offered no favors as the steed jolted her aim with every stride it took.

"Useless," she cursed. She knew it was time for a change in tactics. With a swift motion, she secured the bow and drew one of her slender blades.

The first Orc wolf rider was closing in. Its mount's jaws snapped hungrily, trying to tear into the back right flank of Ariella's steed.

"Get back!" Ariella's voice shot out as she leaned off the side of her mount, plunging her blade into the wolf's snout before ripping it back across its eye. The beast let a blood-curdling yelp loose as it reared its head back.

The Orc atop the wolf lost his balance and tumbled to the ground, a mess of leather and limbs. Ariella righted herself atop her mount with a grin. "One down, two to go," she thought to herself.

But her moment of victory was short-lived. The sharp thud of an arrow piercing flesh shattered her focus as her horse cried out. As if in slow motion, the noble creature's legs buckled, sending it tumbling forward, rolling onto its side with earth-shaking force.

Ariella was thrown forward, her body sailing through the air before crashing into the muddy riverbank. She slid through the wet earth as adrenaline surged through her veins.

With both blades drawn, she shot up from the water and mud, her auburn hair flaring around her head like a fiery halo as it caught the dying light of the day. Then came another Orcish arrow, this one landing square in her left shoulder.

Twisting toward the blow, she felt the bite of the projectile as it sank into her flesh. The impact caused her to drop her left blade and stumble backward, her knees buckling beneath her, forcing her to the ground once more.

Ariella's vision blurred as the mud and water began to drip over her eyes, but she concentrated her focus on the advancing threat. The slow thud of paws upon dirt grew louder as one Orcish wolf walked steadily towards her. Time seemed to slow as the rider drew back another massive arrow before releasing the string.

With a swift motion born of desperation and skill, Ariella's right arm lashed out, her blade catching the shaft of the arrow mid-flight. Her heart hammered in her chest, breath coming in ragged gasps, the pain in her shoulder throbbing in time with her pulse.

The Orcish rider pulled back on the reins, halting his mount with a snarl. He dismounted with a thud, his boots sinking into the soft, earthy mud of the riverbank.

A chilling scene caught her eye. The second Orc rider was allowing his wolf to gorge on the flesh of the first fallen Orc, blood covering its face as organs were ripped from flesh. *Is this my fate?*, She thought bitterly, *to die here, alone, as feed for overgrown monstrosities?*

The remaining Orc approached, slowly, sword in hand. "She Elf, serve me now," he grunted in broken Common Tongue.

"I'd rather die," Ariella shouted defiantly, as she swung at his exposed throat with what strength she had left.

But the Orc was quick, powerful. With a brutish sneer, he caught her wrist mid-swing. Then came the punch, a devastating blow landing squarely in her stomach, driving the breath from her lungs, her body refusing to breathe.

Gasping for air, Ariella's vision darkened around the edges. She attempted to lift her left arm in a feeble attempt to fight back, but the Orc was merciless. With a swift, callous strike, he slammed his palm onto the arrow still embedded in her shoulder, pushing it deeper.

"Elf serve now," he growled again, his eyes seething with anger.

Pain exploded through Ariella's body. She wanted to scream, to curse, to fight—but no sound came out. Her throat constricted, and her limbs refused to respond.

The bloodlust in the air was palpable as the third Orc rider, a hulking brute adorned with jagged armor, dismounted his wolf. Cold and calculating eyes surveyed Ariella's form, her once vibrant auburn hair and creamy skin now a tangled mess of blood and mud.

"This one is important to the Queen," he rumbled authoritatively.

"No, this one is mine. I caught this one," his counterpart argued, approaching far closer than anyone, or anything, should to an Orcish wolf still under bloodlust.

The authoritative Orc uttered a single word, "Kill," and the beast did not hesitate. With savage efficiency, it lunged, tearing the disobedient Orc's head from his shoulders in a spray of crimson.

Ariella watched through a haze of pain and disbelief. These were the ruthless games of Orcs, where strength ruled and mercy was a weakness.

Without ceremony, the surviving Orc retrieved a length of rope from his saddlebags before tossing it at Ariella's feet. "Tie."

Pride and defiance surged within her as she rose to her knees. Locking eyes with her would-be captor, she let out one final defiance. "Go. Fuck. Yourself," she said with perfect enunciation, before spitting a mixture of blood, saliva, and mud into his face.

The Orc stood firm, then raised his massive hand and delivered a devastating backhand, swift and merciless.

Ariella's body spun before it went limp, then slowly crumpled into the river, eyes forced shut, and then there was only darkness.

Within the crystalline heart of Stonefire Mountain, Rider and Kael reached the end of their labored task. They had spent what felt like hours meticulously carving shards of crystal and gemstone.

"Kael," Rider grunted, handing over the final piece of crystal.

Kael's palm glowed softly as he conjured a small orb of light, inspecting how the prismatic colors passed through the crystal. "Well done, Rider," he said, before continuing. "Focus now," Kael instructed, as he set the crystal aside with the others. "Now we begin the transmutation."

"Transmutation?" Rider echoed.

Kael nodded. "These crystals, once joined, will form the Astralan Arcane Focus. A nexus of energy to amplify and stabilize the raw magic of this place."

"Stabilize?" Rider queried.

"Raw arcane energy can be extremely dangerous," Kael explained. "You saw what it did to Ragnoc's body when he destroyed the natural focus the mountain created for itself."

"Right," Rider responded.

"The arcane focus serves not only as a conduit for the energy in the surrounding space, but a stabilizer for their world," Kael continued. "Once fused with a leyline, it creates an access point that future magic wielders can use to feed, consume, or commune with. Rider, each world is unique. Each will require a different number of leyline access points, and arcane focuses, depending on its size and arcane output."

"To what end?" Rider replied, before continuing. "All I've seen so far is how Drakzeneth, or others, can use these access points to destroy or enslave an entire world."

"Rider," Kael responded, "Once stabilized, a world can enter an age of magical blessings and wonder. One where, like Astrala, everyone's needs can be met through simple magic. Hunger, disease, homelessness, all of these concepts are lost to time, if the people of those worlds can come together and use their blessings appropriately. That is why we travel. To learn, to guide, to help."

Rider absorbed the weight of Kael's words. Magic was more than just power; it was responsibility.

"Let us begin," Kael declared.

"All right," Rider replied, stepping opposite Kael amidst the pile of gemstones.

"Follow my lead," Kael instructed. "Just as before, with Ariella."

They stood together, not merely crafting an object, but potentially shaping the fate of this world. An unspoken trust passed between them; though from different paths, their journey had led them here, together.

"Repeat after me, move exactly as I do," Kael began. He raised his arms slowly, palms facing downward, wrists loose, and then continued his slowed pace as he began moving them independently, each arm in its own opposite, circular motion. Then he began the chant, *"Terra'kael Elixen, Arcana'eth Vessar,"* never stopping his motions.

"Terrakael Elixen, Arcana'eth Vessar," Rider repeated, mirroring Kael's movements. Their hands traced intricate patterns in the air, weaving unseen threads of energy.

The crystals responded, humming with a frequency

that vibrated the surrounding area. Lights sparked, then blazed, engulfing the gemstones in a radiant glow.

"Keep going," Kael urged, his eyes locked onto the burgeoning light.

"Terra'kael Elixen, Arcana'eth Vessar," they continued in unison, voices merging with the magic that swirled around them.

A crescendo of light and sound enveloped them. Rider felt a surge of heat, followed by an icy chill. The elements themselves seemed to bend to their will, coalescing into a final flash of light.

"Open your eyes, Rider," Kael's voice cut through the dwindling echoes. Before them lay the culmination of their work, the Astralan Arcane Focus—a pentagonal pyramid of fused gemstones gleaming with inner light.

"By the stars..." Rider breathed, his voice filled with awe.

"By our hands," Kael corrected gently.

The two men shared a look of accomplishment, understanding that their bond had been sealed not only by friendship, but by the shared creation of something greater than themselves.

"Okay, Kael," Rider began, urgency returning to his tone. "The faster we deal with Drakzeneth, the faster we can return to provide it with some of my Spark."

"No, Rider," Kael responded. "This is not going to be like the access point at Reshu's academy."

"What?! Why not?" Rider asked.

"This leyline was not simply drained, Rider." Kael replied. "When Ragnoc destroyed the chamber's center stone, he severed its connection with Etonya. Ragnoc needs to return the energy his body is holding, to the heart, to the focus we just made, so it can begin reconnecting with Etonya itself."

"But, Ragnoc—" Rider started.

"Ragnoc will make the sacrifice his people require of him, Rider," Kael interjected. "He serves his people well."

"OK, then," Rider responded. "Let's go help him deal with those Dragons."

"Indeed," Kael responded.

The two heroes began their ascent up the stairs, through the smithy's hidden doorway, and exited the building. Two Royal Guards stood ready at the entrance.

"Have you completed your work?" they asked.

"Yes," Rider replied. "Where's King Ragnoc? We need him."

"He's with our men, holding back Queen Vyshaan's forces," the guard responded.

"Take us to him immediately," Rider replied.

"This way, Sir. Follow me," the guard said with authority.

The guards escorted Rider and Kael out of the smithing district and toward a nearby rampart leading out of the mountain.

"King Ragnoc should be just beyond the mountain's expanse," one of the guards yelled, looking back toward the heroes as he exited the mouth of the cave leading to the outside world.

Just as he crossed the threshold and stood outside the cave, he was consumed by a stream of fire. Kael and Rider, shocked by the sudden attack, halted in their tracks as they covered their faces from the heat. Together, they stood helpless, unable to do anything for the Dwarf as they watched him melt into a pile of liquid metal and bone.

"Kael?" Rider questioned, shock still lingering on his voice.

"Dragon fire," Kael answered. "He's done it. He's recreated a Red Dragon."

As the liquid fire cooled, the mound hardened before them. Kael, Rider, and the remaining guard, all approached the exit cautiously, peering toward the sky for any sign of danger.

As they stepped onto the rocky terrain outside the mountain, a scene of chaos unfolded before them. Plumes of smoke rose from various points on the mountainside, evidence of the Dragon's fiery onslaught.

Suddenly, a group of King Ragnoc's Royal Guards came into view. They had just killed a pair of massive Orc warriors. One of the Royal Guards pulled his axe from deep within the Orc's chest, ripping through its crude armor and tough flesh as he retrieved it.

Rider and Kael rushed to the Dwarves' side, their faces etched with concern and urgency.

"Where is King Ragnoc?" Rider asked, his voice carrying a tone of authority.

The Dwarf guard wiped sweat and Orc blood from his brow, his breath heavy. "We were all headed up the mountain to man the ballistas," he explained. "We got separated by Orcs and that damn Dragon. It's been a bloody mess."

He gestured toward the smoldering corpses littering the rocky terrain.

"We've been pinned down by those Orc bastards," another guard chimed in, his armor dented and bloody. "Every time we try to send someone up after the King, that cursed Dragon flies back and turns them into a molten pile of flesh."

Rider met Kael's gaze of concern before instructing the Dwarves, "Stay here and stay safe. Do not let a single fucking Orc into that mountain." Rider's face hardened as he continued, "We're going to get Ragnoc. When he comes back, you escort his ass straight to the Heart."

The guards all grunted a Dwarven military agreement

before standing at attention. Rider and Kael gave an approving nod to the soldiers before they sprinted from behind the boulders toward the mountain's peak.

As they climbed higher in search of King Ragnoc, the battle below the mountain came into view. Rider's stomach sank as he witnessed the Dwarven military being overrun by a sea of Orcish warriors, a military force he believed they had already defeated when claiming Kor Stronghold. The size of this Orcish force, however, dispelled any belief Rider held about how impactful that victory was over Drakzeneth's.

Rider and Kael exchanged looks, a silent conversation passing between the two over what course of action they should take.

"Rider, go get Ragnoc, we need his Spark to repair the heart."

"Kael…," Rider replied with a pause. "You can't take on that entire army, you've only restored a fraction of what you sacrificed to save Ariella and me."

"Maybe not," Kael replied. "But it's the right thing to do. My people's magic created this monster and I won't stand by while his army finishes erasing the Dwarves from this world."

"*Our* people," Rider responded. "*Our* people," he repeated, extending his arm.

A grin crossed Kael's face as he clasped hold of Rider's extended forearm. "*Our* people," he repeated with pride.

Kael released his grasp and began his descent toward the battle below.

There, on the face of the ancient Stonefire mountain, Rider stood alone. He looked up toward the sky and saw the mighty red Dragon spiral downward as it began spewing fire toward the mountain's peak.

"I'm coming, Ragnoc," Rider said to himself as he began to run once more.

He scrambled over boulders and leaped across the small rocky caverns that littered the path's surface. Finally, as he crested a rise, he spotted a small group of Dwarves clustered around a series of melted heaps of Dwarven metal. The ballistas had been destroyed.

In the middle of the group stood Ragnoc Blackhammer, his white beard now stained with foreboding patches of blood and soot. He looked up as Rider approached.

"About damn time you showed up," Ragnoc growled. "We've got our hands full up here."

"We've fixed the heart," Rider announced. "We need you to return and give back the energy your body took when you destroyed it."

"I will not leave my people in their time of need," Ragnoc shouted. "First, we deal with that damn beast," Ragnoc continued, pointing toward the crimson Dragon above.

"You need to trust me, Ragnoc," Rider urged. "I will take care of the Dragon, but I need you to go back."

Ragnoc stared into Rider's eyes, judging the man before him.

Rider met Ragnoc's gaze and placed a hand upon his shoulder before speaking, "Only you can make the sacrifice that's necessary."

"Men," Ragnoc shouted. "Back to Stonefire. You better be right about this, Rider," Ragnoc said before he issued his final command. "Give it hell."

Rider watched as King Ragnoc and his men sprinted back down the mountain. The Dragon, however, had other plans.

The crimson Dragon's wings beat against the air as it descended toward the fleeing Dwarves. The fading sunlight reflected off its scale like dull rubies. The beast's eyes were glowing with fiery intent, locked onto its prey.

Deep within the Dragon's chest, an inferno stirred. Flames flickered up its neck, building in intensity with each passing second. The air around the creature shimmered with heat as it tucked its wings and dove closer.

Ragnoc risked a glance over his shoulder, his eyes widening at the sight of the Dragon preparing its deadly flame. The beast's maw opened wide, the glow emanating from deep within its throat, each moment growing brighter and more intense. The air crackled with energy as the beast unleashed a torrent of liquid fire.

The stream of fire hurtled toward the fleeing Dwarves. In unison, Ragnoc's Royal Guards halted their descent and immediately raised their shields in a desperate attempt to ward off the flames from their King. A brilliant burst of blue arcane energy erupted from the top of the mountain, colliding with the path of the Dragon's fiery breath, causing the liquid flame to scatter through the air past the Dwarves.

Rider stood atop a rocky outcropping, his sword pointing at the Dragon from beside his face in his right hand, its blade gleaming with an otherworldly light. His left hand was outstretched toward the beast, wreathed in smoky blue tendrils of raw arcane power.

The Dragon roared in fury as it banked sharply, its wings stirring up dust and debris as it turned its attention toward Rider. The beast's eyes narrowed, recognizing the threat that stood before it.

The crimson beast's wings beat the air with thunderous force as it hurled itself through forward. Smoke and embers trailed from between the beast's scales as it landed, preparing to unleash another torrent of liquid fire.

Rider stood his ground, his sapphire eyes locked onto

the approaching threat. The Dragon opened its jaws wide, revealing the inferno building within its throat. With a deafening roar, the Dragon released a stream of molten flame. The liquid splashed against Rider and the surrounding landscape, its fury unrelenting. The ground around where Rider had stood was reduced to molten slag, the rocks melting and flowing like lava.

As the Dragon's breath ceased, and the smoke began to clear, a blue glow pierced through. Rider stood untouched, a beacon of defiance against the Dragon's onslaught. His sapphire eyes blazed with determination, his blue flame aura simmering atop his armor. With two simple words, he began his clash with destiny. "My turn."

CHAPTER XXVIII
SKYFALL

With a mighty surge of arcane energy, Rider's aura grew larger as it sent the remaining flames scattering in all directions. Rider dashed toward the colossal creature at blinding speed, both hands gripping his sword.

The creature, shocked by the speed of the stream of azure light headed in its direction, slammed and buffeted its wings toward the ground as it took flight. It was too late. Rider had already started his assault. Leaping toward the Dragon, Rider swung his sword, as he prepared to deliver a devastating blow. Scales shattered, sending tiny shards of the ruby Dragon's armor flying. Rider's blade tore through the creature's hide and muscle until finally striking home deep in the beast's shoulder bone. The Dragon let loose a deafening roar as pain and anger left its throat.

Rider landed from his aerial assault before pivoting on his heels, looking skyward to see where the beast would land next. There wasn't much level ground near the peak of the mountain, and he knew he'd have to make the beast land if he wanted to keep it from joining the battle below.

The Dragon flapped its injured wing as it sought to

reposition itself on the rocky mountainside. Its molten blood spewed forth from the wound, which widened with each stumbled attempt to move further through the air. The blood sizzled as it hit the earth, melting into the dirt and stone it landed upon. The beast's feet caught rock as it slid, more of a crash than a landing, before locking eyes with Rider who stood near where the beast originated its failed flight. It attempted to flap its left wing twice more, the tear growing larger with each attempt, before finally turning its head and biting into its own flesh. With a disgusting sound, the beast ripped its own wing from its body before throwing it at Rider.

The wing flew through the air as its blood sprayed about, littering the rocky terrain. As the massive wing approached, it blocked Rider's view of the Dragon and surrounding landscape, but he could hear the beast approaching. Rider swung his sword upward, catching the wing mid air and splitting the flesh as the weight carried it beyond. As the final flap of flesh was severed, restoring Rider's view, the Dragon's maw appeared, turned on its side, as it aimed to engulf Rider. Rider quickly released his left hand from the blade and shoved it forward, the maw almost surrounding him, and shot forth another azure blast of arcane force.

The beast's head reared back from the impact as Rider used the opportunity to slide through the Dragon's cheek, connecting with its jaw bone. Quickly, and out of desperation, the Dragon spun about, swinging its tail. Rider leaped skyward in an effort to dodge the assault, but the creature's body was too large.

The tail slammed into Rider, hitting him harder than anything he'd experienced before. His vision went black as he flew backwards. The sensation was foreign, he could feel the wind, he knew he was moving, but he could not control his body.

Rider crashed like a felled tree as his body rolled and tumbled upon the now cooled bloodied dirt. The only sound Rider could hear was the ringing in his ears, but the vibrations he felt were clear. The earth trembled under the claws of the stampeding Dragon, the shaking growing stronger as it approached… Then suddenly it stopped. Rider started to regain control of his body, but as his vision flickered back to life, he could see only in pieces. Griffins were swooping in and out as they performed diving attacks against the Dragon, upon all but one of their backs were Wood Elf warriors, barraging the monstrosity with spears from above.

"Laucian," Rider thought to himself, he's made it.

Rider stumbled to his feet, still regaining full control of his limbs. The ringing in his ears was replaced by the loud screeches of the Griffins. The majestic animals were relentless, sharp claws tearing at scale and flesh, others attempting to land on the beast's back and gouge at its flesh with their mighty beaks. The Dragon, however, had not given up. It continued to flap its remaining wing as it buffeted javelin strikes back and swung at the flying onslaught. Its tail and claws connected every so often, hurling Elven warriors and Griffins to the ground or off the cliff faces.

Rider, now fully alert, ignited his aura as he sprang toward the beast with a guttural yell. "RAAAAAAAH!"

The beast turned to face the reawakened threat before him and attempted another mighty tail strike.

Rider, with no blade in sight, raised both his hands and shouted, *"FERASTEL!"* A massive bolt of lighting erupted from Rider's very soul, his Arcane Spark. It collided with the Dragon and sent it hurtling backwards up the mountain toward its peak. Rider could no longer see the Dragon as it crested the peak, but he heard the tremendous crash it caused upon landing. Just then, a familiar creature landed beside him with a mighty screech and show of triumphant wings. The very same Griffin that Rider had ridden twice before.

"I really need to learn what to call you," Rider said with a nod as he met the creature's gaze. "For now, how about we just go with Talon?"

The creature let out a screech in agreement as it batted its wings in the air.

"Talon it is," Rider said with a grin. "Now let's go finish this."

Rider climbed upon Talon's back and was ready to depart as another Griffin landed beside them.

"Rider," an Elven warrior called out. "I spotted this when we arrived," he continued as he presented Rider's blade, "and I believe it belongs to you."

Rider gripped the hilt of his longsword and couldn't help but feel a piece of him had been returned. "Thank you, warrior," Rider said as he returned the blade to its sheath upon his back. "Now go," Rider commanded. "Rejoin the others and help the Dwarves below. I'll handle what's left up here."

The warrior gave Rider a reassuring nod before the two of them led their Griffins forward, leaping skyward in opposite directions.

As Rider soared toward the peak of the mountain's volcano, he could see the Orcish threat now engaged from all sides. The Wood Elf and Dwarvish armies clashed against the Orcs from opposite ends of the battlefield, while Griffin riders continued their aerial assaults from above. The tide of battle was turning in their favor. Now it was just up to Rider to ensure their victory.

As Rider rose above the crest, he was met by waves of blazing heat. He knew he would be at a disadvantage here, but he had no choice. The Dragon came back into view as Rider's eyes caught the horizon, its red scales now bearing scorch marks from where Rider's electric blast made contact. The beast's breath came in ragged motions as it struggled to return to its feet.

"Thank you," Rider said as he dismounted the landing Griffin. "Go now. Find and protect the Dwarven King."

Talon screeched in acknowledgement and quickly turned, sprinting toward the nearby edge before leaping into the fray, followed by a diving motion toward the battle below.

"It's just you and me," Rider said, addressing the mangled creature as he strode toward it, unsheathing his blade. "Come on!" Rider yelled as his blue-flame aura erupted around him, now seemingly in full control over when and how he called forth his Aetherion Ascension.

The Dragon's face dripped blood and tore further as it opened its maw and unleashed another hideous roar.

The two opponents charged forth at one another knowing this would be their final clash. As the Dragon approached, it reared its body back, raising its head and claws high in an attempt to stop Rider from gaining any height advantage, but failed. Rider threw his left hand toward the ground as he approached, commanding his arcane inheritance to come forth. "*Vor'ethra!*" Rider shouted, as a blast of pure arcane force shot from his palm, launching him skyward in an instant. Rider passed between the Dragon's claws as they slammed down upon the ground where he once stood. The Dragon's left eye followed as his adversary flew past skyward. As Rider reached the apex of his ascent, dark storm clouds began to form above as if the arcane energies of Etonya could sense his next move.

"*VALKORIN!*" Rider screamed with all his heart as he raised his sword high above his head, gripping it with both hands.

In an instant, lighting surged across the clouds. What followed was a crack of thunder as multiple large bolts of electricity gathered into Rider's sword from above like a lightning rod. As the last bolt struck, Rider flipped forward from the apex and dove straight down toward the Dragon below. In a last attempt at survival, the Dragon raised its head and leaped skyward with its maw open to swallow Rider. The inferno within, growing in intensity, reflected against Rider's sapphire eyes as he disappeared deep within the creature's throat.

The Dragon's body exploded before it could descend back toward the ground below. Molten fire and blood erupted into the air above the volcano. Chunks of flesh, scale, and bone shot skyward across the mountaintop, falling to the battlefield below like flaming meteors. The falling debris caused chaos and confusion as it plummeted atop warriors from both sides of war, melting flesh and crushing souls. It could only be described as the second great eruption of Stonefire Mountain.

Kael looked skyward in fear, hoping to find Rider in his sights. What came next was a saga that would be etched in the memory of every warrior for ages to come.

Rider's body tumbled and spun through the air, his dark hair whipping around his face as he plummeted toward the battle below. His armor was scorched and dented, but his grip on his longsword remained steadfast. Smoke trailed from Rider's body as the Dragon's Arcane Spark struggled to merge with his own. Crimson and azure energies crackled and writhed around him like dueling serpents. With each pulse, his body jerked and spasmed uncontrollably, thrown about by the warring magics.

Flaming chunks of Dragon flesh hurtled past, searing the air with their heat. Jagged shards of ruby scales sliced through the sky like a storm of bloodied razors that clattered against Rider's armor as he fell.

The battle below stilled for a moment as all eyes turned skyward, watching in awe and horror. Orcs, Dwarves, and Elves alike scattered, desperate to avoid the deadly downpour. Shields were raised in futile defense against the sizzling onslaught.

Kael's heart seized in his chest as he spotted Rider among the falling debris. He watched helplessly as his friend was buffeted by the arcane blasts, his body contorted in agony with each surge of power.

As Rider neared the ground, the energies reached a crescendo. A final, massive eruption of crimson and azure light engulfed his form, blinding all in the vicinity. The shockwave rippled outward, flattening nearby combatants as the falling Dragon turned from flesh to ash.

Then, as suddenly as it began, the light faded. Rider's body, still wreathed in tendrils of dissipating magic, slammed into the blood-soaked earth with a sickening thud, sending up a plume of dust and dirt. He lay motionless, his sword still clutched in his hand.

Kael sprinted toward his fallen friend. All that mattered was to see if Rider still drew breath. Fear and desperation quickened the mage's steps, when suddenly a screech came from above, and Talon swooped low and gently took Kael into its claws.

Talon released Kael from his grasp, allowing him to skid to a halt beside Rider's prone form. Falling to his knees in the churned mud, Kael reached out with shaking hands, feeling for a pulse, any sign of life. The seconds stretched into eternity as he searched, silently pleading to the stars above. Finally, he felt it. A faint beat beneath his fingertips. Relief flooded through Kael, a shaky breath escaped his lips. Rider was alive, but only just. The warring magics had taken their toll, leaving him battered and broken.

With a surge of determination, Kael gathered Rider into his arms. Talon, sensing the urgency, lowered his body to the ground, allowing Kael to carefully drape Rider across its back.

"To Stonefire, with haste," Kael commanded. "Rider's life hangs in the balance."

Talon let out a piercing screech of understanding, his powerful wings unfurling as he prepared to take flight. Kael climbed atop the Griffin, positioning himself behind Rider to keep him secure. With a mighty leap, Talon launched into the sky.

As they soared above the chaos, Kael caught glimpses of the battle. The Orcish army, already in disarray from the Dragon's fiery demise, found themselves outflanked and overwhelmed. The Elven archers rained down a hail of arrows, each one finding its mark with deadly precision. The Dwarven warriors, their spirits bolstered by the sight of the Dragon's fall, surged forward with renewed vigor, their axes and hammers cleaving through Orcish armor and flesh. The battle raged on, the alliance's victory now all but certain. Talon's wings carried the heroes swiftly over the mountainous terrain, the wind whipping past their faces as they raced towards Stonefire.

As they neared the Dwarven stronghold, Kael could see the commotion below. News of the Dragon's demise and Rider's fall had already reached the mountain, and a flurry of activity greeted their arrival. Dwarven healers and attendants rushed forward as Talon touched down in the main courtyard, their faces etched with concern and determination. Kael dismounted, carefully lowering Rider into the waiting arms of the healers who carried him swiftly into the infirmary.

Hours had passed. King Laucian and King Ragnoc returned to Stonefire and officially announced their victory over Drakzeneth's Orcish horde. Celebrations erupted around Stonefire as the Wood Elf and Dwarven people shared in their triumph. Kael, however, stood idle throughout the night and into the next morning as he kept guard over Rider's unconscious body.

Ragnoc entered the infirmary and saw Rider laying on the bed. The guards standing watch quickly stood at attention as they acknowledged their King, "Your majesty, we were not aware you'd be coming by."

"Good," Ragnoc grunted. "Glad to see you both are still dutiful when not expecting me."

"For the Spellsword who saved Stonefire," one declared, "It is our pleasure, not our duty."

Ragnoc gave the duo a nod and then turned to the caregivers.

"Has there been any change?" he asked.

"No, my King," the lead nurse responded. "His pulse is steady, but we are unsure why he has yet to awaken."

"I may have an idea," Kael chimed in. "I fear the massive amount of energy his Arcane Spark has absorbed may be to blame."

"Stormbringer," Ragnoc responded as he turned his gaze to Kael, "I admit I do not understand magic as you do, but my Kingdom and its resources are at your disposal.

Do not hesitate to ask for anything you believe may aid in his recovery."

"I fear only time can—" Kael started before stopping mid sentence. "King Ragnoc, if the heart of the mountain is restored, the leyline itself may be of assistance."

King Ragnoc's gaze switched from Kael to Rider and lingered there for what felt like an eternity before he spoke.

"Very well, Stormbringer," Ragnoc said at last. "Not only did this man save my Kingdom, he saved my life. Allow me to make some preparations and I will meet you there before the hour is over."

"Thank you, Your Majesty," Kael replied.

Ragnoc switched his attention to the guards at the door. "Assist this man in any way he requires."

The two guards fisted their right hands and crossed them over their hearts in salute. "Yes, Your Majesty."

Kael and the two Royal Guards escorted the caregivers as they transported Rider's unconscious body through the city. As they traversed the streets, many citizens stopped to kneel or bow their heads in respect to the fallen hero who saved their kingdom, the last Kingdom of all Dwarven kind. By the time they reached the main gates of the smithing district, they had amassed a small parade of followers waiting to see what would become of their hero. King Ragnoc had a company of guards waiting to halt the citizenry that followed as they arrived.

"My people," Ragnoc began as he addressed the masses. "I know you are all here out of respect for The Spellsword. However, I must ask that you wait here as our healers do what they can for him."

Ragnoc stepped back behind the guards toward Kael and demanded the healers swear an oath of secrecy to what they were about to witness. Once all had agreed,

Ragnoc ushered them all toward the blacksmith's shop and down the hidden chamber toward the heart of the mountain.

As they reached the crystalline chamber, Kael gave instructions where to place Rider and where King Ragnoc should stand. Ragnoc dismissed the healers back up the chamber, leaving the trio alone in the heart.

"Your Majesty," Kael began, "This ritual typically requires at least those being attuned to the magic forces of their world to be present. I want you to be aware of the risks."

"Stormbringer," Ragnoc replied. "I gave you my word that anything you needed would be provided. Now, let us begin."

"Very well," Kael nodded. "You will need to repeat my words and mimic my motion as closely as you can. When I stop, you continue until the leyline opens up and accepts your Spark. Let me be clear, you are returning what you've taken. All of it."

"I understand, Kael," Ragnoc said quietly, then after a breath added, "How long will I have…afterwards?"

"Impossible to say," Kael replied. "Have you made arrangements?"

"I have," Ragnoc confirmed. "Begin."

Kael and Ragnoc performed the same counter ritual that Ariella and Rider had helped Kael with before. Upon its climax, Ragnoc's power was deposited into the Astralan Arcane Focus with a bright flash and a stream of energy that eventually dissipated. Afterwards, Ragnoc stood, drained but resolute.

"How do you feel?" Kael asked as Ragnoc steadied himself.

"Different, unburdened perhaps… tired," Ragnoc muttered.

"Let's get you back to your people," Kael suggested. "I'm going to stay here with Rider."

"That's a fine idea," Ragnoc gave him a weary nod, his voice sounding a bit older.

Ragnoc made it about halfway up the chambers pathway before Kael heard him call for assistance from his guards and healers. The ritual had taken its toll, but it was yet to be determined if it would have the effect on Rider they'd hoped for.

Kael placed his back against the wall closest to Rider and slowly slid down next to his friend before placing his hand on his shoulder. Only time would tell if Rider would recover, but he would remain one way or the other.

Deep within Rider's soul, a battle was unfolding within his Arcane Spark. The dreams and memories of all the Dragons he'd slain and absorbed power from took over, attempting to replace his own. Flashes of the Dragon's dark deeds once again flooded his mind, quickly shifting back to his own recent memories as his mind and soul attempted to maintain their own existence. He saw Bael-gor. He saw Kael. He saw himself through the eyes of the Dragons he'd faced, the fear he'd instilled in them.

Meanwhile, Kael began to notice how the arcane energies in the room flickered into streams, swirling and penetrating the Astralan Focus, eventually making their way toward Rider before swirling around him and entering his chest.

Rider's mind raced with the changing memories before eventually seeing an image of Ariella's face. However, this image was not a memory of his own. Rider's mind pulled back the memory, forcing all others to stop as it focused solely on this moment. She was caged and being tortured. Queen Vyshaan was releasing dark tendrils of magic into her as she casted a series of spells, trying to turn her into a

Dragon. The small portion of Kael's donated Spark was saving her, fighting back against the spell, but she was growing weaker as the Spark was depleting.

Rider's eyes shot open as a single word left his lips. "Ari."

Kael, overcome with joy and relief, collapsed his arms onto Rider's chest as tears began to form in his eyes. "Thank the stars," he said, fighting through tears.

"Ari," Rider repeated as he tried to sit up. "We need to save her."

"Save her?" Kael questioned as he sat up, surprised. "What are you talking about?"

"I saw her, Kael," Rider explained. "Vyshaan has her. She's been captured, and Vyshaan is trying to transform her into a Dragon."

Kael's eyes turned from sorrow to rage. "Where is she?"

"Brightspire," Rider answered as he rose to his feet. "Your Spark is protecting her, fighting back against the spell, but she doesn't have long. Let's move."

Rider and Kael traveled up the chamber and met the Royal Guards at the entrance. Cheers erupted as Rider came into view. The parade of people outside the smithy district heard the cheers of the Royal Guards, and celebration erupted in the streets.

The Spellsword had returned.

Rider and Kael were escorted to the King's chambers, where Ragnoc lay in his bed, his features less vibrant and aged.

"So it worked," Ragnoc said as Rider and Kael entered the room.

"Indeed it did, Your Majesty," Kael responded.

Rider approached King Ragnoc's bedside as the healers moved away.

"Ragnoc," Rider began, "The sacrifice you've made, your people will know a life free of struggle and loss. I promise you, we will usher in a new age for all Etonians. The generations of Dwarves that follow will be blessed beyond measure."

Ragnoc sighed as a smile drew across his face. "I'm not dead yet, boy," he smirked. "Let's not talk like I won't be around to see it."

"Of course," Rider said with a half-smile of his own.

The doors to the King's chambers opened as an escort announced an arrival. "King Laucian Amakiir, Your Majesty."

"Rider," King Laucian greeted. "I heard you had recovered, a wonderful blessing indeed!"

"Thank you, Your Majesty," Rider replied. "However, we do not have time for celebration. We need to make our way to Brightspire with haste. Queen Vyshaan has taken Ariella and is already attempting to create more Dragons."

King Laucian appeared to stand taller for a moment. "My forces are diminished, but whoever can march is yours to command. I'll speak to the Griffins at once and see if they are willing and able to continue."

King Laucian turned and departed from the chambers with haste.

Rider turned back to King Ragnoc. "Your Majesty, I must ask."

But Ragnoc was already ahead of him. "My kingdom, and all my forces, are yours to command, Spellsword. Use them well."

"Thank you, Ragnoc," Rider replied. "Rest now, honorable King."

With that, Ragnoc closed his eyes and waved a hand instructing his guards to escort Rider and Kael from the chamber.

As Rider and Kael departed into the adjoining throne room, King Laucian entered from the other side, meeting them in the middle of the court.

"Two Griffins wait on the balcony and have agreed to carry you both to Brightspire. The rest shall remain to assist the armies on their march."

"Wonderful news," Kael responded. "Rider, let's not waste any time."

"Thank you, Your Majesty," Rider said, addressing King Laucian with a courteous bow before heading to the balcony.

As the doors to the balcony swung open, Talon's eyes caught sight of Rider and a joyous screech rang through the air as he reared onto his back legs and fluttered his wings in delight. Rider approached the Griffin and embraced him with a hug around his thick mane of feathers.

"Thank you," Rider said as he embraced the majestic creature. "Someone very dear to me is in great danger. I need to get to Brightspire as fast as you can carry me, please."

Talon locked eyes with Rider, understanding radiating in that deep, intelligent gaze, and gave him one long deter-mined nod. He was ready.

Rider and Kael mounted their respective Griffins and set forth to Brightspire, a flurry of feathers fluttering from the sprinting creatures as they took flight.

CHAPTER XXIX
DRAKZENETH

Rider and Kael soared through the air on the backs of their Griffins, flying high over the Stonefire range and across the vast stretch of the Emerald Forest. From their aerial view, they could see the Human forces of house Bloodmane and Reshu gathered at the base of the mountain pass leading to Brightspire. Rider led the Griffins downward, drawing his sword as they soared over the Human forces. The sight of the Spellsword brought a surge of cheers from below, igniting morale like a wildfire.

Rider and Kael landed at a series of tents bearing the banners of both great houses, positioned near the rear of the gathered armies. They were met by cheers and the hollering of troops as they dismounted. Jarl Bloodmane and Reshu emerged from a central tent to witness their arrival.

"Spellsword!" Jarl Bloodmane bellowed as he approached and embraced Rider with firm grasps to his forearm.

"Stormbringer," Jarl Reshu said with a knowing nod as she met Kael's presence.

"Thank you, but we have no time," Rider said in haste. "Queen Vyshaan has Ariella and is already trying to raise more Dragons. I need you to move your forces onto the castle at once."

"Hold on a minute," Jarl Bloodmane interjected. "If she raises even one Dragon, we won't have the numbers to defeat both it and the Brightspire military."

"Bloodmane!" Rider shouted in anger. "I am a Jarl of the plains, you have sworn allegiance to our trinity. Ariella is in danger and I have called you to action. Will you answer?"

Jarl Bloodmane took a quick step back at Rider's fierceness. His guards drew their blades.

"Sheath those blades!" Jarl Bloodmane shouted back towards his men. "You'll need them by the end of the hour." Then, with a sharp command to his army, Bloodmane shouted, "Forces! To Brightspire!"

"You heard him, Mages!" Reshu yelled, "To war!"

Rider and Kael returned to their Griffins and took flight as the armies of man descended the final hill toward Brightspire. House Bloodmane's Lancer Corps calvaries galloped onward. Brightspire's military, already in battle formations outside the grand port, unleashed flaming spheres and frozen icicles that rained from the sky above.

Rider and Kael flew above the elemental onslaught and could see the dark smoky tendrils that rose above Brightspire's military below. The entire military was under the control of Drakzeneth, helpless to resist, and forced to carry out his commands.

As the battle raged below, Rider and Kael made their way to the city above. As they peered below, they witnessed the damage and destruction Queen Vyshaan had unleashed on her own people. Buildings were destroyed, mangled bodies lie in the streets, and draconic abomina-tions ran rampant as the remaining citizens either fought for survival or ran in panic. Rider glanced back at Kael and then down to the city below. Kael ushered his Griffin to dive, casting a series of spells at the abominations as he landed in the streets below.

"All right, Talon," Rider said as he leaned toward the Griffin's ear, "Help me find her and the queen."

Talon screeched in response as he banked around spires and dove between buildings in search of Ariella or the Queen. They continued scanning the streets and court-yards from above before Rider steered Talon upward toward Queen Vyshaan's castle. That's when he saw Queen Vyshaan and a series of royal guards carrying a cage across the north end of the port.

"Dive," Rider commanded. Talon obeyed as wind rushed across Rider's face. Feathers flew behind the pair as they descended. The noble Griffin let loose a valiant cry as they approached from above, but it proved to be the majestic creature's final act of defiance.

Queen Vyshaan, alerted by the cry, turned and fired a spear of energy into the air. Talon pulled back in an attempt to dodge, but it struck with deadly aim as it pierced Talon's chest, spraying blood and feathers as it connected.

Rider tried to maintain his grip as Talon tumbled toward the port below, but it was no use, his majestic steed had already departed from this world. Rider let go, tumbling across the stone pathway of the port below. He caught himself just in time to see Talon's body slam against the water with a horrifying splash as it sank to its watery grave.

Rider rose to his feet, his sapphire eyes ablaze with fury

as Queen Vyshaan's guards approached. In one fluid motion, he drew his longsword from the sheath on his back, its steel singing.

With a roar of rage, Rider lunged forward, his blade a blur of motion as it cleaved straight through the first guard's sword. Sparks flew momentarily as the weapons collided, the metallic clang brief but loud as Rider's blade sank into the collarbone. Rider delivered a swift, yet forceful kick, freeing his blade as the guard fell into the water.

The second and the third guard charged forward, thrusting their spears toward Rider's heart. Rider twisted his body, and parried them upward, cleaving the tips of the spears from their poles. Before the guards could react, Rider's spinning elbow connected with the second's jaw, sending him sprawling to the stone floor. The third attempted to return a strike, but was met by the vicious arc of Rider's blade as it came back around, sinking into the side of his helmet, finally stopping halfway into his face.

Rider placed his free palm against the guard's chest as he turned his gaze toward Queen Vyshaan and whispered, *"Vor'ethra."* The body flew from his blade as a small azure explosion came forth from between his palm and the guard's chest.

The second guard stumbled back to his feet, blood dripping down his visor, as Rider simply swung his sword upward, cleaving head from shoulders.

Queen Vyshaan watched as her guards met their death, one by one. *"Dra'kesh Drakonos,"* her voice rang out with authority, a slender hand raised.

The two guards standing watch over Ariella's cage twisted in agony as their bodies ripped apart, new limbs sprouting from under their skin, muscles gurgling forth from the torn flesh. Two large, four-legged reptiles now stood, ready to obey. "Leave the cage and bring me his head!" Queen Vyshaan commanded.

They rushed forward, tongues slithering from their open mouths, fangs bared. Rider's eyes narrowed as he assessed the new threat, his grip tightening on the hilt of his longsword. Then with a grin, Rider's aura erupted forth. A shockwave of force sent the reptiles stumbling back before they regained their footing.

Rider dashed toward the beasts in a streak of light, his sword aglow with azure energy. Rider's blade connected, cleaving one reptilian body in half, its body sliding apart with the sound of slick wet meat separating.

The second beast let loose a disturbing half-growl, half-hiss as it skittered towards Rider with deadly intent. Effortlessly, Rider spun around the approaching creature and sliced it in two large chunks, separating its chest from its rear. It gurgled forth another hiss as it attempted to crawl its front half forward before Rider plunged his blade into its skull, ending its misery.

Rider removed his blade, gave it a flourish to remove the blood, then turned as he began his march toward the queen.

"Think, child," Vyshaan began, locking eyes with Rider. "Think about all we could accomplish together. The power we could amass. This world is just one of many we could rule if you would simply see the bigger picture."

"I thought you would have learned by now. For *Her*, I'd burn this whole world down," Rider replied without missing a single step. As the final words left his lips, Rider's aura erupted ever larger as he continued his march.

"You think you know power," Vyshaan spat. "You're not the only one who's mastered ascension."

Rider halted in his tracks.

Queen Vyshaan let out a chilling laugh that echoed like

cracked glass in the dark, before her voice fractured into a chorus of disembodied whispers, each one layering over the next in a dissonant murmur. Then came the spell. *"Drakonir Val'amerith."*

Just as the guards before her, Queen Vyshaan' body began to ripple and contort. First were her legs, each splitting in two as they broke apart, flesh torn asunder, pairs of claws forming at the end of each half. The transformation continued up her body: her back split open as her royal gown burst into the breeze. Her spine shattered as bone and vertebrae flew from her body and wings began to sprout. Her head was last. Her skull began to open from the top before carving down the middle, hair and flesh falling aside. Four snouts began to rise, each attached to its own spiraling neck.

Rider stood in shock at the sight of the grotesque transformation that unfolded before him. A monstrous four-headed Dragon continued to grow from the corpse of the once mighty Queen Vyshaan.

The four-headed Dragon now loomed over Rider and most of the port, each neck twisting and writhing like serpents. The green head let out a guttural roar that shook the foundations they stood upon. Glowing, malevolent eyes fixed on Rider as the beast advanced, its massive clawed feet cracking the stone beneath.

As Rider gripped his sword tighter, the azure glow of his aura began to flicker; something wasn't right. He had pushed himself without rest, but he couldn't falter, not with Ariella's life hanging in the balance.

The black head reared back, its maw opening wide. Rider barely had time to dive out of the way before a torrent of acid sprayed forth, sizzling and hissing as it ate through stone and metal alike. The stench of melting rock and corroding steel filled the air.

Rider rolled to his feet, only to be met by a blast of arcane force from the maw of the blue head. Rider was flung from his feet, tumbling across the pier.

The red head wasted no time as it sent forth a stream of molten fire. He dove into water, the flames scorching the ground where he'd stood a moment before.

Rider knew he couldn't keep this up forever. Each attack drained him further, and his ascension was beginning to waver. He needed to end this, and fast.

Mustering his strength, Rider sprang from the water with an arcane blast of his own. He slashed at the black neck, his blade biting deep. Inky blood sprayed from the wound as it slid down the neck.

Before he could press his advantage, the Green head whipped around, catching him in the chest with a brutal headbutt. Rider flew backwards, slamming into a stone wall with a sickening crunch. Rider tumbled to the stone platform beneath as he struggled to catch his breath.

The Dragon advanced, all four heads hissing and snarling as blood continued to spew from the black neck. Rider forced himself to his feet, spitting blood. He had to keep fighting.

He dashed to the left, then right, but his magic failed him halfway through his maneuver. He turned as the Dragon seized its chance, and Rider was swept into the air by its massive tail. His vision went black under the force of the blow.

He'd lost his ascension, and its protection.

Rider's vision returned as he made contact with the stone slabs of the port once more. He struggled to catch his breath and roll to his stomach, but it was no use. He could see the beast approaching. Through its legs, he could see Ariella's cage, her Elven body laid against the bars with her eyes shut, either unconscious or under a spell, he knew not which, but at least she wouldn't see his demise.

The beast approached and all four heads began to open their maws as a mix of colors grew in the enormous creature's chest. Just then, a cannon rang out. A blast slammed against the beast's raised chest, sending it stumbling backwards. Then another, and another, and another. A volley of cannon fire barraged the mighty beast. Rider turned his head back toward the source. It was the Wail, leading a small fleet of black sails. Hawke and his crew made good on their promise. The Pirates of the Crystal Sea would not miss their chance at fortune and glory.

"Get up, Rider!" Hawke's voice rang out between cannon fire. "How am I supposed to pay these men if you're dead?" he joked, firing rounds from his black powder pistols.

"Fire at will! Don't let up, keep that thing pinned down!" Volley after volley continued to rain forth as the ships turned and sailed into Brightspire's massive harbor.

The Dragon staggered under the onslaught, its massive body recoiling with each blast. Eventually it spewed breath attacks at anything it could hit. The port and piers became ablaze with various elemental energies. Ships and stone sizzled with acid, half broken ships were set ablaze, green poison clouds floated above the water, and lightning danced across the waves. Finally, it struck true, and one of Hawke's ships caught fire and then exploded in a plume of gunpowder.

Rider regained his composure, his confidence that they could prevail renewed by Hawke and his crew's arrival. He looked around the battlefield, but the chaos of elements and smoke limited his sight. A screech rang out and Rider's eyes shot toward the sky. It was Kael.

"Kael!" Rider yelled, catching the mage's attention. "Get Ari outta here!"

Kael nodded once, then banked over the rising clouds of smoke.

"Okay, Rider," he growled under his breath. "One more fight. For Kael, for Ari. For everyone this fucking Draconin ever hurt."

Rider's battle cry echoed across the harbor as he charged headlong towards the monstrous form of Drakzeneth that loomed over the smoke. Azure energy swirled around him, crackling and pulsing with raw power. It enveloped his body as an aura of electricity played along the contours of his armor in jagged bolts. The enchanted metal plates crackled and hissed, barely able to contain the energy coursing through them. As Rider's pace quickened, his eyes blazed with otherworldly light, twin spheres of azure fire that burned with the intensity of his rage. With each bounding step, Rider left scorch marks upon the stone, as he drew upon the deepest wells of his Aetherion Ascendance.

Four heads swiveled to face him, their serpentine necks coiling and twisting, poised to strike. Malice gleamed in their monstrous eyes. Drakzeneth's maws opened wide, wisps of elemental energy dancing between them.

Rider did not relent. With a final, earth-shattering roar, he gathered his power and leapt skyward, his ascendant might nearly propelling him into flight. He soared upwards, wind whipping at his hair and cloak, the force of his movement sending ripples through the billowing smoke.

Brilliant streaks of lightning unfurled behind him, etching jagged paths across the chaos of the battlefield. The thunderous crack of each bolt was lost amidst the cannon fire and clashing magic, yet their radiance lit up the harbor in flashes of blue-white luminescence.

At the apex of his mighty leap, time slowed and the world fell away beneath him.

He drew back his arms, muscles coiling beneath his armor. In a single, devastating motion, Rider hurled his longsword at Drakzeneth with all his strength. The blade sang through the air, a spinning blur of razor-edged steel and arcane might. It tumbled end over end, the polished metal catching the eerie light of the flames and magical discharges.

The spinning longsword streaked through the air, a brilliant comet of steel and arcane energy hurtling towards its monstrous target. It sliced through the billowing smoke, leaving a shimmering azure trail in its wake.

Drakzeneth's four heads reared back, jaws snapping shut as the Dragon sensed the approaching threat. The beast was too late.

Rider's blade struck true, sinking into the central point where the Dragon's four necks converged. There was a sickening crunch, a wet squelch of parting flesh and shattering bone. A geyser of dark, steaming blood erupted from the grievous wound, splattering the stone below in a rain of sizzling ichor.

The Dragon let loose a deafening roar of pain and fury from its four throats. It thrashed and writhed, its massive form crashing against the surrounding buildings and ships, sending stone and timber flying. Drakzeneth's heads whipped about in a frenzy, belching spurts of elemental energy in all directions.

Rider hit the ground hard, his boots skidding across the blood-slicked stone. He stumbled, nearly losing his footing. His chest heaved with exertion; sweat and grime streaked his face. But in his eyes there burned a fierce, unyielding determination.

Something in his soul guided him as he thrust out his

hand, fingers splayed, and barked an Astralan word of power. "*Veng'ath!*"

He'd never heard this word, but somehow, he knew what it meant. *Revenge.*

The lodged longsword pulsed with arcane light, then a searing torrent of azure flame erupted around the spot where it was planted. The Dragon's flesh sizzled and blackened around the embedded blade, the stench of charring meat mixing with the acrid tang of dark magic.

Drakzeneth's movements grew more erratic, more desperate. The beast's massive tail lashed out, smashing through stone structures like a battering ram. Its wings unfurled, beating at the air in a maelstrom of smoke and debris.

Rider advanced, step by laborious step, his aura flickering and pulsing around him. He could feel his Spark sputtering, his ascendance might pushed to its very limits. But he would not yield. Not while the faintest hope remained.

Behind him, Hawke's ships continued their relentless barrage, cannons thundering in rhythm. Fiery projectiles arced through the air, pummeling the Dragon's thrashing form. Explosions bloomed across the creature's hide, scales cracking and splintering under the onslaught.

High above, Kael soared on his Griffin's back, scanning the chaos of the battlefield. His eyes caught a glint of metal amidst the smoke. Ariella's cage, half-buried in rubble.

Kael urged his Griffin into a steep dive as they plummeted towards the shattered remains of Ariella's prison. With a mighty flap of its wings, the Griffin landed, talons scraping against stone.

Kael leapt from the saddle as he sprinted towards the

twisted bars of the cage. "Ariella!" he called out, his voice hoarse with desperation.

A weak moan drifted from within the wreckage. Kael's breath caught in his throat. She was alive. Battered and bloody, but alive. He thrust his hands forward, arcane syllables tumbling from his lips. A shimmering field of force coalesced around the mangled metal, and with a gesture, Kael wrenched the bars apart.

Ariella lay curled within, her once lustrous hair matted with blood, her skin marred by bruises and cuts. Kael dropped to his knees beside her, gathering her gently into his arms. "I've got you," he whispered. "You're safe now."

Her eyelids fluttered open, her unfocused gaze settling on his face. "Kael..." she breathed, her voice barely audible above the din of battle. "Rider...is he...?"

"He's fighting for us all," Kael assured her, his eyes glistening with unshed tears. "And he's going to win."

Across the harbor, Rider stood tall amidst the maelstrom, his azure aura a beacon in the darkness. Drakzeneth continued to thrash and wither, its movements growing weaker, more erratic. Rivers of steaming ichor slowed their pour from its wounds, staining the stones black.

Rider raised both his hands, fingers splayed wide. He could feel the last dregs of his spark, the final embers of his ascendant might.

It had to be enough. It would be enough.

With a roar heard by all, Rider unleashed the full might of his remaining power. A blinding surge of azure energy erupted from his palms, a flashing beam of pure arcane fury. It lanced through the smoke and flames, searing the air.

The beam struck Drakzeneth's chest, the point where Rider's embedded sword still smoldered. The Dragon's hide split and cracked, the weapon acting as a conduit, channeling the raw power deep into the monster's malformed flesh.

Rider poured every last ounce of his strength into the attack. The air around him shimmered with heat, and stone cracked beneath his feet. His eyes blazed with righteous fury, reflecting the azure inferno that consumed his foe.

Drakzeneth's four heads whipped about in agony. Its shrieks rose to a deafening crescendo, a sound of pure, unadulterated suffering. The Dragon's flesh blackened and charred, sloughing off in smoldering chunks.

And then, with a final, earth-shattering roar, Drakzeneth exploded. A cataclysm of fire, lightning, and dark magic erupted outward, engulfing the harbor. Ships were hurled through the air like children's toys, shattering against the stone piers. Buildings crumbled, their foundations pulverized by the shockwave.

Rider stood at the epicenter, his aura a dying spark. As the explosion reached its zenith, he felt his Spark gutter and die, his ascendant might utterly spent. The force of the blast lifted him off his feet as Drakzeneth's Spark began its transfer, overwhelming him with the influx of raw, arcane power.

Rider could feel the energy coursing through his veins, a maelstrom of magic threatening to consume him. The dark power of the Dragon Lord's essence was seeking to subvert his own.

Rider struggled to maintain control, his muscles straining with the effort, but the magnitude of the transfer proved too much to withstand. The dark energy surged through him like a raging torrent, setting his nerves alight with searing agony. It felt as if his blood was boiling within his veins, his flesh threatening to burst asunder from the force of the arcane might that now resided within him.

He could feel Drakzeneth's consciousness pressing against his own, a malevolent presence seeking to dominate and subjugate. The Dragon Lord's will was a suffocating darkness that threatened to extinguish the light of Rider's soul. It whispered seductively in his mind, promising power beyond imagining if he would only submit, only surrender.

As Rider's body convulsed with the influx of tainted magic, his vision dimmed and his strength faltered. With a final, agonized cry, Rider's mind shattered.

In the months following Drakzeneth's demise, Rider's body, in a state of permanent slumber, remained in Brightspire under the care of healers from across all the great races. Brightspire itself was ruled by a joint council consisting of King Ragnoc, King Laucian, Jarl Reshu, Jarl Bloodmane, and Lady Ariella. The council pooled its resources and individual strengths to repair and aid the people of Brightspire while they waited to appoint their new leader.

Kael and Jarl Reshu investigated the Brightspire leyline and found that the Iron Sorceress had been draining its power for generations to help maintain her control, dominance, and magical sight over the other realms. Drained, but not completely broken. Kael instructed the Council on how to monitor its recovery over the coming years, just as they would need to do for the leylines within their own kingdoms.

Ariella worked together with each member of the Council to scour Brightspire and eradicate any remnants of Drakzeneth's cult. Once complete, they worked together to build a campaign of enlightenment to help people understand who Drakzeneth was and why his promises of power were misleading. The council agreed that they would hold a joint celebration each year in remembrance of Drakzeneth's defeat. They hoped that this, combined with their campaign of enlightenment, would help prevent Drakzeneth's cult from ever taking root in Etonya again.

Once the Council agreed its work was complete, they planned a grand celebration to honor the rebirth of Brightspire. They unanimously agreed to dismantle the Council and crown Ariella as Brightspire's new Queen. The members of the Council presented their ruling to the gathered masses of Brightspire, citing her aid and the honor she demonstrated toward the other kingdoms during her journey with Rider. Ariella vowed to usher in a new age for the High Elf kingdom and immediately removed all sanctions on the study and practice of magic, except one.

No person, living, dead, or otherwise, may attempt, in any manner, to intervene with the restored leylines.

Deep within Rider's shattered mind, he relived the memories and actions of those whose Sparks he absorbed. He experienced the invasion of Astrala, the enslavement of their people, their deaths and their suffering, over and over again… Until one vision creeped through, different, brighter.

He witnessed the Astralan hero's first ascension. His defeat of the Dragons. Although he didn't destroy the Draconian leylines as Rider had been taught, he drained them instead. He was corrupted by them…. He came to Etonya…. He was losing control…. He found a beautiful High Elf woman…. She calmed his mind, healed his soul….they lived together for over a 1000 years…. He finally grew old… His mind grew weak… He started reliving the memories of those he'd absorbed… He left to the stars to keep his wife safe…. He never told her he was leaving…. She never told him…. She was with child…

Ages began to flash, the world of Etonya began to shift, mountains grew, oceans rose and fell, forests expanded…. Drakzeneth arrived. He was on the lost island, he appeared from the leyline access point. The people worshiped him… he enslaved them… he transformed them… they moved across the sea… the Great War flashed before him… Stonefire erupted… Rider was born… he was a babe… he looked at his mother, a High Elf. Then to his father, a Human… they were simple farmers…. Visitors arrived… beggars…. They gave them shelter…. It was night now… his mother rushed into the room. She was crying…. She grabbed him from the cradle, one of the men walked through the door…. He was bloody…. He was holding a sword…. There was blood on the sword…. His mother turned… she was struck down…. The beggar raised the sword at Rider…blue light flashed… it was day now… he was crying…. A woman arrived…. She held him….calmed him… She took him to the orphanage… his childhood flashed through his mind… then his youth… then Ariella….

The first time he saw her eyes… the first time he made her smile at the Silver Harp… Their first night of passion…. Vorathor… Her light fading… His first ascension … The Banshee's Wail… Their room at Amakiir… Leaving her on the ferry dock…. Her crying… he hears her heartbeat….she's holding her stomach…. He hears a second heart beat…

His eyes open.

Rider bursts into Queen Ariella's throne room as she's in the middle of session. She sees the double ornate doors open. Ariella runs down from her throne. The people part as her guards push everyone aside as she approaches Rider. The two embrace in tears and kisses.

Rider's hands move down to her stomach and he looks at her with tears of joy. Her smile changes from joy to sadness and she shakes her head, "no".

One word leaves Ariella's mouth, "Drakzeneth." The lovers fall to the floor as they lay crying in each other's arms.

EPILOGUE

Rider's boots scuffed the polished floors of Brightspire, each step echoing the weight of his heart. Sunlight from stained glass windows splashed colors on his path, but the vibrancy failed to reach him. His days melded with the nights in a continuous cycle of healing and tending to an inner wound no magic could close—the loss of a child he'd never held.

"Another day, another whispered prayer," Ariella said, her voice a silken balm as she joined him. Her presence was like a warm breeze through the chill of his sorrow.

"Prayers feel empty, Ariella," Rider confessed, turning his gaze toward her—a flame against the cold marble.

"Yet we stand. We breathe. We honor our loss by living fully." Her words, wrapped in the scent of roses and pain, settled over him like a shroud.

"Kael needs me. The leylines won't mend themselves," he uttered, the decision firming within him like steel tempered in fire.

"Then we go, with hearts heavy, but hands ready to

build anew," she agreed, her slender fingers intertwining with his.

With a shared nod, they summoned the arcane energies. A swirl of light enveloped them, the teleportation spell specific to Reshu Academy igniting with a crackle.

Emerging into the sun-drenched grounds of the academy, Rider took a deep breath, the air rich with the musty scent of ancient tomes and the dusty breeze of the plainlands. They walked, their steps crunching on gravel as the grandeur of the library loomed ahead, its towering spires reaching for the sky.

They pushed open the ornate doors, and the familiar scent of leather-bound books and dust-laden shelves greeted them. Kael stood amidst this fortress of knowledge, his back to them, the very air around him shimmering with latent energy.

"Didn't anyone tell you those books are for the students?" Rider called out, his voice bouncing between the rows of endless literature.

The blonde mage turned, his face lighting up with recognition and relief. "By the cosmos!"

Kael caught Rider in an embrace that spoke volumes of their shared trials and the bond forged between them. His shoulders shook as he clung to his friend, the shimmering blue of his eyes now glistening with unspoken relief. "I feared the worst," he admitted, his voice trembling.

"Death would have to be a lot stronger to keep me from this moment," Rider stated, thumping Kael on the back before releasing him. The words were light, but they carried the weight of his recent ordeal.

"Let's mend the broken strands of our world," Rider said, determination lacing his tone. Ariella stepped forward, her presence a silent pillar of support.

Together, the trio descended into the bowels of Reshu Academy, where the walls hummed with unseen power. The leyline access point was a cavernous chamber, its air charged with arcane potential, the ground veined with pulsating energy that beckoned them forward.

"Stand clear," Rider instructed, rolling up his sleeves, revealing forearms etched with the scars of the trio's recent stories. He positioned himself at the heart of the access point, feeling the raw surge of magic rise within him from beneath his feet.

"Are you certain?" Ariella asked, her violet gaze locked onto his. She could almost see the Spark within him, burning brighter as he prepared for the transfer.

"Never been more," he affirmed, nodding to Kael.

Kael raised his hands, and his voice echoed through the chamber, weaving words of power that danced around them like leaves caught in an autumn gale. The symbols adorning his armor glowed in response, illuminating the darkness with celestial light.

Rider closed his eyes, focusing inward, calling upon the core of his being where his Arcane Spark lived—a fierce, crackling ember waiting to be unleashed. He envisioned the leyline before him, fractured and dim, yearning for the lifeblood of magic to flow once more.

Rider slowly rose off the floor as he offered a portion of his essence, a sacrifice to the ancient magic that connected all things.

The air thrummed as power surged forth from Rider, swirling in a maelstrom of color and sound. It poured into the leyline like a river returning to its course, stitching together the torn fabric of the world's magic.

Ariella's breath caught at the sight, her senses overwhelmed by the swirling energies cradling her lover's weightlessness in the air. His Spark began to diminish before the transfer ended in a crescendo that resonated deep within her soul.

Rider's descent to the floor was more of a fall than a controlled landing. "Done," Rider gasped, sagging with the effort. Power still crackled around him, but he was now more depleted of magic than he'd ever been since embarking on this journey.

The leyline was whole once more, its connection restored.

"Rest now, friend. It will take some time to see exactly how much energy you've given back to your world," Kael said, offering Rider a hand to steady him.

"Come," Ariella urged softly, aware of the toll taken. "Let's return to the light."

They ascended from the depths, leaving behind the echoes of their feat, the leyline now a vibrant artery of magic coursing unseen beneath the academy—a beacon of hope rekindled.

"Kael," Rider spoke, his voice bearing the weight of the world they had just saved. "I owe you a life's debt."

"Think nothing of it. We are bound by more than debts, my friend." Kael clasped Rider's shoulder with solemn warmth. "But now, I must return to Astrala. I need to share what we've learned about the Draconin and warn the Council of Astrala."

"Kael?" Rider's eyes pierced Kael's, a silent question hanging between them.

"Your secret about ascension is safe with me," Kael assured, his tone steadfast. "Your sacrifice and your gift will remain known only to those who hold your trust."

"Thank you," Rider said, relief evident in his weary smile.

"Until we meet again," Kael nodded to Ariella before embracing her with a warm hug.

"Safe travels, Kael Stormbringer," Ariella whispered, her voice carrying the strength of their shared past and the uncertainty of the future.

With a final nod, Kael invoked the words of departure, ancient and powerful. *"Astiria'k Ven'solara, Astrala'en Satai'el."* *

A shimmering portal materialized before him, and he stepped forth, vanishing into the cosmos.

---

* *This incantation intertwines "Astiria'k," representing the expansive cosmos and the act of traversing across the stars, with "Ven'solara," denoting the journey from one world to another. "Astrala'en" signifies the destination, the mystical realm of Astrala, while "Satai'el" evokes the notion of returning or coming back. By weaving these potent words together in the resonant chant "Astiria'k Ven'solara, Astrala'en Satai'el," practitioners can invoke the ancient magic needed to teleport seamlessly across vast cosmic distances, bridging the expanse between worlds and returning safely to the cherished realm of Astrala.*

Thus the phrase became more than a spell—it became a vow: **"Across the stars I travel. To Astrala, I return."**

THE END...FOR NOW

The Astrala Saga will continue…

PRONUNCIATION GUIDE

Harmoniael Festivion (*Har-MOAN-ee-uhl FESS-tiv-ee-on*)
Essentiael Verdonar, Luminar Pavilia (*Eh-SENT-ee-uhl VUR-doh-nar, LOO-mih-nar Puh-VEE-lee-uh*)
Aerovien Zephyra, Caelum Arcili (*AIR-oh-vee-en ZEFF-ee-ruh, KAY-lum AR-sih-lee*)
Telathrin Caelinor Velorian (*Teh-LATH-rin KAY-lih-nor Veh-LORE-ee-un*)
Gor'makh Ghash (*GOR-mokh GASH*)
Vorathor (*VOHR-uh-thor*)
Aetherion Ascendance (*Ay-THEER-ee-on Uh-SEN-dunce*)
Vor'ethra (*Vor-ETH-rah*)
Vistara el'lythos amin'karyn (*VISS-tar-uh el-LITH-ohs ah-MEEN-kah-rin*)
Avelor en'dur (*AV-eh-lore en-DOOR*)
Vel'ethrae, Vri'shanar, Leyarin'sol, Ar'kanon (vel-ETH-ray, VREE-shuh-nar, LAY-uh-rin-SOHL, AR-kah-non)
Asha'khel, Nol'shivar, An'arae, Spar'kannon (AH-sha-kell, NOL-shih-var, An-AHR-ray, SPAR-kan-on)

Aer'leth, Talasen, Vael'shara, Solan (AIR-leth, TAL-uh-sen, VAYL-shuh-rah, SOH-lan)

Dra'kesh Drakonos (DRAH-kesh DRAH-koh-nos)

Drakonir Val'amerith (DRAH-koh-neer Val-ah-MEH-rith)

Veng'ath! (VEN-gath)

Astiria'k Ven'solara, Astrala'en Satai'el (Ah-STEER-ee-ak Ven-soh-LAH-rah, As-TRAH-lah-en Sah-TIE-el)

ACKNOWLEDGMENTS

Wow, there are so many people I want to thank. Firstly, I'd like to thank my wife Cali. Without her constant love and support, neither I or this book would be anywhere near as well rounded. Furthermore, without her I would never have been blessed with my princess Evelyn. To my child, my love, my future. Although you are too small and innocent to read this today, I know one day you will break the rules and read it anyway. You are the reason this book exists. You wanted a story one night in bed and I was so tired, but your sweet voice begging for, "just a small one from your brain" spawned this entire saga. You are the reason I wake up everyday and strive to be a better version of myself. Your love for magic, dragons, fairies, unicorns, and every mystical and wondrous thing you encounter is so refreshing and pure. Watching your eyes light up and your beautiful smile shoot across your face everytime I began telling you about the newest adventure of Rider, the boy with the special heart, empowered me to continue and strive to make each chapter more epic than the one that came before it.

To my MOTHER and FATHER; Lee and Stan Yarbro. I would not be anything I am today without you. You took in a troubled, orphaned, self-made foster child and never gave up. You saw my potential and helped me mulligan the hand I was dealt in life. You are beyond any doubt, the best mother, father, mentors, guardians, caregivers, and examples of selfless love and family I have ever seen or been blessed to experience. I can never repay you for the life you've provided me and the world you helped me experience. You literally took this kid from the gutter to the penthouse. Thank you for always loving and supporting me. Through the mistakes, the disappointments, and the successes, I never once doubted your love.

To my greatest ally, friend, and brother beyond blood, Jacob Lee Davis. I love you man. We've been through a lot together, we've seen each other rise, fall, break, and put ourselves back together. There is no person I would rather have by my side in the heat of battle. You and your daughter will be forever cared for, forever protected, and forever welcome in our kingdom. When the world, the journey, or the battle looks too large to concur, remember you are never alone.

To my Editor and friend, Vanessa. Thank you for not throwing away the turd I first sent you. As someone who was approaching this journey for the first time, your help and honesty has been incredible. Your mastery of your craft is impressive. Your ability to see what someone is trying to express, polish it, and present it once again without changing their voice is genuinely amazing. Thank you for putting up with my constant questions, changes, and worries about timelines.

Last but not definitely not least, to my friends and family in B3. Thank you. This book would not be here without you. You challenged me, pushed me, and sometimes forced me, but I love ya'll for it. Thank you for being my biggest hype squad, promoters, and fuelers of chocolate during the struggles to cross the finish line. You're going to do amazing things for so many others as you embark on your own journey. I cannot wait to see where you land among the stars.

ABOUT THE AUTHOR

David (D.A.) White was born in 1986 and is the youngest of three siblings. His lifelong love of all things fantasy and sci-fi was inherited from his older brother, Robert. Robert is responsible for exposing David to the genres, series, and games that would not only shape his personality, but teach him that no one is defined by where they start in life. You simply need to complete the hard quests, gain experience, and level up. Looking for a life beyond homelessness and hunger at fifteen, David walked into The Bill Wilson Center in Santa Clara, California. After years of legal proceedings, counseling, and foster homes, there was light at the end of the tunnel. David found his forever family, bound by love and choice.

David Graduated from California State University, Fresno with a Bachelor of Science in Psychology and Academic Honors. After graduating, David returned to Santa Clara to begin working as a Youth Counselor at the Bill Wilson Center, the very shelter he stayed in during his earlier years. David spent the next few years working with a variety of organizations focused on helping youth become the best version of themselves before entering adulthood.

David eventually got married to his beautiful wife, and started a family of his own. His recent years have been spent focusing on raising his princess. When not striving to become the best father this world has ever seen, he enjoys reliving and exploring the classic genres and stories his late brother Robert exposed him to such as, Star Wars, Lord of the Rings, Highlander, Dungeons and Dragons, Stargate SG-1, Magic the Gather, and many more.

tiktok.com/@author.dawhite

instagram.com/author.dawhite